CHECKMATE

CHECKMATE

A Neighbor From Hell

R.L. MATHEWSON

Edited by: Jessica Atchison, Stephanie Shaw, Jodi Negri, Jennelyn Tabios Carrion and R.L. Mathewson

Cover Design by: Rochelle McGrath

eBook ISBN 9780988573208
ISBN: 1482318687
ISBN 13: 9781482318685

OTHER BOOKS BY R.L. MATHEWSON

SPECIAL
THANK YOU TO......

To L.D. Davis, Gitte Doherty, Ricki Fieldberg Wieselthler, Rick and Nicki LaCuesta and many others that I stalk for my own entertainment, thank you for making my adventures on Facebook more interesting.

And last, but not least, to Kayley and Shane, my little buddies, the bullies who beat me and steal my chocolate, I love you both and I hope like hell that you never read any of my books.

PROLOGUE

Twenty-five years earlier.........

"Rory's a boy's name," the mean little boy, who'd pushed her off the swing only seconds earlier, announced as he glared down at her accusingly.

Never taking her eyes away from the bully, Rory slowly got up as she wiped dirt off her shirt and jeans. When she finally stood up all the way she was forced to tilt her head back slightly so that she could continue to glare at him the way that her older brothers had taught her.

"It's a girl's name," she said, taking a deep breath and shoving him back.

One thing she'd learned thanks to having five older brothers was never to let anyone push her around. Once you did, you'd have to sleep with one eye open and keep an eye out for snakes in your bed, spit in your cereal, and toenails in your mac and cheese. She might have to put up with five big bullies at home, but that didn't mean that she had to put up with it at preschool, she decided as she gave the boy that had all the girls giggling and calling cute, another shove.

"You're ugly!" he practically sneered as he reached over and pulled one of her pigtails, hard.

"Well, you smell like my brother's butt!" she said, shoving him hard, because she really couldn't call him ugly since he was kind of cute with honey blonde hair and green eyes.

"Well, you look like my uncle's butt!" he said, yanking the other pigtail hard enough to make her eyes sting.

"Well, you-"

"That's enough of that!" Mrs. Fitzpatrick, the mean woman her father had left her with, said as she grabbed them both by the arm. With a firm tug, she dragged them towards the large multicolored building that her father said looked like a rainbow had taken a shit on. She wasn't sure what shit was exactly, but she knew that no matter what it was that her father was probably right.

"She started it!" the boy pointed out as they were dragged to the small table in the far corner with the scary clown painted on it.

"That's enough of that, Connor," Mrs. Fitzpatrick said sternly as she planted them both on wobbly, red-blotched stools. "You will both sit here and think about what you did while the rest of the children enjoy free play."

Rory narrowed her eyes on the little boy that had cost her a turn on the swings as he narrowed his eyes on her.

"*You'll pay for this,*" he promised tightly.

"No, you will," she said, knowing the second, the very second, that Mrs. Fitzpatrick turned her back on them that the large jar of pink glitter by the window was going to find its way into Connor's hair.

———

Twenty years earlier..........

"Give it back, Connor!"

He held it up higher, making little Rory James jump for it. She tried to glare at him, but unlike the other boys at school he wasn't afraid of her or her big brothers. As far as he was concerned, little Rory James had been put on this earth solely for him to torture and torture her he did.

"Give what back?" he asked innocently, waving her notebook in the air above the brown pond water just to taunt her. Not that he was going to give it back to her, he wasn't. In a minute or two when he got bored with this, he fully planned on throwing it in the water with the hopes that she'd go after it.

"My notebook, you jerk!" she said, giving up on trying to get it back and moving on to the kicking phase, but he was ready for that. After five years of making her life a living hell he knew what to expect and he knew that if he gave her a chance she'd kick him between the legs and drop him to the ground. Then she'd probably make him eat dirt, again.

"Just give her the notebook," Zack, the annoying boy from Mrs. Plumes' class who'd been following after Rory for the past two weeks like a puppy dog, said. Connor hadn't minded the kid before he'd started following after Rory. He was a decent basketball player and knew how to make an awesome spitball, but he didn't like anyone getting between him and Rory.

"I can take care of myself," Rory said, never taking her eyes away from him, which pleased him immensely, but he was still pretty annoyed with the interruption.

"Why don't you come take it for her?" he suggested to the boy as he reached out and palmed Rory's face and shoved her away before she tried to kick him while he was distracted. With a curse that would probably have her father reaching for a bar of soap, she stumbled backwards, fell over a dead log and landed in the mud. Connor would have laughed, but he had other things to do at the moment.

"Fine," the only slightly smaller boy said as he stormed over and made a move to grab the notebook. With a bored sigh, Connor held the notebook higher and further away. As soon as Zack reached out for it, Connor hooked his foot between the boy's legs and pulled up just as he turned, causing the boy to lose his balance and take a header into the dirty water.

"Next time mind your own business," he said, laughing as the boy started to cry. Crying over a little dirty water, what a dork, Connor thought. Rory wouldn't have cried. She never cried, which he took as a personal challenge.

"And next time," Rory suddenly said as he felt her small hands press against his back and shove, "don't touch my math homework." With that, he went stumbling forward and landed in the water right next to the big crybaby.

Connor rolled over and spit a mouthful of murky water at Rory, laughing when it hit her bare leg. Deciding that wasn't nearly good enough, he used her now soaked notebook and splashed her until she was as wet as he was.

He wasn't entirely surprised when she launched herself at him instead of running off and crying like most of the girls he knew would have done. There was no running off and crying for Rory James, not when she could try and kick his ass.

As they rolled around in the muddy water, trying to make the other one eat a handful of mud, he couldn't help but smile. She was just so much fun to torture, he thought as he forced a handful of mud and god only knows what else in her mouth.

———

Fifteen years earlier.........
"There's no talking in detention," Mr. Williams snapped.

Rory shoved her green, black, and pink paint splattered hair out of her face and wondered, not for the first time, why the school hadn't let them either use the showers in the locker rooms or sent them home to wash up and start their two weeks of detention tomorrow. It would have made more sense and would have saved them from having to stand at the back of the room on newspapers so that they didn't get paint everywhere as well as the embarrassment of having the other kids laughing at them.

"That's what I told her, Mr. Williams," Connor said, discretely reaching out when Mr. Williams became distracted by a spitball flying past his head and shoved Rory, making her stumble off their newspaper and onto the pristine white tiled floor.

"You bastard!" she hissed out as she jumped back onto the newspaper, but not before her paint soaked stocking feet left large smears of black and red paint all over the floor.

"Just wait until detention's over, Rory. You're going to pay for making me miss practice," he said, shoving her again, but this time she managed to stay on the newspaper.

"We wouldn't be here if you hadn't shoved me into the art room," she said, shoving him back, causing him to stumble, slip and slide on the floor, leaving an impressive streak of green and pink paint behind.

"If anyone should be mad, it's me. You made me miss work!'" she said, giving him another shove that added a little bit of black paint to the mix.

After this little episode she'd be lucky if she still had a job. Her father told her that if she pulled any bullshit she was fired. She hoped that he meant any bullshit on the job, because otherwise she was screwed since she couldn't seem to go a day without getting into it with Connor.

Over the years their parents, teachers, the priest at their church, their coaches, and even the Neighborhood Watch had gone out of their way to keep them apart, but nothing worked. Absolutely nothing. In the past ten years they hadn't been placed in the same classroom at school or CCD at church. They weren't allowed to play on the coed teams after school out of fear that they'd beat each other with baseball bats, and Neighborhood watches all over town blew those damn whistles whenever the two of them were spotted together.

It was really annoying.

They hadn't gone a day in the last ten years, not even when she was laid up in bed with the flu last year, without giving each other hell. She still remembered waking up at two in the morning to find Connor short sheeting her bed while she was still in it! To this day she didn't know how he'd managed to sneak into her room for two weeks straight. It wasn't like her room was on the first floor or she'd left her windows unlocked. No matter what she did the jerk always found a way to break in and piss her off into a speedy recovery so that she could kick his ass.

When he was laid up for two weeks after she'd gotten over the flu she'd made damn sure to return the favor.

"Oh please, it's not like you have a real job. I bet your *daddy*," he said mockingly, and he was the only one with the balls to do it, "has you fetching his drinks."

She had to snort at that. Her father worked her to the bone. She did everything her brothers had to do and more, because she had a talent and skill with the saws that none of them could touch. Every day after school, she joined her brothers and father wherever he was working that day and they worked their asses off until dinner time. Then they went home, made dinner, did their homework and passed out.

Even though she knew that her father worked them hard because he wanted to keep them out of trouble, she didn't care. She loved working with her family and earning her own money. It also didn't hurt that she was learning a job that she hoped to do after high school.

"At least I know who my father is," she said, knowing it was a low blow, but then again so was sitting on top of her so that he could pour gallon after gallon of paint on her.

"Well, at least my mother didn't run off with the milkman," he said, getting in her face and just like that she snapped. It didn't matter that there was twenty witnesses in the room or that extra month of detention that would no doubt be added onto her time. All that mattered was wiping that smug look off the bastard's face.

"It was the mailman, you bastard!" she said, lunging for him.

"Same damn thing," he muttered as he put her in a headlock and took her to the ground.

———

Ten years earlier.......

"But I love you, Connor," Jill, Jen, or whatever the hell her name was, said.

"Uh huh, that's nice," he said absently as he watched the asshole who'd been hanging around Rory for way too long, wrap his arm around her shoulders and kiss her. "Now if you'll excuse me, I have something very important to do," he said, not caring if she heard him over the loud music.

"Connor!" she said, grabbing onto his arm to stop him from leaving her. With an annoyed sigh, he gently removed her hand from his arm and walked away. He damn neared rolled his eyes when he heard her profess her undying love for him.

He couldn't help but wonder what the hell was wrong with her. They'd had sex, not even good sex, once. There had never been any promises or declarations of love, but for some reason she thought that meant they were meant to be. Why in the hell did women get so damn clingy? It wasn't as if he hadn't made it damn clear that he'd used her for sex.

"Whoa! What the hell was wrong with Rick inviting you and Rory to the same party?" Ted, a guy he'd gone to high school with, asked, laughing as he held up his beer to Connor in salute.

"No clue," he answered without taking his eyes off his prey since he had about five minutes before Rick and his buddies tried to remove him. Two hours ago he'd been too tired to crash this party, but then he happened to stop for some gas and a cold soda and overheard the prick in front of him brag to his frat buddies that he was going to fuck a virgin townie tonight and earn twenty points.

Normally, he wouldn't have cared what one of the asshole college kids did, but when he heard Rory's name, he of course decided that he had to do something. She was his to screw over, no one else's and especially not some fucking college punk's. It didn't matter that they were no longer kids, she was still the best part of his day and he'd be damned if he let some other asshole cause her grief when it was still his damn job. Once upon a time he'd hoped for something else, but.......

It was never going to happen and it was pointless to wish for something that common sense told him would never happen. He'd fucked up big time and made damn sure that there would never be anything more between them a few months ago. For now, he'd have to settle for keeping an eye out for her and enjoying their daily antics, which did entertain him immensely. Since this was all they would ever have, he made damn sure that he enjoyed himself.

A minute later he smoothly stepped in their path, blocking them as they tried to leave. He ignored Rory as she glared up at him since he had more important things to deal with at the moment. His eyes dropped to their entwined hands before settling back on the prick's face.

"Did you earn your twenty points yet, Mark?" he asked, drawing everyone's attention and not giving a damn.

Mark's eyes widened. "I-I don't know what you're talking about," the little shit said, lying.

"That must suck having a short term memory problem, especially in college. Should I refresh your memory?" he asked, barely aware that someone had shut off the music and not really caring.

"I-I-I...," the man stammered nervously as he dropped Rory's hand and stepped away from her.

"Mark?" Rory asked, glancing between the two of them.

"I-I-I..," he continued to stammer.

"Good answer, Mark," Connor drawled, wondering where she found these losers. The last one made this one look like fucking Einstein, but he hadn't been this much fun to fuck over.

Rory sighed long and heavy as she gestured for him to get on with it. There was no drama or theatrics with this woman. She knew the game as well as he did and wasn't going to freak out over the impending blow. They'd screwed each other over enough times that they were pretty much immune to public humiliation by now. That didn't mean that she was going to take this lying down. He fully expected some sort of retaliation.

"Seems your little boyfriend here is trying to pop your cherry so that he can earn some points with his frat brothers," Connor said, trying to hide how surprised he'd been to find out that she was still a virgin. Then again, he did fuck up her life on a daily basis so maybe he shouldn't be that surprised. He'd lost track of how many losers he'd run off in the last five years.

She was quiet for a moment before she frowned up at Mark. "Is that true?"

Connor snorted at that. As if he'd lie. She really should know better by now.

"I-I......it was......" Mark noticeably swallowed as he backed away from Rory with his hands up in a pacifying motion. "It was just for fun, honestly. It's no big deal."

"I see," Rory mumbled, but didn't make a move to run away or cry like most women would. She simply stood there glaring at the man.

"You're not going to hit me, are you?" Mark asked, sounding like a pussy.

Rory simply shrugged. "I don't have to."

Mark frowned, dropping his hands. "Why not?"

"Because they will," Connor answered for her, grinning when five huge men broke through the crowd and started to circle Mark, looking ready to tear him apart and they probably would.

"But it was just a-" Whatever he would have said was cut off by a fist from one of Rory's brothers.

"Thanks for the head's up," Rory said as she passed him.

"No problem," he said, following after her. He was more than ready to go to bed and get some sleep. He was exhausted, which was probably the reason he didn't see it, or rather her, coming.

As soon as he stepped outside he realized that Rory was nowhere to be seen. He really should have known better, he thought as Rory dumped what had to be a gallon of piss warm beer over his head.

"Thanks again," she said pleasantly as she handed him the empty jug and headed towards her car.

"No, problem," he said, fighting back a yawn as he headed after her, only pausing long enough to snatch a large bag of ice out of someone's hand.

ONE

"Come on, come on, come on," Rory mumbled as she waited for the only traffic light in town to turn green. Just as it did, she sighed with immense relief, which abruptly ended when Mrs. Church, Golden, New Hampshire's oldest citizen, took the green light as the signal to walk across the street, using her walker.

Her eyes shot to the dimly lit clock on her dashboard and whimpered. She was five minutes late! She could not be five minutes late. Not today. Normally it would just irritate her, but today it felt like it was a life or death matter. She needed Mrs. Church to haul her ninety-six year old ass across the street before the light turned red.

Rory tapped her thumbs against the steering wheel as she stared intently at Mrs. Church in an effort to will the old woman to move quickly. It only seemed to draw Mrs. Church's attention. The older woman stopped right in front of Rory's new, well new to her, Jeep and smiled and waved at Rory.

Fighting back the urge to gesture for the older woman to move her ass, Rory forced a smile and returned her wave. After a few seconds, Mrs. Church slowly turned back around and raised her walker, set it a few inches in front of her and shuffled. Rory watched as she raised the walker again, gained six more inches and shuffled.

The light turned red.

She groaned as Mrs. Church turned and sent her another friendly wave. Rory debated getting out of the car and helping her across the street, but she knew that would only encourage Mrs. Church to stop in the middle of the street and brag about her great grandchildren.

All thirty-four of them.

Two red lights and three green lights later, Mrs. Church was safely across the street and Rory was gunning it. Two minutes later she was in front of McGill's main office on Center Street, waiting for a minivan full of kids driven by a woman, who looked like she was going to snap if she heard "The wheels on the bus goes round and round" one more time, to pull out of her spot.

As she waited for the van to pull out, Rory put on her left blinker, officially declaring her claim on the spot while she took the opportunity to calm her breathing. It probably wouldn't look professional to go in there sweating and panting like a woman who needed a cocaine fix, although she really could go for a large cup of hot cocoa with a large spoonful of fluff in it, her one true weakness. Maybe after this she could-

Her thoughts were cut off when she realized that her spot was free and clear. Sighing with relief, Rory started to turn into the space when a black pickup cut her off and took the spot.

Rory could only stare for a moment, shocked that someone had ignored the universally agreed upon parking spot rule of the blinker. Perhaps he hadn't seen her blinker?

All thoughts about this being a simple mistake flew out of her head when *he* stepped out of the truck. She ground her jaw as she pressed the "down" button for the passenger side window. Once it was down, she politely asked the bane of her existence to move his truck.

"Move your ass, O'Neil! That's my spot!"

The bastard smiled. Smiled!

"Oh, is this your spot?" he asked, feigning innocence, but Rory knew the man was anything but innocent. He was a bad boy, even his looks gave him away, and that damn smile of his let him get away with everything. The life-ruining bastard!

"Yes!" she snapped. "You know damn well that's my spot! Why else would I have been sitting here waiting with my blinker on?"

He sighed dramatically. "Yes, I did see that now that you mention it."

"Then move!" she said, not caring about playing their usual game of pissing each other off today. She had a huge contract to sign, damn it!

He nodded as he fixed his tie and leaned into the cab of his truck. Rory tapped her thumbs against the steering wheel once again happy that the man had enough sense to skip the bullshit this morning. Maybe today would be-

"I'll move it," he said, pausing as he stepped away from his truck with a folder in his hand and shut his door, "*right* after my meeting."

Her jaw dropped as the life-ruining bastard walked away laughing.

———

"Ah, good times," Connor sighed happily as he stepped inside the office. Taunting a woman shouldn't be so much fun, but it was. It always had been where Rory was concerned. Hell, he'd even enjoyed screwing with her back in preschool.

Sure there were about a dozen other little girls that he could have tormented with paint, paste and pushed down into the mud, but why bother when there was always little Rory James around? She was just asking for it with those two little pigtails, tomboy clothes and little know-it-all attitude. As the school bully, it had been his job to make her life a living hell and he'd taken his job quite seriously all those years ago. Hell, he still did.

There was just something about screwing with her that brought a smile to his face. That was probably why three years ago he'd bought the run down house right next to hers. Sure there were other fixer-uppers that he could have bought for half the price, but none of them would have provided him with entertainment of living next door to Rory.

He ran a hand over the back of his head, smoothing down his hair as he headed towards the little blushing secretary that was trying to pretend that she wasn't watching his approach.

"Good morning, Mary, how are you this morning?" he asked in his most charming voice.

She nodded, shyly averting her eyes. "Mr. McGill will be with you in a few minutes, Mr. O'Neil. Please have a seat and help yourself to some coffee," she mumbled quietly while she gestured to the small waiting area with three chairs lined up against the wall and a gourmet coffee table with one of those insanely expensive coffee machines that used mini cups of ground coffee to make single cups.

Connor winked. "Thank you." He walked over to the waiting area and decided a good cup of coffee would help settle his nerves, not that he doubted that he was getting the job. There was no doubt that he would get it this time. He'd put in the time and had his work to back him up. No one within a hundred miles could match the price. This job was as good as his.

He was reaching for a single cup serving of gourmet French vanilla coffee when a single brown serving cup caught his eye. Picking it up, he couldn't help but smile as he held the last serving of gourmet hot chocolate in his hand. Not that he was particularly fond of hot chocolate, he really wasn't, but he knew a certain someone that was.

A minute later he was sitting down with a cup of frothy hot chocolate. Not as good as coffee, but not too bad. He placed his folder on the empty chair next to him and sipped his drink while he waited.

He didn't even bother trying hide his amusement when Rory half stumbled into the reception area and made a beeline for Mary's desk, almost falling over seven times in the process. Why she'd tried to walk in those heels he would never know. She was already tall, taller than most women in town and a good majority of the men at five-ten. He was not one of them since he had a good five inches on her. She really didn't need the heels, but he rather liked what they did for those beautiful tan legs of hers. Although, he would never admit that she looked good, really good, in that little business outfit that accentuated her size D's, and he would bet his life they were D's, and the high heels that she clearly didn't know how to walk in, she was easily the sexiest woman that he'd ever seen.

He noticed that she wore a little bit of makeup today, interesting. She looked good, but then again she always looked good. He especially liked her hair, always had, even when it used to be pulled up into pigtails. There was just something about wavy caramel hair with natural blonde highlights with those sky blue eyes that drove him nuts.

Connor watched as Mary informed her that Mr. McGill was running behind and gestured for her to sit in the waiting area. Rory didn't look happy about the wait, but she looked decidedly pissed off seconds later when she spotted him. Her eyes narrowed on him as she walked, stumbled, over to the complimentary coffee table all while glaring at him.

Connor sipped his cocoa, watching as Rory searched for her precious hot chocolate.

"Mary, is there any hot chocolate?" the little addict asked, sounding anxious for a fix.

"Sorry, hun, if it's not there, then we don't have it."

Sighing, she nodded and carefully walked the ten steps over to the waiting area only to stop abruptly and glare at him.

"Is something wrong, Rory?" he asked, acting as if he didn't know what had her panties in a twist.

"You're sitting in the middle," she bit out.

He made a show of looking down around where he sat and then at each chair beside him. "Hmm, look at that so I am," he said in an amused tone.

"Move," she demanded, gesturing impatiently for him to move his ass.

Sighing, he took a sip of his drink. "I can't."

"You can't or you won't?" she demanded.

"Both."

Rory glared at him, then at each empty chair before looking around desperately for another chair. When she couldn't find any means to distance herself from him, which he knew that she was dying to do, she sat down as far as she could in the chair to his right.

Sighing loud and long to annoy the shit out of her, he stretched his right arm out and then dropped it along the back of her chair.

"Do you mind?" she asked, looking pointedly at his arm.

He shook his head. "No, not really."

She opened her mouth, probably to tell him off for the millionth time, shut it and shook her head, muttering, "I don't have time for games today."

That was too bad, because he rather enjoyed their little battles. He made a show of sipping his drink. "Mmmm, that's good cocoa."

Rory first glared at him then at his cup.

"You took the last hot cocoa?"

"Uh huh," he answered, taking another sip.

She nodded slowly. "I see."

"I'm sure that you do."

Just as he went to take another sip of that rather creamy cup of hot cocoa that was tasting better and better with each passing second, she jabbed him in the side with a finger the same time she made a grab for his cup. He tried to pull the cup away, but she just dug that damn finger harder into his side.

Shit! That really hurt!

Deciding that it was better to give up the cocoa than to let her make his eyes tear up, he released the cup. Rory twisted her finger harder into his side, digging deep for good measure before backing off. Glaring at her, he rubbed his side while she happily sipped *his* cocoa.

Damn, there were a lot of things in life that he regretted and right now showing her that little trick in sixth grade when she wouldn't let him cut her in the lunch line was one of them. He winced as he rubbed the sore spot. Well, it looked like she'd perfected that move.

"I spit in that you know," he lied.

She simply shrugged when most women would have probably screeched, gagged, and shoved it back at him. Not Rory James. She made a show of taking a huge sip of the cocoa.

"I think I've been immune to your germs since the ninth grade," she pointed out, making him smile.

Ah, good times. For six months he'd found ways to spit in her food and drinks without her and her little band of geeks, nerds, and dorks finding out about it. His friends of course did their part by distracting her so that he could break into her locker and took pictures of the act.

On her birthday, he'd placed all those lovely pictures in a small box, gift wrapped it, and placed it inside her locker. Then he leaned against the locker across from hers and waited with all his friends and half the school for her to open it. Everyone watched as she opened her locker, waiting for her reaction. She first looked surprised to find the present in her locker and of course that turned to horror as she flipped through the pictures. She hadn't been able to hide that little gag sound that she'd made.

Everyone laughed.

He remembered standing there cocky as hell, waiting for her to finally react like a girl and cry. Instead, she calmly put the pictures back in the box, gagged louder, and returned it to her locker. She grabbed the lunch that he and all his friends spit in, hey it was her birthday after all, and walked over to him.

Instead of crying and screaming at him or even threatening to tell her daddy and her rather large brothers, she'd kneed him in the balls. When he was down on the ground she forced half her lunch down his throat while his friends fell over themselves, laughing their asses off, but it had been worth it. Even the month of detention that followed couldn't take away the joy he'd received from that little prank.

"Mr. O'Neil? Miss James? He's ready for you."

TWO

Rory sat in the padded chair, trying to hide her annoyance at being seated next to the bastard. She couldn't understand why Mr. McGill was handling their bids this way. She'd known a month ago when she'd placed her bid on this job that Connor was planning to place a bid. It hadn't been a big deal then, because they were in the same business and usually went after the same jobs.

Usually these things were handled more privately. She couldn't remember ever being in the room with her competition before when the client announced his decision. The only thing that she could come up with was that the client was hoping to use their well-known animosity towards each other to start a bidding war.

It wasn't going to happen. As much as she would love to get her hands on Strawberry Fields Manor, she wasn't about to get into another embarrassing public confrontation with Connor. The one they'd had last month at the Strawberry Festival still made her cringe.

Things probably wouldn't have gotten out of hand if their dates had just stayed out of it, but once Mary Lee decided to get in her face and Jeff took it as his cue to get into Connor's, things had kind of gone downhill quickly. Okay, so she may have started it when she'd dumped the bucket of mashed strawberries over Mary Lee's head, but in her defense, she could only hear "'stupid bitch" so many times before she snapped.

She still didn't understand why the festival committee banned them for a year, especially after they'd paid for all those strawberries they'd wrecked. At least she was still allowed to have a booth at next year's festival for her business, Shadow Construction. Granted, one of her brothers would have to man the table and that probably wouldn't go well, but at least her company would be represented during the town's biggest event.

Connor shifted in his chair next to hers, probably just as nervous as she was. A thought occurred to her, one that pissed her off. If he actually went along with this and tried to outbid her, she was going to pants his ass on the way out.

Her lips twitched at the memory of the last time she'd done that. Granted, it had been a week after he'd done it to her, but at least she hadn't been wearing pink boxers with hearts all over them at a bar like a certain someone that she wouldn't mention. It really had brought such joy to her and her brothers' lives as they'd watched guys hit on Connor and send drinks his way all night. She'd been sixty percent sure that he was going to kill her with his bare hands that night.

"As you both know," Mr. McGill started, bringing her attention back to him, "we've had problems getting permits and the heavy rain season has pushed our plans back by six months."

They both nodded.

"I know that you're both probably very confused as to why I've asked Shadow Construction and Highland Construction for a joint meeting." Thankfully, he didn't leave them in suspense for very long. "My partners and I would like Strawberry Fields Hotel up and running by November."

"That's five months," she blurted out before she could stop herself. Connor threw her an annoyed look, probably for stating the obvious. Not that she cared if she aggravated the bastard. She could care less about that. What she did care about was the fact that there was no way that her company could get Strawberry Fields Hotel up and running in five months. A year? Yes, and that was only after hiring ten extra men and going overboard with overtime.

Five months was not doable.

"Yes, it is," Mr. McGill agreed with a nodding in agreement. "As I'm sure that you both know, Strawberry Fields Manor needs a bit of work." Rory just barely stopped herself from snorting her disbelief out loud.

Strawberry Fields Manor was going to need a complete overhaul. The manor was going to have to be completely gutted, the long driveway was going to have to be torn up, and the landscape fixed. Those were just a few of the major things that were going to need to be worked on. She had a fifteen-page list in her office of all the small problems that needed attention and those things were going to be the one that took the most time.

"I know that this is highly unusual, but we'd like to hire both your companies to work together and finish the project," he announced with a nervous smile, shocking them both into absolute silence. She wasn't even sure that she was breathing or knew how to at that moment.

He really couldn't expect the two of them to work together. Could he? They'd kill each other! The entire town knew that. Hell, there were several betting pools over how they were going to kill each other.

This could not be happening.

As much as she would love to work on Strawberry Fields Manor she really wasn't sure-

"If you're both able to do this and meet our deadline, you will each be paid a bonus of fifty-thousand dollars on top of the twenty percent we've already decided to add to your bids," Mr. McGill announced. "As long as both of you believe that you can work on this project together without any problems," he stipulated, giving them a pointed look.

She looked at Connor only to find him staring at her. They narrowed their eyes on each other, trying to decide if that amount of money would be enough to keep them from killing each other. After several tense moments they both nodded, slowly.

For that kind of money she was more than willing to do a lot of unpleasant things, like let the life-ruining bastard live.

———

Grinning hugely, Connor walked into O'Malley's tavern. He really couldn't help but smile. Not only had he landed the most sought after project of the decade, but he was going to be getting a very nice bonus when he was done. He spotted five very large men sitting to the far right, glaring openly at him and was reminded of the little problem that he would have to quickly rectify.

No doubt the little tomboy thought that they were really going to work this project together. That was just sad, because really, at this stage of the game she really should know better.

This project was his and the sooner she figured that out the better off everyone would be. Sure, he'd keep her around for appearances' sake. She could fetch his lunch or something to make herself useful, but she would be staying away from his project. The use of her men was certainly a nice little bonus.

Even he had to admit that he hadn't been looking forward to hiring temporary workers. There wasn't time to sort through applicants right now and this project was definitely not something that he wanted anyone green to work on. He needed seasoned workers and he'd reluctantly admit that Rory's crew was good. His eyes darted over to the five men, who looked torn between kicking his ass and eating their appetizers.

Having the James brothers working this project was like winning the lottery. Not that he would ever admit this, but the James brothers were the best, even better than his team. They worked hard, always finished their projects on time, and their work was unquestionably the best in the area. He'd never admit any of that of course. Not when he was their main competition. His boys were good, very good, but they didn't have that extra edge that the James boys brought to the job.

What he wouldn't give to have even one of them on his crew. Hell, running his crew. Over the past five years, he'd seriously considered risking war with Rory and going after one of her brothers on more than one occasion. If he could get one, just one, he could probably lure the rest of them over to his side. His eyes moved over to the oldest brother, Craig. He was the clear leader of the group. If he came over the rest would follow.

He still couldn't figure out how they'd managed to end up working for their baby sister. Any of those men could have easily started his own company and given Connor a run for his money, but they hadn't. There was no doubt in his mind that they worked for Rory out of fear of old man James. His boys might be grown men, but he still ruled the family with an iron fist. He'd probably told the boys to help their sister and they'd jumped to do it, afraid the old man would kick their collective asses. Hell, even Connor wasn't foolish enough to turn his back on the sixty-year-old man.

Then again, if any of the James brothers decided after working on this project that they'd rather work for him, who was he to argue?

"Did we get it?" Andrew, one of his oldest friends and one of his foremen, asked as he sat down at the round tavern table in the back. The four other men stopped talking and sipping their beers to watch him expectantly.

"Oh yeah," he said, grinning, looking towards the James brothers. "Maybe even more."

———

"Did you know that Connor was gay?"

That question had Rory stumbling even though she'd changed into her work boots, jeans, and customary gray tee shirt. Before she went head first into the brick wall, Sean reached out and grabbed her by the arm to steady her, which was actually pretty impressive since he'd never taken his eyes off the huge plate of food in front of him.

"Thanks," she said, taking the empty seat next to Brian.

"No problem," Sean said around a huge bite of his cheeseburger.

"Well?" Bryce demanded as he pushed a still steaming mug of hot cocoa towards her while Craig gestured to Luanne, their waitress.

"Well, what?" Rory asked before taking a fortifying sip of cocoa. Not as good as hers, but still doable.

"*Did you know he was gay?*" Sean hissed as Luanne placed a large cheeseburger platter with extra fries, onion rings and coleslaw in front of her.

Connor O'Neil gay?

That was actually laughable. She snorted as she took another sip of cocoa and picked up her knife. Just as she'd finished cutting her burger in half, Brian reached over and took half of it. When she raised the bun of the remaining half, Johnny took her onions. Sean and Bryce took her French fries while Craig and Brian split her onion rings. When the only food left on her plate was the coleslaw and half a burger, each man in turn dumped his side salad with extra creamy French dressing on her plate.

It had taken her a few years, but she had them nicely trained, she thought with a content little sigh as she took a bite out of her burger.

"Why do you think he's gay?" she asked, spearing a delicious looking French dressing-covered cucumber slice onto her fork.

"He keeps looking over here at us," Brian said, gesturing with a nod behind him.

Sipping her cocoa, Rory leaned to the left to look between two of her very large brothers. Sometimes she felt like she had her very own entourage of linebackers. Having large muscular brothers definitely came in handy when she needed help moving or someone to open a pickle jar.

"He's doing it again," Johnny hissed, moving to the side so she could get a better look and sure enough, he was looking over at them. Actually, so were his little buddies. They were talking and gesturing towards them. No doubt the men were pissed at the news. So was she, but she was willing to suck it up as long as he stayed out of her way.

As if he'd sensed her thoughts, he turned his eyes on her and narrowed them dangerously. She narrowed her eyes on him. Everything around them disappeared as they glared at each other. Sure it was childish, but she would not look away first, damn it! Even when people walked between them neither one of them looked away.

The glaring was actually starting to make her feel dizzy, but she would not look away first! Not this time! She would-

"They're probably just gloating. It's okay, baby girl. We'll get the next one," Craig said, pulling her attention away from the glaring bastard. She looked away, but not before she caught his triumphant grin.

The bastard!

"We got it," she said, taking a quick sip of cocoa.

The men actually stopped eating to frown at her, which was pretty amazing since there was still food on the table and these were the James brothers.

"We got it?" Brian asked, looking confused.

She shrugged. "I signed the contract less than a half hour ago. It's ours."

The men looked over their shoulders and then back at her in unison. "Then why do they look like they're celebrating? I can't imagine Connor being happy about losing to you," Bryce pointed out, staring longingly at the burger left on her plate. So maybe they hadn't entirely forgotten about the food, she rectified.

"Yeah, he looks damn happy for a man that just lost a million dollar contract," Johnny said as his hand inched, almost as if it had a mind of its own, towards her burger. With an annoyed sigh, Craig slapped his hand away.

Johnny gave her a sheepish smile and a shrug. She knew that he couldn't help himself. It was something she'd understood even when they were kids. Her brothers had been able to eat their father out of house and home by the time they were six and often had. Considering that by the time they'd turned six they'd all been the size of a twelve year old, that wasn't too surprising. If it hadn't been for Craig, she probably would have starved to death. He'd kept his younger brothers in line and made sure she that she'd had enough to eat.

"Yeah, well, he kind of sort of got the contract too," she said quickly, wincing in anticipation of their reaction.

Instead of cursing and slamming the table with their fists like she'd expected, they just sat there staring at her. Finally Bryce spoke. "You're kidding, right?"

She shook her head, taking another sip of cocoa. Again, her brothers looked over their shoulders and this time the life-ruining bastard had the balls to salute them with his beer and a cocky grin.

Rory discretely flipped him off. Connor's cocky smile quickly turned to a tight frown as his eyes once again narrowed dangerously on her. Her brothers returned their attention to her, clearly wondering what she'd done. She just gave them an innocent smile as she sipped her cocoa.

"I don't understand," Sean said. "How could you both get the contract?"

Darting her eyes away, she said quietly, "We'll be working with Highland Construction on this job."

Stunned silence met her announcement. She chanced a glance up at her brothers, who were now looking at her as though she'd grown an extra head. She cleared her throat and continued.

"We each got the contract with a twenty percent markup and a nice bonus if we finish by the November deadline," she explained, watching as the information sank in.

Each of her brothers cursed vividly as they turned and shot another scowl to the man that was once again smiling smugly in their direction. Slowly, her brothers turned back to face her, glaring.

"Why didn't you tell them that we could do it without Highland Construction?" Sean demanded. This time when Johnny tried to snag her burger, Craig didn't stop him.

Great, the big babies were mad at her. Whatever. They'd get over it.

"Does it look like I want to work with him?" she asked, making them frown. "I didn't have a choice. Even if we hire extra men, we won't be able to train them in time for them to be useful. We wouldn't make the deadline. If we did this alone we'd also blow our profit margin on extra equipment. Extra equipment I might add that Highland Construction has. All we have to do is go in, work our asses off just like any other project, meet the deadline and that's it. The only downside is that it will be with the bastard, but if I can handle it, then so can you."

Her brothers looked thoughtful as they considered what she'd said. Finally with a shrug, Craig said, "Fine, as long as he leaves us alone to do our job and lets us lead we won't kick his ass."

THREE

"That's it, boy," Connor cooed as the hundred and fifty-pound pain in the ass cocked his head to the side and studied him. "Come on, big guy, you know you want it," he said, holding the hot dog he'd dipped in peanut butter up higher as he moved it slowly from side to side, trying to entice the little bastard.

The demon spawn that Rory liked to call a dog licked his lips hungrily as his eyes zeroed in on the tasty treat. Grinning, Connor leaned over and reached for the laptop bag that he'd foolishly set down on the ground ten minutes ago so that he could grab his brief-case and files only to turn around and find the pain in the ass lying across it.

Connor tossed the tasty treat onto Rory's property. The dog sent him one last glare before he took off. Connor didn't waste any time, he reached down and grabbed his laptop, knowing damn well that the damn dog would be back. Sometimes it seemed as though the damn dog liked screwing him over more than Rory did.

He was just about to head inside his house when a familiar red four-door sedan pulled in Rory's driveway. Hadn't he already chased this loser off? It had been what.....three or four weeks since he'd last saw this asshole sniffing around Rory? Then again, most of the men Rory dated, all losers in his opinion, stopped coming by her house shortly after meeting him, which was just the way he liked it.

But clearly he hadn't done his job if this one was coming back for more. As he watched the asshole step out of his car, smooth his hair back and straighten his obviously new shirt and slacks, Connor couldn't help but wonder how dumb the man really was.

When he spotted Connor, he froze on the spot and noticeably swallowed. A loud menacing growl had the man taking a step back. Because that too pleased him, he pulled the second peanut butter dipped hot dog out of the baggy and tossed it to the dog Rory dared to name, "Bunny." With a grunt, the dog swallowed the treat whole, but never took his eyes away from the asshole who refused to step away from behind his car.

Like that would protect him, Connor thought with a sigh as he walked over to the corner of his large white Victorian home, which happened to be a mere twenty feet away from the corner of Rory's house, an almost identical house. When the homes had been built over two hundred years ago they'd been identical in every way, except the direction of the layout of the houses were completely different. The Master bedroom suite of each house had its very own open porch that extended past the walls of the house by a good ten feet and cut the distance between the two houses.

It wasn't exactly a surprise that the homes had been built together since the houses had been built by identical twins. The brothers had built the homes for their wives only to discover that their wives couldn't stand each other, at least that's what his realtor had told him. Whether or not it was true didn't really matter to him. All that mattered was that he could look forward to aggravating the piss out of Rory each and every night when she sat out on her porch to relax.

When he'd first bought the place, the small strip of land that separated the two properties held not only a tall wood fence that started at the street and ended at the back of the property, but also large arboreta trees that were nearly as tall as the house, completely blocking Rory from his sight. Since he'd bought the house for the entertainment value alone, he'd had the fence and trees taken down the very next day.

Rory had been pissed at the time, but she soon got over it and focused her attention back on renovating her house while he'd done the same with his. It took him two years to get the house the way that he wanted it, but it had been well worth it. When he'd first bought the place he'd considered giving it a more modern look, but after his first night in the place he'd decided to go with what he thought it might have looked like when it had been originally built. It took extra time, money and a lot of guessing, but he was happy with the results.

When he'd originally bought the property, he'd planned on fixing it up and selling it, having Rory around to torture was just a bonus while he'd worked on flipping the property, but once the renovations were finished he hadn't been able to part with the house. He knew that it had been the same for Rory. Although he'd never seen what she'd done with her house, and God how he wanted to see what she'd done, he knew that she had changed her mind about selling when the renovations were complete, because she'd fallen in love with her house.

"Is Rory here?" the man asked, shifting nervously near his car.

"Is she expecting you?" he asked, leaning back against his house as he discretely reached behind the rosebush that one of his ex-girlfriends had insisted on planting, and flipped the switch on what he liked to call his "Little Box of fun." He settled his fingers over the three black buttons that made up the small panel and waited.

"That's none of your business," the man snapped, noticeably bristling.

"Then I guess you'll just have to find out for yourself," Connor said with a careless shrug as he watched the man shoot him a scowl just before he stormed up the walkway and damn near jumped out of his skin when Bunny decided to block his path.

"Easy," the man said anxiously as he backed away from the dog. Even though it probably should be enough that the dog probably made the man piss his pants, Connor felt that he needed a little extra incentive to get the hell out of here and never come back.

"What the hell!" the man yelled as Rory's sprinklers came on full blast. Connor waited until the man ran back to his car, only falling twice and ruining his clothes with mud and grass, and was peeling out of the driveway before he turned her sprinklers off.

Best damn thing he'd ever built, he decided as he gave his partner in crime a mock salute and headed for his front door. It really was too bad that he couldn't stand her dog since he did come in handy from time to time.

———

"Why are you covered in mud, sweetie?" Rory asked as she bent down and cupped Bunny's mud splattered face. When she caught a whiff of peanut butter and hot dog, she knew exactly how her poor baby had got all dirty.

"*Connor*," she bit out, momentarily forgetting that she couldn't kill him for at least five months.

"You called?" the annoying bastard said, sounding amused.

She looked up, not surprised to find him standing on his second floor balcony, shirtless and holding a bottle of beer. Sometimes she really wished that he hadn't cut down those damn trees. At least she could have pretended that he wasn't next door and probably would have been able to enjoy her porch more if she didn't have to worry about seeing him everyday. Then again, he would have just found some other way to annoy the hell out of her.

"You want to tell me why you felt the need to soak Bunny?" she asked, resigning herself to waiting another hour or two before she ventured out onto her porch. Not that it would make much of a difference since he'd just come back out again to aggravate her, but after three years she'd become used to the jerk wrecking what should have been the best part of her day. She also loved her time on her porch too much to really care most of the time.

"I will if you tell me why you named that poor dog, Bunny," he offered, taking a sip of his beer.

Because the dog was her little honey bunny, but she would never tell *him* that. "Forget it," she said, sighing as she headed for her front door.

"Come up here and join me," he called after her.

"I'll pass," she said, wanting nothing more than to enjoy a hot cup of cocoa as she went over the new plans McGill had given her earlier and figure out a way to work them into her plans before she called it a night. She also needed to figure out ways to speed up this renovation. Even with Connor's men and equipment they were looking at long hours and she needed to figure out how to get it all done without destroying their profit margin with overtime.

"Don't you think that the two of us should sit down and go over the plans for Strawberry Manor?" he asked casually, but she wasn't stupid. She knew the only reason he wanted to talk to her was so that he could pick her brain and discover what resources she had at her disposal. It's exactly what she would have done if she hadn't managed to corner one of his men an hour earlier and sweet talk him into spilling his guts about Highland Construction's equipment, men, and their skills. Now she just had to work all of that newfound knowledge into her plans.

"Not really," she said as she unlocked her front door and sent up a silent prayer, asking for a Connor free night. Of course her prayer was ignored. They usually were where Connor was concerned.

"That's too bad. I guess I'll have to tell McGill that you're not willing to fulfill your end of the contract," he mused loudly.

She didn't say anything as she slammed the door behind her, because there was nothing to say. He knew that he had her in a tight spot and he had no problem screwing her over. If she didn't play nice he would cost her the contract and more importantly, her reputation.

Clenching her jaw, she stormed into her kitchen and dropped her things onto the light oak country table. If she was going to deal with Connor and not kill him, then she was going to need a hot cocoa fix. As she waited for the water to boil, she fed Bunny and sorted through her notes. If he wanted to pretend that they were going to play nice then that was fine with her since none of this bullshit mattered anyway.

The real battle wouldn't begin until tomorrow and she was more than prepared to kick his ass. So, if he wanted to play these pointless little games now that was more than fine with her. After she mixed up her special hot cocoa, took a sip and sighed happily, she grabbed the top folder and made her way through the house.

If she didn't absolutely adore her house she would have sold it and moved away from Connor a long time ago, but she did, so she couldn't. This was her house, her baby, and nothing and no one was ever going to make her give it up. As she'd restored the house to its original condition she'd fallen in love with the large old house and couldn't imagine living anywhere else. Her only hope was that Connor got sick and tired of these games and decided to sell his house and move far, far, far, far, far away.

Just the idea of having a Connor free day made her giddy. Now if it would only come true she might actually cry tears of joy, she thought as she headed up the back stairs to her room. As she walked across her large bedroom, she wondered if Connor was going to use their new situation to his advantage and make her life a living hell over the next five months. Then she snorted at her own stupidity.

Of course he was going to make her life a living hell. He'd been doing it for over twenty-five years now and wasn't showing any signs of boredom yet. Every single day for the last twenty-five years he'd gone out of his way to make her life difficult. It didn't matter what she was doing or where she was, Connor found a way to leave his mark on her day.

She still couldn't forget her eighteenth birthday. It had started off great. Her brothers had woken her up at two in the morning by tying her up and gagging her, a James tradition and one that her father tried to make her brothers skip that year. Thankfully, they hadn't thrown her in the trunk of Craig's car as tradition dictated. Instead, they'd tossed her in the backseat, thrown a black pillowcase over her head and teased and tormented her for ten hours by refusing to tell her where they were going.

When they'd finally pulled the hood off her head and she saw where they'd brought her, she squealed happily as she gave all of her brothers bear hugs. Really, how many brothers were sweet enough to bring their sister to Canada on her eighteenth birthday to get her drunk?

Best. Brothers. Ever.

For the first four hours everything had been perfect. After she'd ate, because her brothers refused to let her drink unless she had food in her stomach, she tried beer, wine and hard liquor. Her brothers had taken turns watching her, but by the time the first hour had come and gone she'd been too drunk to really care that her brothers were hovering over her like mother hens.

She'd been happy and giddy as she'd danced to every song. Well, she'd danced when she wasn't drinking. All the men at the bar had been super nice, too. They'd bought her drinks so that she didn't have to spend a cent of her own money and they'd all jumped at the chance to dance with her. The night had been going perfectly until she thought she'd spotted Connor lurking in the corner, watching her.

When she couldn't find him again, she just shook it off as an overactive imagination and yummy alcohol. A little while after that, things kind of got fuzzy. From what little she could remember of that night, she knew that it was all Connor's fault that she'd woken up the next morning handcuffed to *him* on a bench while a Mounty with a fresh black eye glared at them from across the room.

If it hadn't been for Connor, she wouldn't have needed to be placed in a cell for her own protection while her father had tried to plow through a dozen officers so that he could wring her neck. The only pleasure she'd got out of that awful experience had been watching her father take a swing at Connor, who must have been hung over, because he'd just stood there and took it.

"Stay," she told Bunny as she pushed back the dark thick curtains that gave her a false sense of peace and unlocked the sliding glass door.

"Took you long enough."

"What the hell are you doing on my porch?" she asked, not really caring. As long as he didn't break into her house, and surprisingly he didn't, then she really didn't care.

"For our meeting," he said, leaning a hip against the banister as he sipped his beer.

"We don't have a meeting," she said even as she allowed her eyes to quickly, and discretely, run over his rather impressive chest and a set of abs that most men would kill for. While her brothers were huge and muscular, Connor had the type of body that any Hollywood leading man would kill for. Not that she would admit this to anyone, but he was by far the best-looking man that she'd ever seen.

Her eyes moved back up to his chest and paused at the black Celtic tattoo that started on the left side of his chest and ended at his shoulder. It was large, beautifully drawn and unbelievably hot, the tattoo, not the man. She hated the man, but on any other man she would have been hard pressed not to trace that tattoo with her fingers or better yet, her tongue. As she forced her eyes elsewhere, they landed on part of the tattoo that to this day remained a mystery.

She knew that she wasn't the only one who wondered who "LRJ" was and reason why Connor had the initials placed in the middle of that tattoo. There were a few betting pools going around about the identity of LRJ, but as far as she knew, no one had been able to figure it out. Connor certainly had never told anyone. If someone asked, and damn near everyone had asked at least a dozen times, well everyone but her, he simply shrugged it off like it was nothing.

"How many men do you have working for you full-time?" Connor asked, drawing her attention away from her rather disturbing thoughts.

"Fifty and I have another ten men that I already screened and interviewed for the job," she answered, not caring if he knew any of this. They were working together, kind of, so they'd have to share a few things.

Connor nodded as he digested the information. He placed his now-empty beer bottle on the banister behind him. "How many are certified?"

"All of them."

"Can paint?"

"All of them."

"Interesting," Connor mumbled, but she really didn't think that it was. Her father made damn sure that she knew how to build a house from top to bottom and she'd made sure that all of her employees did as well. If they didn't know how to paint, drywall, put up siding, or do masonry work then she made sure that they learned. Since every man that worked for her knew how to do every position, she never had to put up with delays or waste money by hiring outside help. She also never had to waste time stressing over schedules or try to figure out who knew how to do what since all of her men were trained to do whatever was needed of them.

"Anything else?" she asked, itching to get back inside and go over the plans.

"Are you in a rush?" Connor asked, chuckling.

"No," she said, shrugging. "I just don't like you."

"I'm the best part of your day and you know it," he said and she knew that he truly believed that.

"Whatever helps you sleep at night, big guy. Are we done yet?"

But Connor wouldn't let it go, he never did. "Admit that I'm the best part of your day," he said, crossing his arms over his chest as he gave her a cocky smile.

"I can honestly say with absolutely no hesitation that you, Connor O'Neil, have never been the best part of my day," she said, wondering, not for the first time, what horrible things she'd done in a past life to deserve having him in her life.

"Puhlease, that's bullshit and we both know it. I bet you fall asleep every night thinking about me and wake up every morning smiling and eager to see me," he mused, sounding smug, too damn smug.

"Actually, you have that backwards," she said, taking a sip of her perfect hot cocoa.

"Really?"

"Mmmhmmm," she murmured around another sip of cocoa.

"How so?"

"Well," she said, placing her cup of delicious hot cocoa on the small patio table, "I fall asleep every night smiling, because I no longer have to worry about seeing you for at least eight hours and wake up every morning thinking about how to avoid you."

"But you're still thinking about me and smiling when you do it," he said with a wink, leaning over and swiping her hot cocoa before she could stop him.

"Hey!" she said, trying to grab the cup out of his hands, but the bastard simply cupped the top of her head and held her back as he downed her delicious hot cocoa. She hated when he did this to her. It made her feel foolish and little and as soon as she got the chance she was kicking his ass.

"You *bastard*!" she hissed when he made a big show of smacking his lips.

"That was a damn good cup of cocoa, Rory. Thanks," he said, handing her back the cup as he dropped his hand away from her head.

"How could you?" she mumbled as she looked longingly down at the now empty coffee cup where her delicious hot cocoa had once been.

"Are you ready to admit that I'm the best part of your day yet?" he asked, leaning back against the banister.

She glared up at him before looking back down at the empty coffee cup in her hand and then back up at him.

"Aw, shit," he said, turning and jumping over the banister. He crouched down on his own porch just as she let the coffee cup go flying.

When it missed his head by a few inches she groaned. So damn close, yet not close enough, she thought as it slammed into the side of his house and shattered.

"Well, I guess we'll have to continue this conversation tomorrow night when you're in a better mood," Connor said, standing.

"I'll make sure to bring plenty of coffee cups," she said sweetly.

"Good," Connor said, sauntering towards his sliding glass door, "because I could really go for another cup of that delicious cocoa," he said, laughing when his beer bottle sailed through the air towards his head.

"Damn it!" She groaned when she missed again.

When the hell was her luck going to change?

FOUR

Connor couldn't help grinning as he took the turn for Strawberry Manor. His eyes darted to his rear view mirror to check on the long line of employee trucks and equipment following him and then to the dashboard clock. It was almost seven o'clock and there hadn't been a sign of Rory or her team anywhere on the way over here.

When he'd snuck out of his house an hour ago he'd been shocked to find her Jeep still in the driveway. He'd really thought the eager little thing was going to give him a run for his money, but she hadn't. Hell, she hadn't even rigged his truck so that it wouldn't start. After he'd let the air out of her tires he'd left for work, wondering if he even had to worry about her getting in his way after all.

As far as he was concerned, this early bird definitely caught the worm, the worm being Strawberry Manor of course. Clearly he wanted this project more than Rory. If she wanted it half as badly as he did, she would have had her beautiful ass up at the crack of dawn, getting everything set up, and making an official claim on the project. But, she didn't and hadn't, so this project was his. He couldn't wait to see her face when she realized that he'd stolen the lead.

He thought of all the different ways he could rub this in her face as he drove his truck over the broken road leading up to Strawberry Manor. The half-mile road and parking lot would have to be replaced soon so they could get equipment and materials up here safely. The thick brush that hugged the private road would also have to be pruned back, not too much though. His client wanted to keep the little trip from the road to the hotel looking beautiful. It wouldn't be too hard, he thought as he took the last curve on the private road. They could cut back the trees and shrub ten feet on each side to widen the private road. Then they could-

"Son of a bitch!" he practically shouted as the hotel and grounds came into view.

This was not happening!

This was not fucking happening!

A horn honking behind him made him realize that he'd come to a complete stop. Cursing Rory James to hell, he pulled off to the side to where an impromptu parking lot had been created and parked between two pickup trucks. He jumped out of his truck and looked around in disbelief as his crew found parking spots.

Not only had she managed to beat him here this morning, but she also had the entire construction site set up. Where he'd planned to place his office trailer tomorrow, she had one with tan vinyl siding that looked newer and larger than his. Thanks to the overgrown vegetation and uneven terrain and large equipment there was nowhere for him to place his trailer now.

His eyes quickly ran over the rest of the property. Her large trucks and equipment were lined up along the west side of the property. There were four large dumpsters placed close to each end of the mansion with a makeshift dirt road leading to the cracked parking lot. Hell, she already had several equipment sheds placed as well as latrines.

Was that a coffee truck?

"How the hell did she do all this?" he mumbled to himself as he grabbed his hardhat, briefcase, and tool belt before slamming his truck door shut and stormed off in the direction of the trailer.

He was barely ten feet away from the trailer when the door opened and Rory James stepped out, looking innocent as she sipped what had to be a cup of cocoa.

"Good afternoon, Connor," she said brightly when her eyes landed on him.

"It's morning," he bit out as he stormed past her and into the rather comfortable looking office.

"Oh, is it? It feels more like afternoon, but that probably has something to do with the fact that we've been here for hours," she mused.

"I can see that," he said, shooting her secretary, her *male* secretary he might add, a glare as he walked through what appeared to be the waiting room and into the back room that he'd figured was the office and he was right.

The office was large, but not large enough. There was hardly enough room as it was for the large desk, drafting table, chairs and filing cabinets that took up the majority of the room. This wouldn't do.

Not at all.

He turned around, not at all surprised to find the little cocoa addict leaning against the doorway, sipping the cocoa that he was tempted to snatch away from her.

"You need to have the trailer towed out of here," he explained in what he thought was a reasonable tone.

"No," she simply said with a shrug.

"Move it or I'll tow it myself!" he snapped.

"Not going to happen," she said, taking a slow sip of her cocoa.

"Yes, you will," he said, getting in her face.

"It's so sad that you think that you can push me around," she said, patting his cheek condescendingly before she stepped past him.

"You're going to have to move your trailer, Rory. I need my office," he bit out through clenched teeth.

"So do I," she said.

"What for?" he demanded, tossing his shit on the small loveseat by the door.

"To work, what else?" she asked, throwing him a frown.

"To fetch my drinks and be at my beck and call?" he asked, shaking his head. "Nope, you don't need an office for that. All you need is a little chair in the corner and I think we can manage that."

"Be at your beck and call?" she asked, sounding amused and pissing him off.

Why in the hell did she think that he was joking about something like that?

"Yup, and if you do a good job I might just let you wash my truck," he said, feeling generous.

"How long exactly have you been this delusional?" she asked as she leaned over to grab something from one of her desk drawers.

"About a month, give or take a few weeks," he mumbled distract-edly as he watched one of the first fantasies he'd ever had come to life.

Was he dead? he wondered, but quickly decided that he really didn't care as Rory pulled off her black tee shirt and tossed it aside like it was nothing, revealing a flat, lightly tanned stomach that he'd love to lick, kiss and caress. He swallowed hard as he took in the tight fitting black sports bra with the large breasts that threatened to spill out.

He should probably care or at least wonder why she was stripping in front of him, but he didn't. The only thing that mattered was that she was in fact stripping in front of him and none of the fantasies that he'd had over the years about her body were even close to the real thing.

"Rory, I-" her secretary started to say as he walked in the office.

With a muttered curse for interrupting his fantasy come to life, Connor shoved the man out of the room and slammed the door shut in his face before turning a glare on Rory.

She frowned at him as she pulled on a grey Shadow Construction tank top. "What was that about?"

"What the hell is wrong with you stripping in front of your employ-ees like that?" he demanded, barely resisting the urge to yell at the woman.

Rory rolled her eyes as she fixed her ponytail. "It's just a sports bra, Connor. Nothing to get excited about," she said and he just barely stopped himself from correcting her.

"You shouldn't be stripping in front of your employees. What if he sues?" he demanded, barely reigning in his temper when all he wanted to do was throttle the woman for covering up.

"I would never sue!" her secretary yelled from behind the door. "I'm willing to sign a waiver!"

"Go away!" Connor snapped in no mood for this bullshit. They had work to do and if Rory decided that she'd be more comfortable wearing something else then he would just have to suck it up and be a gentleman while she changed her shirt again.

"I need to get to work," Rory said, stepping around the desk and walked towards him, "so unless you can walk and bitch at the same time, I'd say that this conversation is over."

He leaned back against the door, blocking her only exit. "You're not leaving until we get a few things settled." He crossed his arms over his chest as he glared down at her, hoping that for once in her life that she'd act like a woman and be intimidated enough to do as he asked, but of course he was an idiot for even considering it. With a small sigh, she reached up and latched onto both of his flat nipples and twisted.

Shit!

That was definitely one trick that he hadn't showed her. No doubt she'd learned that from watching her brothers beat the shit out of each other. Biting back a pained groan, he quickly moved to the side, deciding that he'd let her have this round. When he was well out of the way of the door, she gave him a smug little smile and another twist that threatened to drop him to his knees before releasing him.

With a satisfied sigh, Rory grabbed a tool belt off the small couch and put it on as she sauntered out of the room. When the pain in his nipples subsided he went after her. He caught up with her at the coffee truck.

"That was a violation of the code, woman!" he bit out, barely resisting the urge to grab a handful of ice and press it against his poor abused nipples. The woman fought dirty and he'd been a fool to forget that.

A little smile tugged at her lips at the reminder of the "Code." Neither one of them had been happy to call a temporary truce to their war, but they'd had no choice after the eighth grade dinner dance when things may have gone a little too far.

No matter what the cops said, he really didn't think that what happened had warranted the two of them being placed in adjoining cells all night. Yeah, everyone left the gymnasium screaming, there were one or two dozen minor injuries, but he really didn't think what they'd done justified being charged with inciting a riot. It had all been a simple misunderstanding that had gone horribly wrong.

So while they'd waited in their cells for their parents to kill them, well her father to kill her and his mother to bail him out, they'd come up with a few rules to help avoid a repeat of that night. They'd come up with the "Code."

"Your nipples are not protected by the code," Rory simply said as she grabbed the last Milky Way and a bottle of water and stepped up in line to pay the cashier.

"Well, they are now," he said, deciding that it was better late than never to protect his poor nipples.

"Sorry, veto," Rory said with a shrug, not sounding sorry at all as she paid for her snack and drink.

Damn. He'd forgotten about the veto rule. They were only allowed to change the code if they both agreed. Well, that was fine with him, he decided as he snagged her candy bar out of her hand and ripped it open as he headed towards the large hotel to make sure that Andrew was able to get all his men set up.

"Give me that back," Rory demanded as she walked by his side, not trying to attack him for the candy bar, he noted with satisfaction. She was trying to keep up a professional appearance for the job. That was fine with him, but only because it worked for him.

"Nope," he said, taking a huge bite out of her candy bar. Maybe it was just him, but food stolen from Rory always tasted so damn good. Even those plain peanut butter sandwiches he used to steal from her when they were in preschool had been out of this world.

"Bastard," she muttered as she opened her bottle of water and went to take a sip, but of course the chocolate had made him thirsty so he swiped it out of her hand and downed it.

"Shouldn't you be hauling your little ass back to the office and arranging for your trailer to be removed?" he asked as they headed towards her brothers and his men, who appeared to be arguing.

"Yeah, I'll get right on that," she said dryly as she sauntered past him.

His eyes dropped to her heart shaped ass and he just barely bit back a groan that would probably get his ass kicked by at least two of her brothers.

"What's the problem?" Rory demanded as she neared the men.

"Tell your men to get out of our way so we can get some work done," David, a man he may have mistakenly promoted, snapped at Rory.

As one, all five of her brothers stepped forward as they scowled down at the much smaller man. "Watch how you talk to our sister," Bryce said softly, but the threat was clear.

David noticeably swallowed as he took a healthy step back. He shot a look of panic Connor's way and as much as he'd love to start shit just to piss Rory off, he couldn't. He needed to keep the James brothers happy if he was going to have any chance at getting them to come work for him when this project was finished.

"With our companies working together this might become a little difficult," he said to Rory, but his eyes were on the James brothers who looked more than eager to teach his foreman a lesson. That was one thing he'd learned early on, the James brothers had a zero tolerance policy when it came to their sister. They'd never gone after him, but that was only because Rory thought she could handle him.

Sad, but true.

"Until we figure things out, David and the rest of my supervisors are going to check in with Craig and his men since they were here first and have a better understanding of what requires immediate attention," he said, shocking everyone into silence.

Rory frowned, but he didn't really care what she thought. As long she stayed out of his way, fetched his drinks and food, he would tolerate her presence. David looked pissed and ready to argue, but he didn't really care about that either. The only thing that he cared about was the five large men sharing questioning looks.

He knew that they hadn't expected him to give in so easily. Hell, they probably expected shouting, arguments and a lot of chaos, but they wouldn't get any of that. He wanted these men to come work for him, and what better way to convince them to do that than letting them start now?

FIVE

"What are you doing?"

Rory didn't bother looking at Connor while she said, "Working. What does it look like?"

"It looks like you're getting in the way of my men."

She stopped what she was doing and looked pointedly around the large roof where four of her brothers were checking for weak spots and marking the area.

"Exactly how am I getting in the way of your men if none of them are up here?" she asked, leaning over to mark a weak spot in the roof with a can of orange spray paint.

Connor glared at her as he stepped up onto the arched roof. Rory cocked a brow as she looked him over from his baby blue shirt with the dark blue tie pulled lose at the neck, to his dark tan cargo khakis and finally down to his black leather hiking boots. Only a man as hot as Connor would be able to pull off that look, she thought with disgust as she returned her attention to marking the roof.

They were going to have to replace the entire thing thanks to poor upkeep, but they liked to know which spots to avoid when it was time to rip it off. They'd learned that lesson years ago when they'd still worked for their father. Brian hadn't marked the roof before he'd started working. He fell through the roof, broke his arm and got his ass chewed out by their father in the ER while his arm was being set in a cast, scaring off more than a few nurses in the process.

Brian had sat there quietly, taking it, because he'd known that he'd fucked up. He hadn't even bothered complaining when their father made him do all the grunt work for the next three months. It was a

- 33 -

job they all hated and worked their asses off to avoid, but once you got grunt work, you knew that you'd royally screwed up. They worked hard to avoid grunt work, real hard.

"Because they should be up here doing this instead of you," he said, stepping onto the roof and gesturing for her to get off. With an amused snort, she continued to check the roof.

"And what exactly should I be doing?" she asked, not bothering to look up as she tapped her blunt metal pole against another spot.

"Getting my coffee. What else?" he asked in that cocky tone that always rubbed her the wrong way and worst of all, he'd said it in front of her brothers.

She looked up, hoping that they were getting offended on her behalf and moving to throw Connor's ass off the roof, but of course they only let out amused chuckles as they continued to work. For a moment she glared at them, wondering not for the first time, why they hadn't beaten the crap out of Connor for her since they beat everyone else up that screwed with her.

Whenever she'd asked them about that, they'd either shrugged it off like it was nothing or told her that she was handling Connor well enough on her own. She secretly suspected that they said and did nothing because they got a kick out of this sick and twisted rivalry she had going on with Connor. Even her own father, who hated it when a man looked at her the wrong way never mind made her life a living hell, said and did nothing.

There was something seriously wrong with the men in her life, she decided as she marked off another area. When she stood up, she nearly jumped off the roof, but Connor's grip on her hips kept her firmly in place. That was good, because it meant that it wouldn't take a year to heal in order to kick his ass. She could do it right now.

She moved to turn around and let him have it, but he held her firmly in place. "You don't belong up here, Rory," he said, keeping his tone light even as his hands tightened on her hips.

"I'm not fetching your coffee, Connor, so drop it," she said, taking a step forward only to have the jerk move with her.

"I don't care what you do as long as you get off the roof and let some of my men up here," he said, keeping his hold on her as they continued to move forward with her ramming the end of her pole against the roof with a little more force than necessary. When she found a soft spot, she bent down without thinking and placed her bottom firmly against the front of his pants.

As soon as the action registered in her mind, she stood up, praying that no one else noticed the blush creeping up her cheeks, and tested the area around the weak spot. Connor's soft chuckle in her ear made the blush worse.

"Don't you have anything better to do?" she asked him as she tried to ignore just how good the brief contact had felt.

"Well, I do have about a hundred things that need my attention, but at the moment I'm trying to get a pain in the ass woman off the roof so that my men can get to work. As soon as she moves her ass I'll be out of your hair," he explained, sounding amused.

"I'm not going anywhere," she said stubbornly as she bent, making sure that she bumped into him hard and was pleased by his pained grunt, and marked off another area.

"Then neither am I," he bit out tightly when she stood up.

She shrugged as she focused on her work and not on the large hands at her waist. "Suit yourself." It was a difficult task, but she somehow made it through the next hour without tossing him over the side of the roof. Of course, when they were done the life-ruining bastard insisted that he go down the ladder first and waited patiently until she moved her ass and joined him on the ladder.

"Careful," Connor said, making her grind her teeth together as she glared up at her brothers as they nearly fell off the roof while they laughed their asses off at her. It would serve them right, she decided as she was forced to move at Connor's snail's pace as she climbed down the ladder. Once they reached the bottom, the bastard actually had the nerve to place his hands on her hips as if she needed the help.

She'd been seven when her last babysitter had quit after a rather unfortunate incident at the playground between her, Connor and the McCaffie's dog, Snowflake. Since no one else in town had the guts to watch her, her father decided that she was more than old enough to work. He'd started her off with grunt work and he hadn't taken it easy on her because she was a girl or only seven.

It figured that the one man that treated her like a woman was the one that made her wish that she was a man so that she could kick his ass. Ever since she could remember she'd been treated like one of the guys. Even her boyfriends treated her like one of the guys.

They'd never once told her that she was pretty, brought her flowers, chocolates or did a hundred things that other women took for granted. When they went out it was to a fast food joint or a bar. For movies they'd always picked action movies or horror flicks, never once asking her if she wanted to see whatever romantic comedy was playing, she didn't, but it would have been nice to been asked. For gifts, she got tools and nothing but tools. She liked tools, but she could have gone for some sexy lingerie or something equally feminine.

The fact that Connor seemed to be the only man on earth that remembered that she was a woman, even as he tortured the hell out of her, annoyed her. She didn't want him to notice her and she sure as hell didn't like the fact that on some level she liked it. She hated him and always would.

"Where are you going now?" he demanded as she shoved him away.

"I need a drink," she bit out between clenched teeth as she headed for her trailer.

"Hold up! We need to talk," he said, but she didn't stop.

Oh no, if anything she moved faster. If she didn't get a drink soon, she was afraid that she was going to do something stupid like strangle the bastard. Then she'd lose the contract on Strawberry Manor and as good as she knew that it would feel to do it, she couldn't. She'd waited too long for this project and she wasn't about to let him wreck it.

By the time she reached her trailer her nerves were frayed and she was trembling with the need to kick Connor's ass. She stormed inside the trailer, and ignored Jacob's questioning look as he spoke on the phone, probably handling one of the hundreds of boring things that she hated doing. She walked over to the coffee cart that she paid Jacob well to keep stocked and turned on the electric kettle.

While the water was heating up, she scooped out a large amount of hot cocoa mix and placed it in a super sized coffee cup. Once it looked like enough, she opened the mini-fridge and grabbed a small carton of coffee creamer. She poured a dab of creamer into the cup. She stirred the cocoa powder and creamer until the mixture was nice and creamy. Then she added a spoonful of fluff and mixed it until it was well blended. When it was done, she stood there with her hands on her hips as she glared at the electric kettle, urging it to hurry up.

"I hate to tell you this since you're already in a bad mood," Jacob said as he stood up and approached her.

"I'm not in a bad mood," she said tightly as she narrowed her eyes on the kettle, making all sorts of mental promises to sell it for scrap metal if it didn't hurry up so that she could make her precious and much needed hot cocoa.

"Then why are you having a large hot chocolate during a work day, hmm?" he asked, stepping up beside her and with an amused smirk that she could have happily bitch slapped off his face at the moment. He reached over and plugged the kettle in.

She clenched her jaw tighter as she fought against the urge to release a frustrated scream. Jacob smartly said nothing about the kettle as he leaned against the paneled wall.

"I have some bad news."

"Does it have to do with the life-wrecking bastard?" she asked, wondering just how much more she could take before she lost it. The fact that the first day wasn't even over yet and she was close to a breakdown hadn't escaped her notice.

"No," Jacob said, shaking his head before frowning at her. "Are you ever going to tell me why you call him that?"

"No," she said evenly while she continued to direct her focus on the kettle that was just now starting to release steam.

"Alrighty then. I guess this is the part where I tell you that your father just called to let you know that he's on his way," he said, taking a healthy step back just as Rory's glare swung from the kettle to him.

"*This is how you tell me?*" she demanded in disgust.

Jacob shifted nervously under her murderous glare. "He just called." When she looked towards the door, wondering, heck hoping that she could make a run for it before her old man came, he added, "He was on his cell phone when he called and less than two minutes away."

She couldn't do this. Oh God, she really couldn't do this. Not today. Not when Connor already had her contemplating manslaughter. Her eyes shot back to the kettle just as it began to whistle. Wasting no time, she picked up the kettle, filled the mug and stirred it until the creamy concoction was perfect. She picked it up, gave it her customary thirty-second blow and sipped.

When she felt the hot creamy chocolate go down her throat and into her stomach some of the tension in her body disappeared. Three long sips later, she felt close to being able to face the day. By the time half the cocoa was gone she was in her special place, the place where everything was fine and she could face anything including Connor and a visit from her dad. By the time she finished the rest of the cocoa she'd be able to keep this calm façade going for the rest of the day, but of course she was going to need a second cup. She quickly made another cup and was just about to take a sip when the trailer door flew open and Connor stormed in, looking pissed.

"I told you that I needed to talk with you," he said, tossing his hardhat on one of the guest chairs as he stormed over to her. Her lips barely touched the brim of her cup when she found the large mug suddenly ripped out of her hands.

For a moment she could only stare in disbelief as Connor drank, more like chugged, her cocoa down. When he was done, he handed the empty cup back over to her and gestured for her to go into her office, but she couldn't move. She just couldn't.

She looked down at her empty mug as her mind struggled with the knowledge that not only had he touched her mug, but he'd also drained her hot cocoa, again. All those calm feelings she'd had a minute ago quickly vanished as she looked up and glared at the bastard who dared touch her much-needed hot cocoa.

"*You.......bastard,*" she bit out slowly in a harsh whisper as she took a step towards him, quickly closing the distance between them. "Do you have any idea how much I needed that?"

"She really did," Jacob agreed, retreating back to the safety of his desk and for good reason.

"Too bad," Connor said, moving impossibly closer to her as he leaned down until they were practically nose-to-nose.

Her fingers flexed by her side with the need to slap that smug look off his face. Just one slap, that's all she was asking for. She really didn't think that she was asking for too much. Connor's smile became knowing and the urge to slap him shifted to the need to throttle him.

"I tell you what, Rory," he said in a seductive whisper that would probably make other woman tremble with need, but only managed to set her rage off another notch, "if you're really good I might just let you make me some hot cocoa instead of just fetching my coffee."

That was it! She was going to kill the bastard, she decided just as Jacob cleared his throat. She glared at Connor for ten more seconds before she moved her glare to her assistant, who had the balls to look amused.

"I probably should remind you that your brothers said that they wouldn't bail you out of jail again for the next three years after what happened the last time *and* that if you kill him then you'll probably lose this contract," Jacob reminded her, which is of course was the reason that she kept him around. He kept the business running smoothly and kept her from doing anything rash, most of the time anyway.

Fortunately today was one of those days that he managed to stop her from doing anything particularly stupid like lose the contract for Strawberry Manor because she killed the bastard.

"*Fine,*" she gritted out, hating the fact that she'd have to resist the urge to throttle the man until the project was done. "Then I'm going back to work," she said, moving to step around the jerk, but he simply shook his head, grabbed her by the arm and hauled her ass towards the office.

"Let me go!" she snapped, trying to pull her arm away, but he refused to release her.

"Not until you and I go over a few things," he simply said as he opened her office door.

"Let go!"

"No."

"Don't worry. I'll hold your calls," Jacob said, sounding amused and if she didn't rely on the man so damn much she would have fired him then and there, but she did, so she couldn't.

Stupid job security, she thought as Connor hauled her ass inside her office.

SIX

"Let me go!" Rory snapped as he kicked the office door shut behind him.

"Sure thing," he said, releasing her just as she tried to yank her arm free. The move sent her stumbling back and muttering a few choice words about him and his ass, which he easily ignored. He walked around her desk and sat down in her surprisingly comfy chair.

"Get the hell out of my chair," Rory snapped as she walked around the desk and glared down at him. Perhaps he shouldn't have stolen her hot cocoa since the little addict seemed on edge. Then again, he did enjoy ruffling her feathers so to speak.

"I'm sorry. Did you want to sit down?" he asked innocently.

"*Yes*," she hissed out as her hands clenched and unclenched into fists.

With a shrug, he reached out and grabbed her hand, giving it a good yank and taking her by surprise. With an adorable little squeak, her beautiful ass landed on his lap. Before she could move, he had his arms wrapped around her waist and pulled tightly against him so that her side was pressed up against his chest and her legs hung over his.

"Now, I think we should probably go over your duties, don't you?" he asked brightly, loving the murderous scowl she sent him.

"The only duty I have at the moment is to kick your ass," she bit out, practically shaking with rage that he of course ignored as he settled more comfortably in the chair.

"The most important thing that you need to remember is that I take two sugars in my coffee and just a splash of half and half," he explained as he allowed his eyes to roam.

Was it just him or did she look hotter when she was pissed? His eyes ran from her beautiful neck with a few tendrils of damp hair plastered against it, down to the beautiful tanned skin of her shoulders, to the pair of large breasts that stretched the shirt's material to perfection. She truly was magnificent.

"My eyes are up here," she pointed out.

"Uh huh," he said, not bothering to look up.

With an exasperated sigh, she cupped his chin and forced him to look up and meet her eyes. "Stop pissing me off or I'm going to have to kill you," she said in a low even tone, sounding as though she'd meant it and he knew that if she could figure out a way to hide his body that she'd probably would do it. Then again, she'd been saying that same damn thing to him since they were six so he really wasn't too concerned.

"That's nice," he said absently as he shifted her on his lap and pulled her closer. "I tell you what, Rory. If you do a really good job and stay away from my site, I might just give you a special bonus when this is all done. How does that sound?" he asked in his most patronizing voice, unable to help himself even though he knew that he was pissing her off.

"This is my project, too," she said, glaring daggers at him through narrowed eyes.

He nodded in agreement as he continued, "Which is why you should be a good little girl and stay out of the way so that we can get this project finished on time."

She tried to climb off his lap, but of course he wouldn't let her. Not when he was comfortable and well, that's all that he really cared about, but apparently she couldn't give a damn about his comfort. Kind of selfish of her, he thought as she went for his nipples. With a curse, he released his hold on her so that he could protect his poor little nipples before the vicious woman could tear them off.

"Do the rules mean nothing to you?" he demanded, feeling like an idiot with his hands plastered against his chest. He dropped his hands away as he came to his feet and stood so that he could glare down at the woman.

"As long as I'm stuck with you on this project and you try to get in my way, anything goes," she said, stepping into him as she met his glare and he just barely bit back the groan that was threatening to escape as her large, warm breasts pressed tightly against his chest.

Somehow he forced himself to ignore them and focus on the little problem at the moment.

Rory.

He leaned down further until their noses were practically touching. "Is that a fact?" he demanded evenly.

"*Yes,*" she practically hissed as her eyes narrowed on his.

"You're only here because of my generosity, Rory. Push me and you might just find yourself locked in the trunk of a car on a ferryboat headed off to Nova Scotia......*again,*" he said softly, loving the way that she practically shook with rage against him.

"I knew that was you, you bastard!" she snarled, looking torn between going for his nipples again or flat-out killing him.

"You deserved it," he felt obligated to remind her.

She scoffed. "I was twelve!"

"You superglued my shorts to my ass!"

The smile that teased her lips transformed her face from pretty to breathtakingly beautiful in a matter of seconds. He was damn thankful that she didn't know the effect that had on him or she'd do it to bring him to his knees and God help him, but he'd love every fucking second of it.

She chuckled softly as she moved to put a little space between them. "I'd actually forgotten about that."

"I haven't," he bit out tightly, pissed that she'd moved away from him and took her warmth with her.

"I'm sure that you deserved it," she said with a shrug like it was no big deal that it took a month, five specialists and about a hundred experimental procedures that took a pound of flesh from his ass before they were able to remove every last scrap of his basketball shorts off his ass.

"I didn't!" he snapped, unable to remember exactly what he'd done to piss her off enough to break into the boy's locker room and squirt superglue into his shorts, but he was sure that he hadn't done anything to deserve it. As far as he was concerned, that prank had been unprovoked and he was the innocent party in all of-

"Now I remember why I did that," she said, looking angry once again. "You snuck laxatives into my food and then locked all the girl's bathrooms in the school with bicycle locks so that I was left with no choice but to use the boy's bathroom where you and your stupid friends locked me inside without any toilet paper or paper towels, you jerk!"

Huh, he'd actually forgotten about that one, he realized with a careless shrug. "Whatever. The point is, Rory, this is my project. I've busted my ass to get it and I'm not about to let you fuck it up for me."

"This is *our* project," she said, getting back in his face where she belonged, "and as long as you remember that we'll be fine, but the next time that you try to stop me from doing my job I will kick. Your. Ass."

He leaned in closer. "Your job is to fetch my coffee, food and whatever else I need and as long as you remember how I like my coffee everything will be fine."

"You can shove your coffee right up your-"

"There's a problem," Rory's assistant said as he burst through the door.

———

"We're not finished talking," Connor said.

Rory didn't even bother slowing her pace or looking back as she shot him a one-finger salute. His deep chuckle that followed did not send a delicious shiver throughout her body that had her fighting the urge to lick her lips.

It didn't.

She sighed heavily as she adjusted the tool belt around her hips. It really wasn't her fault that her body betrayed her the way it did when Connor was around. He might be a life-ruining bastard, but he was a hot life-ruining bastard and her poor neglected body didn't realize that it should hate him as much as her heart and brain did. One day her body would be on board, but until that day came, and she prayed that it came quickly, she was just going to have to ignore her body's response to him.

"What's going on?" she asked as they stepped outside.

"Work has come to a halt," Jacob announced as he gestured with his clipboard towards Strawberry Manor.

One look and she knew that he hadn't exaggerated. There were no men manning the equipment, the scaffolding that was supposed to be completed by now was left incomplete against the outer walls of the manor, and it appeared that every single one of their employees were in the middle of the yard, having a shouting and pushing match.

Great, she thought dryly, just what they needed.

When she spotted the familiar beat up red pickup truck parked near the coffee truck she nearly cried. Why did he have to come here today of all days? Why couldn't he have come when she had this situation under control? The last thing she wanted him to see was this or the fact that Connor was treating her like some weak woman.

"You planning on handling this?" her father asked as she stepped past the coffee truck.

She looked to her left to find her father leaning back against one of Connor's trucks with his impressively large arms crossed over his standard black tee shirt covered chest and a hint of annoyance in his blue eyes as he looked past her toward the men arguing.

"Just give me a minute, Dad," she said, wondering when all this nonsense would end so that she could focus on Strawberry Manor. Right now she should be inside assessing the water damage in the attic, but thanks to Connor, she was stressed and needed a hot cocoa fix soon or she was afraid that she was going to kill someone. If that wasn't bad enough, it seemed as though all hell was breaking loose among their employees and having her father around to witness it was just the icing on the cake.

He nodded firmly as he pushed away from the truck. "I'll be in the building looking the old girl over when you're finally ready to get down to work," he said, making her inwardly cringe at the unspoken criticism. She wasn't handling the job right and her men were not only wasting her money, but they were also wasting time and that was something that her father taught her never to do.

Relieved that he was going to let her handle this without an audience, she walked around the crowd, stole the bullhorn from one of Connor's men since the man was just standing around looking useless, and moved to stand between the manor and the large crowd of men. As she turned the bullhorn on and scanned the large crowd she couldn't help but wonder where her brothers were. They should have handled this.

"You have exactly sixty seconds to go back to work or you're fired," she announced, keeping it simple and direct.

Her men noticeably startled. Not even ten seconds later they were shoving Connor's men aside as they rushed back to work. One thing that she made sure of was that everyone that worked for her understood on the first day that they were hired was that she always backed up her word. Whoever wasn't working in sixty seconds would be fired. She didn't play games and she definitely didn't have time for her men to be screwing around.

With an annoyed sigh, Connor took the bullhorn from her hands and made his own announcement, "Get back to work or leave," he said before tossing the bullhorn back to his supervisor, who was still standing around looking useless.

"Try to keep your men in line, okay, cupcake?" Connor drawled as he walked past her.

"Don't call me that," she bit out as she yanked out a pair of pliers from her tool belt and moved to catch up with him, careful to wait for just the right moment and when that moment came she didn't hesitate.

"Son of a bitch!" he snapped as she sauntered past him, whistling a jaunty tune as she returned her pliers back to her tool belt.

She sighed with relief as she made her way past the men hustling to get back to work. It never ceased to amaze her how torturing Connor always seemed to calm her down. It wasn't as good as a hot cocoa fix, but it would do.

When she spotted her father waiting for her in a half-gutted room with his arms crossed over his chest and his lips drawn into a frown she was tempted to hit Connor with the sledgehammer that was close by. Her fingers literally twitched with the need to get one good hit in. But that went against the rules. They weren't supposed to do anything that left permanent damage, pity.

"Rule ten," Connor said, chuckling as he walked past her.

She glared at his back even as she wondered how he knew. Then again, they'd been at each other's throats since they were kids so he probably could sense these things.

Now that she thought about it, she realized that perhaps the sledgehammer was a bit of an overkill. The only thing he was guilty of today was annoying her, she realized as she pulled her needle nose pliers out of her tool belt and walked towards her father, loving the startled little groan Connor let out as her pliers accidentally pinched him on the ass. He didn't say anything as she walked past him and she didn't expect him to, but she would have to keep her guard up for the rest of the day, because if there was one thing that she knew about Connor, it was that the man loved immediate retribution.

SEVEN

First his poor defenseless nipples and now his ass, Connor thought with disgust as he barely resisted the urge to rub the sore spot on his ass as he narrowed a glare on Rory's retreating back. If that wasn't bad enough, her men were already causing problems for his and cutting into the workday with their bullshit. Not only was he going to have to find out what her men had done to interrupt his workday, but he was going to have to find a way to get his trailer brought onto the property. There was no way that he was going be stuck doing his paperwork in his truck while Rory had a large comfortable trailer to work in.

Oh, she was going to pay for this shit.

When his eyes landed on her old man he knew exactly how to get the little brat back and the hell out of his hair. As long as he had the use of her men and equipment he'd be able to get this project done on time. What he didn't need was the little pain in the ass getting in his way and he knew just the man to help him with this little problem.

If there was one thing that he knew about Mr. James, besides the fact that the man absolutely hated him, it was that he took the job very seriously. Everyone in town knew the man didn't believe in bullshit at work and he stressed that rule big time on his kids. It didn't exactly take a genius to figure out that Mr. James was pretty pissed off about what just went down with their employees so of course he had to cash in on that.

"If you can't handle your men then I suggest that you find someone that can," he said to her back, loving the way that she suddenly went tense and stumbled over her own two feet. He wasn't at all surprised when she threw a murderous glare over her shoulder or mouthed a few unpleasant words in his direction as her father's scowl intensified.

"We have a deadline that we need to make and we're not going to be able to do that unless you get your men organized and under control," he said firmly as he sent Mr. James a nod of acknowledgement before he headed off to see what his men were up to and of course, to hide his shit-eating grin.

Was it wrong that he enjoyed making Rory's life a living hell? He really didn't think so. In fact, he decided that if he was going to get her out of his hair then he was going to have to up his game.

———

"This is a big project," her father needlessly reminded her quietly, but not low enough that she missed the familiar disapproval lacing his words. "Maybe you should step aside and let one of your brothers handle this just to make sure that it's done right," he said, confirming her fears.

Even after all these years, she still wasn't good enough in his eyes. Why she thought landing this project would mean anything to him, she didn't know. She was neither a daughter nor a son in his eyes, but something in between. When she was little she hadn't been girly enough in his eyes to be a daughter and growing up she hadn't exactly been boyish enough to be treated like a son.

Nothing she did ever seemed to be good enough for him. When she was a kid, she'd busted her ass just as hard if not harder than her brothers, but instead of telling her that she did a good job he simply grunted and told her that she needed to move her ass faster or work harder. When she'd mastered the skill saw and far surpassed even his abilities he'd made her practice more. It hadn't seemed to matter what she did, he always found a flaw or pushed her to do better. Nothing she did ever made him happy.

When she'd started Shadow Construction she'd thought that he'd be happy that she was following in his footsteps, but instead of being proud of her, he'd sighed heavily and suggested that perhaps she should go work for one of her brothers instead. Her brothers, who had been proud of her, had all gone deathly silent at their father's announcement. Then, one by one, they'd each told her that they'd be working for her and that she damn well better not try bossing them around or they'd kick her ass.

It was one of the sweetest things her brothers had ever done for her.

"I have it under control, Dad," she said, forcing herself to sound casual when all she wanted to do was scream at him.

"This is a big project, Rory," he mused as his eyes shifted to follow the life-ruining bastard as he walked away. "Maybe you should let Connor take the lead," he said, shocking the ever-loving hell out of her.

She couldn't believe how much it hurt to hear her father say that. It was one thing to constantly have him second-guess her, but quite another for him to suggest that the one person on earth that he knew that she couldn't stand take over her dream project. In that moment she realized something, in her father's eyes she might not be good enough, but Connor was.

"He's got a great reputation and as much as I hate to say this, his work is some of the best that I've ever seen. The boy has talent, Rory and maybe it would be for the best if you let him take the lead on this one," her father said, stunning her into silence, because really there was no way to respond to that without crying.

"Where are you going? I thought you were going to give me a tour?" her father asked as she walked away. She knew that she was being rude, but she couldn't help it. If she didn't get away from him now she knew that she'd do something stupid like cry and that wasn't happening. Her father might think that she was weaker than the boys, but that didn't mean that she had to prove him right.

———

"Where's your sister?" Connor asked as he stepped into the once impressive kitchen, but was sadly nothing more than a room full of broken tile, rust and debris.

None of the James brothers looked at him, never mind paused in demolishing the room and the connecting pantries. That really didn't surprise him since the whole family seemed to hate him. Not that he could really blame them. He did seem to go out of his way to make Rory's life a living hell. He was actually surprised that none of them had tried to kill him yet.

"She's checking the attic," came the deep voice that used to give him nightmares as a kid. It was a little unnerving that the man still had the power to make him want to run and hide.

He forced himself to relax as he turned around and once again forced himself to stay where he was when blue eyes very much like Rory's, but colder, so much colder, locked on him.

"She shouldn't be up there by herself," he said, ignoring the disbelieving snorts from her brothers.

"Oh? And why's that?" Mr. James asked in a bored tone as he crossed the still impressively large arms of his over his chest.

"Because she could get hurt," he said with an annoyed sigh as the James boys once again snorted and chuckled. "She's also getting in the way and holding back this project," he said firmly, never taking his eyes off the man in front of him. He wasn't an idiot after all.

"Oh, puhlease," Brian said, chuckling. "You're acting like she's some chick."

Connor blinked. "Because she is," he said slowly, wondering what the hell was wrong with these men. Of course her brothers laughed while Mr. James considered him with a hard glint in his eyes.

What in the hell was wrong with them? They overprotected her everywhere else in life except for this when they should be dragging the damn woman away from tools and dangerous conditions. Hell, it was taking everything he had not to run up to the attic and drag her ass away from his job site. She had no business here.

He wasn't a sexist pig or anything, okay, maybe just a tad, but Rory had no business working here. It wasn't because she was a woman, but because it was Rory. He had several women working for him that could easily keep up with the men, but Rory………

For some reason he just couldn't stomach the idea of her doing this. Not only because she was going to get in his way, but because he didn't want to see the damn woman get hurt. Sure, he liked to torture her and make her life a living hell, but he'd never done any permanent damage and that was really all that mattered.

This was the biggest project of his career and if he could pull it off it would mean bigger and better things for Highland Construction, but that wouldn't be happening as long as Rory James was around. He didn't want her screwing with his site and he sure as hell didn't want to have to worry about the stubborn woman getting hurt and judging by the amused smirks on her brothers' faces he was the only one that was concerned.

Hell, he was never going to get any work done while she was around.

The only choice he had was to drive her off, just her. He still needed her men and equipment if he was going to finish this project on time after all. With an inward sigh, he decided that he was going to have to go ahead and make her life a living hell.

"Sunday," Mr. James said, interrupting his thoughts.

"Sunday, what?" he asked, unable to hide his confusion even as he noted the looks of shock on the rest of the James men's faces. They'd all stopped working to stare at their father in disbelief.

"Dad, you can't be serious," Johnny finally said.

Mr. James never took his cold eyes away from him as he addressed his sons. "Last time I checked, I was still head of this family and if I decide that Connor needs to join us this Sunday then he's going to join us," he said firmly, giving Connor the impression that he wasn't exactly being asked to come, but commanded.

Since this actually worked in his favor, Connor didn't argue. "What's going on Sunday?"

"Every Sunday, rain or shine we go fishing as a family at six," his eyes narrowed ever so slightly as he added, "no women allowed. We take our fishing seriously. If you bring a woman you better make sure that she knows that she stays at the house with the rest of them. While we're fishing you can tell me about the plans you have for this old house."

He nodded even as he thought that over. Huh, no Rory......that could actually work for him. He'd be able to get her old man on his side and work on starting to convince the James brothers that their lives would be so much better if they came to work for him. This could really work in his favor, he thought as he looked at the men in question and had to bite back a smile. Oh yeah, the James boys were as good as his.

———

"We're having Dad committed," Bryce said in way of a greeting as he climbed up the rickety steps to the enormous attic that she was even at that moment making plans for. The client wanted the roof fixed, a new attic floor, fix the stairs and update the utilities, but they were passing up a golden opportunity with this space and she was going to convince them to allow her to make three large luxury suites out of the space and she was going to make damn sure that Connor stayed away from the area.

It was going to be her signature touch to the hotel, the thing that drew people to this hotel and the thing that came to mind when Strawberry Manor was mentioned and it was going to be Shadow Construction that got all the glory. She had a meeting set up this Friday and she was going to convince them to stretch their budget just a little more to accommodate her dreams.

While other little girls had been day dreaming about their wedding she'd been thinking about all the things that she would do to this large old mansion to make it perfect and now that it was all hers, well, half hers, to renovate she was going to make damn sure that it lived up to her dreams.

"Did you hear me? I said we're having Dad committed," Bryce said as he carefully stepped on the plywood she'd laid down for safety and glared at her.

"Yeah, I heard you," she said distractedly as she looked at the ceiling and frowned at the structure beams that were going to have to be replaced. She'd hoped that they could salvage some of them to help get the new roof on faster, but it looked like they were going to have to tear the entire roof off and start from scratch. Actually, that could work for her, because-

"Don't you even want to know what he did?"

"Nope, just tell me where to sign," she said, wondering if she would be able to convince some of Connor's men to do a little side work for her, only the ones that met her standards of course. She didn't tolerate sloppy work and she sure as hell wouldn't tolerate substandard work on this project. Unfortunately, she already had a feeling that she was going to have to have some of her guys double check Connor's men's work.

"You really don't care?" he asked, eyeing her suspiciously as he stepped up to stand beside her.

"Not at all," she said as she considered using skylight windows and just as quickly dismissed the idea. The whole point of this project was to give it that eighteenth century feel and placing modern day sky-lights on the roof would wreck the effect. No, it was better to go with her original plan, she decided.

"Fine. Then I won't tell you," Bryce said, clearly fighting back a smile as he crossed his massive arms over his chest.

"Uh huh," she said absently, earning a loud drawn out sigh of annoyance from Bryce and probably an eye roll.

"Shouldn't you be working?" she asked as she checked her watch. It was a quarter to five and she was too excited to call it a night. Not that she would and she doubted that her brothers would either. They'd probably put in another three or four hours until hunger forced them to head home.

"Probably," Bryce mused.

"Is there a special reason why you're not?" she asked as she turned to face him.

He shrugged. "We wanted to know if you wanted us to handle Connor's men the next time they pull any bullshit or just let him deal with it," he said, reminding her of the earlier mutiny that she'd been forced to handle in front of their father.

"What the hell happened?" she asked, walking over to a rotting post and grabbed her bottle of lukewarm water. "And most impor-tantly, why didn't you guys handle it?"

He gave her a "duh" look as he said, "We had our hands full with the fire inspector."

"The fire inspector was here?" When he nodded, she gave him her own version of the "duh" look. "Why the hell didn't someone come get me?"

"Because they were all fighting over petty bullshit. It wouldn't have been too bad, but Connor's foremen are incompetent and started bitching about who was in charge. We got sick of their bullshit and decided to let them beat the shit out of each other while we made sure that we weren't shut down."

She bit back a groan. Being shut down this early in the game would kill their schedule. They needed to get off the ground running. "Did he shut us down?" she asked, trying to stay calm.

Bryce snorted. "He almost did, but lucky for you Dad showed up."

"Shit."

"Yup, seems the fire inspector wasn't too happy having to duck out of the way of morons shoving each other and leaving equipment running and unmanned. Lucky for you that dad took him aside and convinced him to ignore the bullshit. He's coming back Monday so I suggest that you and Connor come to some sort of an agreement before this bullshit gets us shut down."

She sighed heavily as she ran her hands down her face. "I don't want to have to deal with Connor. Can't you do it?" she asked, knowing that she was whining and not really caring.

Bryce chuckled as he reached out and hooked his arm around her neck, pulling her tightly against his side as they headed for the stairs. "Relax, Rory. I don't think it will be that bad."

"But I hate him," she mumbled pathetically. "He makes my life a living hell."

"I know, but if it makes you feel any better, I think that you do a fair job of making his life a living hell, too."

Well, that was something, she thought as she carefully stepped over a missing step.

"At least you'll probably get a break for the next five months from all of his bullshit," Bryce said, sounding hopeful. "He'll be too busy with this project to give you a second thought."

"Oh, I'm sure I can make time for you," Connor drawled from the bottom of the stairs. Their gazes locked and in that moment she knew, just knew that there would never be a break from the daily bullshit. In fact, if that little wink he sent her way before he sauntered off was any indication, she could count on it getting worse and there wasn't a damn thing that she could do to stop it.

EIGHT

Later that night.......

"Looks like he let the air out of your tires," Sean said, chuckling as he pulled up in front of Rory's house.

"That's not too bad," she mumbled, glancing around her dark property, wondering what else he had in store for her. At this point in their lives, letting air out of her tires was child's play and she knew, just knew, that he wasn't done. Oh no, not Connor, especially not since that look he'd shot her earlier told her as much.

That was fine, more than fine actually. She could handle anything he dished out and probably do worse in return. She no longer got nervous at the prospect of Connor settling a score, because she knew that he would at least make sure that he didn't do any permanent damage. That was something at least, she mused as she grabbed her lunch cooler and empty hot chocolate thermos.

"Are you going to need a ride in the morning," Sean asked, sounding amused.

"Yes, and an apple fritter or two," she said, throwing him a wink as she climbed out of his truck.

"I'll see what I can do," he said, chuckling as she shut the door.

She sent him one last wave as she walked towards her Jeep and sighed. She was just too tired to mess with the air compressor right now and was glad that Craig had given her an AAA membership last year for Christmas. Bunny came running around the house as she pulled out her cell phone. He jogged over to her and sat by her feet, obediently waiting for her to finish her phone call.

With a promise of an hour wait, she gave Bunny his customary ear scratch and headed for her front door, forcing herself not to look around like some paranoid chick in a horror flick. Whatever happened, happened. She wasn't about to live the rest of her life looking over her shoulder. He just wasn't worth the effort. Besides, she was too tired at the moment to really care.

After feeding Bunny, she went upstairs and took a quick shower. Normally she would have taken her time and allowed the hot water to ease the ache in her sore muscles, but tonight she really needed a hot cocoa fix. She quickly dried off, pulled on a light blue tank top that ended just above her belly button and pulled on a pair of Craig's old grey gym shorts with a fading Mickey Mouse on the leg and tied them off so that they wouldn't fall off, and headed towards her much needed fix.

Ten minutes later she was carrying an extra large mug of her cocoa as she walked up the stairs with Bunny on her heels. She walked down the hall, releasing a loud yawn as she gestured Bunny towards her bed. As she pulled back the thick curtain she sent up a silent prayer for a Connor-free night and nearly cursed when she spotted the bastard in question lounging on his deck with a bottle of beer and a magazine.

Hopefully, he would be too exhausted to annoy her. For a moment she considered going downstairs and relaxing on her couch, but it wasn't the same. She liked relaxing on her deck after a long day and wasn't about to let Connor take that away from her. She took a sip of her cocoa for fortification and opened the door and stepped out onto her porch.

Connor didn't so much as bat an eye in her direction. Hmmm, that was interesting, she noted as she took another sip from her cocoa before setting it down on the small table. Well, maybe she got her wish and he was too tired to do anything, she thought as she sat down on her lounge chair and stretched out.

When he still didn't say anything a few minutes later she became a little nervous and shot him a look only to find him taking a sip of his beer as he continued to read his magazine. It was a little unsettling and unexpected, but if he was willing to let it go for one night, then so was she. Perhaps he'd realized that they needed to get along for the sake of the project.

"Are you going to move your trailer tomorrow?" Connor asked in a bored tone, never taking his eyes off his magazine.

Maybe not.

"No," she said on a sigh.

"Okay," he said, shrugging.

She cocked a brow at that. "Okay?"

"Yup," he said absently as he took another sip of his beer.

She narrowed her eyes on him, wondering what he was up to. He never gave up this easily, never. Not even when they were fourteen and she may have pantsed him in front of the entire school one afternoon and he may have broken his arm in an attempt to pull her out of the air duct where she may have been hiding. He'd simply waited until the cast was dry and his mother was looking the other way before he'd snuck out of the exam room at the clinic over on Chestnut and made his way to the waiting room where he'd known her father would make her wait so that she could give him the customary muttered "sorry."

As soon as Connor stepped into the waiting room she knew that she was in deep shit. She'd barely turned to run and hide when he'd clamped his good hand around her wrist and dragged her kicking and screaming into the staff kitchenette where he found a strawberry yogurt three years past its expiration date hiding in the back of the fridge. For the next ten minutes he sat on her back while he'd forced her to eat the brown concoction and even when the doctor, three nurses and his mother tried to drag him off of her, he'd still managed to shove a large spoonful of the fuzzy gunk in her mouth.

No, he was definitely up to something, she thought as she picked up her mug of cocoa and gave it the attention that it deserved. Since there really was no way to prepare herself for his little antics, she didn't even bother trying. Whatever he did, she would make damn sure that she did something ten times worse to him.

"I'm drawing a blank here and I was wondering if you could help me out," he said in a thoughtful tone and just like that the small hairs on the back of her neck stood up, but she refused to visibly react for him in any way.

She didn't answer and he didn't seem to care as he continued, "What was the name of that guy, you know the one that you bitch slapped at McGill's Bar last year for no reason at all?"

Rory wasn't sure where he was going with this, but she was sick of people, especially Connor for some weird reason, thinking that she'd attacked the jerk for no reason at all like she was some crazed bitch with a bad case of PMS. She hadn't told her brothers why she'd slapped the man, because she thought that she'd taken care of it, but obviously she'd been wrong. By the next morning he'd spread rumors all over town that she begged him for a quickie in the bathroom and that he'd turned her down, making her look pathetic and slutty. Her brothers' fists had taken care of the rumor, but men still thought that she was easy thanks to him.

"Oh, you mean the guy that cornered me in the small hallway near the jukebox and grabbed my breasts while demanding that I give him a blowjob in the bathroom?" she asked in a bored tone even though the memory of that night still had the power to make her feel weak and vulnerable, something that she didn't like.

Connor paused just as he brought the beer to his mouth. He looked thoughtful as he took a slow sip and placed the beer down on his small table. "He attacked you?" he asked in a deceptively calm tone that didn't match the way that his jaw clenched tightly as a little muscle ticked just below his eye.

"You didn't really think that I would slap some jerk for no reason, now did you?" she asked with a shrug.

He sighed heavily as he took another sip of his beer. "No, I didn't, but I didn't know the asshole was that stupid," he said, shifting in his seat to look at something over his banister. "Speaking of the asshole, you called triple A to take care of your tires?" he asked, conversationally.

"You mean for my tires that mysteriously deflated sometime after I got home last night?" she asked dryly. "Yeah, I hoped they'd send someone else, but it figures that they'd send him," she said, not even bothering to get up to look since she didn't need to sign anything for him to fill up her tires.

She didn't need any added drama to her night and she sure as hell didn't want to face Barry tonight. The guy was a prick and took being shot down a little too personally. As far as she was concerned, he should just be grateful that she hadn't told her brothers what he did, because he would still be eating through a straw if she had.

"Hmmm, looks like he's towing you," Connor said in an innocent tone as he watched Barry do whatever he was doing.

"Yeah, right." She snorted in disbelief. It was really sad that Connor had to resort to lame jokes to try and scare her. Seriously, like she'd believe Barry was really stupid enough to tow her truck away. There was no way that Barry would ever.......

Did she just hear chains rattling? she wondered, trying not to panic as she quickly climbed off her lounge chair and made her way over to the railing just in time to see Barry throw the switch.

"Stop!" she yelled, looking around desperately for a way to get down there and stop that madman before he took off with her Jeep. "What the hell are you doing?" she asked, even as she contemplated climbing over the railing and jumping.

With her paved driveway right below her, she didn't want to take a chance of twisting her ankle or breaking something. She uselessly waved to get Barry's attention, but the damn man was too busy looking down at his clipboard to see her. Groaning in frustration, she shoved away from the banister and ran towards her room.

She ran across the room, startling Bunny, down the long hallway and down the stairs, taking them two at a time and damn near falling to her death several times in the process, before she ran across her small foyer. She threw the front door open, ran outside and across her freshly mowed lawn to the tow truck just as Barry set the locks on the back wheels of her Jeep, the Jeep that was now firmly secured on the back of the tow truck.

"Get it down! What the hell are you doing?" she demanded.

Barry shrugged helplessly. "I have orders to tow it."

"What the hell are you talking about? That's my Jeep! Put it back!" she ordered, resisting the urge to punch that smug little smile that was playing on the corners of Barry's mouth off.

"Sorry, you'll have to take that up with the city," he said, not sounding sorry at all as she followed him around the truck to the driver's side.

"City? What the hell are you talking about?"

"Jeep's being impounded for unpaid parking tickets," he said with that damn shrug again.

"Tickets? I don't have any tickets. I just got this thing," she pointed out to the stubborn man as he opened his door and threw his clipboard in the truck's cab.

"Like I said before, you'll have to take it up with the city," he said, looking past her and gave a slight nod. "Thanks for the tip."

"Not a problem," Connor said from somewhere behind her.

Slowly, she turned around to face her nemesis. "You did this?" she demanded, barely holding back her rage.

"It was my civic duty," he said with an exaggerated sigh.

"I just bet it was," she said, forcing herself to walk past him.

This battle was lost and she knew it. Barry wasn't about to unload her Jeep and she sure as hell wasn't going to give the neighbors anything else to gossip about.

"*Motherfucker!*" she heard Barry wail as she reached her front door, but she was too focused on what needed to be done to care. If Connor wanted to play this game then that was more than fine with her.

———

Early the next morning............

"What the hell!" Connor yelled as he came fully awake in under three seconds flat. He reached over and slammed his hand down on his alarm clock, silencing it on the first hit and glowering when he saw what time it was. He hadn't set his alarm for two. Why the hell was it going off?

"Oh, good. You're awake," Rory's said, sounding upbeat and chipper as his bedroom lights were thrown on, momentarily blinding him.

"It's two in the morning, Rory! What the hell are you doing?" he demanded as he opened his eyes, wincing as his eyes adjusted to the suddenly bright light filling the room and when they did, they narrowed on the woman sitting on top of his desk, looking amused and oddly triumphant.

"Just thought I'd swing by and thank you for having my Jeep towed," she said, smiling sweetly.

"Uh huh," he said slowly as his sleep hazed mind worked to take everything in, "you woke me up at two in the morning to thank me?" he clarified with a sigh.

Clearly the woman was losing her touch. It was annoying and a bit frustrating to be woken up this early, but once he tossed her ass out onto his balcony and crawled back into his warm comfortable bed, he'd fall back to sleep without a problem. He moved to do just that when something near his foot caught his attention.

She couldn't have…

After throwing her one last glare, he tore the sheets away, uncaring that he was only wearing a pair of boxers, and glared at the evidence that the damn woman had lost her mind.

"You chained me?" he asked in disbelief as he examined the handcuff clasped around his ankle and the thick chain that was attached to it.

"Mmmmhmmm," was Rory's only reply as he jumped off the bed and followed the chain to his bathroom where the crazy woman had tied it off around the base of the toilet with three padlocks. He tried to pull it up, but she hadn't left any slack in the chain. After a minute, he realized that trying to get the chain off the toilet was useless and focused his attention on the cuff around his ankle.

Thankfully she hadn't placed the cuff too tightly around his ankle to cut off circulation, but it still wouldn't go down over his ankle. With a muttered curse and a few promises of violence to her beautiful ass, he grabbed a bottle of shampoo and coated the damn cuff. The only thing the shampoo seemed to do was make a mess.

By the time he washed his foot off in the shower and stormed out of the bathroom he was ready to kill her with his bare hands. He kept his eyes locked on her as he stepped around the bed and headed for the desk.

"You went too far this time, Rory," he bit out tightly even as he imagined wringing her neck. He would take his time and savor it, he decided.

"And what are you going to do about it?" she asked tauntingly, making no move to run away, he noted.

"I'm going to-*what the hell?*" he roared with rage as his chain stopped short mere feet from his prey. Maybe he could still reach her, he hoped as he reached out to grab her and drag her over to him only to discover that she was safely out of his reach.

"Un-fucking chain me, Rory," he snapped, standing up. Every muscle in his body literally ached to go after her and drag her over his knee and give her the spanking that she was practically begging for.

"Well," Rory said brightly as she ignored him and got to her feet, "as much as I'd love to hang out with you, I'm afraid that I have to get some more sleep since I have a big day ahead of me." She walked over to the sliding glass doors with a pleased smile on her face.

"Don't do it, Rory," he warned as he yanked at his restraint.

She blinked, looking innocent as she pulled the remote to his stereo out of her back pocket. "Do this you mean?" she asked seconds before the most frightening song in the history of mankind started playing.

"*Mmmmbop, mmmbop, mmmmmmbop,*" blasted throughout the room, taking his rage to a whole new level.

"Don't worry!" she yelled over the incoherent noise, "I set it to repeat so that you don't have to worry about it ending!" With a wink she left.

He rushed over to the stereo only to discover to his horror that it was out of his reach. After a quick search, he discovered that the little brat had taken his cell phone, his house phone, and his tools.

Oh, Rory James was going to pay for this shit. He'd make damn sure of it.

NINE

"Where's Connor?" Craig asked as Rory handed him a crowbar. "I, um," she had to swallow back a chuckle and force herself to keep a straight face as she continued, "I think he's taking the day off."

"Are you serious? The second day on the job and he's taking the day off?" Craig asked in disgust.

"It's shameful," Rory said, struggling not to laugh.

"It's bullshit. We have enough to do without adding supervising his men to the list," Craig said, sighing heavily as he grabbed a pair of work gloves off the shelf of their doublewide portable storage unit.

"It won't be that bad," she said, initialing the order form before tossing it back to Eddie, one of the few supervisors she had working for her that wasn't blood related. He looked it over before nodding and heading out to get the supplies they needed. "Decide which of his men are qualified to help you with the roof today. Have Sean put the rest to work on gutting the first and second floor. I don't want anyone working outside unless they're on roof detail. We don't need accidents this early in the game," she explained, knowing just how quickly accidents could happen when people swarmed areas that should be kept cleared.

Today and probably for the next few days they'd work on taking the old roof off. The last thing they needed was men working on the grounds around the manor where boards, nails and shingles were going to fall. They'd have a small ground cleanup crew working the property that was trained to move their asses and knew better than to take any chances.

The rest of the men would work on gutting the walls and checking for damage to the frame. While they were doing that she was stuck with basement duty. She'd been looking forward to getting to work on the roof, but McGill had called this morning while she was on her way to work and asked if she could reconfigure the plans for the basement. Apparently after a talk with his partners, they'd decided that they wanted to double the size of the planned wine storage.

Even though it changed her plans for the day, she'd agreed to look into it today and draw up new plans for the basement. Having the client call up with changes this early in the project was not a good sign, but she wasn't about to complain since it meant more money for Shadow Construction and it made the client happy, which is what she really cared about since she needed them to okay her plans this Friday. As long as they allowed her to design and build the attic suites, she'd bite her tongue and nod when they suggested something that irritated the hell out of her.

"That sounds fine," Craig said, heading for the open double doors. "Do you want me to send any of the men to help you in the basement?" he asked over his shoulder.

She shook her head as she grabbed a flashlight. "No, I shouldn't be more than a few hours. I'm going to measure the rooms again and see what I can shift around," she said, biting back a sigh. A few hours was being optimistic. She had a feeling that this particular project was going to take up most of her day. "As soon as I'm done I'll come up and help," she promised as she grabbed her water bottle and headed towards the manor that was already bustling with activity.

As she made her way through the large foyer she wasn't at all surprised to find a decent amount of her men already working on gutting the first floor and tearing down the old grand staircase. Her men knew what was expected of them. When things needed to be done they did them without having to be told. It was one of the benefits that she found from treating her men like equals and making sure they knew the game plan from start to finish. She also kept them updated of any changes.

She wasn't too surprised to find a few of Connor's men standing around, talking. Honestly, she didn't know how he'd built the reputation he had by having slackers work for him. The majority of his men were hard workers, but the rest of them left a lot to be desired. From what she'd seen it was his friends, the men he'd made foremen who caused most of the problems.

When Connor wasn't around they seemed to give up the pretense of working, instead choosing to hang out while the rest of the men worked. Connor must have to micromanage the hell out of each project, she realized, nearly wincing in sympathy for the man. She couldn't imagine the kind of time and effort it would take to go around supervising each part of the job or having to take the time out of her day to explain each and every job as it came up. She didn't have time for that nonsense.

"Gentlemen," she said, gesturing to the men standing in the foyer and getting in the way of the men working, "if you're not working then you need to leave the site."

"We're waiting for Connor," Andrew, Connor's oldest friend and one of the biggest assholes she'd ever met, explained.

She hadn't liked the jerk back in school when he'd been nothing more than one of Connor's lackeys and she sure as hell didn't like him now. He was cocky, arrogant and lazy. As much as she hated Connor, and dear God did she hate the life-ruining bastard, she thought he could do better. She wasn't sure why Connor kept this asshole in his life for so long, but that was his problem. As long as they didn't interfere with this project she didn't care what they did.

"Then wait for him outside," she said, gesturing to the wide-open battered doors that were going to have to be replaced sometime today since constructions sites had the unfortunate luck of drawing vandals.

With a nod, they headed for the door. They'd probably bitch and moan to Connor the next time they saw him, not that he was going to need much encouragement to flip out on her. The last time she'd checked on him, he was making all sorts of promises to her ass that didn't sound like fun for her so she'd left him where he was.........

After she'd taunted him one more time of course.

R.L. MATHEWSON

Not only had she gotten back at Connor first thing in the morning, but she'd made damn sure that he wouldn't be bothering her for at least a day....or two. She'd definitely have to let him go before the forty-eight hour mark passed just so she could avoid someone filing a missing person's report on him since the last time that happened hadn't exactly ended well for her.

Then again the judge clearly agreed with her that the circumstances of his "imprisonment;" hadn't really been her fault. No one had forced Connor to follow her into the old shed on the back of her uncle's property. Just because she might have "accidentally" locked the padlock and ignored his demands to be released didn't make her responsible.

Of course, the judge may have thrown the case out because they'd only been seven at the time and he had kind of asked for it by chasing her with his pet python. It also hadn't hurt that the judge thought that Connor's mother had overreacted to the whole thing. Not really a big surprise since the woman had always overreacted to everything.

It hadn't mattered whose fault it really was, it was always Rory James' fault according to Janice O'Neil. Her son had been a perfect angel and had only acted up because of Rory. It never mattered how many witnesses there were or if the incident had been captured on camera, it was Rory James' fault and Janice made damn sure that everyone knew it. Not that anyone had believed her, they hadn't, but that hadn't stopped Janice O'Neil from bitching about Rory since the first time Rory and Connor came to blows.

The only thing that had saved Connor from a broken nose for all the trouble his mother caused her was the fact that he seemed embarrassed by his mother. Again, not that she could blame him. The woman gushed over him and treated him like a baby up until about five years ago when she'd passed away. It had always been that way. She knew that it had embarrassed Connor when his mother showed up at school or at one of his games and fussed over him, making a huge scene if someone got too close to her son on the football field. So of course Rory made sure that his lovely mother had a front seat at all of his games and then sat back and laughed her ass off at him.

She turned on her flashlight and opened the thick oak door leading to the large basement. She closed the door behind her as she carefully navigated the old stone stairway. The stairs were in pretty good shape, but like the rest of the house they'd been damaged over the years by wear and tear and needed a little TLC. She was reminded of that fact several times as her foot landed in ruts where rocks were supposed to be and she almost went flying on her ass.

Thankfully, the designers of this basement had the foresight to add plenty of windows so that the area wasn't pitch-black, but she still needed her flashlight to get around. Although she knew the measurements of the entire manor by heart as well as the layout, she still needed to look around the large basement rooms to get a better idea of how she was going to work a much larger state of the art wine room into the plans.

A half hour later she still wasn't sure how she was going to do this without causing some serious damage to the foundation. She looked over at the cracked plank door of what she assumed was used as a storage room since it still had a wall lined with old crates. Maybe she could break through that room and keep the original spot she had planned for the wine cellar, but that all depended on what was behind those crates. If it was stone then she'd have to come up with something else, but if it was wood then she'd have the space she needed and could go up and help the guys with that roof. She'd change the plans later tonight.

Eager to get this over with and help the guys with the roof, she made her way over to the crooked door and pushed it open with her shoulder. She swung her flashlight around the damp dark room, praying that she wasn't about to have a run in with some furry little friends or some of the eight-legged variety. When nothing came running out or dropped from the ceiling, she focused her flashlight and attention on the wood crates stacked against what she was hoping was a wall constructed of wood.

She placed her flashlight on the floor against the opposite wall with the beam of light pointed on the crates. With a resigned sigh, she set to work moving the top crates first. The crates were empty and she was able to remove them quickly and stack them on the other side of the room. When she had the crates cleared at chest level she squinted her eyes, trying to see what she was dealing with. She was almost positive that it was-

"This ends now," Connor suddenly said, scaring the living hell out of her.

Rory whirled around, hand to chest, heart pounding violently as she fought to calm her breathing. "What in the hell is wrong with you?" she demanded, taking a deep breath to calm herself as she looked at Connor.

He stood in the doorway with a flashlight in his hand and even in the dim light she could tell that he was having a hell of a time stopping himself from crossing the small room and throttling her. She had to give him credit, because if she had been in his place there would be no stopping the ass whooping that he had coming.

"You went over the line today with that bullshit, Rory," he said, taking a step into the dark room.

She had to roll her eyes at that. "You're only pissed because you didn't think of it first," she said, turning her back on him and effectively dismissing him. She didn't have time for his whining today. She needed to make sure that the whole wall was made of wood and then go up on the roof and help the guys.

"That's bullshit," he snapped. "You chained me to a toilet, Rory, and took away any way to call for help. What if there had been a fire?" he demanded.

"I paid Mr. Henderson fifty bucks to watch the house and keep an ear out for you," she said in a bored tone as she started hefting more crates over to the other side of the room.

"Mr. Henderson is ninety years old and wears a hearing aid the size of my fist. How the hell was he supposed to hear me screaming for help over the garbage you left blasting?"

She picked up a crate and moved it to the other side as she said, "He had his binoculars."

Connor snorted in disbelief. "Of course he had his binoculars! He can't see without them!"

"Obviously nothing bad happened," she said with a shrug as she grabbed the second crate from the top, not mentioning that she'd also paid Katie, her seventeen year old neighbor who specialized in babysitting, fifty bucks to also keep an eye on Connor's house. Then again, she wouldn't be paying Katie that extra fifty to call and alert her when Connor broke out.

Oh yes she would, she realized a moment later, sighing as she reached for her cell phone and remembered that she'd put it down on her desk when she'd changed and forgot to put it back on her belt. Damn, a warning would have been nice, too.

"What about kicking my men off the site? What's your excuse for that?" Connor demanded, sounding truly pissed.

"You mean the men standing around and getting in the way?" she asked, wondering when he was just going to give up this line of questioning and seek his sad little revenge.

"I don't care what they were doing-"

"Well, you should," she cut him off as she reached for another crate.

He simply continued as if she hadn't spoken. "Those men work for me. If there's a problem then I'll handle it," he said tightly.

"But you weren't here," she pointed out in innocently, knowing that would drive him crazy. It was probably wrong of her to enjoy tormenting him, but she didn't care. It was one of the few pleasures in life that she allowed herself.

"If it hadn't been for you, I would have been here and my men wouldn't have been delayed," he snapped, sounding more irritated.

With a sigh, she removed the final crate and brought it over to the other wall. "You shouldn't have to babysit your men, Connor. It's a waste of time and resources," she simply said as she walked back to the area she'd just cleared and inspected the wall.

The wall was made of wood, rotting wood, but that would work. She frowned as she looked down at her feet. Although the area matched the rest of the room's floor, dirt mixed with a heavy layer of dust, it didn't feel like dirt beneath her feet. Was it a wood floor, she wondered idly as she dragged her foot across the surface, shifting the dirt and sand to the side to reveal old rotting wood.

"Don't tell me how to handle my men, Rory. In fact, I'd appreciate it if you just stayed the hell out of my way completely," Connor snapped.

"That's going to be kind of hard to do with us working together, don't you think?" she mused.

"We're not working together, Rory. I'm running this site with the use of your men and equipment. You're going to stay the hell out of my way. If you can manage to do that and cut the bullshit like this morning then you'll come out of this a very rich woman," he said, ramming his fingers through his hair in frustration.

She ground her teeth together as she reminded herself that she had to play nice, well, at least while they were at work. Outside of work she didn't have to take his bullshit. "We signed that contract together, Connor, so whether you like it or not I will be working on this project and if you don't like that then you can-"

She never finished that sentence as the sounds of planks cracking beneath her feet cut her off. Before she could move so much as move a muscle, the floor beneath her gave way and she found herself falling into darkness.

"Rory!" she thought she heard Connor yell, but she wasn't really sure since she couldn't hear much of anything above her own screams of agony.

TEN

"Rory!" he yelled again as he gripped the edge of the splintered wood floor and pulled, uncaring that the dry rotting wood was tearing into his hands, as he widened the hole she'd dropped through. "Answer me goddammit!"

Nothing.

"Shit," he muttered, yanking his two way radio off his belt. He knew that he should call 911, but he needed help now. Besides, he wasn't about to leave Rory wherever she'd just landed alone so that he could run outside and try getting a signal on his cell phone.

"Andrew!" he said, clicking off and dropping the radio by his side so that he could widen the hole while he waited for a response. When one didn't come quick enough he tried again with the same results.

Cursing his foreman to hell, he switched the radio to the channel he knew the James brothers used. "Craig, I need someone to call an ambulance and I need help down in the basement, fourth storage room to the right," he said, releasing the button with a *click* and praying that someone heard that.

"*Connor, what the hell is going on?*" Craig returned almost immediately.

"Rory's hurt. I need an ambulance and help," he said, quickly releasing the radio to set back to work on the hole.

"*If you hurt her, I will-*"

"I didn't hurt her!" he snapped, feeling his patience fray as his body shook. Please let her be okay, he prayed as he ripped another chunk of wood away with one hand. "Call a fucking ambulance and send some men down here now!" he snapped, tossing the radio aside, promising to kill the bastard if he didn't move his ass.

Not even a minute later he heard the sounds of men running in his direction.

"Rory!" he heard Bryce yell.

"In here!" he answered as he ripped another piece of wood off, but it wasn't wide enough.

Shit!

He tore off another piece and then another until he was sure the space was big enough for him to fit through. He grabbed her flashlight off the floor where it had fallen, aimed it into the hole and squinted. He couldn't see anything but a set of stone stairs.

"Rory!" he called down, but there was no answer.

"Shit!" he snapped as he dropped down onto his ass and shifted until his feet were in the hole. He shoved the flashlight in his pocket and moved to go after her.

"Where the hell is she?" Sean asked as he ran into the room with three of his brothers close behind him. He didn't need to look to know that Craig wasn't with them. The last he'd seen of the oldest brother, he'd been on the roof tearing it apart. He also knew that Craig probably wasn't too far behind them.

"Rory crashed through this hole. Make sure they send Fire and Rescue with that ambulance," he said as he quickly lowered himself into the hole, ignoring the sharp shards of wood that sliced his skin as he went.

"Get the hell out of there and let one of us go. It's our sister down there," Johnny said, reaching to grab his arm and yank him out of the hole.

"Back the fuck off. I've got this," he said as he sucked in a breath and worked his way through the opening. Johnny paused in surprise just long enough to give him a chance to work his shoulders through the hole and when he dropped down, he released his hold on the splintered wood and did his best not to fall down the stairs and land on Rory.

With a grunt, he landed on his feet and quickly righted himself before he toppled over into the pitch-black. He yanked the flashlight out of his pocket and turned it on, chasing away the darkness. He aimed the beam down the stairs and nearly dropped to his knees when he spotted her.

"Oh, God......," he mumbled even as he raced down the stone stairs. "Rory? Rory!" he said, trying to keep the panic out of his voice, but failing miserably.

He dropped by her side, careful not to brush against her and quickly looked her over with the flashlight. She was on her side. Her left arm was obviously broken, blood trickled down her forehead and onto the dirt floor, forming a small pool beneath her head and she was out. He wasn't sure what else was wrong with her so he didn't try move her, terrified that he'd make things worse.

"Rory? You have to wake up," he said gently as he pressed his fingertips against the cut on her temple, careful not to apply too much pressure and hurt her.

"Is she okay?" Sean yelled down the hole.

"Her arm's broken, she has a head wound and she's unconscious," he yelled back, never taking his eyes away from her.

He heard her brothers arguing about who was coming down, but didn't pay much attention to them as he placed the flashlight on the ground with the beam pointed at her. With a shaky hand, he pressed two blood-stained fingers against her neck and searched for a pulse.

When he didn't find it, he promised everything that he had and was if she would just be okay. Hell, he couldn't imagine a world without Rory in it, didn't want to think about that happening. The moment his fingers came in contact with the proof that she was still very much alive, he nearly sagged with relief.

"Connor?" Rory said weakly.

"I'm here," he said softly. She was going to be okay. He'd make damn sure of it.

"We're all coming down!" Johnny yelled down.

"She's awake!" he yelled back, noting Rory's cringe from the loud sound. Her head was probably pounding, he realized and having five brothers fussing over her and bickering wasn't going to help with that. "Stay up there and make the hole big enough for the stretcher and EMTs!"

There was a short pause before they started bitching, but thank fucking God they did as they were asked. He looked back at Rory and even in the dim light cast off by the flashlight he could tell that she was pale. Her mouth was pinched tightly and he had no doubt that she was struggling not to scream or cry.

"Where does it hurt, Rory?" he asked quietly, trying to keep his tone soothing even though he was panicking on the inside. What the hell was he supposed to do? He didn't know jack shit about first aid. The one and only time he'd attended a class on First Aid hadn't ended well.

Then again, if the instructor had read the memo the school had given her, she wouldn't have made the mistake of placing them in the same class. She certainly wouldn't have ignored the other students' pleas, shouts and warnings about placing them together in the same group. Of course, he could have said something and Rory sure as hell could have said something, but they'd both been more than eager for a little payback after the incident at the convenience store the night before. It really shouldn't have surprised anyone when a demonstration in the Heimlich maneuver turned into him on his back with Rory straddling his waist and trying to shove a fistful of gauze down his throat or him flipping her off of him and onto her stomach so that he could hog tie her with medical tape.

He still wasn't sure why the principal kicked them out of the class or blamed them for the woman's meltdown. It's not like it took her an hour to spit up all the bits of gauze. Curling up into the fetal position beneath the desk had been a bit much for something so minor. Clearly the woman had no business teaching kids if something like that would set her off into full-blown panic attack that needed five teachers, four cops and the paramedics to get her to come out from beneath the desk.

Now he was regretting not taking that course they'd offered every year at the community center. After this incident he was going to damn well make sure that he went and he'd make his men do it as well. It was stupid not to have all his men trained in first aid, he realized as he grabbed the flashlight and ran it over Rory's body, taking a closer look to make sure that there wasn't any other damage.

"I think my arm's broken," she said, sucking in a breath before she continued, "and a few ribs might be bruised."

"Well, then try not to move," he said lamely, feeling like an idiot.

"Yeah, I'll get right on that," she said dryly as she noticeably cringed.

Her smartass remark helped ease some of his worry, but that only made way for the anger that had been simmering in the background. Now he couldn't hold it back any longer. She'd scared the shit out of him when she'd disappeared through the floor. Then, when she hadn't answered him and he couldn't get to her fast enough, he'd feared the worst.

"What the hell were you doing down here by yourself in the first place?" he demanded as he continued to look her over, ignoring the way his hands shook at the memory of her falling through the floor.

"My job," she said tightly as she sucked in another deep breath.

"You had no business being down here, Rory," he said, noting the way she shivered. He pulled his long sleeve shirt off and laid it over her, leaving him in a white tee shirt.

"McGill called up and asked me to look into making the wine storage room bigger," she explained with a tremor in her voice as she did her best to hold it together.

"Then you should have waited for me, Rory," he snapped, feeling like an asshole for yelling at an injured woman, but he couldn't help it. He knew that he was taking it out on her, but God help him, he really couldn't help it. He'd never been so frightened in his life.

"You were kind of tied up at the moment," she said, smiling weakly.

"And if you weren't interfering with my job, Rory, I would have been here!"

"Stop yelling at me, you insensitive bastard! You had it coming and you damn well know it," she said, forcing her eyes open to glare at him, then immediately winced and closed them right back up again as she assumed her grimace of pain.

"All I know is that better be the last time you pull a stunt like that, Rory. Whether you like it or not, this is my project and if you want to stick around you're going to start doing things my way and that includes not taking bullshit chances," he bit through clenched teeth as he fought against the urge to pull the infuriating woman into his arms and comfort her.

"Doing my job is not taking chances and this is my project as well so you need to get the hell over-*ow!*" she cried out, turning her face towards the dirt floor as though she was trying to hide from the pain.

"Rory?" Brian yelled down the hole.

"She's fine!" Connor yelled back, never taking his eyes off her. Not knowing what else to do at the moment, he reached out and took her good hand in his and held it. He was surprised when she didn't try to pull her hand away, but instead gave his hand a squeeze.

"This is my project too, Connor, and if you can't accept that then we're going to have some serious problems," she said evenly after a minute as she continued to clasp onto his hand like a lifeline.

He sighed heavily. She was right of course. They were going to have problems.

———

"I'm going to kick his ass," Craig said, earning approving nods from the rest of her brothers who were lounging around her bedroom.

"I told you," she said, sucking in a breath as sharp pain shot up her left arm and raced around her ribs as she slowly made her way from the bathroom to her bed, "he didn't do this."

Her brothers grumbled something, but quickly they let it go, which she would forever appreciate. Her head was pounding, her side hurt, she was starving and her arm was killing her. She couldn't wait to get in bed and take a few of the painkillers the doctor had given her.

As soon as she made it to the bed she let out a sigh of relief and proceeded to take her pills. She considered asking her brothers to get her something to eat, but that would mean having them stick around longer. Unfortunately for her, her brothers weren't exactly known for their domestic skills or their ability to be quiet and right now, peace and quiet were the things that she craved more than anything.

Carefully, she laid down and closed her eyes, releasing another sigh of relief. Sleep, she just needed a little sleep and she'd be fine, she decided as she felt the first tendrils of sleep pull at her.

"Who's staying the night?" Sean asked, yanking her right back into reality, but since she was comfortable she decided not to bother with opening her eyes as she said, "No one is staying. Now get the hell out so that I can sleep," she mumbled around a loud yawn.

Her brothers weren't the coddling type and took her at her word. Craig took Bunny home with him for the night and they promised to give Dad an update so that he wouldn't worry. Not that he would. If it wasn't serious enough to warrant a night in the hospital then it wasn't serious enough to worry about, was her father's motto. He'd checked up on her at the ER, spoke with the doctor and when she told him that she was fine, he took her at her word.

Her brothers hadn't been so easily deterred, but giving her a ride home was pretty much the extent of their nursing abilities. They'd made her promise to call them if she needed anything, but other than that they'd left her to get a good night's sleep. That was all she needed, she thought as she drifted off.

It was pitch-black when she woke up, biting back a cry of pain. Why the hell did it hurt this much? It hadn't hurt this badly when it broke and that had definitely been a memorable occasion. Her head pounded with every breath she took and her ribs screamed in protest.

Maybe it hadn't been such a good idea to send her brothers away, she realized as she turned over to bury her face against her pillow and let out a scream of agony. She needed her pills or at the very least, someone to knock her out so that she didn't have to experience this much pain.

"Shhhhh."

She barely heard the whisper or registered the large strong hands on her shoulders as she was turned over onto her back and pills were pressed against her lips. Once she'd accepted them into her mouth, the rim of a water bottle quickly followed. She swallowed her pill as she struggled not to scream out against the pain.

This was too much. She couldn't handle this, couldn't do this, she realized, panicking at the thought that there would be no escaping from this pain. She would have to-

"Shhhh, I've got you," the deep familiar voice said soothingly as she was carefully shifted until she was lying on her right side with her injured arm resting across a firm stomach and her face pressed against a warm shoulder as a strong arm came up behind her and pulled her closer.

"Connor?" she whispered softly, but apparently not softly enough since the sound tore through her already throbbing head.

"Go to sleep, Rory," he whispered against the top of her head.

If Connor was taking care of her, it could only mean one thing.......

"How long do I have?" she asked, squeezing her eyes shut against the pain.

She felt him go still beneath her. "How long do you have for what?"

She scoffed even as she adjusted herself so that she was lying tightly against him, accepting the comfort he was offering during her last hours on this earth.

"Before I kick the bucket. What the hell do you think I'm talking about?" she snapped, immediately regretting the action when it sent sharp pain through her skull.

"That really depends on how much you piss me off," he sighed as he pulled her impossibly closer as if he needed the comfort as much as she did.

She thought over what he said and came to only one conclusion. "So it'll be soon then?"

He chuckled softly. "Probably."

ELEVEN

She was so damn beautiful, he thought as he gently pushed her hair away from the small cut on her forehead that hadn't needed stitches. He hoped it didn't leave a scar, not that it would lessen Rory's appeal, but it would be a constant reminder of the time that he'd failed her.

Instead of stubbornly standing there yesterday while she'd worked, he should have taken over. Then it would have been him falling through the floor and not her. He'd take a broken arm and bruised ribs over the scare she'd given him any day.

After she'd been placed on a backboard, hoisted up through the hole and placed in the back of the ambulance, he'd forced himself to walk away like it hadn't bothered him. He'd spent the rest of the night thinking. Rory was stubborn, holy hell was she stubborn and no matter what he did or said the damn woman wasn't going to stay away from the job site even with a broken arm. He could either fight with her and waste precious time and energy or he could give in, with a few conditions of course.

Rory needed someone to watch over her and since her brothers were too damn lazy to do it, that left only him. Not that it bothered him. He'd been doing it for most of their lives after all. At first he did it because he hadn't liked the idea of anyone else tormenting her and of course it had made it easier to make her life a living hell, but later on when they were both adults he'd done it out of guilt. He'd fucked up her life, big time, and he couldn't stomach the idea of her ever going through that much pain again, not because of him.

He'd tried to apologize several times, but she wouldn't listen to him. She hated him and he couldn't blame her. He'd done it for her own good, but he knew that there was nothing that he could say to get her to see that. So instead, he kept an eye out for her and if anyone hurt her then he stepped in. A few of her boyfriends hadn't treated her right. They treated her like shit, cheated on her left and right, and just made her miserable.

A few times, her brothers had stepped up and handled them, but there were a few that had slipped their notice. He'd noticed. The asshole that shoved Rory in the parking lot over on Harrison after she'd dumped his ass ended up in the hospital later that night when Connor caught up with him. The asshole that bragged to his buddies that Rory was a bad lay ended up taking back every last word through a mouthful of broken teeth. He did his best to make up for what he'd done and this time would be no different.

He'd watch after her and keep her out of danger. Keeping an eye out for her would add to his workload, but if it meant keeping her safe then he'd do it. He owed her that much at least. If he hadn't interfered all those years ago she'd probably be head of the PTA by now with a dozen or so kids at home fighting for her attention instead of a pain in the ass dog with a fucked up name. Thanks to him, that's not how things had turned out. Thanks to him, she was doing a job that she had no business doing and she was alone.

Not that he took the entire blame for her being alone. He didn't. Rory was easily the sexiest woman in town. Every man in town with two working eyes agreed. She was Playboy level hot. Great body, beautiful long hair with natural highlights and a face meant to take a man's breath away and she knew it, too.

Rory James knew how hot she was, but she didn't care. Her focus was on her company and that was the problem. If she stepped back or let her brothers take over, she'd be able to find a decent guy to settle down with. Not that he was going to push for that. Oh hell no, she was his to torment. He might watch over her because of the damn guilt that racked him, but that didn't mean that he didn't enjoy their daily antics. He did and he fully planned on continuing with them until she either slapped a restraining order against him or a doctor called his time of death.

Until this project was over, he would have to keep an eye on her. While he did that, he would also continue to work on winning her brothers over. They'd gotten off to a rough start, but now he knew what he had to do. Thanks to her father's invitation to join them this Sunday it was just a matter of time before the James boys ditched their sister and came to work for him, hopefully taking Rory's best employees right along with them.

If Rory needed a job after she lost her business because her best employees came to work for him, then he'd consider letting her be his assistant. She could fetch his drinks and food all while wearing a tight Highland Construction tee shirt and tight jeans that showcased her ass perfectly. He'd be able to keep her safe, keep her close by to torment and really, that was all that mattered.

———

"What the hell are you doing?" Rory demanded as she sat up, a little too quickly, she realized a few seconds later when the dull ache above her temple protested.

Without taking his eyes away from the laptop on his lap, Connor reached over and grabbed the prescription bottle off the nightstand and handed it to her. "I'm working, Rory. What does it look like?" he asked distractedly as he looked at a file that he had spread open on the bed next to him.

"It looks like you're half naked in my bed!" she said, screeching just a tad bit.

He simply shrugged one wide shoulder as he grabbed a bottle of water and handed it to her. Since her head hurt and her arm felt like someone was shoving hot pokers inside the bone, she decided to take her pills before she killed him. She took her pills, never taking her eyes off of him while she did it. Connor simply ignored her as he continued typing away at his computer, only pausing long enough to absently scratch his bare chest.

Her eyes darted down to the pair of charcoal colored sweatpants he wore and then back up to his bare chest and then finally to his face, confirming her first observation, the man really was half naked in her bed.

"Get out," she said, inwardly cringing when pain radiated up her arm as she slowly climbed off the bed and got to her feet.

"Can't," he said, keeping his focus on his computer while she looked around for something to throw at him. When she spotted her boots she considered throwing them, but they really wouldn't get the job done so she settled on glaring at him while she made her way to the bathroom.

"Out," she said firmly as she closed the bathroom door behind her.

He didn't say anything so she decided to take that as an agreement. Now that he annoyed her first thing in the morning he would be content on going about his day and leaving her alone. By the time she stepped out of the bathroom he would be gone and she would unfortunately be spending the rest of the day in bed since the damn doctor had opened his big mouth and told her brothers that she shouldn't work today.

At least she'd get some paperwork done, she thought as she used the bathroom and cleaned up. She hated doing paperwork, but now that she was stuck in bed for a day she had no excuses not to do it. That wasn't entirely true since she was pretty sure that she could come up with a good excuse not to do it. Or maybe she should just suck it up and get it over with, she decided as she opened the door and sighed with relief.

Connor was gone.

She didn't even bother wasting her time trying to figure out what he'd been thinking when he decided to lounge in her bed this morning. It would just be one of those things that was best left alone. Her stomach rumbled as she reached her bed and she tried to ignore it, but it refused to be ignored.

Grumbling and admittedly bitching a little, she padded barefoot out of her room, down the hallway and the stairs as she prayed that her brothers hadn't hit her kitchen on the way out. Her cabinets were mostly empty to begin with, but if her brothers somehow forgot to make a side stop on their way out the door last night she should be able to whip something up with the half sleeve of saltines, half empty jar of olives and scrape a teaspoon or two of peanut butter out of the jar that probably should have been thrown away last year and make something somewhat edible.

Her stomach rumbled approvingly at the thought of an oily peanut butter and olive dip smothered over dry brittle saltine crackers so she quickened her pace only to stop abruptly when she passed the open double doors of her living room. Knowing, hell, praying that she was wrong, she backtracked until she was in front of the open doorway. She took a deep, calming breath and slowly turned around until she was facing her living room.

"They cleaned you out," Connor said as he stared down intently at his computer, which was now on her oak coffee table with about a dozen files scattered around it.

"What the hell are you still doing here?" she demanded as she walked into the living room.

"Working."

"I told you to get out," she reminded him as she crossed, well, tried to cross her arms over her chest, but her left arm apparently wasn't happy with that move. She settled for propping her hands on her hips and glaring down at him as he continued to ignore her.

"I did," he said.

"No, you didn't!"

With a heavy sigh, he sat back on the tan couch and finally looked at her. "You told me to get out and I did."

"No, you only left the bedroom," she pointed out, sounding a little irritated. "I told you to get out so you should have left the house."

"You didn't clarify that," he pointed out with a shrug.

"It was implied!" she snapped.

"It really wasn't."

"Get out!"

"Sorry, can't do that," he said, shrugging.

"Why not?"

"Because I'm waiting for my food to be delivered and you and I have some work to do here since you've decided to lounge around all day," he said, gesturing to the computer and the files before he flicked his hand lazily in her direction.

"I was not lounging around!"

"What do you call sleeping until one in the afternoon then?" he asked with a frown as he once again focused on his computer, clearly dismissing her.

"I call it being knocked out by painkillers, you jackass!" she snapped even as she desperately tried to rein her temper in, but it was always a difficult thing to do where Connor was concerned.

Her stomach wouldn't stop rumbling, her head was starting to pound and her damn arm was killing her. All she wanted to do was get something to eat, grab some aspirin and go back to bed, but she couldn't do that until her unwanted guest left. If he didn't get off her couch and get the hell out of here soon, she was going to-

"Come over here and sit down before you pass out," Connor said, concern coloring his tone as he stood up and gestured for her to sit down, taking her off guard.

"I'm fine," she said, casting a discreet look around the living room as she wondered what his game was. Connor O'Neil was not nice to her, never had been and as far as she knew, he never would be. So she obviously found this little act of concern a little unsettling.

"I need you conscious so that we can get some work done," he said on an exaggerated sigh as if that much should be obvious. While he took her elbow and led her to the couch, she guessed that maybe it should have been. He wouldn't do anything unless it somehow benefitted him. Still........

Having Connor nice to her for any reason was unsettling so while he settled back on the couch next to her, she cast another look around the room, looking for hidden dangers. Maybe he was going to get rid of her once and for all so that he could have Strawberry Manor to himself, she thought.

"There's no poisonous spiders or snakes ready to leap out at you," Connor said, sounding amused as he handed her a bottle of aspirin. When she remembered a certain incident at summer camp when they were twelve and he laced her chocolate chip pancakes with laxatives she hesitated in taking the bottle from him.

With a sigh and a few muttered words about her being a big baby, he opened the bottle and popped two pills in his mouth and swallowed them dry as he handed her the bottle. Reluctantly, she took the bottle. When he handed her a bottle of water she glared at him and swallowed her pills dry as well.

"No trust," he said, shaking his head in disgust as he took the bottle from her and handed her a file.

"What's this?" she asked, opening the file and nearly groaned when she realized he'd handed her a spreadsheet. Since looking at the numbers aggravated her eyes, she shoved the file back at him and settled for bringing her knees up to her chest and hugging them while she laid her head against her arm.

She couldn't believe how badly her head hurt. It seemed with each passing moment that it became progressively worse. Between that, her arm and ribs, she really wasn't in the mood to deal with Connor's bullshit today. She suddenly felt tired, so tired. Hadn't she just slept all night and most of the day away, she wondered as she felt herself drift off, but she fought it with everything she had.

There was too much to do today. If she gave in and fell asleep then she'd have to deal with a ton of paperwork on top of all her other duties tomorrow and she simply didn't have the time or patience for that. She needed to stay awake, throw Connor out on his ass and get some work done.

"Shhh, go to sleep, Rory," Connor said soothingly as he wrapped an arm around her and pulled her closer, but she resisted until she was too tired to fight. Then with a content sigh, she allowed him to pull her closer. Once her head rested on his chest she found that she didn't want to fight it any longer. He felt too good to push away and oddly enough, she felt safe in his arms. That should have frightened her, but she was too tired to do anything more than curl up against him.

"I always knew that you wanted me," Connor said, sounding smug so of course she called up her last reserve of energy and did what any woman in her position would do.

"Ow! Leave my nipples alone, woman!" he snapped and she fully expected him to push her away. Instead, he pulled her closer, mumbling something about rules and nipples as she fell asleep.

TWELVE

"No," Rory said as she snatched the slice of mushroom and meatball pizza right out of his hand.

"What do you mean by 'no'?" he demanded, snatching back his slice of pizza. He took a huge bite out of it, making his claim on the slice, but of course the damn woman snatched it right back and took a bite out of his pizza. If that wasn't bad enough, she washed it down with his Coke.

"I don't think that's going to work," Rory said, gesturing to his laptop's computer screen with *his* slice of pizza.

Glaring, he snatched it out of her hand and took a huge bite out of it as he pointed at the design he'd come up with while she'd slept. He still didn't know what the hell he'd been thinking. He should have just sent it to McGill without showing it to her, but he needed her co-operation. If he was going to keep her under his thumb then he had to play nice, or at the very least, pretend.

"What about the generator?" she asked, stealing the pizza crust out of his hand and nibbled on it as she gestured to the blueprint he'd designed earlier when she was sleeping. Well, he did that and of course he'd had a look around.

He just couldn't resist. Not that he tried to resist all that hard. For years he'd been dying to know what her house looked like and when she'd conked out and he really had to use the bathroom after a few hours of holding her in his arms he may have taken a detour and explored her house.

The master bathroom had been a bit of a shock. It was a rather pleasant surprise after all these years to discover that there was a secret side to Rory, a very feminine side. Instead of having a straightforward bathroom that met minimal needs like his bathroom, a guy's bathroom, Rory's was without question a woman's dream bathroom.

The tiled wall was comprised of every shade of pink imaginable while the floor was a combination of light pink, dark pink and white tiles. Her shower could easily fit ten people and had four showerheads and a built in marble bench that lined the wall. She also had a two person light pink Jacuzzi bathtub. What really surprised him was her built-in shelves that held dozens of body sprays, lotions and a whole shitload of girly products.

He didn't check out her medicine cabinet or drawers since he wasn't a snoop or some weird pervert. There were some lines that he wouldn't cross even with Rory and snooping through her personal things was definitely one of them. Of course, that didn't mean that he hadn't allowed himself a tour of her house while she'd been knocked out.

The style was very close to what he'd chosen for his own house, which surprised him. He really thought she would have gone for a more contemporary look. Instead, it appeared as though she'd restored the house to its glory days with a few modern touches. He loved her den. It had the nineteenth century feel to it with an eighty-inch flat screen built into the wall that surprisingly didn't wreck the effect. Somehow she'd managed to blend the television in with the rest of the decor. Now, the stack of chick flicks he'd found surprised him since he couldn't picture her watching them, but he decided to ignore those.

Not that he would ever tell her, but he loved her house, maybe not as much as he loved his own, but hers was a close second. There were a few things he would have done differently, but overall the house was truly beautiful. She'd probably raised the value of the house by a hundred grand with all the work she'd put into it. He couldn't help but wonder how much of it her brothers were responsible for. Probably for most of it, which was just another reminder that he had to get his ass moving and convince the James brothers that it would be in their best interest to come work for him.

"You know that they want the 458, but you have the schematics set up for the 310," Rory said, pointing at the small computer monitor as she stole the last slice of pizza. Grudgingly, he allowed her to have it since she'd slept through lunch. Plus, he was a little distracted at the moment to really care.

"What the hell do you mean they want the 458?" he demanded, trying not to get pissed, but it was pretty damn difficult at the moment. He'd spent all day redesigning the wine room and the rest of the basement and now she was telling him that they wanted a refrigerating unit that not only would need a stronger feed, but it also wouldn't be able to fit in the space he'd designed for it. It also meant that he'd just wasted ten hours of his time for bullshit and that he'd be spending the rest of the night and early morning redesigning the basement to meet the rest of their specifications.

"It was in the fax," she said with a shrug as she took a big bite of pizza.

"What fax?" he asked as he considered snatching her slice of pizza away just on principle alone. If there had been a fax then he should have been told about it, especially before he'd wasted his day.

"They sent it yesterday morning," she said, taking another bite of her pizza before she continued. "There's about a dozen changes they want made," she said with a somewhat apologetic smile that did nothing to calm him down.

"Why didn't you give me the fax?" he asked, giving up on glaring at her and stole the rest of the pizza out of her hand.

She rolled her eyes as she snatched it back. "Because you weren't there for one thing," she said, taking a huge bite. "And I planned on having the new plans for the basement done last night so there really was no point in telling you."

"It's my project too, Rory," he bit out slowly.

Another shrug as she finished off the pizza had his glare returning. It was one thing for him to keep her in the dark, but it was a whole different story when she pulled that bullshit on him. This was his project and he should have been told about the fax. Hell, she should have delivered the damn thing to him while wearing a smile and something skimpy, he decided. He forced himself to turn around in his seat and stare at his computer screen as he wondered how he was going to adjust the space for the refrigerating unit and not fuck up the rest of the plans.

"Look, it's really not a big deal. I can fix this," Rory said as she reached out to screw with his fucked up plans.

"No," Connor said firmly as he blocked her good hand with one of his.

"Don't be a baby about this, Connor. It's not a big deal. I remember what was in the fax. I can-"

"No," he said more firmly as he moved his arm to re-block her when the stubborn woman tried to reach past his hand and touch his computer.

With an annoyed sigh, she reached out once again and tried to screw with his computer, but he was ready for her. It was an old move, but one that worked. He palmed her face and gently pushed her back. As she tried to slap his hand away he focused on his plans. Maybe he could readjust the storage unit next to it by a foot and-

He heard her loud gasp of pain before he registered the weak, yet hard, slap on his arm. He turned in time to see her hug her broken arm to her chest and double over in pain.

"*Shit!*" he groaned, feeling like an asshole. He should have realized that she'd forget about her arm when she got pissed enough. Well, there was nothing he could do about it now.

"Looks like it's time for bed," he announced as he stood and scooped her up in his arms.

"Bastard," Rory choked out between gasps.

"That wasn't very nice," he mused as he carried her into the foyer.

"Asshole," of course was the reply.

"Words hurt, Rory," he said with a heartfelt sigh as he carried her up the stairs. "Words hurt."

"I wish," she muttered as she turned her face and buried it against his chest.

Since she was in pain he let it go and focused on gently placing her on the bed. As soon as she was curled up on her side and burying her face against the pillow, he released her and grabbed her bottle of pills.

"Open up for a happy pill," he said brightly as he held one of the pills in front of her mouth.

She opened her eyes just to glare at him as she did just that. When she swallowed, he considered going back downstairs and calling the office to have that fax emailed to him, but one look at Rory had him crawling on the bed next to her and pulling her into his arms. He was actually rather pleased when she didn't fight him. That is until she got her revenge for palming her face.

"Ow! Goddammit, leave my nipple alone!" he snapped, barely resisting the urge to rub it. The damn woman fought dirty, but then again, that's what he liked about her, he realized with a smile. Rory James always managed to keep him on his toes and kept it interesting. It was a rather nice quality in an enemy.

———

"Why did you do it?" she demanded as she yanked back the curtain.

"What the hell is wrong with you?" Connor asked as he grabbed the shower curtain and yanked it out of her hand, but not before she got an eyeful.

The man had a very delicious backside and she was tempted to pull the curtain back to get another glimpse, but she needed to focus.

"Answer the damn question," she demanded, waiting impatiently for him to finish his shower.

"How did you get in my house?" Connor asked instead, making her roll her eyes. It really was a stupid question. "I picked the lock. Now focus, why did you do it?"

Connor sighed heavily as he reached out and snagged the towel off the hook. "I knew you were crazy."

She impatiently waved that off as if it were a given. "Just answer the damn question."

"Couldn't this have waited until we got to work?" Connor asked as he pulled the curtain back and stepped out, forcing her to back up or brush up against him. It actually freaked her out a little that she momentarily considered holding her ground just to see if those glistening muscles felt as good as they looked.

Oh, this was so wrong.

She was not attracted to the bastard. Okay, so that was a lie. The man was incredibly good looking and he knew it. Normally her attraction for him was easy to ignore since her hatred of him usually overshadowed that rather frightening reaction. Since he'd been taking care of her and being nice to her, she'd been having some difficulty ignoring how handsome he was or how much she liked his body and his smile.

That was the reason that she was here. She needed to confront him and find out what sick and twisted reason had made him do it. As soon as he admitted that he'd taken care of her to screw with her head, she'd be able to go back to loathing him so completely that she'd be unable to notice how hot he was or crave his touch. Then of course, she'd kick his ass for making her think of him with anything other than revulsion.

"No," she said firmly as she moved to block the doorway and his escape, but then rethought the plan since it would most likely result in touching. So she marched into his room instead. Once she'd put some space between them she motioned for him to get on with his answer.

With a sigh, he closed the bathroom door and locked it, leaving her fuming. "That lock won't keep me out you know!" she said loudly even as she had to admit to herself that the likelihood of her breaking into the bathroom a second time while he was naked was very unlikely. She needed to keep her wits about her and checking out his ass, no matter how yummy it was, wouldn't help her do that.

"Are you going to tell me what has your panties in a twist?" Connor demanded from the other side of the door.

"You going to tell me why the hell you took care of me?" she snapped back, ignoring the panties comment since she knew that she wasn't overreacting. The man was up to something and she wasn't leaving until she figured it out.

"I think," Connor said, opening the door and stepping into bedroom wearing only a pair of cargo khaki pants that he'd left unbuttoned and may have drawn her attention for a moment before her eyes roamed up, over a set of well-defined abs and she forced herself to look away, "that the better question is why weren't your brothers here?"

"Because I was fine," she said, waving off the comment in hopes that he would just focus and answer her damn question so that she could go back to hating everything about him.

"Fine?" he repeated in disbelief, shaking his head as if he couldn't quite believe what she'd just said. "You weren't fine, Rory."

"Of course I was," she lied, but the truth was that she was grateful for Connor's help. She would have hated asking for her brothers' help mostly because they wouldn't have had any clue on how to go about taking care of her. They were great brothers, but they didn't know anything about taking care of someone.

If she needed her car fixed, help moving, or a million other things, she wouldn't have hesitated in asking her brothers for help. For something like an injury or illness, they would have stood around, looking completely helpless

It wasn't their fault. That's how they'd been raised after all. Each and every one of them had been raised to be self-reliant. They learned early on how to take care of their own scraped knees, and how to threaten the monster hiding in their closets with baseball bats. Their father made damn sure that they could take care of themselves so that they would never need or expect a handout from anyone. They knew how to manage their money, pay their bills, cook, clean and work with their hands. Unfortunately, their father hadn't taught them compassion.

She knew that if she'd asked her brothers they would have tried to help. Actually, if she'd asked her brothers to take care of her, they would have rushed her to the hospital, thinking that she was dying or something. No one in the James family asked for help when they were sick or hurt. It just wasn't done, which made what Connor did for her special.

No one had ever taken care of her before. It made her feel uncomfortable. She owed him and she hated that almost as much as she hated the fact that she liked being in his arms. It was unnatural and she was here to put an end to it.

He walked towards her, not stopping until they were practically chest-to-chest, but she didn't back down. She never would and he knew it.

"Fine?" he asked, looking down at her as if she were crazy. "You had a concussion, five bruised ribs and you broke your goddamn arm, Rory. You weren't fine and you sure as hell shouldn't have been left to fend for yourself," he snapped, sounding truly angry, which only confused her more.

"Why do you care?" she asked, propping her hands on her hips as she did her best to out glare the bastard.

"I don't," he snapped. "But I am seriously considering beating the shit out of your brothers for leaving you alone the other night. What the hell were they thinking?"

"Well, they-" she started to defend them, but he apparently wasn't done yet.

"You shouldn't have been left alone, Rory. They should have made sure that you had your pills and that you were okay!"

"They called several-"

"That wasn't enough!" he snapped, getting in her face and backing her up. She was so stunned by his outburst that she didn't realize what happened until her back hit the wall and he was caging her in.

"Instead of coming over here and getting pissed at me for something that your family should have done, why don't you try saying thank you instead, huh?" he demanded as he got right in her face and before she could tell him to back the hell off or come to her brothers' defense, his mouth was on hers, hard and demanding and God help her but she didn't want him to stop.

But he did.

Before she could do something stupid like kiss him back or wrap her arms around his neck, he was pulling away, jaw clenched and looking even more pissed than before. Without a word, and before she could think beyond what just happened, he grabbed her by her shoulders and steered her out of his room and onto his patio where the cool morning air brought her back to her senses.

"Thank you!" she snapped, irritated with him and pissed at herself, because coming over here hadn't helped one damn bit. Instead of clearing her head of him all she wanted to do was go right back in there and kiss the bastard and that was wrong, so very, very wrong.

"You're welcome!" he snapped back before slamming the sliding glass door shut and pissing her off even more. Would it really have killed him to let her have the last word, she wondered as she made her way back to her patio.

"Stupid, toe curling kissing bastard," she grumbled as she marched into her room, slamming the sliding glass door shut behind her with her broken hand, which of course started a five minute *owie* dance and a mad search for her bottle of painkillers. By the time she'd popped a pill into her mouth, she was no closer to figuring out what Connor was up to than she had been when she'd stormed over there. One way or the other, she would figure out what he was up to and then she would put an end to it.

THIRTEEN

"What the hell did I just do?" Connor muttered as he leaned back against his truck.

Bunny barked his answer, finishing it off with a growl of disapproval.

He sighed heavily even as he nodded his agreement. "Exactly. Women fuck with your head, buddy. Remember that," he told the dog who'd given up his search for the perfect spot to mark five minutes ago to make sure that Connor didn't harass his master, or rather his "Mommy."

"It was a dumb move," he felt compelled to say as he scrubbed his hands down his face, wishing like hell that he could take the kiss back almost as much as he wished he'd never let her go.

There was no denying that he wanted the woman, had since he first hit puberty, but he'd always known that there would never be anything between them. This strange relationship of theirs pretty much guaranteed it. Even knowing that there would never be anything between them hadn't stopped him from fantasizing about her over the years.

There probably weren't many men in town that hadn't fantasized about taking Rory James to bed. She was a beautiful, desirable, sexy woman and he would have been concerned if he hadn't been attracted to her. It didn't matter how badly he wanted her though, there would never be anything between them. There was just too much history and animosity between them to take things further, but apparently that hadn't stopped him from doing something incredibly stupid, like kissing her.

One minute, he wanted to take her over his knee and the next, he wanted her in his bed and before he could stop himself, he'd kissed her. He'd never been a big fan of kissing before. It was one of those things that he did to get a woman to spread, but with Rory he could have happily kissed her all day. Her lips were warm, soft, full and felt so damn good against his that it had taken everything he had not to tilt his head and deepen the kiss. He wanted to do that and more, but he knew that she would never let it happen. Rory James didn't want him and the knowledge had knocked some sense into him. It also hadn't hurt that she hadn't touched or kissed him back.

She was probably going to kick him in the balls for that lapse in judgment the next time that she saw him, which would probably be any minute now, he mused as he shot a look down at his watch. It was almost six in the morning and if they didn't haul ass they'd be late for work. Maybe he should do his poor balls a favor and let her fend for herself, but just as quickly as the thought flashed through his head he shoved it away. Her arm was broken and she really had no business driving.

His eyes shifted to her Jeep and he considered yanking a few cables out of the engine to take the choice out of her hands, but knowing Rory, she probably had some backups in the garage. Then again, she might have called for one of her brothers to pick her up, he realized as he shot a look down both ends of the quiet street. When he didn't spot anything, he settled back against his truck door and waited.

A few minutes later Rory came walking out of her house with a backpack slung over her left shoulder and a large metal thermos that was no doubt filled to the brim with hot chocolate, in her good hand. When she spotted him leaning against his truck she noticeably swallowed. Was that a blush creeping up her beautiful face? It was kind of hard to tell in the early morning light, but he was pretty sure that it was a blush.

Great, he thought dryly. She was embarrassed about what happened. Nothing like the woman who hated you finding out that you were attracted to her. He'd been a fucking idiot to think that she'd settle for kicking him in the balls, although she still might. She was probably going to use her newfound knowledge to bring him to his knees and make him wish that she'd just taken it out on his balls. He really was a fucking idiot, he decided as he walked over to her.

"What do you want?" she asked cautiously as she continued to make her way over to her Jeep.

With a sigh, he gestured to his truck. "I'm driving you to work this morning."

She shook her head stubbornly. "No need. As you can see I got my Jeep back," she said, giving him a pointed look. "Turns out that there was a glitch in the records."

He simply shrugged it off. "You can't drive with a broken arm, Rory," he pointed out.

"I'm pretty sure that I can," the stubborn woman said.

Connor prayed for patience as he stopped himself from grabbing the woman, tossing her over his shoulder and throwing her ass in the back of his truck. "You just broke your arm, Rory. It probably still hurts, which means that you probably took a painkiller and you shouldn't be driving," he explained with forced patience.

Rory paused a few feet away from her Jeep, pursing her lips up as she thought it over. Finally with a heavy sigh she nodded. "I'll call one of my brothers for a ride," she said, placing the thermos on the hood of her Jeep so that she could dig around in her bag for her cell phone.

"No need," he said, snatching up her thermos and headed for his truck, knowing that's all it would take to get her to follow him and sure enough, it worked.

"Hey! Give that back!" she snapped as she followed him, but of course he just ignored her as he walked around the truck and opened the passenger door for her.

"Get in or I drink it," he promised.

With a glare, she snatched the thermos out of his hand and climbed in. When he tried to help her with her seatbelt she slapped his hands away. He let it go since she hadn't rubbed the kiss in his face yet and quickly made his way around the truck and climbed in.

She didn't say anything as he started the truck and backed out of the long driveway. Maybe the kiss hadn't meant anything to her and she'd already forgotten about it, he half-hoped/half-inwardly cringed as he drove towards the site. Then again, maybe she was just waiting until her brothers were around so that they could get in a good laugh at his expense. He opened his mouth to ask her about it, but snapped his mouth shut. If she was willing to pretend that it never happened then so was he.

"Can I ask you something?" she said, destroying all his hopes that she'd forgotten about his little act of stupidity.

"No."

Of course she ignored him and asked anyway. "Why are you being so nice to me?" she asked, confusing the hell out of him.

"What are you talking about?" he asked as he held back a sigh of relief. As long as she didn't talk about the kiss, they could have any asinine conversation that she wanted.

"What do you mean 'what am I talking about'?" she demanded, sounding frustrated. "You took care of me after I fell, held my hand, kept my brothers from making things worse, spent the last couple of days playing nursemaid to me and you really have to ask what I'm talking about?"

He shook his head as he took a turn onto Slade Road, a normally busy road, but at this time of morning there were only a few cars on the road. "It wasn't a big deal," he said, wondering why she was latching onto it. Obviously it was bugging the shit out of her if it drove her to break into his house and interrupt his shower.

"It's a very big deal!" she snapped.

"Why?" he demanded, taking his eyes off the road so that he could look at her.

"Because you're confusing me!"

He had to chuckle at that. "You're acting like no one's ever been nice to you before, Rory," he said, only realizing after the words left his mouth that there might be some truth in that. The dark blush that stained her cheeks and the way that she averted her eyes only confirmed it.

"That's bullshit, Rory," he said as he thought it over, trying to think of someone or something that would prove his words wrong.

He knew that her family loved her, adored her, but they tended to treat her like a weaker brother. The only time that they really watched out for her was when some guy stepped over the line and then they simply beat the shit out of the loser. Her father was pretty much the same way. From what he'd seen over the years, the man obviously cared for her, but he didn't seem to have a clue about how to show it.

There was no point in asking about boyfriends since he knew that they either treated her like shit or like a fuck buddy. He'd never seen anyone act sweet on Rory. Sure they'd flirted with her and were obviously attracted to her, but they'd never treated her like she was anything special. While other women were treated to romantic dates, jewelry, gifts, adoration and expensive meals, Rory was given sensible gifts, brought out for a beer or a burger and treated like a guy.

They were all fucking idiots.

Rory deserved to be pampered, spoiled and worshiped and any man that was lucky enough to earn her notice should make sure that he did all of those things and more. He didn't give a damn what she wore, she was still one hundred percent woman and should be treated as one. He'd never gone out of his way for any of his ex-girlfriends, but at least he'd treated them a hell of a lot better than any of Rory's old boyfriends had treated her.

He really didn't understand that at all. She was beautiful. Well, more like hot, but the guys around her acted like they were doing her a favor by asking her out. They were all fucking idiots. Granted, he knew most of the problem was her overprotective brothers, because asking her out was just as good as asking to have your ass kicked. In his opinion, she was more than worth a trip to the ICU.

"Just forget it," Rory said with a heavy sigh as she moved to take a sip of her hot cocoa. He considered taking it, but somehow managed to resist the urge. She'd probably try to smack him upside his head with her broken hand and he'd be forced to turn the truck around and take her back home. He'd have to take care of her. Plus, he really couldn't afford to lose another day.

They were two days behind and needed to play catch up. He hated taking the time off, especially since they didn't have any time to spare on this project, but he couldn't leave Rory. Yesterday morning he'd had his ass up by four, shaved, showered, dressed and headed down to his truck to get his ass to work thirty minutes later, assuming that she would call for help if she needed it when he remembered something very important.

Rory James was a stubborn pain in the ass and would never ask for help.

While he'd walked back in his house and headed for his bedroom, he made a quick round of phone calls. Ten minutes later he was chucking off most of his clothes and climbing in bed with her and not a moment too soon. She'd been dealing with a migraine that had left her helpless to move. He'd helped her take her pills before he crawled in bed with her. He held her until she'd fallen asleep with that damn dog of hers glaring at him from across the room.

If she hadn't been able to work today, he wouldn't have had a choice in the matter. He had to go to work today, but he'd fully planned on sending one of her brothers to take care of her. He'd also planned on checking in on her during his lunch break. It was probably a good thing that Rory was stubborn and was coming to work so that he wouldn't have to worry about her all day. If it became too much for her, she could always curl up on the couch in her office.

He really didn't think she should be going to work today, but he knew better than to say anything since she'd just ignore him. Well, at least she couldn't get into too much trouble hanging in the office all day, he reassured himself. He'd have that secretary of hers keep him updated so that he could focus on work, where his mind should be.

This was a big project, the biggest project of his career, and he needed to stay focused. Rory James was out of commission for a few months and probably wouldn't be able to do much once the cast was taken off. She could go around and play supervisor when she felt better. At least that would keep her safe while he busted his ass to get this project going.

A few minutes later, he was parking in the makeshift parking lot and preparing himself for the long day ahead. They were at least two days behind and would need to move their asses. Rory sent him a barely-there nod as she climbed out of the truck and headed for her trailer. He followed after her, hoping her secretary was good for something like making a cup of extra strong coffee and keeping his damn eyes off Rory's luscious ass, he thought absently as he watched the body part in question sway slightly side to side.

She had a great ass.

He followed her into the trailer and somehow managed to tear his eyes away from that beautiful ass and headed for the coffee cart set up against the wall near the time clock. He ignored the questioning look her secretary was sending him and focused his attention on finding some damn caffeine before he lost his fucking mind.

"They canceled the meeting," he heard Jacob softly explain to Rory.

As he searched the small cabinets, he couldn't help but wonder what meeting her assistant was talking about, but as he shoved box after box of some weird cocoa product out of his way he decided that he really just didn't care. He needed a caffeine fix and all he could find was cocoa. Oh, they were going to have to change that pretty damn soon or he'd become bitchy.

"Did they reschedule?" she whispered, sounding nervous.

Now *that* had his attention.

He couldn't remember a time when Rory was nervous about anything. Pissed? Yes, but never nervous. What could make a woman like Rory nervous? he wondered as he reluctantly settled on making a cup of hot cocoa and praying that it had a shitload of caffeine otherwise her secretary was getting a new chore added to his duties.

"No, I'm sorry, Rory. They sent back the proposal with an apology. They're not interested," Jacob said with true regret lacing his tone.

He wasn't too surprised when he heard the trailer door slam shut seconds later. Hot cocoa forgotten, he turned around to find her secretary moving to go after her.

"What has little Rory James in a huff I wonder?" he mused, stopping the secretary dead in his tracks.

"It's none of your business," Jacob said firmly as he stood his ground.

Connor couldn't help but chuckle as he moved towards the man. "Did Rory ever tell you what happens when someone comes between us?"

FOURTEEN

"Please don't fire me," Jacob said as she stepped inside the office. She felt her brows damn near shoot to her hairline when her eyes landed on him. It managed to distract her from her current problem of trying to figure out how to make McGill change his mind.

"Why exactly are you duct taped to a chair?" she demanded even as the answer dawned on her.

Connor.

She wasn't really surprised. Well, actually she kind of was since Connor tended to focus on torturing her these days. Sure, he went after the guys she dated, but that never really bothered her since they usually turned out to be jerks and had it coming. She wondered what Jacob could have done as she walked over and started the five-minute process of making a double cup of hot cocoa.

"Are you going to release me?" Jacob asked, sounding unsure, which only piqued her curiosity since most of the men that Connor dealt with would usually be pissed and threatening to call the police by now.

"How long ago did he tie you up?" she asked as her eyes shot to the clock on the wall. She hadn't seen Connor since this morning so she was going to just go ahead and take a guess about the time.

"Five hours ago," Jacob muttered pathetically, confirming her suspicions.

"And what did you do?" she asked casually as she added a spoonful of vanilla and caramel flavored creamer.

There was a telling pause before Jacob muttered, "It wasn't my fault."

"What wasn't your fault?" she asked, pouring a dab of cream in her mug.

"H-he knows."

"Knows what?"

"About the plans, meetings, suites, everything," he admitted, making everything in her go still.

"Where is he?" she asked in a bored tone even as panic shot through her.

She realized that he would have found out about the project sooner or later, but she was kind of hoping on it being later, after she had a signed contract with McGill so that he couldn't interfere and take over. Now she was going to have to hunt him down, kick his ass and make sure that he knew that this was her project and that it was off limits to him. Then she would be right back to trying to figure out how to convince them to let her do this. Maybe she could -

"I think you and I should have a talk," Connor announced as he stepped in the office, holding a thick folder.

Thankful that he'd saved her the time of having to hunt him down to kick his ass, she grabbed her drink and headed for her office, knowing that he'd be right behind her.

"Hey, what about me?" Jacob asked, but she ignored him. "Seriously, I have to use the bathroom. If you could just make a little tear in the tape, I'm pretty sure that I could-"

Connor closed the door behind him and moved to sit in her chair, but she was faster. She sat down and couldn't quite bite back the smug little smile that came along with besting Connor. It seemed as though this meeting was starting off on the right track, she mused seconds before he snatched the hot cocoa out of her hands, placed it on her desk, grabbed her good hand and gave it a yank.

"Hey!"

He ignored her as he took her seat and yanked her back until she was sitting on his lap. Once he had her settled, meaning trapped, he reached around her and picked up her cup of cocoa.

"Don't even think about it," she bit out evenly as she struggled to get off his lap, but the arm he had wrapped around her waist held her right where he wanted her.

He ignored her and finished off her cocoa as she was forced to sit there, watching as her precious cocoa was devoured. Once he finished, he placed the coffee cup back on the desktop with a little more force than she felt was necessary and shifted her on his lap so that she was facing him.

"Anything you feel like sharing?" he asked as he leaned back in her chair, making himself comfortable as he studied her.

"You're an ass."

"Anything else?" he asked in a deceptively calm tone, but there was no missing the anger in his eyes.

"Yeah, stop touching my cocoa," she said as she tried to climb off his lap, but he refused to let her go.

"No. Anything else you want to tell me, Rory?" he asked, reaching up and pushed a strand of hair away from her face.

"I hate you?" she offered with a sweet smile.

For a moment he didn't say anything as he studied her, finally he leaned forward and grabbed the folder he'd dropped on the desk only minutes earlier and handed it to her.

"What's this?" she asked as she cautiously opened it, this was from Connor after all.

"My bargaining chip," he said, sounding arrogant, a little too arrogant for her comfort.

With a feigned casualness, she opened the envelope and pulled out the crisp white papers inside. She ignored him as he shifted her on his lap, and looked over the papers. With one glance, she knew that she was looking at a contract and a few seconds later she realized that it was a contract from McGill. When her eyes landed on the third paragraph she felt her brows pull together and her jaw pop.

"You…..son……of…..a…….*bitch*!" she bit out with barely controlled rage as she jumped off his lap and turned on him.

"Checkmate, sweetheart," Connor said with a wink and that sexy grin of his that had her seeing red.

"*Checkmate?*" she repeated in a strangled voice as she fought against the urge to jump him and go for those damn nipples that she was becoming so fond of. "You stole my project, you son of a bitch!"

"Did I?" he asked in a bored tone as he leaned back in the chair and appeared to think it over. "I think you just might be right about that, Rory," he said with a shrug.

"You've gone too far this time, Connor," she said, slamming the papers down on top of the desk as she continued to glare down at him.

"Oh, but I'm not even close to being done," he drawled as he reached over and picked up the contract, making a show of looking it over.

"What are you talking about?" she asked, reminding herself that this was the way the game was played and that she couldn't make her move until he'd laid all the cards on the table. When he was done, she was grabbing her pliers and going for his balls this time.

He'd done a lot of horrible things over the years, but stealing her project was by far the worst thing that he'd ever done, besides ruining her life that is. How was she supposed to explain to McGill that this was her project and that Connor had stolen it from her without sounding like a child and creating a lot of drama? There probably wasn't, so she was just going to have to settle for using the pliers until Connor promised to back out of the contract so that she could take it over.

"You arranged a meeting and tried to go behind my back, altering my project. For that," he paused, meeting her glare, "you're going to have to pay."

"It's my project, Connor. I worked my ass off designing those suites and I had every right to go to McGill and present them. Those are my designs, Connor, and you had no right stealing them!"

"Do you want to yell some more or are you ready to cut the shit and get down to business?" he asked and God help her, but she considered slapping that smug little smile right off his face.

"Yes," she grated out.

"The project is yours, Rory."

"For what price?" she asked, already knowing that Connor was going to make her work her ass off for it and probably put her through hell while doing it. If she didn't want this contract so badly she would have just shrugged and walked off, but she did. She might have to share Strawberry Manor with the jackass that she'd mistakenly started to like, but this project was *hers*.

"I'm glad you asked," he said with a content little sigh that had her right eye twitching and her hand inching towards her tool belt.

"I have a few conditions of course-"

"Of course you do," she said dryly, cutting him off.

"-but once you've completed them to my satisfaction, then you can start building your suites, have full use of my men and equipment and Shadow Construction will get full credit for it," he explained as he watched her, expectantly.

Having the use of his men, the ones she hand selected of course, would help as would having the use of his equipment. It would save her time and most importantly, money. This was a good deal and she'd have to be an idiot not to see that. Then again, she didn't know what he wanted in return so she wasn't even sure that she could go through with it.

"And in return, you're going to be my doting girlfriend," he announced and just like that he found the deal breaker.

"I'm not sleeping with you, Connor. I'll find another way to get my project back," she said, shaking her head in disgust as she snatched the contract away from him and headed for the door. Maybe her lawyer could find a loophole or she could just flat out sue the bastard and get an injunction to stop him from starting work on the suites. It would take time, but hopefully she could get this cleared up in time before Strawberry Manor's deadline.

"This has nothing to do with sex, Rory, so relax," he said, making her pause as she reached the door.

"Then what is the point of this little scheme of yours, Connor?" she asked, not even trying to hide her skepticism or her revulsion. This was a new low even for him.

He stood up and walked around her desk only to lean back against it as he explained, "I'm sure you've noticed that this little relationship of ours has caused a lot of.....," he pursed his lips up thoughtfully before he said, "problems."

That was an understatement if she ever heard one. Their relationship, or rather their hatred for one another had caused them get be banned, gawked at, bet on, and blamed admittedly for a lot of damage that they had inadvertently caused and for things that had absolutely nothing to do with them. She was still pissed about the summer that she was banned from the town pool because someone blamed them for breaking the slide. It had been broken before she'd managed to tackle Connor and pants the jerk.

"You're going to play my loving, doting girlfriend and help turn all of that around, Rory," he said with a shrug as though what he was suggesting wasn't really a big deal.

It was a very big deal!

She was more likely to kill him than dote on him and he damn well knew it!

"No, sorry, not going to happen," she said, shaking her head emphatically with each word. "Come up with something else."

"This isn't up for negotiation, Rory," he said firmly. "You will play my girlfriend in public and make sure that people believe that you not only like me, but love me and in return you get your project."

Her jaw nearly dropped to the ground with that declaration. "You expect me to act like I *love* you?"

"Mmmhmm, to the point that you can't keep your hands off me."

"They'll be firmly wrapped around your throat, you jerk!" she snapped. "Why do you really want to do this, Connor?" she demanded as she moved towards him and gestured with her broken hand in the direction of Strawberry Manor, "you don't care what anyone thinks so why are you screwing with my plans?"

He smiled tightly. "My reasons are my own, Rory. All you need to know is that if you want this project you'll do as I ask. You'll go out with me, hang on my every word and public displays of affection are not only encouraged but expected and you'll keep this deal of ours between us," he announced as he headed for the door. "You have one hour to make your decision. If you don't, then Highland Construction will be building three very elaborate suites and getting all the credit," he said with a wink as he left, shutting the door behind him and leaving her fuming.

She let out a scream of frustration as she kicked her desk and then spent the next two minutes muttering "owie" as she hopped around on one foot. When the pain dulled, she dropped down on her chair and groaned. She could not believe that he did this and she sure as hell couldn't believe that he wanted her to play this little game. She'd known that he was up to something and unfortunately that something had just kicked her ass.

This project meant everything to her. It was going to be Strawberry Manor's signature attraction and now Connor was dangling it in her face and leaving her with no other choice but to go along with this sick and twisted plan of his. She was going to have to play along, she realized with a pathetic whimper as she forced herself to get to her feet and walk out the door, knowing that what she was about to do went against nature, but for this project she would do it.

"If you let me go, I'll make you a triple chocolate hot cocoa," Jacob offered, sounding hopeful, which was really kind of pathetic.

"Consider this your punishment for having such a big mouth!" she snapped, knowing that she was letting him off easy by leaving him tied to his chair, but she couldn't help it. The man did make a delicious cup of hot cocoa.

"He made me tell him!" Jacob whined as she headed for the door.

"Uh huh, you can sit there and think about what you did, mister," she said sternly as she opened the door, "and just so you know, I'm not changing my shirts in front of you for a year for this."

His shocked gasp was rewarding enough as she closed the door behind her and headed towards the coffee truck where Connor was talking to some of his men, to do the unthinkable. She marched right up to him, ignoring the curious looks his men were sending her and reached up, cupping the back of Connor's neck and yanked him down for a kiss that sent shivers down her spine. She ignored her response, the startled gasps around her, and the whispers of people wondering if hell had frozen over as she pulled away.

"Pick me up at eight," she said, moving to walk away so that she could go kick something.

"Seven, and wear something sexy, sweetheart," Connor said with that damn cocky tone that was going to get him bitch slapped.

FIFTEEN

Oh, he was going to hell, but what a way to go, he thought with a chuckle as he grabbed the bouquet of baby pink roses off his coffee table and headed for the door, pausing only long enough to check his hair in the antique mirror hanging in the foyer.

Admittedly, he hadn't been in a good mood when he'd discovered what Rory was doing behind his back, but once he'd realized the possibilities, he hadn't been able to stop smiling. He owned her ass now. He had something that she wanted and he was going to use her to get what he wanted. He was also going to enjoy everything that he put her through along the way.

For the past week he'd been wracking his brain trying to come up with a way to win over her brothers and lure them over to his company and Rory, bless her little backstabbing, betraying heart, just handed him the solution on a silver platter. He'd get to her brothers through her, not that he wouldn't enjoy having Rory on his arm, he would, but she was simply a means to an end.

Finding out that she was lying and going behind his back to deal with McGill was the wakeup call that he'd needed. Over the past couple of days he'd been hoping that they could put their little feud behind them and call a truce, but obviously he'd been foolish to think that Rory could ever let go of the past and move on.

If she wanted to continue playing these games then that was more than fine with him, because he would end this bullshit once and for all. Once Strawberry Manor was done and he had the James boys working for him then he was going to sit back and enjoy the show as Shadow Construction went out of business. It would be the final blow and end this game of theirs.

A minute later, he was knocking on her front door and more than eager to start the final chapter. He was also looking forward to having free reign to touch her and holy hell, did that make it all worth it. Well, that and the fact that she had to pretend to adore him. Really, could life get any better? he thought as he knocked again.

"You're early," Rory said with an annoyed sigh as she opened the door.

"I'm on time," he murmured absently as he scanned her body and frowned. Why was she wearing a tight baby green tee shirt and jeans when he'd specifically told her to wear something sexy? Sexier, he amended a moment later when he was forced to shift slightly to the right to accommodate his growing erection.

"I told you eight," she said, crossing her arms beneath her large breasts and practically shoved them towards his hungry eyes. Did she know what that did to him? He sure as hell hoped not.

"And I told you seven, Rory."

She simply shrugged as she gestured to the flowers in his hand. "What are those?"

His irritation forgotten, he frowned down at her. "They're flowers." She rolled her eyes at him. "I meant, what are they for?"

"For you."

"Why?" she asked, eying the roses as though she was afraid that they were going to attack her.

Christ, she was acting like she'd never received flowers before and it took him a second to realize that she probably hadn't. If he didn't want her brothers to come work for him so badly he'd be tempted to kick their asses for this bullshit.

"Because that's what I do for my dates," he lied. He'd never bought a woman flowers before, but for Rory he made it a point to pick up the flowers on his way home even though it meant that he had to rush to get ready. It just felt wrong not to get them for her.

"I'm not really your date, Connor," she pointed out as she took the flowers, looking and acting like she didn't care, but he didn't miss the pleased little smile or the way she smelled the flowers as she turned around to place them on the small table next to the front door. Now he was kicking himself for not stopping off and getting her a box of chocolates. Next time, he promised himself as he stepped aside so that she could lock her door.

"Um, what are you doing?" she asked as she looked down.

"Holding your hand," he said, quite enjoying the feel of her smaller hand in his. He'd never been one for PDA, but with Rory he was willing to make the exception, especially if it got him what he wanted.

"Why?" she asked, trying to pull her hand away, but he simply ignored her as he walked with her around his truck and opened the door for her. With a roll of her eyes and a muttered, "I could have done that myself," she climbed in and buckled up.

He had to bite his tongue as he closed the door for her. It always irritated him when he saw other men treating her like she was one of the guys, but it absolutely pissed him off that she had such low expectations of how she should be treated. Well, he'd fix that. He'd use this time to show her exactly how a man should treat her so that when he was through with her, she would at least know that she deserved better. It was the least he could do for her after all, he decided as he climbed in the truck.

"Would you stop doing that?" Rory asked a minute later as she tried to pull her hand free, but he ignored her since he knew that she just didn't know any better, but she'd learn, he told himself.

"No."

"No?" she asked, giving up on trying to free her hand to glare at him.

"No, so you'd better get used to it, Rory. For the next five months you're mine," he said, liking the idea more and more. It really was too bad that sex wasn't involved in this deal, but he'd have to settle for the small bonuses like holding her, touching her, and kissing her.

"Ah, no. For the next five months I'm going along with this sick and twisted charade while we're in *public* to get my project, which by the way I'm going to start soon since I've more than earned it," she informed him, yanking her hand back and trying to take him off guard, but he'd been ready. He had her hand firmly in his and refused to let go.

"When it's just the two of us I don't have to do anything but try to figure out a way to get rid of the body without the police figuring it out," she said, giving her hand one more good yank that he easily ignored before she gave up.

"No, I have to hold your hand to help stay in character," he said with a shrug as he turned into O'Malley's busy parking lot. He'd planned on taking her out to a nice restaurant and then out for a drink, but Rory apparently had different expectations for the night judging by her attire. That was fine, more than fine actually. He'd help build up her expectations so that when the next guy came around, and he'd probably beat the shit out of him just on principle alone, she wouldn't put up with cheap assholes that didn't have a clue about how to treat a woman.

"Stay in character?" she said slowly as though she couldn't quite believe what he'd said.

"Exactly," he said absently as he drove towards the back of the large parking lot since he didn't feel like wasting twenty minutes waiting for a prime spot to open up. Besides, he didn't like taking those spots. He'd never feel right if he took a spot up front and forced a woman to park in the back of the parking lot where the street lights didn't quite reach and where any asshole could be hiding in the woods that bordered the parking lot.

"I think we should set some ground rules," she said absently as she shot an anxious look over her shoulder towards the busy restaurant.

Rory James afraid? He never thought he'd see the day when that happened and he couldn't help but feel satisfied that he was responsible for it. She was always trying to be tough and act as though nothing ever fazed her. It was nice to see her act human for a change.

"You're absolutely right," he said with a firm nod of agreement. When she opened her mouth, no doubt to cut him off and start sprouting off a bunch of rules that he would only ignore, he decided to save them both a lot of time and aggravation by just explaining to her how this was going to play out.

"For the next five months you're going to play my sweet, loving girl-friend. I don't expect sex," but he sure as hell wouldn't turn it down from her. "I do expect you to act like you enjoy being with me. If that means that I'll have to suck it up and hold your hand, have you sit on my lap, and kiss you in order to do that then that's just what I'll have to do," he said with a careless shrug that he knew would just piss her off.

"Look," Rory practically hissed, "there's no need to continue with this sick and disturbing plan of yours. We can just call a truce and move on and eventually everyone else will as well."

He pretended to think that over. "You really think so?"

"Yes!"

"I guess we could do that……," he said, purposely letting his words trail off and biting back a smile when she sighed with relief. She really should have known better. "But we're not going to."

"I. Hate. You."

He chuckled as he opened his door. "You'll have to do better than that if you want that project of yours," he reminded her before he shut the door.

It wasn't exactly a surprise that she sat there fuming as she glared at him, her expression clearly telling him what she'd liked to do to him, but he simply ignored her since he was in such a good mood. He was just too pleased with himself to care. For tonight and for the next five months, Rory James was his.

The only thing that would make this whole arrangement better was having her in his bed, but that would never happen. If she hadn't liked him before, and really at this point there was no questioning that, then she absolutely hated him now. In fact, he was willing to bet everything he had that she was even now considering the pros and cons of kicking him in the balls and being done with it.

Then again, he knew that she would never risk her project. If her assistant hadn't spilled everything he knew about the project while Connor duct taped him to the chair then her designs would have. They were meticulous, detailed and well presented and they'd made him feel guilty until he'd managed to focus. He knew that once he had McGill on board that his plan would work.

It took some time convincing McGill to take the chance on Rory's plans, but once he did, Connor knew the James boys were as good as his. He'd been foolish to think that he could win the James boys over on his own. They might have refrained from trying to kick his ass over the years, but it didn't mean that they liked him any more than their sister did.

The looks they gave him when he'd climbed out of that hole and went to help the paramedics, reminded him where he stood with them. Then again, the fact that they'd shoved him out of the way and scowled in his direction any time he got too close, meaning within twenty feet, of Rory told him that his plan would never work. He knew then that if he continued this little war with Rory that he would probably ruin his chance to steal the James brothers.

Now, as Rory's boyfriend……..

That was a different story altogether. They'd be suspicious and rightly so, but it would get his foot in the door and that's all he needed. If they saw him treating Rory with respect and taking care of her the way that she deserved, then he'd win them over.

Not that it would be a hardship treating Rory like a queen, it wouldn't. Sure, he'd screwed her over and enjoyed making her life a living hell, but he always made sure that she was okay, always. When they were seven and a bunch of stuck up little girls made fun of the way that Rory dressed and acted, he made sure that those three girls had a run in with a very large mud puddle in the playground. Over the years he'd lost count of how many little boys, teenagers and grown men he'd taken care of for her after they'd treated her like shit. It probably made him a hypocrite to enjoy screwing with her and then beating the shit out of anyone who hurt her, but he just couldn't stomach the idea of Rory being hurt in any way. Not that he would ever tell her that, especially since she wouldn't believe him.

That was also the reason that he hadn't bothered trying to trick her into dating him. Not that she'd go for it, she wouldn't, but he didn't like the idea of hurting her. Stringing her along so that he could get her brothers to come work for him just felt wrong. At least by blackmailing her, he was being honest with her so that he was free to enjoy screwing her over without any guilt.

He opened the door for the furious woman and didn't bother hiding his grin as she muttered a few violent words about his balls. Biting her lip, she shot another nervous glance at the increasingly busy restaurant as she slowly climbed out of the truck. She looked so cute when she was nervous, still hot as hell, but still cute.

"Um, maybe we could," she noticeably swallowed as she took a step back, "do something else?"

"Would that make you feel more comfortable with this arrangement?" he asked, sounding concerned. He forced back a smile when she noticeably relaxed. She gave him a quick nod, never taking her eyes away from the restaurant as she sighed with relief.

It was really pathetic that she didn't know him by now. Then again, knowing that she didn't want to do this just made the situation too damn irresistible to ignore.

"Fine. We can go home," he said, biting back a smile when her shoulders slumped in obvious relief and she moved to open the truck door. "Right after we eat, play a few games of pool and hang out for two or three hours," he said as he took her good hand in his and headed for the door, not really caring that he was practically dragging her behind him.

He had a game plan after all and she was the key to making it work.

"I really hate you," she muttered, but he decided to ignore that since it was just her crankiness and her severe disliking of him talking.

SIXTEEN

"H-h-how many?" Amber, the hostess and a woman who'd graduated two years ahead of them in high school, asked as she noticeably struggled to tear her eyes away from the sight of Connor holding her hand. That was understandable, because right now Rory was struggling with a nervous breakdown.

Connor O'Neil was holding her hand, in public, on purpose, and she liked it, a little too much, but sadly that wasn't the worst part. The most frightening? Yes, but not the worst part. No, the worst part was that every single person in the bar had stopped talking, eating, dancing, and drinking to stare at them. It was actually a little bit unnerving to be able to hear the jukebox playing Kelly Clarkson's *Mr. Know It All*, which she normally liked, but right now it was creeping her out as everyone stared at them.

They were never going to be able to pull this off. Not that she really cared. She really didn't. Although, it would be nice to be able to go a day without someone pointing at her or being asked to leave a store or restaurant because Connor was already there and the establishment was one of fifty-seven that had the damn rule about not allowing both of them inside at the same time. It was really an inconvenient little rule and one that she wouldn't mind having lifted. Having the no trespass orders lifted wouldn't exactly hurt either, but none of that was worth this little nightmare.

Unfortunately for her, Strawberry Manor was worth it. Otherwise she wouldn't be here at the moment. She'd probably be back at the site putting in a couple more hours before calling it a night if it wasn't for his asinine plan. Not that she could do much with her arm broken, but it was still enough to bring them one step closer to their goal.

If they didn't meet the deadline not only would their reputations be marred, but they'd lose the bonus money and, she wasn't about to let that happen. She'd worked her butt off for years building her reputation for running a dependable company and she wasn't about to let the project of her dreams change that. They would finish this project on time along with those suites and Shadow Construction's reputation would be set for life.

"How many?" Amber asked, shooting a nervous look over to Phil, the manager, who was acting as the backup bartender for the night.

Rory nearly sighed with relief. Phil ran a tight ship and had several strict rules when it came to them and thankfully he was one of the fifty-seven establishments that wouldn't allow them in at the same time. He was going to throw her out on her ass and she couldn't wait. So, when Phil only shrugged a moment later she nearly stomped her foot in frustration. What the hell kind of manager was he that he couldn't even follow his own rules? Rules were made for a reason!

"Two," Connor said as he released her hand and before she could sigh with relief or make a run for it, he had his arm around her shoulders and was pulling her closer.

She felt her cheeks burn as every eye in the restaurant watched that move. Oh, she was never going to live this down. This moment of stupidity was never going to be forgotten. Years from now people were still going to talk about this. She couldn't do this. She couldn't go through with this farce. She couldn't-

A collective gasp sounded throughout the restaurant, but she couldn't really force herself to care about that, not with Connor kissing her. One thing she could say about the life-ruining bastard, he sure knew how to kiss, and well, very well, she thought as he moved his lips against hers one more time before pulling away. He didn't go far before he leaned back in and pressed one last rather sweet kiss against her lips and then one to her cheek before he whispered in her ear, "Relax, Rory."

"This is so going on my Facebook page," someone said, drawing her attention away from Connor and his surprisingly soft lips. She looked past the shocked hostess in time to see several people putting away their phones.

Great, her humiliation was about to go viral, she thought with a little whimper that had Connor chuckling as he once again took her hand in his and pressed a rather sweet kiss to the back of it. Damn, the man was good, she thought as she allowed him to lead her through the crowded restaurant towards a back booth where the waitress waited, looking a little more relaxed as she ran an appreciative eye over Connor.

Not that Rory could really blame her. The man did look especially yummy tonight, she decided as she was forced to walk behind him so that they could squeeze past a couple of tables full of gawkers. She used the opportunity to run an appreciative eye over Connor.

She'd seen a lot of good-looking men in her life, but none were as hot as Connor. Of course, her brothers and cousins would argue that since they were all arrogant bastards, especially her cousins, she thought with a fond smile, but she didn't care. Connor O'Neil was the first boy she'd noticed and he'd only gotten better with age She ran her eyes up his long legs, over his firm behind perfectly encased in light brown pants, and up to his well defined back, wide shoulders and perfectly combed honey blonde hair.

After she was done with her perusal, her eyes dropped back down to his backside while she fought back a groan of embarrassment. He was dressed up while she was wearing a tee shirt and jeans and for the first time in her life, she wished that she'd taken the time to find a pretty dress, shoes and done her makeup instead of just taking a shower, blow dried her hair and threw on the first thing she found when she'd opened her bureau. She knew that she was beautiful and normally she didn't really care, but tonight she kind of wished that she'd played it up a bit.

Not that this was a real date. It wasn't, but that didn't mean that she wanted this to look like he was going out with her out of pity. If anything, people should be wondering why *she* was out with *him*, not the other way around.

"You look beautiful tonight," Connor said with a secret smile as though he could read her mind and he probably could by this point, she thought as he pressed a kiss to her forehead before gesturing for her to slide into the small cozy booth.

She fought the battle to look over her shoulder and lost several times. Sure enough, everyone in the bar was now openly watching them. Several people were actually leaning forward, resting their chins on their fists as they watched her and Connor like they were the best thing on television. She was used to people watching them as they waited to see if they were going to kill each other, but this was ridiculous.

"Your waitress is, Susan," Amber said distractedly as she threw Connor a wistful glance.

Well, that was kind of insulting. As far as everyone here knew they were on a date. Granted, it wasn't a real date, but they didn't know that. She'd bet a huge cup of cocoa that Amber was going to find a way to slip her number into Connor's hand before the night was over.

"I'm not interested," Connor said, dragging her attention back to him.

He leaned back on the bench across from her and nodded towards Amber's retreating back as if she'd asked or cared. She really didn't. He could kiss every woman in town and she wouldn't bat an eye. Nope, it wouldn't bother her at all, she thought absently as she considered kicking Connor beneath the table and wiping that knowing look off his face.

"So, you want to tell me why you're really doing this?" she asked, deciding that she'd had enough of his games over the past week. He wasn't worried enough about how they were treated to force her to go through with this farce. It probably aggravated him and he'd probably be happy if it stopped, but that wasn't the reason that he was pulling this bullshit and they both knew it. So, the question remained, what exactly was he up to?

"I told you why," he said, reaching out and taking her good hand into both of his and for the moment, she allowed it.

For whatever reason, it was important to him that people believed that they were together and she really had no choice but to go along with it. Maybe if she figured out what he wanted, she could turn the tables on him and get her project free and clear.

"Fine. Don't tell me the real reason," she said with a bit more attitude than she'd meant to, but she couldn't help it. She was tired, her ribs and arm were still a little sore. She'd missed her nightly hot chocolate fix when she got home, and to make matters worse, the way Connor was looking at her, kissing her and couldn't seem to stop touching her was seriously screwing with her head.

Connor laced their fingers together as he gestured for Susan, a pleasant woman in her late forties, who used to teach the fourth grade until an unfortunate incident involving the two of them and a fire hose during a school assembly years ago had ended her career. Rory had to admit that it was nice to see the woman smile again and the limp was barely noticeable these days. Not that she took the blame for her injury. She didn't. To this day she still didn't know why Susan had taken off screaming when she'd spotted them.

At least she'd been able to put her past behind her and move on, Rory thought seconds before Susan noticed Connor trying to get her attention. Her smile quickly disappeared as an expression of pure terror took its place. She shook her head in disbelief as she stumbled back, mumbling to herself before she blindly reached out for Amber as the other woman moved to walk past her. Rory watched as Susan whispered something to Amber as she gestured wildly in their direction. When Amber nodded, Susan tore off her apron and took off running through the crowded restaurant.

Rory really hated when that happened.

"Do you want to dance?" Connor asked, drawing her attention as she watched Susan shove a couple out of the way in her desperate attempt to get away from them.

"Dance?" she asked, shifting her eyes to the right to find everyone still watching them, but at least now they were trying to pretend that they weren't.

It really shouldn't bother her, but it did. She didn't like being on display. While she would have normally jumped at the chance to dance since she didn't get to do it often, probably because no one ever asked her, she didn't want to tonight. She wasn't a very good dancer, probably from lack of experience, and she really didn't feel like giving the gossips something else to talk about.

She was just about to tell him no when Phil walked up to their table and sighed heavily with obvious annoyance. "You have to leave."

"And why's that?" Connor asked casually as he gave her hand a gentle squeeze.

"Two of my waitresses just quit and the other six are refusing to come out of the kitchen until I swear on my balls that I won't make them serve you," he explained with a shrug.

"See what I'm talking about?" Connor asked with a sigh as stood up, never releasing her hand as he did. It didn't surprise her that he hadn't argued with Phil since it was pointless. They were being kicked out and nothing they said or did would change that.

"It's only because we're in here together. If I had come alone, I would already be on my second cup of cocoa and making fun of you with the waitresses," Rory felt obligated to point out.

Instead of glaring at her or getting pissed like he normally would have, Connor simply shot her a grin and a wink as he wrapped his arm around her shoulders. They followed after Phil, who was making sure that they actually left. Connor seemed relaxed and carefree and heaven help her, but she actually liked him this way, which of course only made her want to kick his ass even more.

He was up to something, something big and she wished he would just get it over with and stop screwing with her head. She didn't want to like him and with every touch and smile, he was making it difficult to keep hating him.

———

"Please tell me that you're not actually following me," Rory said, abruptly stopping and almost causing him to crash into her since his eyes had been locked on her ass and not her stone walkway.

He caught himself just in time and even managed to look up before Rory had the chance to turn around and catch him staring at her ass, again. It didn't help that the effort caused his eyes to roam over her chest and since they were there, they may have taken a moment to appreciate what Rory had to offer. What he wouldn't give to see Rory naked and have five minutes just to appreciate her body. She was so beautiful and he had absolutely no doubt that her body was just as perfect. As his mind registered Rory cupping his face, he couldn't help but wonder if his fantasies over the years came close to the real thing.

"Care to explain why you're following me?" Rory asked once his eyes moved the rest of the way up her body and met her gorgeous eyes.

"To say goodnight," he said, frowning and wondering why she even had to ask.

"Uh huh," she said, returning his frown. "Didn't we say goodnight in the truck?"

"You mean when you climbed out of the truck, slammed the door shut, and walked off without a word?"

"Yes," she said, nodding.

"How exactly is that a proper goodbye for a date?" he had to ask.

"Because this isn't a real date," she said in an exasperated tone that he simply chose to ignore since he was too busy trying to hold back an annoyed sigh.

Why did she have to be so difficult?

"Of course it is," he said, taking her good hand in his and gave it a gentle tug as he headed for her front door where he planned on giving her a proper goodbye, for appearances of course. He was not looking forward to taking her into his arms.

Not at all.

He was only doing this for the neighbors hiding behind their curtains and blinds as they spied on the two of them and for the neighbors standing in their driveways and on the sidewalks, holding flashlights as they openly watched the two of them. Since they had to appear to be a couple in love then he really had no choice in the matter, he thought with a smile. He had to kiss Rory James.

Poor him.

"No, it's not," Rory said, stepping up beside him in front of her door as she shot a nervous look towards their neighbors.

"Of course this is a date, Rory," he said, drawing her attention back to him where it should be.

This was his time with her and he'd be damned if he shared it with anyone else. He might need their neighbors and the rest of the people in town to spread word to her brothers that they were dating, but that didn't mean that he'd allow them to fuck this up for him. Rory James was his for five months and he fully planned on enjoying his time with her, especially since she'd probably never talk to him again after he stole her brothers from her and ran her out of business.

"How exactly was this a date, Connor?" she asked, shooting another glance towards their nosy neighbors, who were really starting to aggravate the shit out of him.

"I picked you up, took you out to dinner-"

"We didn't actually eat," she mumbled distractedly as she frowned at something behind him.

He looked over his shoulder and nearly groaned when he saw several of their neighbors, and some people that didn't even live in their neighborhood, gathering in front of her house and holding cameras trained on the two of them. With a sigh, he shifted in front of her, giving them his back and effectively blocking their view and bringing Rory's attention right back to him.

"That's not my fault that we didn't get to eat, Rory," he felt obligated to point out. He'd taken her to a restaurant, hadn't he? It wasn't his fault that they were asked to leave because of some bullshit rule that better get lifted and soon.

"How is that not your fault?" she demanded, yanking her hand free so that she could prop her hands on her hips as she glared at him.

"You're the one that got us banned from that restaurant in the first place!"

"No, I wasn't," he said, mostly because he couldn't remember exactly why they'd been banned from O'Malley's, but he was sure that it was Rory's fault.

"You made my date have a nervous breakdown!" she snapped, but that didn't really help him since several of the guys that she dated had that unfortunate response when he got involved.

"How exactly would that get us banned?"

"They had to call a priest to come talk him off the roof!" she snapped.

He shook his head and with a shrug and said, "Still not seeing the problem."

With an eye roll and a muttered, "I give up," she turned to let herself inside the house and end their date, but he wasn't about to let that happen. Whether she liked it or not, she was his date and he wouldn't be denied the best part of the evening.

The kiss goodnight.

SEVENTEEN

"**W**hat are you doing?" she mumbled nervously as Connor cupped her face in his warm hands and leaned in.

"What does it look like I'm doing, Rory?" he asked with that bad boy smile of his that *did not* make her stomach do funny things.

"I-I'm not really sure," she said in a daze as her mind registered that he was going to kiss her. Instead of getting pissed or at the very least, disgusted by the idea, she was surprised to discover that she wanted to kiss him.

She wanted to kiss Connor O'Neil.

This was so wrong, she thought as his lips came in contact with hers. The contact was brief, sweet and not nearly enough. When she placed her hands on his shoulders and leaned into him, it was only because of their deal. For her project she had to kiss the hottest man in town. It was a hardship, but at the moment she decided that she'd just have to suck it up and deal with it.

As long as they kept it to kisses and perhaps a few touches then that was fine. She could handle that, but sex was definitely out of the question. She might be attracted to the man, more so lately, but that didn't mean that she planned on whoring herself out for a project.

Granted, most people were just going to assume that she slept with him, but she really didn't care what they thought. The only thing that mattered was that she knew that she wouldn't. There would be no sex with the bastard, she reminded herself even as she used her hold on Connor and pulled him closer until her breasts were plastered against his chest. He let out a sexy growl as he wrapped his arms around her and moved to deepen the kiss.

She'd been kissed by plenty of men in her life, but none of them had prepared her for a kiss from Connor. The first sweep of his tongue had her panting and holding onto his shoulders for dear life and the second had her fighting against the urge to climb him then and there. What the hell was wrong with her? she wondered as she met him stroke for stroke.

Instead of enjoying this, she should have kept it simple with a quick peck on the cheek, gone inside, grabbed a mug of cocoa and tried to come up with ideas on how to get out of this deal and keep her project. She definitely should be doing that now. It wasn't too late, she absently thought as she suckled on Connor's tongue.

"Oh my god!" a woman whispered loudly. *"They're going to do it on the front lawn!"*

She felt Connor go still against her as mortification set in. During her little make out session with Connor she may have forgotten about their audience. She'd never been one for PDAs and here she was practically swallowing Connor's tongue. This was bad. This was very bad, she thought as they pulled apart.

"Goodnight," Connor said tightly and as much as she'd love to kick him for making her forget about their audience, she was still a little breathless from their kiss and mortified by the knowledge that everyone in town would probably know about this little slip in judgment by tomorrow morning. This was the last thing she needed right now.

With an absent nod, she turned around and opened her front door, barely aware of Bunny slipping past her, his growl or Connor's curse as she shut the door and ran for her kitchen. Once she was in her kitchen, she didn't hesitate in making a double chocolate, extra large, extra creamy cup of cocoa. When it was done, she closed her eyes and sipped the hot tasty liquid until she'd consumed every last drop.

This was very bad, not the cocoa, that was really good, but the fact that they'd been interrupted and she actually wanted to scream in frustration and drag Connor into her house, push him down on the couch and mount him. She hated him, hated everything about him, she tried to remind herself as she reached out to grab the cocoa mix and make herself another mug of cocoa since the first one apparently hadn't done the trick.

Connor was a very bad man that she didn't want, who made her life a living hell and was a hell of a kisser, and blackmailed her into a situation where she had to suffer through the hottest kisses of her life. As long as she remembered all of that she would be-

A startled gasp escaped her as she suddenly found herself turned around and pressed back against the counter and in Connor's arms as he picked up where they'd left off. It actually frightened her how fast her arms wrapped around his neck, her chest pressed tightly against his and she welcomed him. How could something so wrong feel so good, so right? It shouldn't. Heaven help her, but this felt too good to stop, but she knew that somehow she'd manage to do just that.

In a little while.

Right now she was too busy getting into character as Connor suggested. This was for the good of the project, her dream and now that Connor was gently suckling on her tongue she realized that this was an excellent idea. If they were going to pull this off then they needed to behave like a real couple. What better way to do that then to kiss, and he damn well better keep kissing her, she decided as he grabbed her hips and picked her up, placing her onto the edge of the counter.

If she hadn't been so focused on kissing him, she'd probably be horrified at how quickly her legs parted to welcome him and the way she sighed in pleasure as he took her up on her invitation. When he gripped her hips and dragged her the half inch or so until she was sitting on the edge of the counter she might have whimpered. When she felt him hard, heavy and pressed exactly where she needed him, she may have moaned and wrapped her legs around him.

"No sex," she said against his lips as she struggled against the urge to roll her hips against him. Kissing and enjoying the way it felt to be in his arms was fine, and as long as she remembered that this was only meant to help create the illusion of a relationship, then everything would be fine.

"No sex," Connor agreed against her lips as his hold around her tightened and he once again deepened the kiss. When he didn't push for anything else or try to argue, she felt herself relax.

Maybe this deal wouldn't be so bad after all.

"We should get going," Rory said, pulling away only to come right back again and kiss him in a way that should be illegal.

"Yeah, we should," he said, placing his hands on her hips and helping her move until she was straddling his lap. When she settled herself on his lap, he wanted to groan in pleasure at how good she felt and roar in frustration, because he knew that this was as close as he'd ever get to her.

It was enough, more than enough, he told himself as he did his best to ignore the little moans she made as she struggled not to move on his lap. When her breathing sped up and her grip on his shoulders tightened he had to stop himself from putting them both out of their misery by thrusting up against her. It was difficult, surprisingly even more difficult than it had been last night, but what a night that had been.

They'd made out in her kitchen, in her living room after they'd managed to pull apart and agreed that they'd practiced for long enough. Then he'd made the mistake of sitting down on her couch and boom, Rory was somehow back on his lap and they were making out like teenagers. Two hours later, Rory pulled away and they said goodnight, from a distance. He was willing to call it a night, but then he spotted Rory out on her patio and one thing led to another and he somehow found himself on her lounge chair and on top of her, kissing her.

When they'd finally managed to part, several hours later, they both agreed that they definitely had the kissing aspect of their relationship down and should probably just kiss only when it was necessary. The moment she'd stepped out of her house this morning, he felt that it was very necessary, for appearance sake of course. It didn't matter that it was six in the morning and that no one else in their quiet neighbor-hood was around to witness the kiss, he had to kiss her.

Once they managed to break apart, ten minutes later, he stole her hot chocolate thermos and once again drove her to work. Well, at least halfway there before he had to stop at a red light and just like that, they were at it again. They'd probably still be at it at that intersection if Mr. Jenkins, the seventy year old crossing guard, who used to blow that damn whistle anytime he saw them walking on the same side of the street, hadn't blown that damn whistle right outside his door.

After they'd separated and went to their respective sides, he real-ized that he was starving and he decided to pick up some coffee and donuts. Once they placed their order-

"Um, excuse me?"

With a sigh, Connor pulled his mouth away from Rory's so that he could glare at the pimple-faced bastard that had interrupted them.

"Your order?" the kid said, shifting nervously as he held up two white bakery boxes.

Instead of freaking out or getting embarrassed about getting caught making out in the drive-thru line, Rory grabbed the twenty he'd been holding in his hand and passed it over to the kid. She took the boxes of donuts and moved off his lap, their kiss forgotten as her attention turned to the chocolate dipped glazed donuts that she'd demanded he order for her. He ordered them, but only after she gave him a kiss.

He waved the change away as he threw the truck in drive and started to pull out of the parking lot when a parking spot near a copse of trees caught his eye. It was well away from the other cars, had decent shade and looked perfect for-

"Don't even think about it," Rory said, sounding amused as she nibbled on her donut.

"It's really not safe to eat while driving," Connor pointed out inno-cently as he headed for that well-secluded spot.

"Then I guess it's a good thing that I'm not driving," she said, laughing as she broke off another piece of donut.

"Are you planning on drinking your hot cocoa?" he asked, nod-ding towards her canister of hot cocoa.

"Of course," she said with a snort as she tore off another piece of donut.

With a sigh, he drove over to the semi-secluded spot and parked. "Then I have no choice but to park here so that you don't spill any hot chocolate and burn yourself."

"I see," she said, trying to bite back a smile. "You're just trying to save me from a trip to the hospital, is that it?" she asked, dropping what was left of her donut on a napkin and placing it on the dashboard.

"That's exactly it, Rory," he said, reaching for her as she moved to climb back on his lap where she belonged.

"This is just to stay in character," Rory explained as she settled on his lap.

"Of course," he agreed as he wrapped his arms around her.

"We're not really dating," she said, leaning in and brushing her lips against his. "This is just for show."

"Exactly," he agreed even though he was pretty sure that no one would be able to see what they were doing, but he wasn't about to point that out.

"As long as you remember that I hate you," Rory mumbled against his lips.

"I'll remember," he promised.

"And you hate me," she reminded him as she continued to caress his lips with light, teasing kisses that had his arms tightening around her and his body trembling with the need to consume her.

"With a passion."

———

"We're thinking of having you committed," Bryce announced as he pointed to where he needed her to sign.

"I see," Rory said absently as she looked through the paperwork describing all the lovely problems they were already encountering.

Thanks to her accident they'd lost two days of work. The day of her accident, all of their men had been ordered away from the manor as the rescue crews worked to get her out of the basement. After she was safely on a backboard and on her way to an ambulance, the fire inspector had apparently showed up and closed them down, something she was just finding out about now. The next day her brothers had worked their asses off to get the fire inspector to come back and allow them to return to work.

He had, but they'd lost most of the day. Her brothers and surprisingly a good majority of Connor's foremen did their best to keep the project going even though they were forbidden to set so much as a foot in the mansion. Instead of working on the roof, gutting the house or the few dozen major things that needed to be done immediately, their men worked on clearing the land and tearing up the mile long private road that led up to the old mansion.

By the time the fire inspector showed up and cleared them to continue to work, it was already late and their men were exhausted. She wasn't happy about the lost time, but there wasn't anything that she could do about it now. She just wished that someone had told her. Starting off a project of this size two days behind this early in the game was not a good sign. As she looked down at the paperwork authorizing overtime, she was tempted to authorize work on Sunday, something she'd never done before.

Sunday was supposed to be a day for rest. That was one of many rules that her father had shoved down their throats over the years and one that she'd never been able to ignore. Her men worked hard, sometimes too hard. Working seven days a week would not only kill her budget, but it would also exhaust her men, make their work sloppy and increase the chance of accidents. So as much as she would love to make up for those two lost days immediately, she couldn't.

"Anything else?" she asked, handing the clipboard back over to her brother. She pulled on the sling that her doctor demanded that she wore when she worked so that she wouldn't do anything stupid like try to use it.

"No, that's it," Bryce said with a careless shrug, immediately drawing her attention and making her nervous.

As far as her brothers knew, she was dating Connor, a man she'd despised since she was a child. Sure, he idly threatened to have her committed, but he'd sounded more amused than anything. Besides, if they were really going to have her committed he wouldn't have said anything. They would have just tied her up and dropped her ass off on the front lawn of a mental hospital with a few grunted "good lucks."

Since they hadn't said anything or even threatened to beat the shit out of Connor as a standard warning, she was understandably concerned. They always threatened the guys she dated, even if they liked the guys they were well warned, but as far as she knew they hadn't done that to Connor. The fact that she was supposedly dating Connor really should have elicited some kind of rage-fueled response, but it hadn't.

Her eyes narrowed on her brother. "You're up to something."

"Damn straight," Bryce said with a shit eating grin.

"Are you going to give me a warning?"

"The only thing that you need to know is that we have your back and we figured out a way to make up for the time we lost," he said dismissively as he headed for the coffee truck, leaving her with no choice but to follow after him.

"How?" she asked a minute later when she managed to catch up with him.

"Don't worry your pretty little head, Rory. We took care of everything," Bryce said with a smug little smile that did not bode well for her or the project.

It was bad enough that she'd made a deal with the devil and was apparently addicted to his kisses, but now she had her brothers going behind her back and orchestrating something that couldn't possibly end well for her. When had her life started spiraling out of control? she wondered as she turned around and headed for her trailer and a much needed hot chocolate.

EIGHTEEN

"What's going on with you and Rory?" Andrew asked as soon as they were out of listening distance of the rest of the men.

"We're dating," Connor said with a shrug as he dragged the large barrel the rest of the way to the chute they'd installed after they'd ripped out the window.

"Since when?" Andrew asked, moving to grab the bottom of the barrel and help him dump the plaster and old horsehair insulation down the long chute, but a warning glare from Connor had his friend sighing with aggravation and backing away. He knew better and if Connor caught him pulling that bullshit again he would kick his ass.

"Why does it matter?"

"I'd like to know when you became suicidal, that's all," Andrew said as he grabbed the barrel and pushed it to the side.

"What are you talking about?" Connor asked as he walked over to the large blue cooler that he had filled with ice and bottles of water to make sure that his men didn't pass out from this heat.

"Her brothers are going to kill you," Andrew pointed out, shaking his head in disbelief.

He simply shrugged as he drank his water. Since they hadn't tried to kill him when they'd caught him kissing Rory behind the coffee truck a few hours ago, he doubted that they were going to kill him. Kick his ass? Absolutely, and they probably planned on doing it tomorrow when he joined their old man for fishing and Rory wasn't around to get in the way.

That was more than fine with him. He'd take a few hits if it meant that he could prove that he was serious about Rory, which he wasn't. It was all part of his plan and so far his plans were moving along rather nicely. He'd use her and then-

"Honestly, I never thought Rory was that desperate," Andrew said, grabbing his attention.

"What the hell are you talking about?" Connor demanded, tossing the empty water bottle in the barrel as he glared at his best friend.

"Well," Andrew mused as he crossed his arms over his chest, "she hates you, she's hot, and did I mention that she hates you?"

"She doesn't hate me," Connor said with a snort.

"Then what do you call it?" Andrew asked, grabbing a bottle of water for himself.

"Severely disliking me to the point that she's actually considered doing me bodily harm?" he suggested, chuckling when his friend flipped him off.

"It makes me wonder why she'd agree to go out with you," Andrew mused as he lightly tossed him another bottle of water.

Connor had to snort at that as he caught the bottle of water and opened it. "Because she's desperately in love with me."

Andrew simply shook his head as he said, "No, that's why you're with her."

Connor couldn't help but laugh at that announcement. "Yeah, okay, buddy," he said, taking a sip.

"Wow, did you actually think that I was going to forget about that fateful little trip of yours to Canada all those years ago?" Andrew asked, cocking a brow in question as Connor choked on his water.

Yeah, he actually had.

"A good friend would forget moments of pure stupidity and never bring them up again," he pointed out with a scowl as he tossed the half-empty bottle of water in the barrel and headed back towards the rooms on the far side of the mansion where his men were working when Andrew's next words stopped him.

"She doesn't remember, does she?"

"There's nothing to remember," he said, forcing his mind away from one of the most painful and dumbest moments of his life.

"You never did tell me what happened. Did you end up telling Rory?"

Yes, he had.

It had been one of the most frightening moments of his life, but he'd managed to get the words out of his mouth without making a complete ass out of himself. When the words were finally out, Rory gave him the sweetest smile seconds before all the alcohol she'd consumed during the night before made a second appearance. After that rather momentous occasion, he spent the rest of the night helping her to the jail cell's toilet, helping her drink water and waiting for the moment that the alcohol wore off. When that moment came, the look on Rory's face said it all. She didn't feel the same way and probably wouldn't appreciate hearing that he was in love with her, so he kept his mouth shut.

"It was just a childhood crush," Connor said with a shrug.

It had been a painful and gut wrenching experience, but one that he'd managed to get over with time and a lot of beer. He'd learned to appreciate their little antics, kept an eye out for her, but the palm sweating reaction he used to get just from thinking about her was long gone. It probably also didn't hurt that he'd inadvertently ruined her life that night.

There were a lot of things that he wished that he could change about that night, but following her out of that bar was not one of them. If her brothers had been keeping a better eye on her, they would have seen that asshole leading Rory, who could barely stand at the time, out the back door. The only thing that he regretted was not getting Rory out of there before the bastard managed to pull a knife on him. If he had……..

Rory's life would be a lot different than it was now. He knew that much at least. He couldn't go back and change things, but he could at least help make her life easier by keeping her safe. He still planned on enjoying himself while he did it and holy hell was he enjoying himself. There really were no words to describe what it felt like to kiss and hold Rory.

He couldn't get enough of her. He must have kissed her half the night last night and he'd been surprised to discover that he hadn't wanted to stop. He'd still love to get her in his bed, but that wasn't going to happen and he had no plans on trying either. This was more than enough for him. He'd enjoy kissing and holding her until the project was done and then it would be time to move on, for both of them.

"You don't really believe that, do you?" Andrew asked, grabbing another bottle of water.

"It's the truth," Connor bit out.

"Then why did you buy the house next to hers?" Andrew asked with a knowing smile.

"Because it was within my price range and it was the only house on the market at the time that wasn't built in the twentieth century," he explained, again. The fact that Rory owned the house next door was only a bonus. He loved his house almost as much as he loved giving Rory hell.

"Okay," Andrew said slowly. "Then why are you dating her if you're not in love with her?"

"The last time I checked, you didn't have to be in love with a woman to date her. Just want her," he said, not bothering to point out that he *really* wanted Rory since his friend probably already knew that.

"True," Andrew said, thoughtfully. "But that doesn't explain why she's dating you."

"Is it so hard for you to believe that she wants me?" he demanded, offended that the man thought so little of him. He was a great catch and the man damn well knew that.

Andrew pursed his lips up in thought as he asked, "Do you want an honest answer?"

"Yes!"

"Then yes, yes it is," Andrew said with a shrug.

"I hate you," Connor snapped as he turned to leave, but of course the man wasn't done yet.

"What did you do, Connor?" Andrew asked, stopping him in his tracks.

———

"She's going to kill you," Andrew said hollowly twenty minutes later when Connor finished explaining his brilliant plan.

"Probably," Connor easily agreed with a chuckle as he grabbed another bottle of water.

"Normally, I stay out of the weird shit that the two you have pulled on each other, mostly because it entertains me, but I have to tell you that I think this plan is going to come back and bite you in the ass," Andrew said, sounding completely serious.

"It's just all part of the game we play," Connor said with a shrug. "She'll understand it." She'd be pissed at first, but eventually she'd realize that he'd simply played the game better than her.

"Connor-"

"It's fine, Andrew. Just let it go," Connor said, feeling his patience begin to fray. The last thing he needed was his friend getting on his ass about a plan that he knew was going to work.

Andrew put his hands up in surrender. "Fine. It's your life, but just keep that in mind when you fuck this up."

"This is a done deal," he replied, heading for the door and knowing that there was absolutely no chance of him fucking this up.

———

"You're still not talking to me?" Rory asked, biting back a sigh when Jacob continued to ignore her.

"You're going to have to talk to me at some point," she felt obligated to point out as she sorted through the large stack of mail that he'd gone to town to pick up even as she noted that Jacob hadn't picked up her customary extra large hot chocolate and vanilla cream donuts that he normally picked up for her every Saturday when he did the mail run.

Apparently he was still in a mood, she thought with a little sigh as she tossed the bills and junk mail on his desk. She really wasn't sure why he was mad at her. She hadn't even been the one that duct taped him to the chair. If he should be mad at anyone it was Connor, she thought, ignoring the delicious little shiver that raced through her body at the mere thought of the man. He had been the one who'd taped him to the chair after all.

Granted, she could have untied him and she'd planned on doing that after she'd made him sweat it out for an hour or two. But, was it really her fault that she'd forgotten all about him when she was busy trying to figure out a way to get out of the deal she'd made with Connor? She'd eventually remembered that she'd left him taped to the chair and sent Bryce a text message to release him. Jacob was probably still upset about the dress and makeup her brothers had thrown on him, or the photos, she mused with an inward shrug as she dropped the rest of the mail on his desk.

"Did the supplies I ordered from Henderson's come in yet?" she asked, wondering just how long the big baby planned on giving her the silent treatment.

He shook his head.

"Uh huh," she said, sighing heavily as she reached out and toyed with the pencils in his old Dunkin Donuts coffee cup as she shot him a hopeful look, but the stubborn man simply continued to type as he ignored her.

"Would you forgive me if I offered you a raise?" she asked, wondering if groveling was going to be necessary to get him to stop pouting.

A shrug.

"An extra week of vacation?" she asked, not really sure that she'd be able to survive even that long without him running things.

That offer earned her a killing glare, which of course was understandable since they both knew that she'd probably run the business into the ground in that short amount of time. Last year when he'd made the mistake of calling in sick two days in a row she'd somehow managed to screw up payroll, crash every computer in the office, order a thousand user manuals in Japanese for a copy machine that she didn't even own, and ran out of hot cocoa by mid-day on the second day, making her a tad difficult to work with.

"If you don't talk to me, I'll cry," she threatened even as she allowed her chin to quiver. It was low, but sometimes she just didn't have the patience for this kind of nonsense. Jacob was temperamental, but fortunately for her, he was also a big pushover.

She usually saved the crying act as a last resort, but today she just didn't have the patience to work her way up to it. They were already running behind, the basement was still considered a safety hazard and therefore off limits until the fire department cleared it, the deliveries that they needed were delayed, and to top it all off, she couldn't stop thinking about Connor. Somehow the man managed to worm his way into her thoughts and as hard as she tried, she couldn't stop thinking about him.

Sadly it wasn't just his kisses, which were freaking fantastic, that she couldn't get out of her head, but the man himself. Somehow he'd managed to get under her skin and not just in the annoying, man slaughtering way that he used to, but as a man that she actually enjoyed being around. If she hadn't been eighty percent sure that the painkillers that she'd taken over the past few days were having a lasting effect on her, she'd probably be panicking a bit right about now.

She knew Connor well enough to know that this was just a game to him and that once this project was done they'd go back to their old ways, earth shattering kisses forgotten. It was what she wanted, she reminded herself as she added a slight pout that she knew would break Jacob in a matter of seconds. This was just another game in a long line of games that they'd played over the years and one that she would win. If she had to endure his kisses and touches then that's just what she was going to have to do, she thought as she felt her lips tug up into a pleased smile.

Okay, so this deal wasn't all bad. She got her project, albeit through Connor, but she would change that as soon as she figured out what he was up to and turned the tables on him. She also had free use of his equipment and could use his men, which would save her a lot of money and time on the project. The only thing that really irritated her was having to let him call the shots, but she'd deal with it.

For now.

There was no doubt in her mind that it was only a matter of time before she figured out what he was up to, took control and made him squirm. It was also just a matter of time before-

"What the hell is that?" she asked with a frown when something shiny to her right caught her attention. Jacob and his pouting quickly forgotten, she turned around and felt her brows damn near clear her hairline as she took in the very large and obviously expensive machine that now took up a good portion of her hot cocoa work station.

Her confusion hit an all time high when she spotted a four-foot tall, beautiful oak cabinet right next to it. She threw Jacob a questioning look, but he was still ignoring her. With an exasperated sigh and a roll of her yes that he definitely deserved, she turned her attention back to the cabinet. She walked over to it and opened it, not really expecting much so when she saw that all four shelves were packed with her favorite hot cocoa products, fluff, marshmallows, etc, she found herself stunned and wondering if this was all a dream, a wonderful hot chocolate-fantasy-filled dream.

"Do you like it?" the seductive whisper teased her ear as large, warm arms wrapped around her from behind and pulled her back into an equally warm body.

"Like it?" she mumbled as she ran her greedy eyes over twenty-five different flavors of hot chocolate, each one sounding yummier than the last.

"Mmmhmm," Connor murmured as he pressed a kiss against her neck that would have normally sent her body into overdrive.

She knew that she should play it off like she did with the flowers, but she couldn't. It just felt so wrong to lie in the presence of the most beautiful sight on earth.

"I love it," she found herself admitting like an idiot. If there was one thing that she'd learned from Connor over the years, it was to keep her mouth shut and never let him know what she liked otherwise she had to deal with the big jerk making her life miserable, but knowing that didn't stop her from letting out a little content sigh as her eyes ran over hot chocolate heaven.

Yup, she was definitely going to pay for this little slip up.

NINETEEN

It shouldn't please him that she liked his gift so much, but it did. When Andrew called him a few hours ago to let him know that Brennagin's, the insanely expensive coffee shop that they'd renovated last month, was arguing over the bill, again, and that they were refusing to pay, he'd decided to go down there and handle the matter himself.

Normally, well, in the past year at least, he'd been leaving that job up to Andrew, but the manager was trying to bullshit her way out of paying. It was causing too damn much drama and stressing Andrew out, which was the last thing that Andrew needed needed. By the time Connor arrived, Cindy, the manager and all around pain the ass, was in Andrew's face and bitching him out. When she caught sight of him, her whole attitude turned from flat out bitch to flirty in a matter of seconds.

Once Andrew made his escape, Cindy invited him into her office where she'd suggested that the two of them talk this little "misunderstanding" over at her house. He'd politely declined and that didn't seem to make her happy so she became more blatant about it. When he'd declined her offer to make him breakfast in bed she'd flat offered him a little relief in her office. She was a beautiful woman and any other guy probably would have fallen at her feet and done anything and everything she'd asked, but he wasn't interested.

It didn't take her long to figure out that Rory was the reason why. Well, she was the main reason, but he would never accept a quick fuck to drop the price of a bill. He didn't play games and Cindy quickly learned that. After she gave up trying to get him off in exchange for a huge price drop she went back to being a bitch. She tried to argue her way out of their contracted price and when he wouldn't budge, she'd cried.

It annoyed the hell out of him and made him wonder why more women weren't like Rory. She wouldn't have cried or tried to play him to get out of the bill. If she didn't think the bill was right, she would have argued it and backed it up with proof. If that hadn't worked, she would have tried reason, but not Cindy. Cindy tried to use every damn ploy that she could think up to get him to drop the price by five grand, but he wasn't about to budge.

He didn't work for free and neither did his men. He offered more than fair prices to his customers and didn't play games to jack up the price. She'd known the price going in and had agreed to it. In fact, if she hadn't added a new office for herself and asked for a carport built at the back of the building to keep her car protected from the elements, the price would have been fifteen grand cheaper. After a half hour of her bullshit, he had enough and told her to deal with his lawyer as he'd headed for the door.

Apparently that was the magical phrase, because twenty minutes later he had a check for almost the full amount. It turned out that she'd spent the money set aside for construction on new equipment for the coffee shop. When he'd spotted the large box with fancy writing sitting in the corner of her office with the magical words, "Hot chocolate" printed beneath the picture, he'd decided to take pity on the woman and do a little bartering. He was out a thousand bucks, but had a professional brewing machine and cabinet for Rory.

He'd meant to give it to her in front of the trailer, make a big show of it so that her brothers would see how well he took care of her. He'd hoped to soften them towards him, but at the last minute he'd changed his mind. He had five months to butter her brothers up to come work for him and so there really was no rush, he'd decided. While her assistant had pouted and glared at him, he'd hauled in her new cabinet and cocoa maker and did a little redecorating. Andrew arrived thirty minutes later with every cocoa product known to man.

Unfortunately, ten minutes after that he had to haul his ass out to the site to deal with the truck driver that was contracted to replace the dumpsters. The driver tried refusing to replace all the dumpsters. He gave some bullshit story about construction materials being a problem and overtime issues. It took an hour to get the driver to remove the dumpsters and replace them. They would have been screwed if he hadn't replaced them. They only had half of the first and second floor torn out and they desperately needed to be able to finish ripping the roof off and if they didn't have the dumpsters to do that, they would have been fucked.

As soon as he'd finished dealing with that bullshit, he'd hauled his ass back to the trailer, anxious to see Rory's face when she saw his gift. He'd missed her initial reaction, but the way she'd settled back against him and sighed contently in his arms more than made up for it. When Rory laid her arms over his, he was glad that he'd saved this for just them. There was plenty of time to butter up her brothers, so he wasn't going to stress over a missed opportunity, not when Rory felt so damn good in his arms.

"What does it do?" she asked in a reverent whisper that had him smiling.

"The machine?" he asked, ducking his head to press a kiss against her jaw.

"Mmmhmm," she said as she absently tilted her head to the side in silent demand for more, which he was more than happy to give her.

He pressed another kiss against her jaw before he slowly ran his lips up to her ear and pressed a kiss just below it. "It makes hot chocolate even creamier."

"Are you sure?" she asked, sounding hopeful.

"Very sure," he said, pressing a kiss just below her jaw.

"And this is for me?" she asked slowly, cautiously.

"Mmmhmm," he murmured, pressing another kiss against her neck. "It's for you," he said, loving the way she felt in his arms. Hell, he could happily hold her for the rest of his life and never grow tired of it.

"Why?" she whispered, tilting her head back and to the side so that she could look up at him as he answered.

"Why what?" he murmured distractedly as he leaned down and brushed his lips against hers, unable to help himself.

"Why did you get that for me?" she asked quietly as she followed his lips as he started to make a slow retreat, but once he felt her lips touch his, he stopped moving back and simply enjoyed the way her lips teased his.

"I can take it back if you don't like it," he teased, his lips twitching against hers when she released a cute little growl.

"Lay one finger on it and they'll never find your body," she swore against his lips and even though she sighed softly in pleasure, he knew that she meant it.

"Does that mean that you don't want me to show you how to use it?" he asked, leaning in for another kiss when he suddenly found his arms empty.

When he spotted her standing in front of the machine, gesturing impatiently for him to get on with it, he couldn't help but chuckle. How could such a sexy woman be so damn cute? he wondered as he dutifully walked over to get the little addict her next fix, pausing only long enough to press a quick kiss against her lips that earned a gagging sound from her assistant.

Rory didn't seem to notice. She was too focused on her cocoa machine, barely able to stop herself from fidgeting as she ran her greedy little eyes over the machine. Since she seemed too distracted at the moment, he decided to give her a hand with her assistant.

"Ow!" Jacob whined when a small canister of Belgian cocoa powder bounced off his head.

Connor couldn't help but shake his head in disgust as he started the machine, pausing only long enough to steal another kiss from Rory. As she returned the kiss he wondered if she was even aware of how quickly they'd settled into this level of intimacy. Kissing her felt like the most natural thing in the world to do and he wondered if it was the same for her.

"Cocoa," she murmured against his lips, making him chuckle.

After pressing one last kiss against her lips, he gave into the addict's demands and showed her how to use the machine. He didn't miss the way her assistant watched his every move and shot him murderous glares each and every time he'd touched Rory. It wasn't too hard to figure out that the man was in love with Rory.

Not that he could blame him. He didn't. But, that didn't mean that he was going to step back and let the man have a shot at Rory. Oh hell no, that shit wasn't happening. He was not about to step back, even though he wasn't really dating Rory, and give some prick who'd already proved that he couldn't protect Rory a chance to hurt her. Wasn't happening and the sooner the man realized that, the better.

"Is it done yet?" Rory asked, shifting from foot to foot as she tried to keep herself from reaching out and snatching up the large tan coffee cup as the flow of hot cocoa slowed down to a drip.

He reached out and picked up the cup, afraid that she'd burn herself, and gestured towards her office. "You can attack it in there while we go over some paperwork," he said, smiling when she pouted. When she reached out for it, almost as if she couldn't help herself, he raised the cup higher and moved to step around her.

Rory being Rory, of course tried to reach up and take it away from him, but he simply shook his head and sighed as he raised it higher and moved past her. He didn't bother to look back to make sure that she was following him since he knew the little addict wasn't about to let the cocoa out of her sight. As he stepped around her desk, he placed her mug of cocoa down and sat in her chair.

His ass barely touched the chair when Rory was climbing on his lap, sitting sideways as she picked up her mug of cocoa and took a slow sip as she settled against him. As he put his arm around her and gently cupped her hip, he couldn't help but wonder if she even realized how comfortable she was around him. Considering their history, she should be a nervous wreck whenever he was within a fifty-foot radius of her. Then again, Rory James never reacted the way he'd expected her to, he thought with a smile as he leaned in and pressed a kiss against her neck, chuckling when she let out a little moan of pleasure.

"That good, huh?" he asked, keeping his hand on her hip as he leaned forward, careful not to disturb her, and opened the manila folder that McGill sent over earlier.

When Rory settled herself more comfortably on his lap and threw her injured arm around his shoulders so that she could turn slightly and look over the files with him, he had to force his mind away from how good it felt to have her here like this with him. Granted, she was only doing this because he was blackmailing her, but that was just a minor detail and he chose to ignore it.

"Did you see this?" she asked, pausing mid-sip to nod in the direction of the file.

"No, I didn't get a chance to look at it yet," he said, pulling the file to the edge of the desk so that they could both get a better look and when he saw McGill's new request he forced himself to go back and read it again, sure that he was mistaken. "Are you fucking kidding me?"

"He wants us to rearrange the entire wine cellar again and-"

"Turn the subbasement room that you fell down into another storage room for wine," Connor finished for her, letting out a frustrated breath as he sat back in his chair.

"That's going to make things a little more difficult," Rory grumbled, taking another long sip of her cocoa.

"Just a little," he said, dryly, mentally calculating the time and cost this addition just added to the project. The materials would be covered by McGill, but this new request could kill this project.

"We're going to have to go overboard on the overtime just to meet the deadline," Rory said, worrying her bottom lip as she placed her mug, which he didn't need to check to know that it was empty, on the desk.

With all the other things that needed to be done in under five months that was an understatement. Even with all the men their companies employed, they were already going to have to bust their asses to make that deadline. He'd already figured the amount of overtime that his company could afford on a weekly basis that would allow them to finish this project and not suffer a loss. With this added project they'd be lucky to break even. They'd get paid more, that wasn't the problem. The problem was labor. That was if they managed to make the deadline.

If they missed the deadline.......

Hell, he didn't even want to think about that. They both had so much invested in this project. Not only would they lose the bonus, but they'd also lose their reputations. The only thing that would save his company's ass would be his plan to steal the James brothers. Even though he planned on running Rory out of business, he didn't want to do it this way.

If this project bankrupted her, she'd lose everything including her house and he wasn't about to let that happen. She'd probably hate him for the rest of her life once this project was over and her brothers left her to come work for him, but that didn't mean that he wanted her out of his life completely. Christ, he didn't even want to think about going a day without seeing her. He still planned on having her come work for him, but it wouldn't be the same and there would be no guarantee that she would take it or even stay in town if she lost everything.

That meant that he was going to have to figure out a way to finish this project so that they didn't end up losing everything they had and unfortunately for Rory, he knew exactly how to do it. She was going to argue it, but in the end she would see that this was the only way.

"We're not going to make the deadline with this new addition," he explained slowly, trying to figure out the best way to break the news to her.

"If you have any suggestions, I'm all ears," she said with a sigh as she removed her arm from around his neck, picked up the file and stood up. He almost stopped her, but decided that space would probably be for the best right now.

He waited a minute before he decided to just get it over with. "Rory?"

"Hmm?" she said, absently, never taking her eyes away from the file as she paced the length of the office.

"We're going to have to postpone building your suites," he explained, knowing that was the only way that they were going to cut back on overtime and supplies and be able to meet the deadline with the new project.

She paused mid-stride to shoot him a frown. "What are you talking about?"

"Your suites, Rory. They're going to have to wait until after we finish this project," he explained once again, getting to his feet. "We can't spare the men or equipment right now. Once we get the manor done, we'll complete the suites, Rory," he explained, knowing that it was going to cause a problem, but not really caring. They needed to finish this project and he knew that Rory would be understandably upset, but she'd pull it together and they'd focus on the manor and once that was done they'd turn their attention to her project. He hated doing this to her, but there really was no other way.

"Let me get this straight," she said, tossing the file on the desk. "You want me to wait until after all the renovations are done to build my suites?"

"It's the only way that we're going to get this project done, Rory," he explained, again.

She met his gaze dead on as she said, "No, it's not."

TWENTY

"What the hell do you think you're doing?" Connor demanded.

"What does it look like I'm doing?" she asked as she picked up her tool belt and dropped it on her desk.

"You're not working," Connor gritted out from what sounded like clenched teeth from behind her.

"It's not your choice," she pointed out as she walked around her desk as she pulled off her shirt, revealing a black sports bra. She dropped the shirt on her desk chair and leaned down to open the bottom desk drawer to grab a grey tank top when she suddenly found herself swept off her feet. Before she could so much as gasp, she was plopped down on the edge of the desk with her legs hanging over the side and Connor standing between them.

"You really think that's true?" he asked as he slapped his hands down on the desk on either side of her hips and leaned in. She almost leaned back, but fought against the urge, reminding herself who she was dealing with here. She would never back down from Connor. Okay, so she did that one time, but that didn't count.

She forced herself to ignore the hard glint in his eyes, the clenched jaw and the fact that he looked close to throttling her and moved into him. The move put their faces a few inches apart and heaven help her, but she wanted to close the distance and kiss that firm line away from the lips that she found herself thinking about more than she should.

This was just supposed to be a deal between them, just one more game. He shouldn't be affecting her like this. No, she should be royally pissed that he'd pulled this crap and part of her was, but there was another part of her that was glad to have the excuse to touch and

kiss him. This whole thing was crazy. Only yesterday she was contemplating murder. Today it was a struggle to stay mad at him and not
wrap her arms around his neck and pull him in for the kiss that she
craving.

There was no doubt in her mind that more than two decades worth
of hate was responsible for this. They say there's a fine line between
love and hate and for the first time in her life she truly understood
what that meant. As much as she hated him, and she really did, she
tried to tell herself, she also loved being close to him, touching him
and kissing him. As long as they had this deal, she was free to do all
those things and after last night, she'd decided that for the sake of her
project and to put an end to the town drama, she would have to do
just that. That didn't mean that she planned on allowing Connor to
call all the shots.

"We might have a deal for the project," she said, placing her hands
on his chest and ignoring just how good he felt beneath her touch,
"but that doesn't mean that you have the right to tell me what to do,
Connor, and if you think that it does then you're going to be in for one
hell of a surprise."

She kept her eyes locked on his as she pushed him back, getting
to her feet in the process. He allowed it, but she did notice his eyes
narrowing even further as his jaw clenched until the vein in his jaw
was throbbing double time. Deciding that she'd made her point, she
turned around, grabbed a shirt out of the bottom drawer and moved
past him, not even sparing him a look as she headed for the door.

"Then let's make a new deal," he said, drawing her attention.

"A new deal?" she asked, slowly turning around even as she prepared herself for the next blow. Oh, she had a pretty good idea of
where this "new deal" was heading and knew that it would probably
cause her to go for his nipples. If he tried to use this project to control
her, she was going to-

He cut off her slightly murderous thoughts with a soft kiss and
chuckle that she refused to find sexy. "Hear me out before you go for
the pliers," he said, taking her hand in his and giving it a slight tug that
had her grudgingly following after him.

"I was planning on going for your nipples, not your ass," she felt obligated to point out.

"That's good to know," he said, sitting down in the middle of the couch and with another slight tug that had her rolling her eyes, she climbed on his lap.

"If you want to talk then why do I have to sit like this?" she asked, sighing in exasperation as Connor's eyes dropped to her sports bra encased breasts and stayed there.

"Cause I think better with you in my arms," he murmured, letting out an appreciative little sigh that had her lips twitching.

"They're just breasts, Connor," she said, pretending that she didn't like his answer. She loved being in his arms, she shouldn't, but she did. She only let him pull her onto his lap for the plan of course. She really didn't want to sit on his lap as she looked into his handsome face.

She really didn't.

"That's blasphemy, Rory," he said, sounding pleased as she moved closer, for safety sake of course. Falls from this height could be very dangerous, she decided as she moved forward until she was sitting directly over his lap, her hands resting on his chest and his warm breath fanning her skin. For a moment, she forced her mind away from just how good he felt and focused on the issue at hand.

"What's this new deal, Connor?"

With a sigh, he looked up and met her eyes, but immediately looked back down, sighed heavily again before finally looking back up. Once his attention was on her face she couldn't help but notice that his expression became even more pleased, looking as though he was truly happy with what he saw.

"Put all the focus on the main project for three months and I promise you that we'll get those suites built by the deadline," he swore softly as he wrapped his arms around her.

For a moment all she could do was to stare at him in shock. Finally, she managed to choke out, "Are you high?" as she tried to climb off his lap, but he wasn't having that. He tightened his arms around her, keeping her right where she was.

"Just listen to me for a minute, Rory. If we put all of our extra resources towards your suites right now, we'll screw ourselves over and even if you manage to finish them on time it won't mean a damn thing if the rest of the hotel isn't completed by then," he explained, making sense.

Damn it!

"You know that I'm right, Rory."

She let out a frustrated groan as she once again settled into him. She'd always hated it when he was right and this time there was no question about it. It didn't matter if she got her suites built. Without the hotel being fully functional in time they would be useless.

"Give me three months," Connor said, leaning forward and brushing his lips against hers, "and I will make sure that you have everything that you need to get those suites done, Rory."

"Fine," she whispered against his lips.

She'd give him three months to get the hotel going and when the time came he better keep his word. Until then she should focus all of her attention on the job, she decided as she tilted her head to deepen the kiss even as her brain screamed at her to stop. This was just a deal. She shouldn't be doing this. They had to stop, she reminded herself, moving to get off his lap, but she couldn't do it.

It didn't matter that none of this made any sense and that they hated each other, always had, always would. The only thing that she cared about at the moment was that she wanted this man so much that just the thought of putting space between them made her body want to scream in agony.

Why did it have to be him? she wondered, threading her fingers through his hair as she struggled not to press down and take what he was offering. She'd always been attracted to Connor. Over the years she'd been able to ignore it thanks to the animosity they'd shared, but now she was struggling not to give in and take what she wanted.

Him.

This whole thing was crazy, but knowing that wasn't stopping her from wanting him. She'd never been this turned on by a man before and if she didn't stop now, she knew that she'd cross a line and she'd end up hating herself. It didn't matter that over this past week she'd come to enjoy spending time with him, found him funny, charming and surprisingly sweet. She just couldn't push past the fact that this was the man who'd changed her entire life one night with his typical bullshit. She was also reminded of one very important fact.

This was all just a game to him.

Not that she could or even would cry or complain about that since she was a willing participant in this game of theirs, but that didn't change things. This didn't mean anything and as long as she remembered that, then everything would be fine. In fact, maybe it would be for the best if she remembered that this was only a game.

It would help her deal with the changes in Connor that she admittedly liked, but were unnerving. He was just getting into character, she reminded herself as she slowly slid her tongue across his, earning a sexy growl that left her aching for more. Perhaps that was the way to look at this.

She needed to kiss, touch and enjoy every inch of his incredible body, for their deal. Not that she was dying to run her hands over him or anything. She had to do this for the good of the project, she thought, releasing a little gasp of pleasure as she allowed herself to settle more comfortably onto his lap. Not only for the project, but to stop the town drama, she reminded herself with a content little moan as she adjusted herself on his lap.

"Have dinner with me tonight," he murmured, brushing his lips against hers as his large, warm hands soothingly ran over her back.

It actually surprised her how badly she wanted to say yes, but she couldn't. "Can't. I have plans tonight," she said against his mouth, because she really saw no reason to stop kissing him so that they could have this conversation.

"Break them," he said, pulling her bottom lip between his lips and gently suckling it, his hands never ceasing as they slowly learned every inch of her back, shoulders and arms.

"I can't," she grumbled against his lips, sounding truly disappointed, which kind of frightened her a bit so she just assumed that she was doing a wonderful job of getting into character. That was good, she thought as she ran her hands down his chest, loving the way that his crisp cotton shirt felt over his impressive chest and stomach, but loving his groan a lot more than she probably should. She didn't even think twice about unbuttoning one of the buttons on his shirt and slipping her hand inside so that she could enjoy running her hand over his warm skin.

"You really can," he said, his muscles rippling beneath her touch.

"Nope," she said on a sigh when Connor broke off the kiss and trailed his mouth down her neck, "I really can't."

"We had a deal, Rory," he said as his mouth trailed lower. The thought of stopping him never even crossed her mind as she sat up on her knees to make it easier for him. She could feel his heart start to race as his lips caressed the top swells of her breasts.

"And I'm upholding my end of the deal," she managed to get out as she had to remove her hand from Connor's chest to get it out of his way. She slipped her good hand beneath his shirt collar and held onto his shoulder as Connor kissed his way to her cleavage.

"No, you're not," he said hoarsely before he ran his tongue between her breasts, earning a choked, "Oh, God" from her as her grip on his shoulder tightened.

Unable to help herself, she looked down and met his beautiful emerald eyes as he did it again, robbing her of the ability to think beyond what he was doing to do her. He kept his eyes locked on hers as he removed his hands from her back and slowly brought them around, giving her plenty of time to stop him. The problem was that she didn't want him to stop.

Her body literally shook with need as he reached up and pulled the front bra clasp together before he started to open it, clasp by clasp and making it impossible for her to remain on her trembling knees for much longer. Even as she lowered herself to sit on his lap he didn't take his eyes away from hers as he undid every clasp, one by one. When her bra was finally undone, she'd expected him to drop his eyes down to see what he'd revealed, but he kept his eyes locked with hers as he held the two ends of her bra together, keeping her covered.

"What are these plans of yours? A date?" he asked in a bored tone that didn't quite match the way that he was watching her.

Was he jealous? she wondered, but just as quickly shoved that thought away. Connor O'Neil didn't get jealous, especially not over her. There was no question that they were attracted to each other. The large erection pushing against his zipper was more than proof enough of that, she thought as she allowed herself to settle more comfortably on his lap. The way he licked his lips hungrily as she did that had her doing it just one more time, for comfort sake of course.

"It's Saturday night," she reminded him even though by now he should have known exactly what she had planned. Every Saturday night she met her brothers at Luke's for dinner, drinks and just to relax. It was a tradition they'd started over ten years ago and she still looked forward to it every week.

She liked going to Luke's on Saturday when the music was live and the beers were ice cold. She could relax and have a good time without worrying about some jerk hitting on her. On Saturdays she was untouchable. If she wanted to talk to a man, she would. Her brothers weren't that overbearing, but if some guy made the mistake of hounding her, he would find himself being dragged out back and meeting the fists of at least one of her brothers before he could so much as mutter a half-assed apology.

"Luke's," he said on a sigh with a nod of understanding.

How he could have forgotten about her Saturday night ritual she would never know. He went there most Saturday nights, most everyone in town did. It was also the one place that they had an unspoken agreement about. They didn't so much as acknowledge the other one while they were there, too afraid of getting banned.

"Fine," he said, using his grip on her bra to pull her forward, "I'll pick you up at seven."

"Um, I go there at eight, not seven and who said that I was going with you?" she asked as she wrapped her arms back around his shoulders.

"We have a deal, Rory, so that means that you're going with me and you'll be ready by seven," he said, leaning in to kiss her as she felt his grip on her bra loosen.

"Eight," she said just as his lips touched hers, not even bothering to try and argue.

What was the point? They did have an agreement. It had nothing to do with wanting to spend more time with this man. She hated him, she reminded herself as she felt his hands move up her sides. He repulsed her, she thought as she opened her mouth in welcome and shifted on his lap, rubbing against the large, hard bulge that was driving her crazy and leaning into him as his hands slowly moved over the sides of her breasts.

Her body trembled as her nipples hardened in anticipation. She'd never craved a man's touch as much as she craved his and if he didn't move his ass and touch her, she was going to-

"Rory! The fire inspector is here!" Jacob announced from behind the protection of the door. Not that the door would keep him safe for long. Once she managed to catch her breath, fix her bra and pull on a shirt, she fully planned on strangling him and judging by the vicious growl that escaped Connor's throat, he was probably having a few violent thoughts of his own.

"Seven," Connor said tightly, averting his eyes to the side as he carefully helped her climb off his lap.

"Seven what?" she asked in a daze as her body mourned the loss of his touch.

"Be ready," he said, sounding pained as he stood up and stiffly walked to the door and walked out, shutting the door behind him without a glance in her direction.

She looked down at herself and groaned pathetically as she let herself fall over onto her side. When her eyes landed on the clock it actually terrified her that she was counting down the hours until seven instead of dreading each passing minute like any sane woman would.

"No! Not the duct tape!" Jacob cried out from the other room, making her lips twitch. One thing that she could say about Connor O'Neill, he'd never left her bored.

TWENTY-ONE

Sixty more seconds.......

He dropped his head back and clenched his jaw tightly shut as ice-cold water hit him. Just sixty more seconds, he swore as his muscles started to cramp to the point of pain. His eyes closed as he tried to focus on anything other than the ice cold water assaulting his body. He thought of the manor, baseball, his old high school locker combination and by the time his mind turned to what he'd had for lunch, he felt his body relax somewhat and the most painful erection that he'd ever experienced in his life start to go down.

A shaky breath escaped him as he opened his eyes and reached out to shut the water off. He knew that he should have taken himself in hand to avoid this torture, but he thought that would have only made it worse. It wouldn't have been enough and would have only aggravated him more. His only saving grace was the fact that he hadn't seen Rory's breasts. His hands brushed against them, but while she'd been in his arms he somehow found the will power not to look down.

He'd planned on watching her as he touched her beautiful, and he damn well knew that they would be beautiful, breasts for the first time. Thanks to the little bastard she'd hired as an assistant, he never got the chance. When he'd stormed out of Rory's office and only found her smirking assistant and no fire inspector he almost killed the man with his bare hands. It was only the reminder that he had Rory half-naked in the other room that had him hauling ass to teach the little bastard another lesson about coming between him and Rory.

By the time he'd finished hog-tying her assistant, Rory was walking out of her office, wearing a new shirt and looking unhappy. Thirty seconds after she'd told him about the text message Craig sent her, he'd become decidedly pissed off. The lumber they'd ordered for the roof, the same lumber that he'd been promised would be delivered by lunchtime, was delayed because the flatbed that was transporting it broke down in Massachusetts.

After a dozen phone calls, it became obvious that they weren't going to be getting their lumber before Tuesday. Normally that wouldn't have been much of a problem, but the forecast for Sunday night into Monday morning was rain and plenty of it. They'd been left with no choice but to send a dozen men into town to buy every last piece of tarp that they could get their hands on. It took about eight hours and a hundred men, but they'd managed to get the roof covered and sealed up tight. He didn't even want to think of the bullshit they'd have to deal with if they hadn't been able to cover the roof. The building had enough problems without adding mold or fresh rot to the mix.

He fought back a yawn as he reached for a towel. After putting in fourteen hours today, he was exhausted. He should be crawling into bed right now, especially since he had to get up bright and early tomorrow morning to go fishing with Rory's old man and start working on her brothers. If this had been a date, not that this was really a date, with any other woman he wouldn't have hesitated in breaking it, but this was with Rory. He only had five months with her and he was not about to waste a single minute of it.

Speaking of his "date" with Rory, he was late, he reminded himself with a grumble as he wrapped a towel around his waist. He needed to move his ass and get dressed. It was already after eight and the place was going to be packed. They'd be lucky to get a table near the bathrooms tonight and that's definitely not how he wanted to spend the night with her. He'd rather take her in his bed and hold her. Actually, he'd rather take her in his bed and make love to her all night, but since that required more energy than he had right now, he was going to have to settle for taking her out and hopefully holding her in his arms a time or two on the dance floor.

He walked into his bedroom, fighting back another yawn when his eyes landed on his bed and what he saw there had him stumbling and doing a double take. Why was Rory curled up in his bed wearing only a pink cotton camisole and panties? Was he dreaming? he wondered and not really caring as he walked over to her.

"Too tired. Not going out," she mumbled pathetically without bothering to open her eyes.

"I see," he said, chuckling as she snuggled against his pillow.

"Good. Now carry me back to my room," she muttered even as she blindly reached out for a blanket. When she didn't find one she let out a frustrated little groan and flopped over onto her other side and curled up.

With a heavy sigh, he walked over to the bed and picked her up so that he could pull the covers back. When he laid her back down, she curled right back up, snuggled against his pillow and released a happy little sigh when he pulled the covers over her. He should be pissed that his plans were being wrecked again, but he wasn't, not when breaking their plans meant that he got to hold Rory in his arms all night.

He would be holding her in his arms all night long, he decided as he quickly pulled on a pair of boxers and climbed in behind her. When he wrapped his arm around her, she grumbled, but didn't stop him from pulling her against him. Once he had her where he wanted her, he closed his eyes and felt his body relax.

A few seconds later he grunted in pain when she abruptly turned in his arms, whacking him in the shoulder with her cast as she snuggled against him. He winced as he tightened his hold on her, telling himself that he was doing it because he didn't want to wake up covered in bruises. She was a violent little thing after all, he mused as he kissed the top of her head. It had absolutely nothing to do with the fact that he never wanted to let her go.

———

He really was handsome, Rory thought with a smile as she gently caressed his jaw. She should leave, but she found that she didn't want to go, not just yet. She could come up with a million excuses, but when it came right down to it, she enjoyed waking up in his arms.

Not that she would admit this, but waking up in his arms while he'd been taking care of her had probably done more for her than the pain medication the doctor prescribed. She'd felt safe, truly safe which of course was laughable considering the fact that this man had done anything and everything to make her life a living hell for over two decades, but she couldn't help it. She also couldn't help but like this Connor.

He made her feel safe, wanted and desired. She knew that it was probably all part of his master plan, but that didn't stop her from enjoying it. She'd been dealing with Connor for the majority of her life and for once he wasn't annoying the hell out of her. This Connor was funny, sweet and made her happy and she'd have to be an idiot not to enjoy this short reprieve. She had five months with this Connor and she was going to make damn sure that she enjoyed every single minute of it while it lasted.

But that didn't mean that she trusted this little plan of his. She didn't. He was up to something and she'd be foolish to go into this blindly. While she enjoyed herself, she'd keep her eyes open and as soon as she figured out what Connor was up to she'd turn the tables on him. Until then........

Well, she decided that she'd play it by ear. As long as he stayed out of her way, focused on getting the manor finished and kept kissing her in a way that she loved, then she would let things continue. It actually surprised her how easily she'd accepted this situation between them. Part of her, the part that still remembered the time that he'd turned her blue when they were fourteen, wanted to fight against this overwhelming attraction that she'd felt for him and fight this deal of theirs, but she realized something last night.

She didn't want to fight this.

He mumbled something as he reached for her, but she wasn't there. When he frowned in his sleep, she couldn't help but smile as she leaned over him and pressed a kiss against his forehead. He let out a soft sigh as he rolled over onto his stomach and she took that as her cue to leave.

She climbed off his bed and took a step towards his patio when something occurred to her. She had free reign of Connor's house. Since she didn't know when an opportunity like this would come again she'd be foolish to pass this up. At least that's what she told herself as she shot a quick glance in Connor's direction to make sure that he was still asleep.

After a quick visual check, she wasted no time in tiptoeing out of his room. Her breath caught as she stepped out of his room and into a dimly lit hallway. It felt as though she'd stepped back into the nine-teenth century. The walls were white with dark trim. Dimly lit electric lanterns lined the wall, casting just enough light in the hallway for the historical house junkie in her to get a rush.

Old houses were her favorite. When she was little she used to love it when her father worked on an old house. She used to walk through each room, ignoring the modern changes and imagine what the house used to look like, should look like. Her brothers would tease her, but she didn't care. There was just something about an old house that spoke to her. She'd always imagined that she'd grow up and design modern homes that looked like they belonged in a previous century, but with all the modern amenities blended into the design.

In fact, she'd planned on going to college to earn a degree in architecture and one day design an entire town with old time stores and houses with an eighteenth century facade, but it never happened. Thanks to the incident in Canada she'd lost her college scholarship as well as her acceptance to several schools. She could have applied to another college, a less expensive college, especially since the charges had been dropped, but by the time she'd had enough money to do just that, her dreams had changed.

She'd decided to open her own construction company and truth be told, she'd never regretted that choice. That didn't mean that she couldn't mourn the loss of what might have been. It was the reason why she bought her house. She considered buying both houses, but she knew at the time that two mortgages and renovations would have been too much for her to handle.

When Connor bought this house she'd been pissed for several obvious reasons, but not really surprised. His house had needed a serious amount of work and everyone in town knew that Connor enjoyed a challenge. At seventeen he'd started to work for old man Thompson, a mean son of a bitch who paid piss poor wages and worked his employees to the bone. Connor started off doing the grunt work as a carpenter's apprentice. He'd put in long hours, got yelled at a lot from what she'd heard, but he'd stuck with it.

It wasn't long before people were calling Connor up and hiring him instead of old man Thompson. There were many things that she could say about Connor, but she could never call him lazy. Everyone in town knew that he'd worked his butt off to get where he was today. He did good work, she grudgingly admitted to herself as she tried not to drool over the cast iron fittings that held the lamps to the wall.

She was so going to have to get a set to replace the lights she had in her hallway, she decided as she walked across the hall and opened the beautiful oak door. As she stepped into the room, she threw the light on and nearly stumbled as her heart skipped a beat. She'd never believed in love at first sight, but right now she was a believer.

"Do you like it?" Connor's sleep rasped voice sent shivers throughout her body as his arms wrapped around her waist and pulled her against him as she let out a dreamy sigh.

Like it?

"I'm going to steal it," she told him honestly as she ran her greedy eyes over the most beautiful bathtub that she'd ever seen. It was one of those old fashioned tubs with clawed feet, a high back and appeared to be extra deep.

"Might be a little heavy," he pointed out with a chuckle as he pressed a kiss against the top of her head.

"That's what brothers are for," she mumbled, making him laugh as if she were kidding.

She wasn't.

In fact, she was pretty sure that she'd only need four of her brothers to get the job done. The other brother could keep Connor distracted while they removed the bathtub and carried it to her house. Her brothers could probably get the whole job done in under an hour. An hour after that she'd be in the tub and it would officially belong to her. Possession was nine-tenths of the law after all.

"Want to give it a test drive before you steal it?" he teased as he released her so that he could step around her. "You should probably make sure that it's worth throwing out your back," he explained with a chuckle as he walked over to the tub and started the water.

It wouldn't throw her back out since she planned on participating in the bathtub theft strictly in a supervisory capacity, but he didn't need to know that. Not when he was offering to allow her to sample what had to be heaven on earth. There was only one problem with this plan as far as she could tell.

"Bath salts," she said, frowning as she looked around the large, beautiful bathroom.

"What about them?" he asked absently as he adjusted the water temperature.

"You don't have any," she said, sounding almost accusatory, but she didn't care. By all rights no one should own a bathtub like this without having a decent supply of salts, oils and bubble bath.

Instead of shrugging it off or bitching about her complaint like most of the men she'd known would have, he stood up and headed for the door. "I'll go grab some from your bathroom. Anything in particular that you want?" he asked, pausing by the door as he waited for her answer, not looking or sounding pissed off or putout at all. Actually, he looked like he was actually happy to do it for her.

"Lemongrass?" she asked, not used to men taking care of her.

When Connor simply nodded and took off, her first reaction was suspicion. After years of screwing each other over, she couldn't help but automatically jump to that conclusion. Her mind raced through all the things he'd done to her over the years, wondering if she was about to experience a repeat of being turned into a smurf, but she quickly dismissed the idea.

He wouldn't do that, not when he needed her for whatever plan he was working. When she heard his patio door slide open from the other room another thought occurred to her, a thought that should have disgusted her, but didn't. What if he was planning on joining her in the tub? And why did the thought of Connor holding her against his naked body make her toes curl?

Because she wanted him.

There, she admitted it to herself. She wanted Connor O'Neill in her bed and so what? She didn't see what the big deal was. For the next five months they were supposed to be in a relationship and what woman in her right mind would date Connor and not welcome him into her bed? He was handsome and had an incredible body. She was stuck working with him and trapped in this deal with him, so why shouldn't she enjoy what he had to offer?

It's not like there would be any confusion or hurt feelings if they decided to have sex. They both knew where they stood and they both knew that they hated each other, but that didn't stop them from wanting to tear each other's clothes off. The only downside that came to mind was that nasty little rumor that followed Connor around everywhere that he went. According to the local female population, Connor was extremely selfish in bed.

Then again, weren't all men selfish in bed?

She couldn't think of a single man that she'd slept with that hadn't been selfish. They all wanted sex their way and only their way. Most of them didn't care if she found her moment since they only focused on their own. Some of the men she slept with cared if she enjoyed herself, but usually once she had a small "O" they went right back to focusing on their own enjoyment. Once they were done they couldn't leave fast enough.

Then again, she'd never heard women complain about the skills of the other men in town as much as they did about Connor. Not that she listened to gossip or anything, but she'd heard that Connor did the absolute bare minimum to get a woman in bed and once he had her there the complaints tripled. He didn't make eye contact, refused to kiss any woman once he got her on her back and hated foreplay. If any woman enjoyed herself it was purely by accident, but she wasn't sure how much of that she believed since the rumors didn't seem to stop women from throwing themselves at him.

It certainly wasn't going to stop her, she thought as she shut the water off and headed for Connor's bedroom. If it was horrible then she wouldn't waste the effort again. They'd go on with this little fake relationship of theirs, but if he managed to keep her interest in bed even a little bit, well.........

Then this deal of theirs would be getting a lot more interesting.......

TWENTY-TWO

"**C**hange your grand larceny plans?" he asked, chuckling when he spotted Rory in the hallway, heading towards his room.

"No," she murmured with a shrug as she stepped up to him and placed her injured hand on his shoulder as her good hand moved to the back of his head.

Before he could ask what she was doing, her mouth was on his and he forgot about bath salts and coming up with an excuse so that he could sneak out in a couple of hours and go meet her father and brothers for some fishing. He had a plan that he needed to work on after all, but right now that didn't matter. Right now the only thing that mattered was the woman teasingly nipping at his bottom lip.

"What's going on?" he whispered hoarsely, groaning when she licked his lip better.

"Getting into character," she said, brushing her lips against his as she pressed tightly against him, making everything in him go still as the plastic bottle dropped out of his hand and fell to the ground with a *thud*.

There was no way that he'd just heard what he thought he did. He knew Rory pretty well and knew that she would never use her sex appeal to get what she wanted. She wouldn't bother wasting the energy for all that bullshit. She would just kick his ass to get what she-

"I want sex, Connor, and as long as you make it worth my while we're going to add it to our deal," she said as she somehow managed to back him up until his back hit the wall before adding with a teasing note, "to get into character of course."

He opened his mouth to make sure that he'd heard her right when she took advantage and slid her tongue in his mouth, taking him off guard and leaving him with no other choice but to give in to the stubborn woman. She wanted him. Rory James, the woman that he'd been fantasizing about since he'd first noticed girls, wanted him and he wasn't going to do something stupid like question it or bitch about her methods.

It took a minute for her words to sink in and when they did, he turned the tables on her and pressed her up against the wall. As he slid his tongue against hers, enjoying the way she couldn't seem to get close enough to him, he placed his hands against the wall on either side of her head. After allowing himself another minute of enjoying her decadent mouth, he broke the kiss, but he didn't go far.

When Rory fisted his hair and yanked him back down for another hungry kiss, he indulged her for another moment before he pulled back. When she let out a rather vicious growl, he chuckled and leaned in, but only allowed his lips to brush against hers. Before she could deepen it, he pulled back.

"Make it worth your while?" he repeated.

"Mmmhmm," she said, moving her good hand down his neck, over his shoulder and down his chest, her touch light and teasing as she traced his tattoo.

"So this is my audition?" he asked, loving the way she touched him.

"Yes."

"What exactly am I auditioning for?" he asked, already having a pretty good idea, but he wanted to hear it from her.

"Well, if you pass-"

"I will," he said tightly, insulted that she expected him to suck in bed.

"-then for the next five months," she continued as if he hadn't spoken all while she ran her hand down his chest, "we're going to give in and enjoy this disturbing attraction that's going on between us."

"Who says that I'm attracted to you?" he asked softly as he looked into her beautiful green eyes.

She smiled coyly as her hand slid down between them and over the erection straining his boxers to get to her. When she gave it a light, teasing squeeze, the air in his lungs rushed out as his legs threatened to buckle. "This does," the tease said as she slowly stroked him through his boxers.

He'd heard several men bitch about Rory's performance in bed. Granted, he beat the shit out of those men, but not before he got an earful. Seems the men that Rory dated didn't appreciate an aggressive woman in bed. They wanted a woman that allowed the man take the lead, call the shots and decide their pleasure.

They were all fucking idiots.

There was nothing hotter than a woman who knew what she wanted and went for it. Nothing turned him off more than a woman that let him call the shots and just laid there while he took her. It was boring and only made him lose interest faster. With Rory, he knew that he'd never get bored and taking the next step with her was dangerous, but he'd worry about that later. Right now he had the woman of his dreams giving him a chance to fulfill every fantasy that he'd ever had about her.

"What are the rules?" he asked, already knowing that Rory had something in mind.

"This doesn't interfere with the project or our lives," she said, licking her lips as she worked her hand between his legs and gently massaged his balls, making him hiss in a breath.

"Fine. What else?" he asked, trying not groan as she continued to drive him out of his mind. His hands clenched into fists against the wall as he struggled not to grab her and turn her around so that he could rip off her panties and bury himself deep inside of her.

"It's just to get into character. It means nothing," she said, leaning up to brush her lips against his and for some reason that pissed him off, but not enough to turn down what she was offering.

He didn't like the idea of her trying to play this off as something that she was going to do just for her project. She wanted him and they both knew it. No matter what she said, she wanted him just as badly as he wanted her. For right now he'd accept what she had to offer, but sooner or later he knew that she'd stop kidding herself. He didn't expect a future with her, but that didn't mean that he was willing to accept anything less than the truth.

"Anything else?" he asked as she went back to caressing his cock through his underwear.

"That's it for now," she said, sounding a little breathless.

"Then since this is my audition," he said, pausing long enough to break away from her so that he could bend down and scoop her up into his arms, "I think it's about time that I show you what I have to offer."

———

"That's really not necessary," Rory rushed to explain, so close to crying.

She'd been enjoying herself. Would it have killed him to let her call the shots? It was probably the only way that she would have enjoyed herself, but like all the guys before him, Connor wasn't interested in what she wanted. It was not a good sign of what was to come, she thought with a small pout. Just once she'd like to find a man that wasn't greedy in bed and could handle a woman that knew what she wanted.

When he placed her on her feet, she prepared herself for a few quick kisses, a couple of gropes before she was expected to lie on her back and accept what he had to offer her. It wasn't exactly thrilling and it was starting to kill the mood. Maybe she should-

"What are you doing?" she found herself asking when Connor dropped his underwear, revealing the most impressive erection that she'd ever seen, and simply stood there, watching her expectantly.

"Letting you call the shots, Rory," he said with a hungry expression that quickly reignited the flame that had been threatening to die out only seconds earlier.

"You're going to let me call the shots," she repeated, clearly not believing him as she ran her eyes over the hottest body that she'd ever seen. She swore that when her eyes landed on the large appendage between his legs that it actually grew, which should have been physically impossible.

"Yes," he said with absolutely no hesitation as realization dawned on her.

He really didn't know how to use that thing between his legs.

As depressing as that thought was, and it really was, she forced herself to push past it and focus on what he was offering. He might not know how to use it properly, but she was pretty sure that she could figure it out. She had to bite back a smile when she realized that this little plan of hers would allow her to use Connor's incredible body in any way that she wanted and she definitely wanted.

She held up her hand and crooked a finger. With one of those sexy grins of his, he walked over to her, pulling her in his arms even as she reached for him. As his lips met hers, she couldn't help but sigh. At least he knew how to kiss, but then again, according to local gossip she shouldn't expect to see much of that skill later. That was fine, because she was sure that she could find other things to focus on, she mused as she dropped her hands away from him.

When she grabbed the hem of her camisole to pull it up, she found her hands gently brushed away. He continued to kiss her as he slowly pulled her shirt up, taking his time to run the back of his knuckles over her stomach and over her breasts. They both moaned as his knuckles glided over her nipples, causing the already sensitive tissue to tighten almost painfully.

He broke the kiss, but only long enough to the pull her shirt off and then his mouth was back on hers, taking his time to tease and caress her tongue as he pulled her closer until that impressive erection of his was pressed against her stomach. He felt good against her, but not good enough. She wanted more and had no problems with taking it.

She just prayed that he'd allow her to enjoy herself before he took back control and she knew that he would. There was just no way that Connor was going to be able to sit back and let her call the shots. His pride wouldn't let him. Until that moment came, she planned on doing everything that she'd ever dreamed of and yeah, she'd thought about getting Connor into her bed a time or two. There weren't many women in town that hadn't, she reminded herself, not really liking the idea of another woman fantasizing about him so she forced it out of her mind.

He wasn't hers and most importantly she didn't want him to be, she told herself as she broke off the kiss and stepped away from him. She watched as his eyes moved from her face and slowly traveled down her body. When they reached her breasts, they became hooded as he licked his lips hungrily.

She couldn't help but wonder just how hungry he was as she turned around and slowly crawled onto his bed. She felt the bed dip behind her and wasn't too surprised to feel him behind her as she lowered herself onto the bed. As she turned to lie on her back, Connor leaned over and took her mouth in a hungry kiss, picking up right where they'd left off as his hand came to rest on her stomach.

As she enjoyed the way he kissed her, she waited for his hand to move, knowing that it was just a matter of time before he tried to take control. When several minutes passed and he didn't move his hand she was surprised and admittedly frustrated. While he'd been kissing her, she'd been imaging just how good it would feel to have his hands roam over her body. It was something that she desperately wanted.

"Touch me," she whispered against his lips, loving the little groan that he released as he moved to do just that.

He trailed his fingers up and between her breasts and just when she thought that he was going to put her out of her misery and touch one of the breasts that craved his touch, he continued to move his hand up until he was cupping her face, gently caressing her jaw and ramping up her frustration.

When she reached up to take his hand and put it exactly where she needed it, he moved his mouth away from hers. His mouth trailed kisses down to the opposite side of her neck as his hand moved back down and cupped one of her breasts. She bit back a small cry as she dropped her head back, giving him more access to kiss, suckle and tease her skin with his lips and early morning whiskers that were driving her out of her mind.

His hand, with a slight roughness from years of hard work, moved from one breast to the other with whisper soft touches that were only interrupted by the occasional kneading or a gentle caress. She wrapped her arms around his shoulders as he continued to worship her and that's exactly what it felt like. There were no rushed or awkward moves. Connor was taking his time learning her body and she honestly couldn't remember ever feeling more wanted than she did in that moment.

But still she wanted more.

Taking a deep breath to steady her nerves, she widened her legs until she felt her right leg brush against his erection. As she hooked her leg over his, she placed her injured hand over his roaming hand and with a slight push he took the hint and allowed her to guide his hand away from her breast, down her stomach and between her legs where it came to rest over the place that she needed his touch the most.

Connor pressed one last kiss against her neck before he pulled away and returned to her mouth as he cupped her possessively. The pressure felt good, but it felt even better when he started to rub his hand up and down, teasing her and giving her what she needed all at once. When she felt his hand start tugging at her panties, she didn't hesitate in raising her hips and helping him pull her panties down and kicking them off when they were low enough.

He gave her one last kiss before he pulled back and looked down to watch as he returned his hand between her legs. A groan escaped him as he traced her slit with the tip of his finger. He licked his lips hungrily as her breath sped up and she registered his erection slowly grinding against her hip.

"You're so fucking wet," he said in a daze as he slid his finger inside her and that was all it took.

If she'd been born a male she probably would have been horrified at how quickly she'd come, but as her body bowed, his name left her lips in a half strangled scream and she felt her body throb almost violently around his finger, she couldn't find the willpower to care. As she screamed through the most powerful orgasm that she'd ever experienced, she barely registered the fact that Connor was no longer by her side.

However, when she felt his tongue replace his finger she definitely registered that move as a second, more powerful orgasm ripped through her body, leaving her helpless to do anything but scream.

TWENTY-THREE

"**I** thought that you were going to let me call the shots tonight," Rory said, panting hard as he continued to leisurely lick her out. "You are," he promised as he pulled back so that he could trace her slit with the tip of his tongue. "Tell me to stop and I will," he semi-lied.

He would stop, eventually, but right now he was enjoying himself too much to really mean it. Making love to her with his mouth was one of the most pleasurable experiences that he'd ever had. He'd be honest and admit this sort of thing normally wasn't one of his favorite things to do for a woman. It was usually something he did for a woman he'd been dating for a while and he only did it when he could no longer pretend that she was the one that he wanted. By the point that he was willing to do this for a woman, it was out of desperation.

No matter what any of his old girlfriends thought, he tried. God, how he tried to feel something for them, to want and need them, but he couldn't. He just couldn't. No matter what they did or said, he could never get past the fact that being with them felt wrong. For the longest time he'd lived in denial and fear as he tried relationship after relationship, but nothing changed.

When he was younger he hadn't cared and never bothered trying, going from one woman to the next had made little difference to him. Over the years, things changed, he'd changed and he'd wanted more in his life, but no matter what he did nothing changed. He'd dated some wonderful women that would make any other man drop to his knees and thank God that he was alive, but not him.

He hadn't been able to return their feelings and it just about killed him when he couldn't force himself to love them. He could easily think of five of his ex-girlfriends that would have probably given him a good life as they grew old together, but he hadn't felt anything for them. He couldn't love them. Hell, he couldn't even get it up for them without thinking about the woman currently running her fingers through his hair as she urged him to continue with soft little moans that had his cock jerking in appreciation.

This was the woman that his body craved day and night and it would accept no substitutes. It was something that he'd have to worry about, but later. Right now he was going to enjoy the freedom to touch her. Whatever happened later he'd deal with it. Right now, nothing else mattered but the woman moaning his name.

"Stop," Rory said, panting hard as she tried to catch her breath.

Stopping was the last thing that he wanted to do, but he did. He wasn't an asshole and would never force a woman to do anything that she didn't want. It was a struggle, but he somehow managed to pull away from her.

As soon as he made a move to go to her and make sure that she was okay, he found himself shoved onto his back. By the time the movement registered in his mind, Rory was already climbing over him and gripping his cock by the base as her pert little ass wiggled above his face. He didn't waste any time in raising his face to continue lapping at her slit as his arms wrapped around her body, holding her still.

"So much better," Rory said on a throaty whisper as she stroked his cock.

When she ran her tongue from the head to the base, his hips jerked up in response. When she wrapped her lips around the tip and lightly suckled, he swore that he saw God. As his head hit the bed he brought her down with him, too greedy for her to allow even a second of separation.

Her hard nipples brushed against his stomach, back and forth as she moved her mouth over his cock, taking it as far as her talented mouth would allow while she rode his mouth. He gripped her ass, restraining some of her movements so that he could slide his tongue in and out of her core to mimic what she was doing to his cock.

He ran his tongue slowly between her slit, loving the moan Rory released around his cock. What she was doing to him felt fucking fantastic, but what he was doing to her was life altering. As they both took their time licking, suckling and nibbling, the only sounds that could be heard in his room were moans, groans and whispered pleas never to stop.

———

A loud cry escaped her lips as she struggled to continue giving him pleasure, but she couldn't. She just couldn't take it any longer. With another strangled cry, she released him from her mouth and was forced to rest her head on his hip less than an inch from the large erection that she'd been worshipping only seconds earlier. Her body tightened as her back bowed, seconds away from what she already knew would be a powerful orgasm.

She bit her lip as she pleaded with her body to hurry before he stopped and she knew that he would stop. He hadn't yet, but in a few seconds he would realize that she'd stopped pleasuring him and he would demand that she continue. Men could be selfish jerks, she thought as she licked her lips hungrily.

Just when she thought that he was finally going to stop, he didn't. Oh no, not even close. His arms tightened around her, holding her securely against him as he devoured her and there really was no other way to describe what Connor was doing to her. It felt good, so good......too good.

She tried to pull away, but he refused to give her an inch. Her good hand clenched into a fist, gripping the soft comforter in a death grip as a scream of pleasure like nothing she'd ever heard before ripped from her throat, taking her breath away. The surge of pleasure that rocked her body left her boneless and barely able to softly cry, "Stop," as Connor continued, making her body prepare for another orgasm that would no doubt kill her.

"Shhh, baby, it's okay," Connor said soothingly as he pulled away and gently rolled her off and onto her back where she lay panting as her over stimulated mind tried to figure out what just happened.

Connor hadn't stopped, hadn't demanded that she continue pleasuring him or thrown a fit. Instead, he did everything that he could to make sure that she enjoyed herself. Why did he have to keep confusing her? she wondered as Connor laid by her side and pulled her into his arms. He gently brushed her hair out of her face as he pressed a tender kiss against her lips all while the proof that he hadn't found any relief pressed against her hip.

"You okay?" he asked, giving her another one of those tender kisses that she was really starting to like.

"Mmmmhmmm," she sighed happily as she found herself leaning in and kissing him. More than okay, she thought as she wondered just what else the women in town had lied about. Clearly someone had lied about his aversion to kissing and foreplay, but now wasn't the time to worry about that. Right now, she couldn't think past how good he made her feel, how much she wanted him, needed him and suddenly nothing else mattered but them.

Connor growled in approval as he returned her kiss and his cock brushed against her too sensitive skin. She reached between them as they took their time kissing and when she found what she was looking for, she didn't hesitate in running her hand over it. She couldn't remember enjoying the way a man felt in her hands like this before. The hot, silky skin that covered the large erection felt incredible and she realized as she took her time running her hand over him that she wasn't in a rush to finish this.

She'd done this for most of her boyfriends, well, the ones that she'd become intimate with, but she'd never really enjoyed the act. It was difficult to enjoy something when all she heard were complaints or aggravated groans. Then again, when she usually did this sort of thing for a man she didn't usually enjoy it, but with Connor she was finding herself aching all over again for him.

It shouldn't be possible, especially not after the incredible orgasms that he'd just given her, but she couldn't help it. The sexy little growls he made every time her hand skimmed over the large head had her shifting her legs as she tried to ignore the need growing inside her until she couldn't ignore it any longer.

They were both breathing hard, the kiss becoming more aggressive as Connor reached between them and cupped between her legs, careful not to get in the way of what she was doing for him. She tried to be good, tried to stay still, but the second that he ran one long, thick finger between her folds she was lost. She shifted her legs, desperate to give him more access. He growled approvingly as he slid his finger inside of her, matching the way she was moving her hand over him. She knew that if they continued like this that they'd enjoy it, but she wanted more.

Unable to wait another minute, she released him and hooked her leg over his hip. With a gentle nudge, she had him turning over onto his back. He removed his hand from between her legs so that he could wrap his arms around her and take her with him, which was more than fine with her.

Better than fine actually.

Praying that he didn't change his mind about letting her taking charge, desperately needing him to keep that promise, she shifted back, rolling her hips with the movement. When she slid over his erection they both groaned long and loud and when she moved to do it again, the large tip of his erection came to rest at her core.

"Are you sure?" Connor asked, against her mouth.

Was she?

"Yes," she said on a harsh whisper as she pushed back, taking the large tip inside her.

His loud groan encouraged her to take more, but the problem was that he was a bit bigger than she was used to, but she didn't allow that to discourage her. She wanted this man and she was going to make damn sure that she had him.

For their deal of course.

They had to appear as though they were really dating and what better way than to have sex? she reasoned as she practically clawed at him, desperate for him. This was crazy, but right now she didn't care. Nothing else mattered, not the fact that she hated this man, that they weren't really in a relationship, or the fact that they were about to do something foolish.

A startled gasp escaped her lips as Connor suddenly thrust, filling her halfway. In the next second she found herself on her back and Connor pulling out only to thrust back in, filling her better than any man had before. As she lay there, digging her nails into his back as he stretched her a little too much, she was torn between screaming in frustration and screaming at him to move. He'd told her that he'd allow her to take the lead, but obviously that was-

He rolled them over until she found herself splayed on top of him. "It's all yours, baby, but you gotta move before I lose my fucking mind," he groaned softly against her lips as his hands moved up to cup her face while he kissed her.

It took her a few seconds to realize what he'd said and done and when she did, she couldn't help but release a satisfied moan as she tentatively rolled her hips. His answering groan was all the encouragement that she needed to continue. She might not be experienced in this position, but she was more than willing to keep doing it until she got it right, she thought with a throaty groan as Connor slid one hand between them and cupped her breast as the other one moved down her back and palmed her ass as she rode him.

"Don't stop, Rory," he said on a groan as he moved his mouth to her neck just as she registered his hand leaving her bottom and moving up her body to palm her other breast.

"Or what?" she asked breathlessly as she picked up the pace, taking him deeper and harder each time.

"I'll wring your neck," he promised tightly as he moved his mouth back to hers, kissing her and sending her over the edge.

She felt him grow larger inside of her and if Connor hadn't suddenly released her breasts to cup her face and keep her mouth right where it was, she probably would have screamed in pleasure, well, screamed louder. He felt so good, sliding in and out of her as the large velvety head rubbed against her in just the right way. She tried to make it last longer, but the second that she heard her name leave his lips in a strangled growl she'd lost it.

A violent orgasm tore through her, leaving her breathless and unable to so much as move as pleasure assaulted her body. She never broke away from Connor's mouth, somehow knowing that it wouldn't be as good without this connection. Everything about this moment felt perfect, felt right. She couldn't explain it, didn't want to look too deeply into it and wreck this moment.

She just wanted to keep pretending that he meant nothing to her and that she wasn't starting to care for him. It was just sex and something that she needed to do for her project, her dream. As long as she could do that then everything was fine.

Long after their bodies were sated, she lay on top of him, kissing him leisurely as she enjoyed the way that he held her. For several minutes she allowed him to hold her, comfort her and make her feel wanted, loved and cherished, but all too soon she realized that she didn't have an excuse to remain in his arms. The sex was easy to excuse since she fully planned on enjoying his incredible body during this deal of theirs, but cuddling afterwards?

No, she couldn't explain that and she'd be damned if she let Connor know just how badly he was affecting her. She allowed herself one more minute in his arms before she broke the kiss off and moved to crawl off him when his arms tightened around her.

"Where are you going?" he asked softly.

"Home. I have somewhere to be," which was actually true. In fact, if she didn't move her ass now, grab a quick shower, feed Bunny and put him out, break a few speed laws and stop along the way to pick up coffee and donuts since it was her week, she was going to have five very pissed off brothers to deal with.

"No, you're staying with me," Connor said matter-of-factly, leaning up to press a kiss against her lips as he turned them over until they were lying on their sides, facing each other.

"No," she said on an exasperated sigh as she tried to move out of his arms only to find herself held securely in place, "I'm not. I have somewhere I have to be."

"Then I guess you're going back on our deal," he said with a little shrug even as he pulled her closer until her breasts were pressed against his chest.

"How exactly am I going back on our deal by leaving?" she asked, cuddling closer to him for warmth of course. It didn't matter that it was probably seventy degrees in his room.

"Because it's part of our agreement," he said as he leaned in and pressed one of those tender kisses that she loved, against her forehead.

"No."

"Of course it is," he said, pushing her hair away from her face.

"No, it's not."

"Yes, it is," the infuriating man said as he reached down and took her good hand in his and entwined their fingers.

"We agreed to sleep together?" she asked, too exhausted to hide the confusion in her voice.

"Yes."

For a moment she couldn't respond as she quickly ran the conversation that they'd had before the best sex of her life, through her head. She couldn't for the life of her figure out what he was talking about. "When?"

"It was part of our new agreement."

"Um, no it wasn't," she said, wracking her brain once again since she had been rather distracted during that conversation, but she was sure that she'd remember agreeing to sleep with him after sex. Not that she was really going to complain, much, since it gave her the excuse that she wanted to stay in his arms.

"It really was though," he said, leaning in and brushing his lips against hers. "Whenever you use my body for sex-"

"For the agreement," she quickly added, not wanting him to get the wrong idea or anything.

He ignored the interruption as he continued, "-then you have to sleep with me."

"What if we have a quickie during lunch?" she asked, wondering if he was planning on making up the rules as they went along. She really should call veto, and she would just as soon as he said something that didn't secretly please her.

"Then you have dinner with me, stay the night and have breakfast in the morning," he explained, turning over onto his back, taking her with him and gently laying her on his other side so that she could curl up against him and rest her injured arm across his chest. With a putout sigh, she did just that.

"Why exactly do I have to do all that just to have my way with you?" she asked, closing her eyes and snuggling up against him.

"How else are we supposed to convince people that we're madly in love," he murmured softly as he placed his hand gently over her injured hand.

"Good point," she said, closing her eyes and pretending that his words didn't make something inside her ache.

TWENTY-FOUR

"I really have to go," Rory said even as she tugged him down for another kiss.

"Then go," Connor said as he wrapped his arms around her and raised her off the ground so that he could give her a proper goodbye kiss before he left.

They'd barely managed to get an hour of sleep before his alarm went off, reminding him that he really needed to move his ass if he had any hopes of pulling off his plan. As much as he wanted to stay in bed with Rory and hold her for the rest of the day, he had to leave her. He had to take her father up on his offer so that he could get some time in with her brothers and that meant leaving her.

It didn't hurt that he knew that she wouldn't be too far away while he was getting in a little male bonding time with her brothers. While he was fishing, she'd be up at the house with her brothers' girlfriends doing whatever the hell it is that they did. Knowing that he'd be able to sneak off and steal a kiss or two was the only thing that got him to move his ass and get in the shower before he did something stupid like say to hell with his plan and focus on keeping Rory in his bed.

He was actually pretty proud of himself this morning. He managed to beat the shit out of his alarm clock, get out of bed and into the shower without giving into temptation. He may have lingered in the shower for a few minutes on the off chance that Rory decided to join him. She had an injured arm after all and might be in need of an extra hand or two to help soap up her incredible body. It was a sacrifice, but one that he was willing to make for her.

After a few minutes, he'd given up and started getting ready. When he stepped into his room, he didn't even bother to bite back his disappointed sigh when he found his bed empty. He'd been hoping that she'd be there, giving him the excuse that he needed to focus on her. A wave of exhaustion had hit him and he'd been tempted to crawl back into bed, but without Rory lying in his arms he hadn't seen the point.

He'd just been resigning himself to spending a few hours without kissing her when he'd spotted her walking towards her Jeep, carrying her backpack and thermos. When their eyes locked, a hot current shot through his body, shooting straight to his heart and stealing the air out of his lungs and before he knew it, he was making his way across their yards and pulling her in his arms.

She went willingly, more than willingly which still stunned him considering that only a month ago she would have gone for her pliers. He'd dated plenty of women in the past, but none of them made him feel the way that she did, whole. On some level she'd always made him feel that way, but after making love to her, something inside of him clicked. He didn't understand it, but he wasn't going to fight it either.

He was done fighting with her.

When this project was over, he was keeping her, deal or no deal. She belonged with him. They were so much alike that it was a little frightening, well, to everyone else. Years ago he'd known that, but he'd convinced himself that they were both better off without the added complication in their lives. It wouldn't be easy convincing her to take a real chance on him, but he didn't care. This morning he had a taste of what it could be like between them and he'd have to be out of his fucking mind to give that up.

He was still going to steal her brothers out from under her and run her out of business, but now he planned on doing it with a little more finesse. Instead of watching her business go under, he was going to step up when the time came and buy her business. That way Rory wouldn't feel like a failure and leave town and she'd be able to spend the day working for him and her nights moaning his name in his ear.

"Tonight," Rory said, sounding out of breath as she pulled her lips away from his.

"Tonight, what?" he asked in a daze as he moved in to pick up where they'd left off, but Rory had other plans. With a teasing smile, she pulled her lips further away from his, but quickly made it up to him by wrapping her legs around his waist

"We'll have to continue this tonight, because I really have to go now or I'm going to be late," she said with a sigh as she tried to pull her legs away from his waist, but he wasn't having that.

He moved his hands from her waist to her ass and kept her right where she was so that he could lean in and steal a kiss before they clarified one or two things. "You're having dinner with me, right?" he asked, even though she really didn't have a choice in the matter.

"I usually meet my brothers for dinner on Sunday," she replied against his lips as her hold around his waist tightened and he was tempted once again to say the hell with everything and take her back to bed, but he had work to do, sad, but true. If he wanted to keep Rory in his bed on a permanent basis, and he did, then he was going to have to learn to prioritize.

Plan and work first and then amazing sex second.

"You're having dinner with me instead," he informed her, since she seemed to think that she had a choice.

She didn't.

But that didn't mean that he was going to be a complete prick about it. "You can pick the place. I don't care if you're brothers are there, but you're going with me."

He wasn't too surprised when Rory pulled back, looking more amused than anything. "And if I don't?"

For a few seconds, he considered threatening not to put out, but then he remembered who he was dealing with and decided that it would probably be best not to take a chance of her calling his bluff. Instead, he carried her the rest of the way to his truck as he said, "You will."

"What if I pick the most expensive restaurant in town?" she asked, tilting her head slightly to the side, studying him as she waited for his answer.

"That's fine with me, Rory," he said, leaning in to steal a quick kiss before he carefully set her on her feet. "You can have whatever you want."

"For the deal, right?" she asked, eying him curiously as she held onto him until her feet touched the ground.

"Yes," he answered, knowing that was the only way that she would accept what was going on between them right now.

"Of course," she mumbled as she looked away.

It was hard to tell in this early morning light, but he could have sworn that she looked a little disappointed. He should just let it go, especially since he couldn't risk her figuring out just how much she was coming to mean to him, but he couldn't do that. He didn't want her to think that she wasn't worth everything that he could give to her and then some.

"I would take you anyway, Rory," he admitted, feeling like a dope.

"Why?" she asked, looking and sounding as though she couldn't understand why any sane man would happily die for the chance to put a smile on her face.

"Because you're worth it," he simply said, cupping her face as he leaned in to kiss her, but her next words gave him pause.

"Because I'm beautiful?" she asked with a touch of acid lacing her words.

He didn't even want to imagine how many times she'd heard some asshole compliment her on how beautiful she was. They probably thought that's what she wanted to hear. It wasn't. Not for a woman like Rory who knew that she was beautiful and didn't care. They really were fucking idiots.

"Yes," he said with absolutely no hesitation and when she tried to pull away from him, her expression a combination of hurt and disgust, he held onto her and continued to move in to kiss her. "But I'd take you because you're the best part of my day, Rory. Always have been and always will be."

He planted a quick kiss on her stunned lips before pulling away from her and opening the passenger side door. "You can decide where we're going while I drive," he said, gesturing for her to climb in and she must have been a little stunned, because she did just that. By the time he'd climbed in the truck, carrying her bag and thermos, she'd worked her way out of her shock.

"I have somewhere to be," she said, taking her things as he turned the truck on.

"I know," he said with a shrug. "Buckle up."

"I can drive myself," she pointed out, only looking slightly confused now as she reached for the door handle.

"You're going to your father's, right?" he asked, throwing the truck in reverse and taking the matter out of her hands.

"I go every Sunday," she said, frowning, but she did buckle up.

"Well, today you're going with me," he explained, taking her injured hand gently in his.

"Umm, why?" she asked, lacing her fingers with his.

"Because your father invited me."

———

"What the hell are you doing, woman?" Connor demanded, chuckling like she was playing around.

She wasn't.

"Oh my God, Connor, turn around! It's a trap!" she demanded, desperately looking around for somewhere to turn the truck around.

"Relax, Rory. It's just fishing," he said, throwing her a wink as he took a left on Chestnut Road.

"No, Connor, you don't understand," she said, trying not to panic, but this was bad, very, very, very bad. "Only family is allowed at my Dad's house on Sunday."

"Afraid they'll kill me?" he asked, teasingly.

"Yes!" she snapped, wondering what the hell was wrong with him. He'd known about her father's family only Sunday rule since he was a kid. He used to get a kick out of sneaking onto the property and tormenting the living hell out of her on most Sundays. She'd lost count of how many times he got her butt in trouble just by letting her father see him. To this day she still couldn't figure out why her father punished her over Connor when he'd known how much she hated him, which brought her right back to the problem at hand.

"Connor," she said calmly, trying not to panic, "you cannot go to my father's house. Do you understand? Just bring me home and let's pretend that this never happened."

"Having a nervous breakdown, are we?" he mused, still smiling like this was all some big joke.

"Connor, my brothers hate you and my dad-"

"Is the one who invited me today," he finished for her with a shrug as if he hadn't just confirmed her suspicions.

They were going to kill him.

"Connor," she said, sounding a little panicked and not really caring, "you are the last person that my father would invite to the house."

"Yet, he did," he pointed out, sounding amused as he took a turn onto Red River Road.

She continued as if he hadn't interrupted her. "There are no witnesses. The closest neighbor lives a mile away. There will be no one to hear your screams for help."

"Except for the women at the house," Connor said, making her frown.

"What women?" she couldn't help but ask, temporarily distracted from her mission to save Connor's ungrateful ass.

"Your father said that if I brought anyone that she'd have to stay up at the house."

"What the hell are you talking about?" she demanded before another thought occurred to her. "Why would he think that you were bringing someone along when we're supposedly dating?"

"I got the invite before we started this plan," he explained as he turned onto her father's road.

She didn't bother correcting him about the whole "we" part about who started this plan since she'd gone back into panic mode. "I am begging you to turn around, Connor."

His answer was an amused chuckle as he turned onto the long, secluded private dirt driveway that led to her father's house and suddenly reminded her of slasher films. This was crazy! Surely the man realized that he was walking into a trap.

"Connor, please turn around," she said, forcing herself to remain calm.

"If I didn't know any better, I'd think that you'd miss me."

She opened her mouth to tell him that she wouldn't miss him, but she couldn't get the words out. She would miss the big jerk. Somehow he'd gone from being an annoyance, an entertaining one at that, to....

Well, she really wasn't sure what he was right now since she was too busy trying to save his ass. When she spotted the old oak tree that she'd once tied Connor to with her jump rope, she realized that if she was going to change his mind and save his obstinate ass that she had to do something now. Begging, pleading and reasoning hadn't worked and she considered going for his nipples, but that might cause other problems like him veering off into the woods so that left just one thing.

Unfortunately for her, she didn't have experience using that "one thing" to get a guy to do what she wanted. But, if it stopped Connor from doing something stupid then she was just going to have to do it, she decided, ignoring the little fact that the idea of seducing him appealed to her a little too much. There was going to be hell to pay for missing fishing with her family, but she was pretty sure that spending the day in bed with Connor would be more than worth it. Knowing that it was now or never, she undid her belt and shifted closer to Connor.

"What are you doing?" he asked, throwing her a curious glance as he continued to drive.

"Stop the truck, Connor," she whispered as she carefully climbed onto his lap, taking the choice out of his hands.

With a putout sigh, he pulled off to the side of the dirt road and threw the truck in park. "I appreciate your concern, Rory, but-"

"I want you, Connor," she said, leaning in to press a kiss against his stunned lips. "I want you to take me home and give me a reason to stay in bed all day. Can you do that, Connor?" she asked in a husky voice that she barely recognized as she teasingly kissed her way down his chin and neck. When he tilted his head to the side and groaned softly, she knew that she had him.

Even better, she knew that she'd be spending the day in his bed.

"You're just doing this to get out of fishing," he said roughly as his hands landed on her ass and he moved in, using his face to move hers so that he could take her mouth in a quick, hard kiss that left her breathing hard and desperate for him in a way that actually scared her.

"Does it matter?" she asked softly as she pressed down against that large bulge in his pants that her trembling body screamed for.

"Not one fucking bit."

TWENTY-FIVE

"The James brothers looked like they wanted to kill you," Andrew commented as he looked around to make sure that they were alone before he opened the small blue cooler perched on the driver's side seat of his truck.

Connor shrugged it off as he looked around the basically deserted makeshift parking lot, playing lookout. It was a job that he'd perfected over the past year and one that he hated, but he knew that Andrew hated it more so he kept his mouth shut and an eye out for unwanted company.

"Does it have something to do with that huge shit-eating grin that you were sporting this morning?" Andrew asked, chuckling as he pulled out the first of many syringes.

"In a roundabout way," he admitted, feeling his lips pull up into that grin that he couldn't seem to keep off his face. Yesterday with Rory had been…..

Amazing.

After somehow managing to drive the truck back to his house without wrecking it, they managed to stumble into his house while tearing each other's clothes off and hadn't left until this morning. They'd made love against the front door, on the stairs, in the upstairs hallway, three times in the bathtub before they managed to collapse in a tangled mess on his bed where he proceeded to make love to her until he swore that he'd never be able to move again. Sex with Rory was incredible, but surprisingly it wasn't the reason why he couldn't stop smiling.

Rory was the reason.

He loved spending a lazy Sunday with her. It didn't matter if they were making love, holding each other, fighting over the remote or trying to annoy the hell out of each other, just being with her felt good. She turned him on, made him laugh and drove him out of his goddamn mind and he loved every single minute of it. She was definitely worth the bullshit that he was going to have to go through to get back on her family's good side after yesterday.

"Oh, fuck," Andrew groaned, dragging his attention away from the most incredible weekend of his life in time to see his oldest friend stumble away from the truck and make his way towards the overgrown brush surrounding the woods where Andrew proceeded to lose his lunch near a patch of poison ivy.

"Stop," Andrew said on a gasp when Connor moved to help him.

He wasn't sure what he hated more, watching his best friend slowly lose this battle or feeling this helpless. It wouldn't be so bad if Andrew wasn't being so damn pigheaded, but he was. Andrew refused to ask for help and Connor feared that Andrew's pride was going to get him killed. He knew that it was Andrew's choice, but he wished he would ask for help, scream for it, but he wouldn't. Andrew was leaving his fate in God's hands and Connor didn't think that was enough, not for this.

"You need to go home," Connor snapped, sick of this bullshit. Andrew didn't belong here, especially if he wasn't going to put up a fight. If this was it, he'd rather see his oldest friend go out with a bang, but Andrew refused to act like anything was wrong.

"Are you still going to pay me?" Andrew asked, sitting back on his haunches as he dropped his face in his hands, no doubt fighting another wave of nausea from the expensive medicine that was supposed to be helping him.

"Yes," Connor gritted out, already knowing where the stubborn man was going with this.

Sure enough, Andrew shook his head as he slowly got to his feet. "Then I'm staying, Connor. I'm not a charity case," he said, pressing a shaky hand to his stomach as he walked back to his truck.

"No, you're a fucking idiot!" Connor snapped as the fear that he'd been fighting for the last year once again crept up his spine. He couldn't lose his best friend. They'd been friends since they were little kids and had always been there for each other. Andrew was one of the best people that he knew. The man was kind, considerate and put up with his bullshit and helped keep him in line. Without him……

Hell, he didn't want to think about that, because it wasn't going to happen. Andrew was going to beat this damn thing and that's all that mattered.

"Love you too, man," Andrew said with a forced smile as he placed the used syringes in a canister and stored it beneath his seat. Andrew carefully placed the cooler on the floor, grabbed his hardhat and clipboard while Connor wracked his brain, trying to figure out a way to fix this. He refused to believe that there was nothing that he could do.

"Let it go, Connor," Andrew said softly.

"I can't."

"You're going to have to, Connor," Andrew said, sounding tired as he walked away.

Connor cursed up a storm as Andrew stumbled on his way back to the site. He wasn't too surprised when Andrew couldn't make it past the flatbeds before he needed to take a break. He was supposed to rest for three hours after taking his medication, but he never did. Andrew didn't want to be sick and didn't want to face what lay ahead of him and Connor couldn't blame him, but sometimes like now, it was too much to bear.

He wanted to yell at Andrew, scream at him until his voice was hoarse and then do it some more. He needed to shake some sense into his friend, tell him how unfair he was being by making him feel this fucking helpless, but he couldn't. Andrew didn't need to hear how scared he was. It wouldn't be fair, but then again nothing about this situation was.

———

"We don't have to do this if you don't want to," Rory said casually even as her stomach fluttered in dread.

"You're not getting out of having dinner with me tonight, Rory," Connor said with a hard glare as he caged her in against the side of her Jeep.

"I'm not trying to get out of anything, Connor," she explained, reaching between them and hooking her fingers through his belt loops.

"Then why do you keep asking if I've changed my mind?" he asked, frowning down at her as he reached over and lightly traced her jaw with his finger.

"Because you've been acting like you have a bug up your ass all day and haven't said more than two words to me since lunch," she said, liking the way his lips twitched as some of the sadness seeped away from his expression.

She shouldn't care if he was upset. This was only a deal after all, albeit a deal that now included incredible sex, but a deal nonetheless. Not to mention that this was Connor, the bastard who'd jumped behind the student driver's ed car while she'd been taking her driver's test and made it look like she'd run him over, causing her to fail the test and her instructor's breakdown when Rory may have "inadvertently" tried to run over Connor for real. If she were smart, she'd figure out what caused him to lose that easy going smile of his a few hours ago and exploit it to get her project free and clear and get out of this deal.

Apparently she was an idiot, because not only did she not want to get out of this deal like any sane woman would, but she was afraid that she was falling for him. She should be wringing his neck and going for his nipples for stealing her project and dangling it in front of her like a carrot on a stick, but instead she wanted to do whatever it took to make him smile in that way that curled her toes and made her heart race. Maybe her brothers should have her committed, she thought as she used her slight hold on his belt loops to pull him closer.

"Is this your way of telling me that you missed me?" he asked softly, his features softening as he smiled.

Yes, unfortunately for her and her sanity, and not to mention her pride, she had missed him. Her brothers, who apparently were not speaking to her at the moment, spent most of the day glaring daggers at Connor and making fun her like she hadn't been standing less than ten feet away from them. When Johnny started chanting, "Connor and Rory sitting in a tree" she decided that it was time to go around and check up on the rest of her men, right after she tarred Johnny's ass to the roof.

"Nope," she lied, her focus moving to his lips, "not at all."

Slowly, his lips pulled up into the cocky grin that she had to admit looked good on him. "You missed me, Rory. Just admit it."

"It's just so sad that you think so," she said, reluctantly forcing her attention away from his lips as she released her hold on him and gave him a gentle push that got the point across.

With a chuckle, Connor stepped back, giving her some space, but he didn't go far. When she moved to the side to open the driver's side door, he was already there, opening it for her. Not that she was surprised or anything. Even when Connor was going out of his way to make her life a living hell, he always seemed to remember that she was a woman. It was something that used to aggravate her, but now she had to admit that she kind of liked it.

"I'll pick you up in an hour," Connor announced as she climbed in her Jeep.

She pretended to think that over as she looked over her shoulder. "That's really not going to work for me. Better make it eight," she said with a shrug, moving to turn around. By the time she sat down, Connor was there, resting his forearms against the hood of the Jeep as he leaned in and pressed a quick, too quick, kiss against her needy little lips.

"One hour," he said, moving to step away.

"Sorry, not gonna happen. I need at least two," she explained, which was true.

She really did need at least two hours to do everything that she had to do, take care of Bunny, clean up her house a little bit, take a long hot shower to relieve her sore muscles, enjoy a hot cup of cocoa on her patio, and get dressed. Actually, what she really needed was a night to herself so that she could get all of those things done plus run a few errands since she hadn't had a chance to do them on Sunday like grocery shopping.

There was nothing to eat in her house, absolutely nothing. She ran out of cocoa last night and Bunny ran out of food this morning. If she was going to be ready in an hour, and she already decided that she was, then she was going to have to move her ass and take a chance with the convenience store down the street for Bunny's food. Sadly, her cocoa fix was going to have to wait until later.

"Be ready in an hour and I'll take you to Brennagin's for a cup of hot cocoa," he said, reading her mind or bribing her, not that she cared which one it was since Brennagin's had the second best hot cocoa in town. Hers was number one of course, but that didn't change the fact that just the thought of having a delicious, creamy cup of Brennagin's hot cocoa had her practically drooling.

"Extra large?" she asked, already planning on ordering two.

They were extremely expensive, but so worth it, at least to her, to her past boyfriends, not so much. They balked at the idea of spending eight bucks on a cup of cocoa for her. Not that she could really blame them since they weren't addicted to cocoa, but it would have been nice if at least one of them had acted like she was worth it.

Connor leaned in and gave her another one of those too quick kisses. "I tell you what, Rory. If you're ready in an hour, I'll buy you an extra-large cup of cocoa before we go out, one before we come home and as many as you want in between."

As many as she wanted?

Dear God, she was in heaven, she thought with a content little sigh before something occurred to her and when it did, her eyes narrowed dangerously on him.

"This isn't some sort of sick joke, is it?" she demanded, because really, this was hot cocoa and she didn't screw around when it came to her cocoa.

He sighed heavily as he shook his head in mock disgust. "So little trust."

"Is it?"

"You'll just have to wait and see, now won't you?" he teased as he moved in and tried to give her another quick kiss, but she was done being teased. When he tried to pull away, she laced her fingers through his hair and kept him right where he was, determined to get the proper kiss that he owed her.

They had to stay in character and by kissing him in a way that let him know exactly what she expected at the end of the night, and she damn well better be having him tonight, she did just that. It didn't matter that they'd spent most of yesterday and this morning making love, they needed to get into character and having mind-blowing sex was really the only way that they were going to achieve that goal. When he let out a sexy little growl as he moved to deepen the kiss she considered saying the hell with it and demanding that he take her back to his bed since Bunny would probably try to rip his balls off if he tried to join her in her bed, but she couldn't pass up a chance at unlimited hot cocoa. It just wasn't humanly possible.

Breaking off from the kiss was more difficult than she thought it would be. Even as she pushed him away, she followed after him, continuing that kiss that probably wasn't appropriate for public viewing. She didn't know when she'd climbed out of her Jeep or when Connor pushed her up against it, or even when she'd wrapped her legs around him, but she knew the moment that they drew an audience because that's when the catcalls began.

More annoyed than anything, she allowed him to break off the kiss and removed her legs from around his waist as she shot their audience, a mixture of his men and hers, a glare that had them moving their asses. The only one that lingered was Jacob as he sent her a hurt look that confused her and reminded her that she really needed to have a talk with him, just as soon as he stopped giving her the silent treatment.

She couldn't figure out what was going on with him. He'd never acted like this when she dated before, not that she was really dating Connor. Jacob usually ignored the guys she dated unless he was making fun of them, but that was usually it. He never really reacted one way or the other, but it was more than obvious that he wasn't happy about Connor. The fact that he'd lied the other day about the fire inspector to interrupt them was proof enough that he had a problem.

It was something that she was going to have to figure out, but not right now. Right now she needed to haul ass since she only had an hour to get ready if she was going to have an unlimited supply of creamy, hot cocoa tonight and she damn well was.

"One hour," she said in warning, not because she was worried that he was going to be late or stand her up or anything, but because in an hour and fifteen minutes she fully planned on enjoying her first sip of an endless night's supply of cocoa.

"One hour," Connor said evenly as his eyes narrowed on her assistant.

Realizing that she was wasting precious seconds, she climbed in her Jeep, biting back a pleased smile when she felt Connor's hands on her hips, guiding her inside, and sat down. Connor leaned in and pressed a quick kiss to her cheek before stepping back and closing her door. She didn't waste any time in driving away. She knew what was at stake and she wasn't going to waste a single precious minute because she knew that if she was even a minute late that Connor would deny her, her much needed hot cocoa fix.

After hitting the convenience store and buying a small bag of dog food, a soda and the box of condoms that they'd both agreed this morning that they should be using, she headed home, planning the remainder of the hour down to the minute. If everything went well, she'd have five minutes to spare, she thought with a content little sigh as she pulled onto her street.

A few minutes later, confusion took over as she was forced to park on the street because of the two semi-familiar black trucks that were parked in her driveway. As she climbed out of her Jeep, frustration took over as she wracked her brain, trying to figure out who owned the trucks. The Yankees bumper stickers should have been a huge clue since most everyone around here was a Red Sox fan. Her family, Connor and a few other die-hard Yankees fans were the exception so it really shouldn't have been too difficult to figure out who owned the trucks.

She threw her bag over her shoulder, grabbed her empty thermos and headed for her door, pausing only long enough to throw the trucks another curious look. Her curiosity quickly turned into apprehension when her mind registered the fact that Bunny wasn't running around her, barking and demanding his customary pat behind the ears. In fact, Bunny was nowhere to be seen and she didn't hear barking or anyone screaming for help.

Concern for her dog had her rushing to her front door when what she should be doing was running to her Jeep and grabbing a crowbar to beat the hell out of whoever had broken into her house, but she didn't want to waste any time. If someone had hurt her little honey bunny she was going to-

"Oh my God, I'm dying!" she heard a very familiar voice groan as she threw open her front door and nearly stumbled over the large body curled up in the fetal position on the floor.

"I told you not to touch the brownies," an equally familiar voice said, sounding bored and making her smile hugely as she used the body on the ground as a stepping stone to throw herself into the arms of the incredibly handsome man petting Bunny behind the ear.

"Ow! Goddamnit, woman! I'm dying!" her cousin whined as one of her favorite people in the world caught her mid-jump and twirled her around, hugging her tightly as Jason, who she was fifty percent sure wasn't going to die anytime soon, bitched about them being insensitive bastards.

TWENTY-SIX

"**W**hy are you people ignoring me? I'm dying here!"

"Oh my God, did the town finally lift the ban?" Rory asked, still pissed after all these years that they'd banned all of her family on the Bradford side over a few simple misunderstanding between her Uncles and a few restaurants, grocery stores, a gas station, a hot dog stand or two, an ice cream truck, and a lemonade stand.

It wasn't as if they'd done any permanent damage. Well, the lemonade stand didn't count. It was made with shoddy craftsmanship and probably wouldn't have lasted another season no matter what the fire inspector had said. She'd only been a baby when they were banned so she couldn't say for certain what happened, but she really didn't believe the rumors that were whispered around town. They were just a bit ridiculous.

True, all the Bradford males, and unfortunately some of the females, had a unusually large appetite and she'd almost lost a finger or two at family gatherings, but really, how could that get someone, never mind an entire family, banned? A few times over the years she'd tried asking her father what really happened, but the conversation always ended with a warning never to come between a Bradford and his food. She'd always thought that making her swear it on a Bible was a bit much.

"That ban is total bullshit," Trevor grumbled as he pressed a kiss against her forehead and placed her back on her feet.

"So they didn't lift it?" she asked, carefully stepping over Jason and started to head for the kitchen for something to snack on, but commonsense had her shaking her head, sighing, and heading for the living room.

There was always a slight chance that her brothers would have missed something, but these were her cousins and they never missed a thing. Not that there had been much to start with. The reminder had her stopping and throwing a curious look at Jason as he groaned and curled into a small ball. He wouldn't have been foolish enough to eat baking soda again, would he?

As much as she'd love to dismiss the possibility, and she would have if it had been anyone else, this was a Bradford that she was dealing with here so she had to ask, "You didn't eat my box of baking soda, did you?"

The glare she earned from him was a little over the top, but again, this was a Bradford that she was dealing with here so she just ignored him and walked into the living room. She sat down on the loveseat and picked up the baby blue shirt lying next to her on the couch. Connor left it here the other night when they'd been working out some of the problems they were already running into with this project.

She loved this shirt on him, but she'd admit that she'd liked it a whole lot better when he took it off. Deciding that it was a little cool in the house, she pulled his shirt on and sat back while she waited for her cousins to explain why they were breaking the law to come see her. She knew it wasn't an emergency, because her Aunt, well, really second cousin by marriage, Megan would have called everyone in the family and told them that someone was in trouble.

That's all it would take to get every Bradford and James to come running. They all stuck together, no matter what. It didn't matter if it was one of the younger Bradford boys that didn't know how to reign in his appetite or arrogance and got himself into trouble or one of their elderly relatives who couldn't manage to take care of themselves any longer, if a Bradford or James was in trouble everyone showed up. They worked it out together, whether that meant kicking someone's ass, bailing someone out of jail, or taking them in and giving them a place to live.

They didn't turn their backs on family. Ever. The only time you didn't show up was if you were in labor, dead or dying. If none of those things occurred and you didn't show up when you were needed, you better change your name, pack your bags and haul ass for the border, because as soon as the crisis was over, every Bradford and James would be coming for your ass and an explanation.

"Well?" she asked as Trevor sat down on the chair across from her, shooting her a grin that she was all too familiar with. It was the same grin that her brothers used seconds before they started spouting bullshit, the one they used to get away with everything and to get women to trip over themselves to please them. Quite simply put, it was the Bradford smile.

It was the same grin that her Grandpa, well, really Great Uncle, Wes used to use when he wanted Grandma, really Great Aunt by marriage, Beth to make him fresh biscuits and jam for his mid-morning snack. She could still remember Grandpa Wes giving Grandma Beth that Bradford smile as he tried to sweet talk Grandma into baking him a double batch of biscuits. Grandma Beth would give him a stern look as she huffed and puffed about all the work it would take to make the biscuits even as she made them. She would smile that sweet smile that belonged solely to her when Grandpa Wes was looking the other way.

God, she missed Grandma and Grandpa. They'd been gone ten years now, but she thought about them every day, especially when her brothers used the Bradford charm. She missed spending time with them and cherished the little time that she'd had with them. She would have seen them more often, but with the ban and all it had limited their time to weekends and holidays. That was the one thing her father never refused them, a visit to their grandparents.

Her father loved them too, which wasn't surprising since Grandpa Wes and Aunt Beth had raised her father and his four brothers after they'd lost their parents in the fire. Just like now, every Bradford showed up the moment word got out and within hours of finding out that her real grandparents hadn't made it out of the fire, her father and uncles had a home, a real home with Grandpa Wes and Aunt Beth and their brood of boys. Things had been tight with thirteen boys to feed and clothe, but her grandparents never complained or let any of the boys know just how badly they'd struggled.

They'd never let anything get them down and always worked hard to push ahead. They'd made sure that every single boy was well prepared to go out into the real world. They'd also made sure that they were there if any of the boys needed a helping hand. They made a lot of sacrifices for all their boys and she knew that they'd done it out of love and not because they'd expected anything in return. They certainly hadn't expected all their boys and the rest of the Bradford bunch to show up one day and demolish their small house.

The place was barely better than a shack and because they'd refused any help from the boys as a thank you for everything they'd done, the boys took matters into their own hands. They had the house demolished in one day, cleared out the next and a beautiful new house built within two months as well as the mortgage paid off. Her father, uncles, and cousins all chipped in and worked on the house on their days off, before and after work and didn't stop until Aunt Beth had the small picket fence and rose bushes that she'd always dreamed of.

Rory hadn't been born when they'd built it, but it had been one of her most favorite places in the world to visit when she was a child. The cottage had been sweet, cozy and filled with love. It also hadn't hurt that it was twenty miles away from Connor and provided her with much needed breaks. Short breaks, but they were enough sometimes to help her calm down before she did something stupid like commit murder.

He'd been such a miserable little bastard, she thought, but a really cute one.

"What's with that little smile of yours?" Trevor asked, drawing her attention back to the problem at hand.

Two fully-grown Bradford males breaking the ban and in her house.

Since she really couldn't afford the "Bradford Fine," she knew that she was going to have to make this quick and get them out of here before her cousins did something to give themselves away and she was faced with a two thousand dollar fine and a night in jail. Yes, the fine was steep, but then again, according to local gossip so was the damage the Bradfords had reportedly done to the town.

"She's smiling because she's happy to see me," Jason grumbled as he stumbled past her, looking like he was in a lot of pain. He pressed his hand to his stomach as he moved towards the end of the couch, but after a slight pause he shrugged and dropped down onto the couch, right next to her.

"Yeah, that's why I'm smiling," she said, dryly, realizing that she was indeed smiling and surprised that it was because of Connor. Not that she hadn't found herself smiling recently when she thought of him, but that was for the sweet, funny Connor that she was starting to care too much about. This was the first time that she'd ever been able to think of Connor when they were kids and smile.

"I know," Jason said on a drawn out sigh as he flopped over onto his side so that his head was resting on her lap and he could curl back up into the fetal position.

"Are you going to tell me what you ate?" she asked, settling back and resigning herself to being Jason's pillow.

"Pumpkin pie," Jason grumbled on a miserable groan.

"For the last fucking time," Trevor snapped, "that was a fudge brownie, asshole."

Rory couldn't help but frown at that announcement, because the big baby curled up on the couch was a Bradford and if there was one thing a Bradford knew, it was food. It didn't matter what color you dyed it, if it was burnt, squished or ten weeks past its expiration date and was growing a fuzzy blue, white and green habitat, a Bradford would figure it out by the first bite and by the second he would know if it would make him sick. Not that they would stop eating it if they figured out that it was going to make them sick, because they wouldn't. A true Bradford would take the risk.

"It was orange, gooey and smelled like pumpkin and nutmeg!" Jason snapped at Trevor before turning a glare on her. "Would it kill you to rub my back? I'm dying here!"

Knowing that he wouldn't stop bitching until she did it, she gave in. After about ten seconds, Jason decided to get a little more comfortable and flopped over onto his stomach and sprawled out on the couch. When she didn't recommence with the back rubbing fast enough he cleared his throat and just in case she didn't take the hint, the bastard reached down and pinched the back of her calf.

"Ow!" she yelped, but she moved her ass and started rubbing his back, knowing that the big jerk would only keep bugging the shit out of her until she gave in and did what he wanted. "Demanding bastard," she muttered as she rubbed his back.

"Nice to see that you're still a bully," Jason grumbled, silently demanding that she rub faster by wiggling until she got the damn hint.

"How am I the bully? You pinched me, you bastard!" she snapped at him, but wasn't foolish enough to stop rubbing.

"Because you called me a naughty, naughty name," Jason said on a huff that was quickly followed by a little sigh of pleasure as she rubbed between his shoulders.

"Called you a naughty name?" she repeated in disbelief, foolishly pausing in her labor and earning another pinch. "Ow! Stop doing that, asshole!"

"Again with the name calling," Jason sighed.

"She was always so mean to us," Trevor mused just as an odd crunching noise caught her attention.

She moved her glare away from the large bastard using her lap as a pillow to the large bastard sprawled out in the chair across from her and snapped, "Oh my God! Stop eating that!"

"Your trail mix tastes funny," Trevor said with a cringe.

"That wasn't trail mix, you bastard! That was potpourri!"

"Well, that explains a lot," he said, giving her a sheepish smile as he returned the large wooden bowl back to the side table. She didn't need to look to know that he'd already eaten half the bowl of potpourri. She didn't even bother asking him what was wrong with him since she knew the answer.

The man was a Bradford.

Enough said.

It was also the reminder that she needed to find out why they were here and throw their asses out before she got caught harboring

Bradfords. She really needed to find out what they'd done to get banned in the first place, but that was a problem for another time. Right now she needed to deal with them, and hopefully she could do that in less than twenty minutes so that she could get in a quick shower and take care of Bunny before she met Connor, and enjoyed her night of unlimited hot cocoa.

"There's that smile again," Trevor said, sounding amused.

"Why are you here?" she demanded, deciding to ignore the fact that she couldn't help smiling when she thought about Connor.

"To help you, you ungrateful bastard," Jason grumbled, snuggling his head near her knees and she was tempted, oh so tempted, to shove him onto the floor and give him the wedgie that he was practically begging for.

"How exactly is having you bitch and whine helping me?" she demanded, rubbing faster when she felt his hand move near her calf.

"I wouldn't be bitching and whining if that bastard's Red Sox-loving wife hadn't tried to poison me!" Jason bit out harshly and she knew without asking that her cousin was more pissed off about the fact that Trevor's wife, Zoe, had a soft spot for all things Red Sox than the actual poisoning.

She still cringed when she thought about last Christmas' family gathering. All she had to say was that Zoe had guts showing up at a Bradford gathering with her twin baby boys dressed in matching Red Sox jerseys. She could still remember the stunned silence that took over the house when Zoe pulled the baby blanket off the twin's and revealed those damn jerseys that her brothers, cousins and she may have accidentally smeared pudding, chocolate and cold gravy on within minutes of the unveiling.

It hadn't mattered that they'd "accidentally" dropped the small jerseys in the fireplace after they'd offered to clean them, the damage had already been done. She'd never seen Trevor look so angry before. Instead of yelling at Zoe like she'd expected, he'd became deathly silent and walked away. It had actually been kind of frightening. For the rest of the night, he'd sat silently in the corner of the room, never shifting his glare away from his wife. It wasn't until Zoe had complimented Aunt Janice on her table arrangement that he'd reacted.

He was up and out of his chair and across the room in seconds, shoving aside anyone foolish enough to get in his way. Without a word, he'd grabbed Zoe's hand, yanked her out of the room and disappeared down the hall. She'd like to say that she hadn't heard the sound of her cousin having sex and that those sounds didn't still haunt her to this day, but she couldn't. The rest of the family found it amusing, but they knew better than to say anything about it.

Everyone else pretended that the incident had never happened, partly because they knew that Trevor would beat the hell out of them if any of them gave his wife any shit, but mostly because they were all deathly afraid of Zoe and her baked goods. So far the small, plain woman who made her laugh her ass off had managed to send a total of twenty-nine Bradfords to the emergency room to have their stomachs pumped. Speaking of Bradfords and emergency rooms.....

"Should we bring him to the emergency room?" she asked, throwing Jason a nervous glance and noting the slightly green color marring his normally healthy tanned skin.

"No, he'll be fine. He only took one bite of the brownie," Trevor said, sounding unconcerned. She opened her mouth to argue, but then with a sigh and a shrug she reminded herself that Trevor would know the danger signs of eating Zoe's baked goods better than anyone.

"Fine, then tell me how the two of you breaking the ban is helping me?"

"Let us worry about the ban," Trevor said with a shrug as he reached for the bowl of potpourri, but one look from her had him pulling his hand back and shooting her a sheepish smile.

"Are you going to tell me why you're here?" she asked, absently as she threw another glance towards the clock. She might have to skip the shower and take one later with Connor, she realized as she calculated the odds of throwing her cousins out, feeding Bunny and at least brushing her teeth before Connor showed up. She had to admit they weren't very good.

"We're here to help you with your project, Rory and we're going to help you build your suites," Trevor announced, grabbing her attention in a big way.

"What?" she asked, dumbly, not sure that she heard him correctly.

"He said that we came to help you with your project. Now, move your ass and get back to rubbing, woman!" Jason grumbled testily, wiggling around in an attempt to get her to recommence with the rubbing, but she couldn't do anything more than sit there like an idiot as her mind quickly wrapped around that announcement.

"You're here to help?" she asked, making sure that she'd heard them correctly.

"Yes," Trevor said with a nod and a shrug as if he hadn't just solved most of her problems.

Where her brothers were good, really good, her cousins were the best. They were bigger, stronger and fast, very fast. Having one Bradford working for her would be like having five extra guys.

"Some of the others will come out when they can to help, but for now it's us," Trevor explained

"Oh my God," she mumbled, feeling her lips pull up into a huge smile. "Really? This is great!"

"If you want, we can go have a look at this project right now," Trevor offered with a shrug.

"That would be great!" she said, shoving Jason off of her lap and ignoring his whimpers and muttered, "Bastard" as she jumped to her feet and practically raced to the door. She was halfway there when one thought had her skidding to a stop.

Connor.

She didn't want to break their plans, but she had to if she wanted to get her cousins caught up on what was going on. She could always sneak into his room later tonight, but she already knew that she'd be too tired to do that. It didn't help matters that she had to get up early in the morning. Skipping out on their plans also meant losing a night in his arms and she really wasn't sure that she could do that.

"Where are you going?" Trevor asked as she abruptly turned and raced up the stairs.

"I'll be back in ten minutes!" she yelled, hoping to be back in five before her cousins did something to give themselves away and land her ass in jail for the night.

TWENTY-SEVEN

"**C**onnor?"

Speak of the devil, he thought, grinning as he wiped his hand down his face, wiping water out of his eyes. He'd just been thinking about her, but that wasn't really anything new. Granted, his thoughts used to run along the lines of screwing her over for his own entertainment or revenge, but now he found himself just thinking about her smile, the way she pouted when he stole the last slice of pizza, and the way that she felt in his arms first thing in the morning.

Fucking amazing

"How much longer are you going to be?" Rory asked, sounding impatient and arousing his curiosity.

"I'm done," he said, stepping beneath the water and quickly rinsing off the bodywash that coated his body before he shut the water off, ripped back the curtain and nearly tripped as he stepped out of the shower and his eyes landed on Rory.

"I need you," she said, giving her bare ass a little wiggle as she looked over her shoulder at him. Blindly, he reached out and slapped a hand against the shower wall. It was either that or take the chance of his legs giving out on him as a surge of lust tore through him, leaving him panting and struggling with the need to step up behind her and take her, hard.

The image of Rory bent over his bathroom counter and offering herself up to him was permanently etched into his brain, but it was her little declaration that had him panting and so damn turned on that he actually feared that his balls would explode. The fact that Rory wanted him so badly that she couldn't wait until the end of the night to have him had him struggling with his sanity. That she was as desperate for him as he was for her gave him hope and had him dropping his hand away from the wall and taking a step towards her.

"Couldn't it wait until tonight?" he asked, absently reaching down and running his hand over his painfully erect shaft as he reached out and palmed one of her perfect cheeks and gave it a light squeeze that had them both licking their lips.

"No," she admitted on a needy moan, surprising him and ramping up his hunger for her.

Never in a million years would he have ever imagined that Rory would be so damn open and honest about how much she wanted him. As he dropped to his knees and kissed one of her beautiful smooth cheeks, he realized that Rory was his. He didn't need this bullshit deal to keep her in his arms, not if she was this desperate to have him. She obviously wanted-

"Hurry, Connor," Rory demanded with a little wiggle of her ass that had him grinning like a fool as he pressed a kiss to the other cheek.

"What's the rush, baby?" he asked, loving how desperate she was for him.

"Does it really matter?" she demanded with a groan, shaking her ass enticingly once again to get his attention right back where it should be.

Did it really matter? he wondered as he tilted his head just enough so that he could lean forward and press a kiss against the moist pouty lips that her position revealed to him. He tried to force himself to be content with that and give her what she obviously craved, a hard, fast fuck when she let out a throaty moan that had his cock jerking and his mouth watering for a real taste.

"More," Rory said, sounding a little desperate as she spread her legs further and arched her hips to the perfect angle, baring more of herself to him.

He moved to give her what they both wanted when a thought had him pulling back. As much as he'd love to take her like this, and he would damn well be taking her like this one day, today was not that day. Her arm and ribs were still sore and leaning like that against the counter while they made love probably wouldn't feel too good and he definitely wanted her to feel good.

"Wait!" Rory rushed out, gesturing for him to put her back down mere seconds after he scooped her up into his arms and headed for the door. "What are you doing? I need really quick, hot sex!" she whined adorably.

"And that's exactly what you'll get," he promised as he carried her into his room and headed to the bed.

Like most men, he enjoyed sex, at least the act, but it had always been straightforward with him and always in a bed. Even when he was a kid trying to work Rory out of his system, he'd preferred a bed. He'd sneak into the girl's room or sneak her into his. His sex life had never been kinky or adventurous and he'd never really cared enough to change that.

Plenty of the women over the years had complained that he wasn't as in to sex as they were. They'd bitched, cried, and did everything imaginable to turn him inside out and make him wild between the sheets. Their attempts only made him realize that things weren't going to work out that much faster. For years, he'd wished that he'd been able to give a woman more, be there for her and want her so damn much that he'd thought he'd die if he didn't have her, but that never happened.

Until now that is.

Right now he wanted to drag Rory back into the bathroom, bend her back over the sink and fuck her until his legs gave out and when they collapsed on the floor he wanted to do it again. He wanted to take her in every room in the house, in a thousand different positions and a hundred times a day. He wanted her, needed her, and he'd be damned if he was ever going to walk away from her.

He was done.

Rory James was his perfect match in every way and he'd been foolish to chalk up his feelings for her as a simple infatuation all those years ago. There was nothing simple when it came to him and Rory. They drove each other crazy in every way imaginable and he wouldn't have it any other way. He wanted her, wanted to be with her, drive her crazy for the rest of their lives and he was damn well going to do it.

As he gently laid her on the bed, he realized what he wanted from Rory, forever. He'd get it too. He was a ruthless bastard when it came to something that he wanted and he definitely wanted Rory James. It became crystal clear to him what he needed to do in order to get what he wanted as he moved between Rory's spread legs and pressed a kiss against her hip.

He was going to marry her.

Acknowledging the fact that he wanted to marry her didn't faze him in the slightest, because he realized that he was still in love with her and that fucking terrified him. For a long time he'd hoped, prayed really, that he'd find a woman that could make him happy, make him feel whole and now that he'd found her, he felt oddly terrified and hopeful.

Terrified because this was Rory James he was talking about here and he would definitely have to sleep with one eye open for the rest of his life if he married her, but it would be worth it. She was worth it. They could have a good life together, not perfect, but good. He knew that he'd piss her off a lot along the way, but that was okay because he knew Rory wouldn't hesitate to reach for her pliers.

The only problem as far as he could tell was this little deal of theirs. It had to go. Things hadn't gone exactly as planned, but he was pleased with the results nonetheless. Rory was in his bed, in his life and it was damn well going to stay that way. He still planned on taking over her company, but he'd do it as her husband now. He'd handle running the sites and she could manage the office or whatever it was that she wanted to do.

First though, he needed to get this deal of theirs out of the way so that he could make his next move, making this permanent. He didn't want to hide behind this deal, didn't need to, he realized. Rory wanted and needed him just as badly as he needed her. Once the deal was off the table, she'd realize that and probably be just as relieved as he was not to have to hide the way she felt any longer.

"If you don't hurry up, I'm going to have to kill you," she warned him, panting hard and making him smile as his suspicions were confirmed.

She definitely wanted him.

"You'd miss me," he said, teasingly as he pressed one last kiss against her hip and moved to cover her with his body.

"Not this time. My aim's getting better," she said, wrapping her arms around his shoulders, pulling him closer.

He chuckled as he settled himself between her legs, loving the way she loosely wrapped her legs around him, ready to keep him locked in place. "And what exactly would you do without me around to brighten up your day?" he asked, leaning down to kiss her as he shifted until he felt the tip of his cock slide over her clit and come to rest at her wet entrance.

"Probably lead a fuller, more productive life and maybe get a hobby or something," she said, moaning softly as she tilted her hips only to bring them right down, taking the tip of his cock inside the hot wet core that he planned on worshipping for the rest of the night.

"You'd die of boredom if I wasn't around," he pointed out.

She laughed softly as she moved her good hand to cup his jaw. "Probably."

"You like being with me? " he found himself asking as he slowly slid inside her, taking his time and watching as she arched her back, licking her lips as she moaned, "More."

He wanted to do just that, needed to do it, but somehow he found the willpower to stop halfway inside her and ask again, "Do you like being with me, Rory?"

"Less talking, more sex," she groaned, cupping the back of his head and trying to pull him down for a kiss, but he refused to be distracted. He wanted to hear her say it.

"Do you like being with me, Rory?" he demanded softly as he looked down into her beautiful blue eyes.

"Do you want me to kill you, Connor?" she demanded, sighing in annoyance as she rolled her hips up to force more of his shaft to slide inside her.

He allowed himself one slow thrust before he pulled back and forced himself to focus, further pissing her off.

"Connor!"

"Answer me," he gritted out, wondering why she was being so damn stubborn at a time like this.

She glared up at him for a moment before she snapped, "I forgot what you asked, you psychotic bastard!"

"Would you like me to refresh your memory?" he asked, smiling as he leaned down and kissed her.

"If it gets you to move your ass!" she muttered against his lips with a pout.

He pressed one last kiss against her lips before he pulled back just far enough away so that he could look into her eyes as he softly asked, "Do you like being with me?"

"Oh my God, that's why you're denying me sex?" she demanded, letting out a frustrated groan as she once again tried to roll her hips to entice him, but he was ready for the move and pulled back just enough to keep her attention.

"Yes, and if you want sex then you're going to answer me," he explained, looking down into her beautiful eyes as they glared back up at him with murderous intent.

For a moment she simply laid there, glaring up at him and he didn't need to ask to know that she was calculating the odds of him doing what she wanted without telling him the truth. He knew the second that she came to the conclusion that the odds weren't very good. The glare disappeared as she slowly exhaled, reaching up and cupping his jaw as she admitted, "Yes, I like spending time with you, but I still hate you. Does that make you happy?"

"You hate me?" he demanded, narrowing his eyes on her as he pulled back until just the very tip of his cock was inside her.

She let out a frustrated groan before she snapped, "Fine! I don't hate you as much as I used to! Are you happy now?"

"Extremely," he said, grinning as he leaned down to kiss her.

"Are you going to tell me why it was so damn important that you had to interrupt sex time for that?" she mumbled against his lips as he slowly sank back inside her.

If he hadn't been so damn distracted by the feel of her hot, wet sheath wrapping around him as he slid back inside of her and so damn happy that she'd admitted that she liked being around him, he probably wouldn't have fucked up and told her the truth.

"Because I'm in love with you, Rory."

Yeah, he was a fucking moron.

"Baby, please calm down," Connor pleaded, tightening his hold on her.

"Let me go!"

"Not until you hear me out."

"I don't want to hear you out, you lying, life-ruining bastard! I hate you, you asshole!" she barely managed to get out through the sobs.

For a moment he didn't say anything and she was thankful for that, but even happier when he finally released her. She quickly stepped away from him and headed for the bathroom door and her escape when his next words stopped her short.

"I'm sorry about that night, Rory. I'm sorry for so many fucking things," he said, his voice hoarse.

"You shouldn't have come that night," she said tightly, forcing herself to face him.

"I regret a lot of things about that night, but I don't regret that," he said, meeting her glare with a hard glare of his own.

"You ruined my life that night," she said quietly, not bothering to wipe the tears away as they streamed down her cheeks.

"I know."

"If you hadn't come that night-"

"You would have had to deal with something far worse than losing your scholarship, Rory," Connor said, cutting her off.

Frowning, she asked, "What the hell are you talking about?"

For a moment he only looked at her and just when she thought that she was finally about to get her answers after all these years, he shook his head and moved to step past her. "Ask your brothers."

No, he was not about to do this to her on top of everything else. They were going to finish this tonight.

"I'm asking you, Connor," she said, stepping in front of him and blocking his path.

"It would be better if it came from one of your brothers," he said, trying to step past her, but she was done playing this game with him.

"It would be better if it came from you and while you're at it, you can tell me why you followed me up there in the first place," she demanded, making it clear that she wasn't moving until he finally gave her the answers that she'd been waiting years for.

"Are you sure that you want to hear this?" he asked, leaning his hip against the sink counter as he waited.

"Yes," she said with absolutely no hesitation. She desperately wanted to know what happened that night, why he was there and why he couldn't just leave her the hell -

"I came up there to talk to you about something, but when I got there you were already the life of the party. For weeks, months really I'd been trying to work up the courage to talk to you, but the moment that I saw you, I lost my nerve," he admitted with a small rueful smile.

"What did you come to talk to me about?" she found herself asking as she leaned back against the door.

"I sat back, not sure what to do," he said, continuing with his story and for the moment she allowed it. "I hung back for a few hours, trying to work up the nerve to approach you," he explained, surprising her. Since when was he nervous about talking to her?

"Just when I decided to put it off, I saw you stumble across the dance floor. It was more than obvious that you were drunk. The guy that you were with had definitely figured that out," Connor ground out, suddenly looking pissed. "I hung out for another minute, hoping that your brothers would step in, but none of them did. So, when the asshole dragged you, stumbling and giggling out the backdoor, I followed."

"I don't really remember any of this," she admitted, frowning as she struggled to remember something, anything about that part of the night, but it was useless.

"I'm not surprised, Rory. You were pretty wasted by that point. You couldn't even walk without help," Connor explained as she noticed for the first time since this whole thing started that he'd pulled on a pair of jeans, but had left them unbuttoned, that along with his casual pose and mussed hair made him look sweet and sexy. He certainly didn't look like a life-ruining bastard or someone who enjoyed screwing around with someone's heart.

"Get to the point," she said, needing to hear how he'd ruined her life so that she could build up a defense around her heart and hate him so that this pain would end.

Connor looked away, his jaw clenched tightly as he said, "By the time I got out to the alleyway, the asshole was trying to shove you down behind the dumpster."

"H-he didn't," she said, stopping to wet her suddenly dry lips when the words refused to leave her mouth. It didn't matter if she remembered it or not. Knowing that some guy had hurt her like that would be difficult to get over. As she waited for his answer, she prayed that Connor had gotten there in time. Please let him have gotten there in time, she hoped as dread coiled in her stomach.

"He didn't have a chance to hurt you, Rory. I promise you that he didn't hurt you," he said softly, but wouldn't look at her.

"What aren't you telling me?" she demanded, afraid that he was lying to protect her from the truth.

"There's nothing else to tell, Rory. You know the rest," he said, shaking his head as he pushed away from the counter and moved to step past her, but she wasn't ready to drop this.

"No, I don't," she said, planting her good hand against his chest, stopping him from ending this conversation before she got the rest of her answers.

"He pulled a knife. We ended up in jail. Case closed, end of story, let it go," he said firmly, gently pushing her hand away and this time he managed to walk away from her and was halfway to his bedroom door when she asked, "And how did we land in jail and him in the hospital if he was the one with the knife, Connor? Huh?" she demanded, walking after him and cutting him off before he could make it to that door and walk away from her, taking the answers that she desperately wanted with him.

"How did my life get wrecked, Connor? Tell me," she demanded. When he clenched his jaw and didn't answer, she screamed it. "Tell me!"

"You wouldn't listen to me!" he snapped, grabbing her by the arms and giving her a shake, not hard enough to hurt her, but it was enough to stun her. "I told you to get your ass back in the bar, but you wouldn't listen! You should have fucking listened to me, Rory!" Another shake. "Do you have any idea how close I came to losing you that night? Do you?" he practically roared in her face as he pushed her back up against the wall and got in her face, clearly done with avoiding this subject.

"I begged you to go inside, Rory, but even drunk you're a stubborn pain in the ass!" he snapped, glaring down at her. "When that asshole pulled out a knife, you got pissed and went to punch him. I almost didn't get between you in time! Do you have any idea how close that piece of shit came to stabbing you? *Do you?*" he demanded, sounding angrier and angrier with each passing second when all she could do was stand there, desperately trying to catch her breath as his words sank in.

"How did he get stabbed, Connor?" she asked, reaching out and grabbing onto him as a wave of dizziness tore through her head with the possible knowledge that she was the reason the man ended up in the hospital having one of his kidneys removed.

"He fell on the knife when I tackled him to the ground," Connor said, his tone more gentle as his grip on her arms turned supportive.

"But in the police report he said that you'd attacked him," she mumbled, desperately trying to wrap her mind around everything he'd told her and figure out how they'd gotten off when it was the other guy who'd ended up in the hospital when there hadn't been any witnesses to back them up. She'd tried to get her hands on the police report a few times over the years, but because the case was closed and she wasn't a Canadian resident, her request had been denied.

"I know what he said, Rory, but his story didn't add up," Connor explained softly.

"What are you talking about, Connor? There were no other witnesses and he's the one that got hurt. How exactly didn't his story add up?"

Locking his eyes with hers, he gently took her good hand off his arm and placed it on the left side of his chest. When she opened her mouth to ask what he was doing, he glided her hand over his chest. It took her a moment before a small raised line registered and when it did, she shook off his hand and traced her fingers over the three-inch scar that she'd never noticed before. Not that anyone would have really had a chance to see the scar with his tattoo covering the area.

When he raised his left hand, palm out, her eyes landed on a long thin scar that ran across it. Without a word, she reached up with a shaky hand and traced the thin scar that ran across his palm that she'd always assumed was from working construction.

"Defensive wound," she said numbly as she dropped her hand to her side.

"Yes," Connor said, pushing away from the wall. When he sat down on the edge of the bed and dropped his head in his hands, it surprised her how badly she wanted to go to him.

"Why didn't you tell me?" she asked, leaning her head back and looking up at the ceiling, desperately trying not to lose it as something occurred to her.

He hadn't ruined her life.

That was all her. She'd ruined her life by getting drunk and going off with some asshole. She'd put them both in that situation and because of her, Connor had been hurt.

"There was no point in telling you, Rory. It was done."

"You were in the cell with me the next morning, Connor. How did you manage that if you were injured?" she asked, trying to find a hole in his story and instinctively knowing that she wouldn't find any. For all his faults, Connor was not a liar.

"I let them stitch me up and then left against medical advice when they wanted me to stay the night," he explained softly.

"Why?" she found herself asking even though she wasn't really sure that she could handle anything more tonight.

"I couldn't stomach the idea of you being in a jail cell like that, Rory. By the time the ambulance came, you were already having problems. I made them bring you to the hospital, but they only kept you there long enough to give you some fluids before they released you back into police custody."

"Why did my father hit you?" she asked, wondering if her father knew Connor's role in everything. She doubted it. Her father would never strike someone that protected one of his children.

"He didn't know what happened. The only thing that he knew was that I followed you to Canada and that you were arrested, facing some pretty serious charges."

"You could have corrected him on that," she said, feeling her eyes tear up once again. She hated crying, didn't want to do it, but damn Connor if he didn't have her close to crying her eyes out.

"You had enough to deal with, Rory. It was simpler for me to take the brunt of his anger."

Taking a slow, steady breath, she dropped her gaze to Connor and for the first time in years she didn't know what to feel when she looked at him. She couldn't hate him, wanted to, but she couldn't. He'd saved her, cared for her and protected her and she'd been an absolute bitch to him over the years, not that he hadn't deserved some of it, but there was no way that he'd deserved all of it.

"Why did you come after me, Connor?" she whispered, praying that he wouldn't say or do anything else that would rock her world. She really didn't know how much more she could take.

"In the top drawer," he said, tilting his head to the side so that he could watch her.

Heart pounding in her chest, she walked over to his bureau. She threw him one last look to find him sitting there with his head once again in his hands and she couldn't help but wonder just how bad this was going to be. After taking a fortifying breath, she reached up and opened the drawer.

It slid out easily, but that wasn't exactly surprising since there wasn't much inside, not much at all. In the middle of the drawer sat a small velvet jewelry box.

"What is this?" she asked, swallowing nervously as she picked it up.

"Your birthday gift, Rory."

Her hands shook so badly that she almost dropped the box, twice, but after a minute she managed to open it. Her chin trembled as she traced the tiny diamond with the tip of her finger. It was the smallest diamond ring that she'd ever seen, but it was without a doubt the most beautiful one that she'd ever laid her eyes on.

She pulled the ring out of the box for a closer look when something inside the ring caught her eye. Swallowing hard, she turned the ring over until the dim bedroom light hit the inscription just right and when it did, she almost dropped it as she read the three letters engraved on the ring.

LRJ

TWENTY-NINE

Him and his big fucking mouth.

If he'd just kept his mouth shut and his feelings for her to himself, at least for a little while longer, they wouldn't be sitting here rehashing all of this bullshit. This wasn't how he wanted her to find out. Actually, he'd never planned on telling her, but he knew the moment that he'd walked into that bathroom to face her that the choice was no longer his to make. Now she knew what a pathetic asshole he really was.

"What does LRJ stand for?" she asked softly as she knelt down in front of him.

"Little Rory James," he admitted with a sad smile, knowing that he'd truly gone and fucked up his one chance with her.

"May I?" she asked, gesturing with her broken hand to his chest. With a small nod, he leaned back and wasn't too surprised when she traced her fingers over the initials that he'd had tattooed all those years ago when he'd had a little bit too much beer and not enough common sense not to tattoo the name of a woman who hated him on his body. He'd been young and foolish and now he just felt old and stupid.

"The suites are yours, Rory," he said when he couldn't think of anything else to say.

"I know," she said softly as she continued to trace the letters, looking mesmerized by the tattoo.

"The deal's off, too," he needlessly explained, licking his lips and trying not to moan when her fingers teasingly traced over his nipple.

"Yes, it is," she said, running her fingers to the other side of his chest while he sat there, trying to remain unaffected, but it was nearly impossible with Rory touching him.

"What were you hoping to get out of this deal?" she asked, slowing her movements as she looked up and met his gaze.

"It doesn't matter," he said truthfully, because none of it mattered without her, not Strawberry Manor, his business, nothing. It might have taken him a while to figure it out, but he knew that the only thing that mattered to him was Rory. Her touches gave him hope that they might have a future, but he wasn't a fool. He'd pissed her off and she'd be justified in toying with him.

"Not going to tell me?" she asked, cocking a brow in question as she moved closer, resting her broken arm across his leg as her other hand slid up his chest and over his shoulder.

"It doesn't matter any longer, because I don't want it," he confessed, unable to stop himself from reaching up with one hand and cupping her beautiful face.

"Then what do you want?" she asked, moving closer until their lips were only a few inches apart.

"You," he simply said.

"Why?" she asked, looking a little confused.

"Because I'm in love with you, Rory," he answered, wondering if she was going to try and kick his ass for saying it again.

"You love me," she said, not asked as she leaned back, robbing him of her touch, but he let her go. What other choice did he have? He knew Rory well enough to know that if he pushed her for something that she didn't want that she'd push right back. For the first time since he met her, he was terrified of pushing her.

"Yes."

"I'm not sure how I feel about you, Connor," she admitted as she stood up and stepped away from him.

"Do you hate me?" he asked, gripping his knees as he struggled to stay where he was and not do something foolish like beg her for a chance, a chance that he probably didn't deserve, but wanted desperately.

"No," she answered, walking away from him and heading for the patio. "I need some time to figure this all out, Connor."

"Take as much time as you need. I'll be here when you're ready," he said, knowing as soon as the words left his mouth that he'd just lost her for good.

Oh, fuck that.

———

Time.

She needed time to think and sort through everything, she reminded herself as she fought the urge to run back inside and throw herself in Connor's arms. A couple of hours ago, she knew where she stood with him. It hadn't mattered that she'd been falling for him, because she'd known that she would never be able to get over what he'd done.

Now..........

Now she didn't know what to think about him. For the first time since he came into her life she didn't think that she hated him, at all, not even a little bit. Actually, she was terrified that she wasn't just falling for him anymore, but was more than a little in love with the man. Before she did anything that she might regret later, she needed to be sure that what she felt was real.

She should kick his ass for confusing her, she thought as she opened the sliding glass door and stepped in her room. Why couldn't she just hate him? It made everything so much simpler to-

"Veto," Connor said as he scooped her up in his arms, took her out of the house and placed her bottom on the patio railing before she could put up much of a protest. He settled himself between her legs just as quickly, placing his hands on her hips to steady her and hopefully stop her from falling over the side. She'd never been afraid of heights before, but after falling into that cellar and breaking her arm, she could now say that she had a very healthy respect for heights.

"Veto what?" she asked absently, reaching up with her good hand and placing it on his bicep to help steady herself as she fought against the urge to look down.

"Space, time, a break, whatever the hell you want to call it, Rory. It's not happening. I've waited too many years to have you in my arms and I'm not about to let you go over some bullshit."

"Wait a minute," she said, frowning up at him as his words registered in her mind. "You can't veto a break!"

"Yes, I can," he said, leaning in and brushing his lips over hers in that soft, fleeting gesture that she both loved and hated. Loved, because it made her feel precious and hated because those kisses always left her wanting more, a lot more.

"Since when?" she demanded, resisting the urge to hit him with her cast when he pulled his mouth away.

"Since now, Rory. You're not allowed to run away, because you're too afraid to face what's going on between us."

"I'm not afraid of anything," she said evenly, using the same response that she'd used when they were kids and he tried to taunt her into doing something asinine, kind of like now.

Taking a chance, a real chance, on him was a huge risk not only because they could wind up killing each other, but if things didn't work out between them, which was a real possibility given their history, she could wind up hating him for breaking her heart. This was a really bad idea, she berated herself inwardly as she looked into his beautiful emerald eyes and worried her bottom lip between her teeth. She should just push him away and end things right now before she got in over her head, but really, when had she ever done the smart thing when it came to Connor?

"I don't think this is such a good idea," she said, needing to at least pretend to show good judgment and think it over, but unfortunately common sense and good judgment were usually never around when it came to Connor. At least this time she wouldn't have to worry about ending up in jail.

"I think it's a great idea," he said, pressing a kiss against her forehead before he leaned back and focused all of his attention on her broken hand. When he gingerly picked up her hand and pressed something onto her ring finger, she couldn't help but frown as she looked down, but between his head and the lack of decent light, she couldn't see much.

"Um, what the hell are you doing?" she asked when she felt him slide something onto her finger.

"Nothing much. Just decided that you and I are getting married that's all," he announced with a careless shrug of his shoulders as he turned his head and pressed a swift kiss against her stunned lips.

"I'm sorry, what's this now?" she demanded, sure that she'd misheard him.

"I'm thinking a November wedding. It will give you plenty of time to plan it and get used to the idea," he explained as if it wasn't a big deal when it was a very big freaking deal.

"I can't marry you, Connor," she blurted out, really not knowing what else to say and wishing that she'd said it with a little more finesse. Then again, she should have known that Connor wouldn't take it personally.

"Yes, you can. All you have to do is show up, sign the license, and say 'I do'" he mused as he leaned in to steal another kiss.

"No, I can't," she said, stubbornly, leaning back away from him, but it wasn't all that far considering that he had her sitting on a narrow banister.

"I tell you what, Rory," he said, wrapping his arms around her and pulling her close until she had no other choice but to put her hands on his shoulders to help support herself and when she did, her breath caught in her throat as her eyes landed on that tiny diamond decorating her finger.

It was so beautiful.

"You give me until November to prove that we belong together and if you still don't want to marry me by the time the manor is done then we'll call it off."

"Oh?" she asked distractedly as she grudgingly accepted the fact that she never wanted to take the ring off her finger. "And how exactly do you plan on convincing me to marry you?"

"I plan on making you fall in love with me, Rory," he said softly as he leaned in and kissed her in a way that wasn't fair.

"Wear the ring and if you don't fall in love with me by November then we can call the whole thing off and I'll never bother you again," he swore against her lips.

After more than two decades of being tormented by this man, the idea of never seeing him again should make her happy, but it didn't. She honestly didn't know how she would function without him in her life. But she wasn't sure if she was ready to promise him forever.

Everything in her world had changed in such a short period of time that she didn't know if she was coming or going. The smart thing would be to put some space between them and ignore his veto, but she didn't want to do that.

"You really think that you can make me fall in love with you in less than five months?" she asked, trying not to smile and failing miserably when she felt his lips kick up into that grin that she loved.

"I know that I can," he promised as he stepped away from her only to scoop her up in his arms, turn and head for her bedroom, but he didn't get far.

"It's been more than ten minutes," Trevor announced as he leaned back against the doorframe, startling Connor, but thankfully he didn't drop her and she truly appreciated that.

"And we're hungry!" Jason yelled from what sounded like her bathroom.

"Who the hell are you?" Connor demanded as he stood his ground, holding her tightly in his arms as he glared at her cousin as if the man didn't have several inches and fifty pounds of muscle on him.

Trevor's curious expression turned amused when his eyes zeroed in on her left hand. "Oh, by the looks of it, I would say one of your future in-laws."

THIRTY

"Why are you glaring at me?" Rory asked, giving him a sweet, too sweet, smile as the two men, no correction, his future in-laws from hell periodically sent him killing glares as they tore through his kitchen and ate every last morsel of food.

"Tell me that you didn't break the ban, Rory. Tell me that there aren't two Bradfords beating the shit out of each other over the last slice of cheese in my kitchen," he pleaded, already knowing and dreading the answer.

It had been a good fifteen years since he'd last seen a Bradford, but that was one experience that he would never forget. He'd been sixteen, pissed and looking for a little revenge against Rory for the bullshit she'd pulled on him the night before at the drive-in. Normally, he would have waited until she came home from her family's annual summer vacation, but that day he'd refused to wait to get his revenge. Well, that and his sixteen-year-old hormone-driven mind was hoping to see Rory in a bathing suit.

It was the latter that had him climbing into the back of Mr. James' truck and hiding beneath a pile of gym bags in ninety degree weather, risking an ass whooping by the James boys if he'd been caught. Somehow he'd managed to make it to their destination without getting caught or passing out from the heat. As soon as he felt the truck come to a stop and heard Mr. James order his kids to unload the truck, he'd jumped out and darted across the rocky makeshift dirt parking lot and dove into what unfortunately had turned out to be a bush concealing a large briar patch.

Once he'd managed to untangle himself from the thorns, he'd followed after Rory, who'd trailed behind her brothers. It pissed him off that her brothers hadn't bothered to even offer to carry her bag for her and he'd made it a point to get back at them later that night with poison ivy stuffed in their bags. He'd trailed after them in the woods until they came to a small clearing by the pond. While they'd set up camp, he went and found himself a little hiding spot. Once that was done, he came back only to get the surprise of a lifetime.

The once peaceful campsite was filled with men, very large men and everywhere he'd looked there was food, massive piles of it. The tents weren't even set up, but they had tables set up with food everywhere. None of them, not even what he'd suspected should have been little boys, were small. He'd always thought that the James boys were freakishly large, but the men that were beating the shit out of each other over food had been so much larger. Most every single one of them had been shirtless and all had been buff, which had made him feel scrawny and made him wonder if Rory thought he was scrawny.

Even though he'd never met them before, he knew that they were Bradfords. The tales of the other side of Rory's family were well known. They were often used to scare little children into behaving. If they didn't, they knew the Bradfords would come and eat them. He was ashamed to admit that it had worked on him when he was a kid. He'd even been warned away from Rory by the other kids on his first day of preschool. They'd known who Rory was. They'd been warned away from her because of the Bradfords and because her brothers would beat up anyone that messed with her, but he hadn't cared. She'd been the prettiest little girl that he'd ever seen and he just had to push her and pull on her pigtails.

"Look, if you expect us to get in a decent day's work then you're going to have to feed us more than scraps," the larger of the two men said as he tossed an empty cereal box on the counter with the rest of the empty packages.

"Scraps?" he repeated numbly. "The kitchen was full of food not even twenty minutes ago!"

"That was twenty minutes ago," the other one said with a shrug as he pressed a hand against his stomach and headed for the door.

"Learn to keep up with the times, Roomie," the larger one said with a mocking smile and a wink as he headed for the door, leaving Connor to process what he'd just said and when he did, he turned a glare back on Rory.

"What exactly does he mean by 'Roomie'?" he demanded as Rory gave him another cute smile that set off warning signals in his head.

"Well, while you were grabbing a shirt we talked it over and decided that it would probably be better if Trevor and Jason stayed with you," she explained, looking at him, but not quite meeting his eyes.

"Why is that exactly?" he asked with his jaw set and his hands clenched tightly into fists as he patiently waited for the woman that he loved to explain why she'd just screwed him over.

"If they stay with me, everyone will figure out who they are and we'll lose the extra help."

"And we'll also face a night in jail, a large fine and community service," he said, dryly, noting her wince.

"I'd actually forgotten about the community service part," she admitted with a frown, but it quickly disappeared as she waved off what he'd said. "Don't worry about it. No one is going to figure out who they are. We'll get the help we need and everything will be fine."

He cocked a brow as he looked pointedly around his now barren kitchen. "How exactly do you propose that we hide this little problem of theirs?"

She worried her bottom lip as she followed his gaze. "It will be fine," she said, but she didn't sound like she believed it. "We'll just keep both houses filled with food and avoid taking them out to eat in public. As long as they don't get hungry, we should be fine."

"How exactly do you propose keeping one Bradford, never mind two, full?"

Her answering smile nearly undid him, but her next words had him cursing up a storm.

"Sam's Club."

"So, you think you're good enough for my cousin?" Jason asked, off-handedly as Connor pulled his truck into the parking spot of the wholesale food store, wondering how Rory had managed to talk him into this bullshit.

He remembered putting his foot down and telling her that there was no way in hell that he was going to harbor Bradfords when the kissing started. He barely remembered the rest of their conversation, but he definitely remembered the way she yanked his mouth down to hers and kissed him until he forgot about her cousins, his empty refrigerator and everything else that no longer mattered. He would have made love to her on his kitchen table if the bastard sitting next to him hadn't stormed back into the house and demanded that they feed him.

"Yes," he answered, deciding to be honest and noting twin looks of surprise on her cousins' faces. No doubt they thought he was going to give them a kiss ass answer, but he didn't play those games and never would.

"Why exactly is that?" Trevor, the larger of the two, asked, looking seriously pissed off by Connor's answer. Well, that was too fucking bad, because it was true.

"Because I piss her off," he said with a shrug, shutting the engine down and grabbing the keys.

Instead of getting angry and tearing into him like any sane relative would have done, her cousins' glares turned into shit-eating grins. They shared a quick look, nodded and focused back on him, which was kind of unnerving and he really wished that they'd ridden with Rory instead. They'd insisted on riding with him and he'd just assumed that they were going to try and kill him. He'd been fine with that, expected it even.

"You're that scrawny kid that crashed our family reunion, aren't you?" Trevor asked, chuckling as he leaned forward and rested his elbows on his knees while he considered Connor.

"I wasn't scrawny," he bit out tightly.

Jason shrugged. "Compared to us you were."

"Point taken," he sighed with a nod.

"You know, you were lucky that Grandma Beth showed up when she did, don't you?" Trevor asked, and Connor couldn't help but wonder if either one of these men was one of the large boys that had been ready to tear him apart with their bare hands all those years ago. A couple of them had managed to get in a few good punches before this sweet little old woman put an end to it. She'd swatted the much larger boys away and even demanded that they help him to his feet. Of course when the boys explained why they'd wanted to kill him, the sweet little woman reached up, grabbed him by the ear, twisted it and dragged him the half mile back to their campsite where Mr. James and a very pissed off and embarrassed Rory were waiting.

By the time she'd released his ear, it had been numb, but at least he'd managed to tell his side of the story. It had probably stopped Mr. James from killing him, but it hadn't stopped the man from grabbing a few of his large relatives and hunting down the real culprits. They hadn't believed that he wasn't the one spying on Rory as she'd changed out of her bathing suit. When he'd showed them that his hands were bloody and raw from beating the shit out of the two men that he'd caught watching her, they'd believed him.

"You really should have told us why you were there," Jason said around a bored yawn. "We probably wouldn't have made you cry like that if we had."

"I wasn't crying, asshole!" he snapped back, still pissed after all these years about those ten hours he'd been forced to wait at the campsite while every single Bradford and James taunted him for crying.

"Really? Then why were tears streaming down your face?" Trevor asked as his attention went to searching the glove compartment for something to eat.

"Because one of you dumb bastards shoved my head in the pond! That was pond water streaming down my face!"

"Are you sure? Because I could have sworn that I heard you sobbing," Trevor said, letting out a disappointed sigh when he didn't find anything to eat in the glove compartment.

"That's what it sounded like to me," Jason agreed, gesturing for Trevor to get out of the truck.

"I was embarrassed for you," Trevor admitted, his tone laced with pity as he opened the door and jumped out.

"I wasn't sobbing, you asshole! I was choking on the slimy pond water one of you forced down my throat!"

"Wow, this is just getting sad," Jason said, shaking his head in disgust as he followed after his cousin. Before Connor could tell both men where they could go, Jason shut the door and headed for the warehouse club, leaving Connor to curse and move his ass as he resigned himself to spending a night in jail.

———

"Hands off, woman!" Trevor demanded, but she ignored him as she shoved him back against the brick wall. She threw a warning glare at Jason as he tried to step away and head for the warehouse that promised unlimited free samples.

She pointed her finger from one man to the other as she leveled a hard glare on them. "I am not going to jail for the two of you so listen up and listen good. You are only allowed to hit each sample cart ten times and that's it."

"*You bitch!*" Trevor and Jason gasped in outrage.

Ignoring them, she continued. "And while we're at it, let's get to the other rules."

"Rules?" Trevor repeated slowly, eyes narrowing to slits on her.

"You are not allowed to eat in any of the restaurants in town or within twenty miles of the town unless I am there with you." At that announcement, Jason's eyes narrowed dangerously on her. "Also, you are not to buy anything that requires you to show your driver's license. If you hit the grocery store, you're each limited to one carriage full of food. You can order in, but you're only allowed to order enough for six people."

"I've always hated you," Jason bit out in a huff as he turned his back on her and headed for the double doors of the warehouse.

"Ditto," Trevor said even as he threw his arm around her shoulders and gave her a reassuring squeeze, or a warning, she wasn't sure which. The warning wouldn't exactly surprise her since she'd basically just put them on a strict diet.

As they walked through the double doors, she pulled her club membership card out of her pocket, hoping against hope that the ban the manager threatened them with seven months ago had only been a warning. She really hoped it was, otherwise they were going to have problems keeping her cousins fed enough to follow her rules.

She really didn't want to spend another night in jail.

"Good evening and welcome to Sam's Club. Can I see your card please?" the smiling greeter holding the clipboard asked as they approached the entrance.

"Of course," she said, making sure to give the man a flirty smile, praying that he just gave her card a quick glance and let them be on their way.

Before she could hand her card over, a large tan hand covered her good hand and stopped her.

"They're with me," Connor said, holding her hand by his side as he handed over his card.

"You folks have a good evening," the greeter said, still smiling as he handed Connor's card back.

"You too," Connor said, giving her hand a slight tug, effectively pulling her away from Trevor's side so that she was walking with him. She heard her cousin's amused chuckle, but ignored it as she walked with Connor to the row of oversized carriages.

Once she was sure that they were out of earshot of the greeter, she asked, "What was that all about?"

Connor let out a long suffering sigh as he pulled a carriage loose. "You're banned, Rory."

"I know that, but so are you, so what the hell was that all about?" she asked, giving him a gentle shove out of the way and stealing his carriage.

"I didn't get banned, baby," he said, swooping in and giving her a swift kiss as he deftly stole the carriage back, "only you did."

"How is that possible?" she demanded, gesturing wildly towards the automotive department. "You were the one that started it!"

His answering chuckle as he walked away had her contemplating running him down with a carriage for old time's sake.

"You got banned from a warehouse?" Trevor asked, coming up to her right side as Jason joined her on the left.

"What kind of loser gets banned from a warehouse?"

THIRTY-ONE

"**O**w! Stop hitting us!" Trevor snapped, grabbing Jason and shoving him towards the slaphappy Rory as the woman let loose on the men that had turned her yearlong ban into a lifetime ban in less than twenty minutes.

"How many samples did I tell you that you could have?" she demanded as she moved to kick Jason in the shin, but before she could make contact, Connor had her in his arms and over his shoulder. That didn't seem to slow her down, not at all.

"How many?" she demanded when her cousins didn't answer her fast enough.

"Ten," they muttered sheepishly.

"And how many did you take?"

The men muttered their answers. Not that it mattered. Rory was too busy flipping out to actually listen to them. "You scared the hell out of everyone in that warehouse! You made men and women cry and run screaming for their lives! And thanks to you, my photo now hangs in front of the building next to the Recall Notice board, you greedy bastards!"

"Hey! It's not our fault that those samples were so damn yummy!" Jason snapped back.

"We wouldn't have had any problems if they hadn't been so fucking cheap with the portions!" Trevor added.

"That's it. Put me down. I'm going to kill them," Rory demanded as she struggled to escape from his hold, but he'd been prepared for her escape attempt and kept his arm firmly locked around her.

He looked past the two pouting men towards the front of the warehouse where the manager and about twenty employees stood on the sidewalk, watching them warily. No doubt they'd already called the police. Not that he could blame them, but he really didn't want to deal with having to tackle Rory when she went for the cop's nightstick so that she could beat the shit out of her cousins.

"Listen," he said, pulling his keys out of his pocket and tossing them to Jason. "There's an all you can eat buffet about thirty-five miles from here."

The two men's pouts instantly disappeared as a predatory gleam took over. "We're listening," Trevor said, intently focusing on him.

"It's in Haverville. There's a map book in the truck. The restaurant is on Copper Street. They close at one in the morning so that should hold you over and keep you out of trouble." Rory snorted at that announcement, not that he could blame her.

"Let yourselves into the house and be ready to work your asses off by five," he said, determined to keep her cousins busy and out of his way.

He wasn't an idiot. He knew why they were here. They were definitely here to help them with Strawberry Manor, but he knew that he was the main reason for their presence. It wasn't difficult to guess that her brothers were behind this one. They probably thought their cousins would manage to scare him off. They wouldn't, but he appreciated the effort.

That didn't mean that he'd put up with this bullshit. He'd keep her cousins busy with work and food so that they didn't come between him and Rory. He had less than five months to convince Rory to spend the rest of her life with him and he wasn't about to let anyone fuck that up for him.

"Put me down, Connor. I need to kick their asses!" Rory snapped, but he simply ignored her as he headed for her Jeep.

"You can kick their asses later, Rory. Right now we have to get out of here before the cops show up," he said, placing her on her feet and stealing her keys out of her pocket. He had the door open and her inside before she could put up much of a fight. Not that he'd expected her to put up much a fight, not with the police on the way. They'd been in this situation enough times to know that it was time to haul ass.

"Fine," she said, sounding tired as she buckled up. "Can we please stop for a cup of hot chocolate before we head home?"

"That's a good idea," he said, not mentioning that he'd already planned on doing just that.

To be honest, he was exhausted as well. It had been a very long night and it was barely eight-thirty. All he wanted to do was enjoy this quiet time with Rory, steal her hot cocoa and hold her in his arms for the rest of the night, but he knew that the night wasn't over quite yet. There were a few things that they needed to clear up before any misunderstandings formed and screwed with his plans to make Rory his wife.

Keeping his eyes on the road, he reached over and carefully took Rory's broken hand into his. When he felt his ring on her finger he couldn't help but smile. It had been a long time coming and to be honest, he'd never really expected this day to come. Granted, he had to earn her agreement to marry him, but he would. Now that he knew that she cared about him, nothing was going to stop him, not even the stubborn woman that he loved.

"We'll move your stuff into my room tomorrow night," he said quietly, hoping that she was too tired and exhausted from the hell her cousins had put her through to catch what he'd said, but of course this wasn't going to be easy.

"Why would I do that?" Rory asked, pulling her hand away from his so that she could toy with her new ring.

"I just thought it would be easier," he said offhandedly as he took a right on Oak Street.

"Why would that be easier?"

"I just thought it would be easier if you started to move in with me now. That way we wouldn't have to worry about moving you out and selling your house after we get married," he calmly explained as he pulled into Brennagan's parking lot.

"Ah, I'm not selling my house, Connor and I'm not moving in with you," Rory stubbornly argued.

"Rory," he said, sighing heavily as he shut the Jeep down, "keeping two houses after we get married doesn't make sense. I suppose we could rent it out, but that's a pain in the ass."

"I love my house, Connor. I'm not selling it," Rory said, shooting him a glare as she threw open her door and jumped out.

He chuckled darkly as he climbed out of the truck. "I know that you don't expect me to sell my house," he said, shutting the door behind him and moving to join her on the sidewalk.

"That's exactly what I expect if you want me to marry you," Rory said with a shrug, effectively dismissing him as she headed for the small coffee shop, leaving him to trail after her as he did his best to rein in his temper.

He should sell his house?

Bullshit.

That was not happening. He'd worked his ass off for that house. He'd taken on extra jobs to pay for it and to fix it up. Did she have any idea how hard he'd worked to restore his house? She'd had help, he hadn't. He'd worked his ass off and he wasn't about to sell his house. But, for now, he'd drop it. There was plenty of time to deal with the simple misunderstanding after they were married. Right now it was more important that he convince her to take a chance on him and if that meant biting his lip and keeping his mouth shut until she was his, then that's exactly what he was going to have to do.

———

"Large hot chocolate?" Beth, the senior barista, asked as Rory stepped up to the counter.

"Make it an extra-large please," Rory said, pulling a ten-dollar bill out of her pocket and tossing it on the counter. "I'll be right back," she said, fighting back a yawn as she headed for the bathroom.

As soon as she got home, she was going straight to bed. She'd deal with Connor and her cousins tomorrow. Normally she'd be worried that her cousins were hitting a buffet so close to home, but tonight she just didn't have the energy to care. She'd worry about how she was going to keep them in line tomorrow. Tonight she was-

"Oh my God, did you hear the news?" a vaguely familiar feminine voice asked, sounding excited and drawing Rory's attention as she went to push open the women's bathroom door. She looked down the small hallway and realized that she was alone and that she was hearing a private conversation coming from the manager's office behind her. Deciding that it was none of her business and that she really didn't care about the latest town gossip, she moved to open the bathroom door when the next words stopped her dead in her tracks.

"Connor proposed to Rory!" the excited woman practically squealed, making Rory cringe as her eyes shot down to the ring on her finger. She should have taken it off before she went out. She softly cursed when she realized that her father and brothers had probably already heard the news. That was just great.

"No, he didn't," a voice that she knew all too well said, laughing off the news.

Cindy, one of the most annoying women in town and was unfortunately the manager of this place. Not because she had a degree, had experience or had worked her way up to the position. Cindy became the manager of the best coffee shop in the area for one very simple reason. She'd screwed old man Webster.

Rumor had it that old man Webster called Cindy into his office on her very first day, within the very first hour, because customers and staff alike had complained about her attitude and inability to get off her ass and do anything. As soon as old man Webster finished firing her, Cindy started negotiations to keep her job and kept it up until Mr. Webster stumbled out of his office a half hour later, smiling and looking more relaxed than he had in years. Cindy walked out of the office looking smug and still very much employed. A year later, Cindy was the manager and still hadn't served a single cup of coffee and Mr. Webster no longer bothered coming to the coffee shop since Cindy had started making house calls. Normally she didn't pay attention to rumors, but a few years ago she'd walked in on Cindy giving the owner of the Donut Shack a reason to smile.

"Megan called and told me that she saw Connor and Rory at Sam's Club and that Rory was wearing this really tiny diamond engagement ring."

"So?" Cindy demanded with what sounded like a sneer.

"So? So, everyone knows that she's been dating Connor! What do you mean by so? This is huge! It's also so sweet!" the other women gushed. "Don't you think it's sweet? I wonder how long they've been in love."

Cindy let out an indelicate snort as she demanded, "And what makes you think that they're in love?"

"How could you miss the way he looks at her?" the other woman asked, sounding confused.

"Oh, and just how does he look at her?" Cindy demanded, mockingly.

There was a slight pause before the other woman answered, "Like she's everything that he'd ever dreamed of and he can't quite believe she's real."

"Oh my god, you've been reading too many of those romance novels! He doesn't look at her like she's anything special!"

"You're the only one that doesn't see it then."

"Really? Then if he loves her so damn much then why did he fuck me last week?" Cindy demanded.

Rory stood there for another moment, feeling numb and barely registering the rest of the private conversation as her mind worked through everything she'd heard. When she settled on a decision, she turned around and walked back down the hall to confront Connor.

———

When he saw Rory walk out from the back hall, looking determined and pissed he knew that he was in deep shit. That was confirmed when Rory ignored the cashier trying to hand over an extra-large hot cocoa and headed for the door, not even looking at him as she passed him.

"Great," he muttered, sighing heavily as he walked over to the counter and took the hot cocoa from the stunned cashier, who was probably wondering if hell had frozen over. Everyone in town knew that hot cocoa was Rory's weakness and as far as he knew, she'd never passed up a cup.

He couldn't exactly say that he was surprised to find Rory waiting for him when he stepped outside. They'd been playing this game for over twenty years so he knew by now what to expect when Rory was pissed at him and she was damn well pissed at him. That little murderous glare that she shot him as she gestured for him to follow her told him everything that he needed to know.

She didn't wait to make sure that he'd follow her as she walked over to her Jeep, climbed in the driver's side and slammed the door shut behind her. Any sane man would probably walk the ten miles home instead of facing this woman's wrath, but he was in love with this woman so that pretty much negated the sane part, at least for the moment.

Resigning himself to whatever Rory had in store for him, he took a sip of her cocoa, walked over to the truck and climbed in. Without a word, he handed over her keys and settled back, sipping her cocoa as she started the truck and drove off. Still she didn't speak and to be honest, he was in no rush to have his ass chewed out right now. It had been a long day and an even longer night and all he wanted to do was go home, climb into bed with the cranky woman and-

"Where the hell are we going?" he asked when Rory suddenly took a right into their old high school's parking lot, their old high school that had handed them each a No-Trespass Order along with their diplomas on the day they'd graduated.

Rory didn't answer him as she drove around the back of the building and parked in the empty, dimly lit parking lot. He was in no mood to spend the night in jail and opened his mouth to tell her just that when she started to take her clothes off. Once she started to pull her pants down, he lost all ability to think, never mind talk.

"You and I are going to have a little talk, Connor, and clear a few things up before I decide whether or not to take a chance on you," Rory calmly explained as she hooked her thumbs in the sides of her panties and pulled them down, revealing chestnut curls between her legs that had his breath catching in his throat.

"Are you going to answer my questions, Connor?" Rory asked as she straddled his lap just as she finished pulling her bra off and dropped it to the side, leaving her naked and gorgeous.

When he didn't respond fast enough, she settled herself comfortably on his lap and teasingly ground her pussy down against the erection that was begging to be freed from his pants. She didn't bother asking him if he agreed again, but simply started asking her questions.

"Do you love me?" she asked, cutting right to the point, which was part of the reason that he loved this woman. She didn't play any of the bullshit games that other women played, didn't use drama to get what she wanted. Granted, she was using his dick against him at the moment, but he was fine with that.

"Yes," he hissed as Rory ground down hard on him.

"Since when?" she asked, placing her bad hand on his shoulder to steady herself as she continued to rub her pussy against him, teasing him and driving him out of his fucking mind with pleasure.

"Since the moment that I saw your father drag you into daycare, looking cute and mean as you tried to glare him down," he admitted as he placed his hands on her hips and dragged them up her sides until he was cupping her beautiful breasts. When she made no moves to stop him, he caressed her breasts as he dragged his thumbs over her nipples until they hardened.

"You really want to marry me?" she asked, moaning as she reached between them with her good hand and started working on his fly. His right hand quickly abandoned her breast to help her free his cock.

"Yes."

"Did you sleep with Cindy?" she asked, pausing with his zipper between her fingers.

"Hell no. She offered sex to get out of her bill," he explained, leaning in and pressed his lips against hers, because he felt like he would die if he didn't kiss her.

"Then you have less than five months to convince me to marry you, Connor. Don't fuck up," she said, sounding almost desperate as she struggled to yank his zipper down. It was difficult to get his fly open with her still grinding on him, but he wasn't complaining. He didn't want her to stop. It felt so fucking good, but it felt better a minute later when they managed, with a lot of yanking and pulling, to clear his fly and get his dick out.

Once it was free, Rory wasted no time in raising herself up and taking the tip inside. They both groaned as she slid down, welcoming him into her swollen, wet sheath.

"If you fuck this up, I'm gonna have to kill you," Rory swore, leaning in to kiss him.

"I'm not gonna fuck this up," he promised as he met her lips in a hungry kiss.

"Good," was the last coherent word that came out of her mouth for a while. By the time he pulled her off and positioned her on the driver's seat so that he could lick her out, she could barely manage to say his name. Even when the police showed up and banged on the window she was barely able to speak, but after she calmed down from her third orgasm he'd given her just as the shouting started and they were being read their rights, she managed to say a few colorful words that had him grinning.

He loved her too much to fuck this up. He had five months to prove to her that he was the man for her, and he was going to make them perfect.

THIRTY-TWO

July

"**A**re you still not talking to me?" Rory asked, shooting Jacob a glance as she sorted through the large pile of mail that he'd left on her desk.

"Yes."

"Are you going to tell me why?" she asked, already guessing that it was going to be another big fat "no."

For the past couple of weeks he'd been giving her the silent treatment. He only answered her when it was absolutely necessary and he made damn sure that it wasn't necessary. His mood had been sour since she'd started this thing with Connor and had only got worse when she'd been forced to call him up at three in the morning to come bail her and Connor out of jail. Grudgingly, he agreed and came down to the police station two hours later with the checkbook for petty cash. He only stayed long enough to bail her out, confirm that she was engaged and send her a glare as he stormed out of the station, leaving her to bail Connor out.

She tried to make it up to him and find out why he was so upset, but the stubborn bastard just kept on ignoring her and sending Connor glares whenever the two men were in the same room. Speaking of stubborn bastards.........

"You need to sign this so that we can have more lumber delivered," Bryce, another bastard that wasn't happy with her, demanded as he stepped into the trailer.

Word about her engagement to Connor had spread very quickly. Her family's reaction varied greatly. Her father simply called her up while Connor was arguing with the guard that had impounded her Jeep. He'd been very direct and unemotional as he asked her if the news was true. She'd been scared to death of his reaction when she'd explained that it was true. There had been a brief pause after she'd told him that she was engaged to Connor. She'd almost asked him if he'd heard her when he simply told her to make sure that she made it next Sunday for fishing and then he hung up.

Her brothers' reactions were a bit different. As soon as she'd managed to make it into work, two hours late, they'd hunted her down in her office and blocked off her exit, demanding to know if she was out of her fucking mind. Johnny went as far as to demand that she take a drug test. After a lot of arguing, a few threats to have her locked away and a few shin kicks, her brothers agreed to let it go for now and get back to work. As they walked out, a few limping, they all glared at her and she'd been fully prepared to keep Connor company in the emergency room that night, but they hadn't touched him. They only glared at him. Okay, there was that one time that Craig had to wrestle a hammer out of Brian's hand when he went to throw it at Connor, but other than that they hadn't beat the shit out of him or harmed him in any way.

The fact that they hadn't sent Connor to Intensive Care actually scared the hell out of her. Every guy that spent time with her got the warning. It used to piss her off, but now she was wondering why the guy that she'd agreed to spend the rest of her life with, if he met her conditions, hadn't received the same warning. Actually, one would think that the man that she planned on marrying would receive a more thorough warning, but so far, nothing. That could only mean that they were trying to handle this a different way and she knew exactly how they thought they were going to do that.

By having their cousins drive her and Connor out their goddamn minds.

Well, that probably was the plan, but it was failing miserably. The first week Trevor and Jason had stayed with Connor. The next week they were replaced by two of her other cousins and every week after, two fresh Bradfords showed up at Connor's door. This week the twins were staying with him. Well, they stayed in Connor's house, but not with him since Connor ended up sleeping in her bed, holding her all night. The first night he'd tried to get her to sleep in his bed with him, but having two Bradfords getting into a shouting match at two in the morning over the last jar of pickles quickly changed his mind. He hadn't brought up who was selling their house and neither had she. She was too happy to ruin it and God, was she happy.

Never in her wildest dreams would she have imagined a man treating her the way that Connor did. He was sweet, funny, attentive, and he went out of his way to make her feel special. The other night they came home after putting in a fourteen-hour day, looking forward to a quick meal, a hot shower and bed. Instead of the relaxing night that they'd hoped for they'd been greeted with a nightmare, a Bradford nightmare to be more exact. They pulled into her driveway only to find a terrified pizza delivery kid stuck up in a tree where he'd been forced to run for his life.

Not that she could really blame the kid for being scared. He had forgotten her cousins' double order of chicken tenders and honey mustard sauce back at the restaurant. It probably wouldn't have turned out so badly if the kid hadn't got lazy and offered a credit for the chicken tenders instead of going back and getting them. At that point, her cousins had been seeing red and the delivery boy was lucky that all he got was the hell scared out of him. She'd actually been pretty scared that their little secret was going to get out and that they were not only going to end up in jail, but lose the extra help that they desperately needed.

Just as the kid in the tree finally managed to pull his phone out and started to call the police, Connor climbed up the tree and snatched the phone out of the kid's hand and somehow managed to talk the kid down. Then of course her cousin Devin just had to go and make the kid cry, again, and sent him right back up the tree. It took Connor an exhausting half hour and a hundred bucks to get the kid to come back down and get him to promise not to call the cops. When Connor was done with that, he sent her cousins off to yet another buffet since Jason and Trevor had unintentionally shut down the last one.

After that, she'd been more than ready to settle for a peanut butter sandwich and bed, but they quickly discovered that her cousins had cleaned out both kitchens to hold themselves over while they'd waited for their delivery. She'd been tired, hungry and was starting to get pretty pissed that she had to run out and hit the grocery store for the second night in a row when Connor, who she knew was just as tired as she was, gave her one of those sweet kisses and told her to go take a shower and relax.

By the time she was done with her shower, dressed, and ready to go get the trip to the grocery store over with, Connor surprised her with a large hot chocolate from Brennagan's and a sandwich with all the fixings from her favorite sandwich shop. As she took her first sip of that lifesaving elixir, Connor kissed the top of her head and told her that he'd be right back, which turned out to be a bit of a lie.

She tried to wait up for him, but she'd been too tired by that point to do much of anything but lie down and once she had, she was out for the night. The next morning she was woken by Connor kissing her and the scent of hot chocolate. The kiss was sweet, but the way he took her that morning had been fast and hard and had her toes curling for the rest of the day.

It wasn't until she went downstairs to feed Bunny that she'd discovered that he'd made two runs to Sam's Club the night before and stocked both their kitchen's with food. He'd also had a word with her cousins and told them to stay the hell out of her kitchen and to get their own damn food from now on. Her cousins hadn't been happy about having to get their own snacks, but they weren't dumb enough to bitch, not with Connor providing them with the names and locations of the buffets and restaurants offering "All You Can Eat" deals.

"Oh my fucking word, you're thinking about him again? Really?" Bryce said, dragging her attention away from the man that she decided that she should have a meeting with in about an hour, a very secret and private meeting that would most likely involve her being bent over her desk with her pants around her ankles, again.

She really loved their lunchtime meetings.

"Rory? Rory!" Bryce snapped, wrecking her little fantasy. So, with a glare and a kick to the shin, she yanked the clipboard out of his hand and signed her name.

"You bitch!" Bryce gasped in pain, but she knew that he hadn't meant it. He'd beaten the crap out of enough guys who called her that for her to know that he wouldn't stand for anyone disrespecting her. She also knew that he'd feel bad once the throbbing in his foot subsided. He would apologize with a large cup of hot cocoa. Connor on the other hand…….

"Mother fucker!" Bryce shouted as he stumbled back, cupping his nose as blood poured down his chin.

"Don't you ever call her that again," Connor said evenly as he stepped in front of her and faced off with her much larger brother.

Was it wrong that this turned her on?

Probably, but damn, it was really nice to have a man love and adore her and treat her like a woman, like she needed protection. She didn't, but it was still nice all the same. She never thought the day would come when Connor's chivalrous behavior would stop annoying her and start making her smile, but here it was, she mused as she shoved him aside and went to help her brother.

"She kicked me!" Bryce said accusingly, his eyes narrowing to slits on her and if she had still been a kid, that look would have her hiding her toothbrush for a month so that he couldn't give it a "special" cleaning.

"I don't care what she did, don't fucking call her that again!" Connor shouted, grabbing a roll of paper towels off the counter and tossing it to the big baby.

"She knows that I didn't mean it," Bryce muttered as he tore off a bunch of paper towels and pressed it against his face, leaving enough of his mouth uncovered so that she could see that he was pouting. He really was a big baby.

"It's fine," she said dismissively, turning her back on her brother and ignoring him as he continued to mumble and bitch.

"No, it's not," Connor said, sending Bryce one last glare, which earned another bout of muttered whining before he turned his attention on her. As soon as his gaze landed on her, his expression softened and he smiled that sweet little smile that seemed to be reserved only for her.

"Miss me?" he asked, taking her good hand into his.

Ignoring Jacob and Bryce's twin sounds of disgust, she shook her head. "Nope, not at all," she said, lying her ass off, but before that smile of his could turn knowing, she quickly changed the subject. "What did you need?" she asked, hoping that he needed her in the office for an early "meeting."

He leaned in and pressed a quick kiss to her lips, which earned more of that damn muttering that was really starting to annoy her. "Sorry, baby, but I was actually looking for the big cry baby behind you."

"What do you need?" Bryce asked, not sounding happy at all about having to deal with Connor, which she knew that he wasn't. Not that she cared. She didn't. For the first time in her life she was truly happy.

It didn't matter that her assistant wasn't on speaking terms with her or that her brothers were up to something and were really starting to annoy her with their daily interventions. It seemed that every time her brothers tried to corner her to talk some sense into her, their plans would get screwed up by whichever cousins were staying with her at the time. The interruption was usually work based and while it pissed off her brothers, they understood that the project needed to be completed.

Sometimes they tried to hold their sad little interventions outside of work, but those all failed as well, mostly because everyone was too damn exhausted to get into an argument. It also didn't hurt that her brothers had to take turns babysitting their cousins. The few times that her brothers tried to stall their cousins into waiting to eat so that they could try and talk some sense into her hadn't ended well. Apparently they hadn't listened when their father warned them never to come between a Bradford and his food, because more than once over the past couple of weeks her brothers had learned that valuable lesson the hard way.

She was still cringing at the memory of what happened last night when her brothers tried to ambush her while she'd been snuggled up with Connor in bed, watching a movie. The twins, Reese and Darrin, warned her brothers several times that they were coming between them and a buffet, which was more than any other Bradford would have given them, but then again, the twins were both police officers so it was probably more out of habit than anything. If her brothers had listened they probably wouldn't have been dragged from her room, screaming and begging for mercy. It was more pathetic than anything, but she hadn't complained about how the twins got the job done since it left her free to snuggle in Connor's arms.

"What do you want?" Bryce asked, tossing the bloodied paper towels into the trash, his glare shifting between her and Connor.

"I need you to take over the third floor," Connor explained, stepping past her and grabbing two bottles of water out of the fridge. He handed her one before he took a sip from his bottle.

"That's your little buddy's job," Bryce said with a bit of a bite, his glare taking on a whole new meaning and for good reason.

If she thought that Andrew was lazy before then she'd been dead wrong. Over the past couple of weeks the man had given a whole new meaning to the term lazy. He was constantly late, left early most days, hung out in the parking lot every couple of hours and several times he'd been found asleep in his truck or on the site. It was also becoming painfully obvious that the man had a substance abuse problem. He'd been seen vomiting several times, having the shakes, sweating profusely after one of his many trips to the parking lot and he'd lost a great deal of weight.

Instead of firing him like any other boss would have done, Connor turned a blind eye to his best friend's downward spiral. They'd actually gotten into a few arguments over it, but no matter what she'd said, Connor wouldn't fire his friend. The only concession that he was willing to give her was that Andrew would not be touching any power tools. It wasn't much and she wasn't happy about it, but she'd take it.

For now.

The moment that Andrew became a danger he was gone. She didn't care if he worked for her or not. She was not about to put her men in danger to make Connor happy. As much as she cared about him, and she knew that she was in love with him, she couldn't keep turning a blind eye to this situation. She was very much afraid that Andrew was going to end up killing himself and she was terrified that it would destroy Connor. It didn't matter that she didn't particularly like Andrew, she loved Connor and this situation was hurting him. She could see it in his face every time he watched Andrew stumble, drop something or head for the parking lot.

"And now it's yours," Connor said, his tone hard, leaving no doubt in her mind that it wasn't up for discussion. Bryce seemed to pick up the hint as well, because with one last glare, he stormed out of the office, slamming the door behind him hard enough to shake the trailer.

"Connor, we need to talk," she said, hoping against hope that this time he would listen.

"Tonight, okay?" he said softly, looking miserable and tired and heaven help her, but she didn't want to make him feel worse so she did something that she knew she would regret later.

She dropped it.

THIRTY-THREE

August

"Stop doing that! We have to go!" Rory said, giggling as she tried to crawl out of his arms and off the bed, but the woman was laughing too hard to be able to put up much of an effort.

"No, we don't, baby. We can tell your brothers that you're too sick to go. Then we can spend the first free weekend that we've had in two months in bed doing nothing more than eating, sleeping and making you scream my name," he said, pulling a very amused Rory back away from the edge of the bed and back in his arms.

She let out an indelicate snort at that. "I have never screamed your name!' she said, lying her hot little ass off.

"Really?" he asked in an offhand tone as he managed to wrap his right arm around her and pull her back against his chest, keeping her there as he used his other hand to tickle her until she was thrashing in his arms and laughing so hard that she could barely choke out his name.

"You bastard!" she gasped, still laughing a minute later when he stopped tickling her.

"Yes, I am," he said, chuckling as he shifted back just far enough so that Rory could turn over onto her back.

As soon as her back touched the comforter she was reaching for him. With her fingers threaded through his short hair, she pulled him down for one of her greedy little kisses that he loved. Her throaty little moan as he slid his tongue against hers had his cock jerking and his balls aching, but he ignored them because making Rory fall apart in his arms was one of the most pleasurable experiences that he'd ever had with a woman.

He loved touching her, loved the way she trembled against him, the way her breathing became uneven as she struggled to hold off coming for one more minute so that she could enjoy his touch. He would never get enough of her, he decided as he skimmed his hand down her flat belly and between her legs, his groan merged with hers when his fingers moved through her folds and found her dripping wet. Using the tip of his finger, he traced her core once, twice before he slid his finger inside and found her sheath tight. She wasn't going to last long, but that was okay, because they didn't have much time.

"Connor," she moaned softly against his lips as he slid his finger slowly inside of her.

When he felt her reach for him, he shook his head, only breaking the kiss long enough to say, "No, baby, just lie back and enjoy this."

After a slight hesitation, he felt her melt back against the mattress. She wrapped her good arm around his shoulder, holding him close as he slid a second finger inside her. When she gasped into his mouth he knew that she was on the brink and he wished that he could lay here with her and take his time making her feel good, but they didn't have much time.

He twisted his hand so that he could caress that little nub that he loved to flick his tongue over and rubbed it with short teasing circles. Rory's nails dug into his shoulders and her breaths quickened. She pushed down on his fingers and he allowed it, taking the hint that she wanted it harder so he gave it to her. By the time he felt her sheath throb and squeeze around his fingers he was ready to explode. He held off as long as he could, but when she started to scream his name he lost it.

Keeping his fingers inside of her, he broke off the kiss and sat up, sitting back on his haunches, damn careful not to interrupt her orgasm as he took himself in hand. He watched Rory burst apart, her back arching as she licked her lips hungrily. The grip on his cock tightening as he stroked himself faster, his eyes never leaving her beautiful face.

When she opened her eyes and looked up at him a shot of pleasure surged through him, tightening his balls and intensifying the pleasure with each stroke. She was so damn beautiful, sweet, feisty, but it was the fact that it was Rory looking up at him that turned him inside out and made his heart skip a beat.

"I love you, Rory," he said, struggling not to close his eyes as his spine tingled and he felt intense pleasure as his orgasm worked its way to his cock.

Rory didn't say that she loved him. She never did, but instead her walls clamped down around his fingers as a second, more powerful orgasm tore through her setting off his own. He forced his eyes to remain open, too greedy to miss this. He watched her scream his name again, enjoying every last second of it as it intensified his own orgasm. It wasn't as good as being inside her, but it would have to do until he could manage to get her alone again.

"We have to get going," Rory said, struggling to catch her breath as she sat up.

Unfortunately, she was right. With a nod and a quick kiss, he climbed off the bed, taking her with him. Together, they walked into the shower, only pausing long enough to enjoy a leisurely kiss. He helped cover her cast with a plastic bag before they climbed into the shower and quickly washed up. He'd just pulled her back into his arms when the banging on the bedroom door started, again.

"We gave you a half an hour! Move your asses!" Sean yelled, making them both groan as he reached for the shower knob and turned off the water.

"Let's stay here, Rory. I was serious about spending the weekend in bed with you," he said, knowing that even if they stayed that he wouldn't be able to spend the entire weekend in bed with her.

Andrew was getting worse and he didn't know what he should do. There was no one that he could turn to and no one to share this burden with. He'd promised to keep his mouth shut and that's exactly what he was going to do even as it slowly killed him inside. He wasn't sure how much longer he could keep this up. Every day was like a brand new level of hell. If only Andrew wasn't so hell bent about being stubborn, but the bastard wouldn't even listen to him and take a chance for him. That asshole was dying and he wouldn't take a fucking chance and God help him, but Connor hated him for it.

"What's wrong?" Rory asked softly, reaching up and running her fingers down his jaw, instantly calming him.

"Nothing's wrong," he lied, turning his head and pressed a kiss against the tips of her fingers as they moved down his jaw. He wished that he could tell her what was going on, ease some of his own pain, but he couldn't. He wouldn't do that to her and he wouldn't break the asinine promise that he'd made to Andrew. He owed his friend that much at least.

"If you're not ready in ten minutes we're coming in!" Johnny yelled, making Rory roll her eyes and him have to bite back a groan at the reminder that he promised to spend an entire day with Rory's brothers and the rest of her extended family.

Oh, joy.

It wasn't that he didn't like her cousins, he actually did. He'd only met a dozen of them so far, but all of them were pretty good guys. They were arrogant as hell and some of them liked to call him the "pretty boy", which he thought was a bit screwed up since he hadn't met a single Bradford that couldn't pass for a GQ model. Then again, being called pretty boy was a hell of lot better than being referred to as the crybaby. He hadn't cried and every time he'd pointed that out he'd earned pitying looks and condescending remarks.

Bastards.

The problem was actually Rory's brothers and father. Since news of their engagement had spread like wildfire all over town, her father hadn't said one single word to him, not one. Not that the man was normally a chatter box, but the way he watched his every move when he didn't think Connor was looking was a bit eerie. He just wasn't sure that he could deal with the glares for a whole day when he barely survived it for five hours fishing every Sunday.

Her brothers were another problem entirely. He really wished that they would cut the shit and kick his ass and get it over with already. Their murderous glares and bullshit warnings about watching his back were getting tiresome. They sent him text messages at all hours of the day, reminding him that they were watching his every move. When they were fishing or didn't want Rory or their father to hear what they were saying, they whispered their warnings or mouthed their threats. They even went so far as to send him drinks when he was at the bar just so they could write down exactly what they wanted to do to him on a cocktail napkin. They used stick figure illustration to explain it better just in case he missed the fact that they were dying to kick his ass.

The only thing that wasn't clear to him was why they hadn't kicked his ass by now. They wanted to, that was obvious. He just didn't know what was stopping them from doing it. If he wasn't so damn worried about Andrew, getting this project finished and trying not to screw up with Rory, he would probably try and find out, but he just didn't have the time or energy to really care.

"You better not be touching our sister, asshole!" Bryce yelled, sounding close to killing someone.

"Go away! We'll be down in twenty minutes!" Rory yelled back, sounding aggravated as she stormed into her room and he really couldn't blame her.

When her brothers weren't trying to warn him off, they were harassing the hell out of Rory as they tried to talk some sense into her. It wasn't working. At least, he hoped that it wasn't working. He didn't want to lose her, not now, not when he was a mere three months away from making her his.

She was marrying him. Rory James was going to marry him and he couldn't wait. He knew that if they finished the project tomorrow that she'd marry him. It killed him to have to wait, but he wasn't going to rush this and screw this up. She needed him to prove to her that he loved her and he would do just that, but the moment that the project was over, she was marrying him.

"We need to get going, because the faster that we get dressed, the faster we can put some distance between us and my brothers for a few hours," Rory said, not sounding any happier than he was about spending the day with her family.

"Okay, baby. I'll go get dressed," he said, giving up on trying to talk her out of going and headed for her patio.

"You really should just leave some stuff here, Connor," Rory pointed out with a shrug as she pulled on a pair of light gray lacy panties that he'd really like to tear off with his teeth, but unfortunately they didn't have time.

He cursed softly as he watched Rory continue to get dressed. He'd been avoiding this kind of thing since he'd decided to drop the subject of selling her house. Truth be told, he'd been hoping to avoid talking about this sort of thing until after they were married and it was time to move her into his house and stake a "For Sale" sign in her front yard.

"I'll think about it," he said, hoping the vague answer would be enough for her to drop it.

"Okay," she said with another careless shrug as she focused on pulling a shirt on, reminding him why he loved this woman so damn much. There was no drama, no pouting, and no whining to get her way. She hated that bullshit almost as much as he did, and that made him breathe a little easier because he knew that when it came time for her to make some changes that she would do them. Rory was a smart girl, she'd realize that selling her house and merging her business with his was the smart thing to do.

"I'll meet you outside in ten minutes," he said, moving once again towards the patio door.

"Five minutes! You have five minutes!" Johnny yelled from the other side of Rory's bedroom door, earning a sexy eye roll from Rory.

"Ten minutes," Rory said with a wink.

Fifteen minutes later he was leaning back against his truck, waiting for Rory and ignoring her brothers.

"You're fucking dead!" Johnny snarled.

"Keep pushing us by touching our sister and see what happens," Craig, who'd just arrived, said, between sips of his coffee and a yawn.

"Better watch your back, bitch," Bryce said as he stole Sean's coffee. Sean, who had just opened his mouth to take his turn threatening Connor, quickly forgot all about Connor and focused on bitch slapping the hell out of his brother and stealing back his coffee while Connor let out a bored sigh.

Oh, he was sure that they meant it and would love to pound him into the ground. Any other man would probably be pissing his pants and running the other way, but after listening to this bullshit day in and day out for the past month it had lost its affect. Not that it ever really had much of an effect on him. It hadn't. He'd gladly take an ass whooping for Rory. She was more than worth it.

"Hey, asshole? Did you hear me?" Brian called out, sounding pissed.

"Yeah, yeah, yeah, you're going to tear my throat out and kick the shit out of me or some other bullshit," he said dryly, daring a glance down at his watch and wondering what was taking Rory so damn long.

"Um, actually no. I was wondering if you had any cream and sugar that I could borrow. They messed up on my order," Brian said, sheepishly as he gestured to the coffee in his hand.

"Help yourself," Connor said, focusing his attention back on Rory's front door.

"Thanks, man," Brian said, walking towards his front door only to pause and add with a shrug, "You know you're a dead man, right?"

"Yup."

"Good, good," Brian said with a nod as he headed for Connor's house.

"That's right, your ass is grass, you little prick," Johnny said, sounding smug which was a little sad.

Connor was just about to go see what was taking Rory so long when her front door opened and she walked out, smiling sweetly when she spotted him. He pushed away from his truck and walked past her brothers, ignoring their muttered threats to keep his "dirty hands off their sweet little sister" and met her halfway down her walkway. He didn't care that her brothers were watching or half the neighborhood, who still hadn't moved on and gotten over the initial shock of the relationship, was also watching, he had to touch her, to kiss her and he did just that.

"Ow!" he winced, stepping away from Rory and rubbing the back of his head where it throbbed. He looked over his shoulder and found all five of her brothers watching them with innocent doe-like expressions on their faces.

"It was a squirrel," Craig said, somehow keeping a straight face.

"Vicious little bastards," Bryce added solemnly.

"You should really be careful," Johnny added before mouthing, "bitch."

Oh, this was going to be a long fucking day.

THIRTY-FOUR

"Can we stop at Henderson's?" Rory asked, noting that it was almost six in the morning and the little dinner/convenience store should be open by now. At least she thought it should. Granted, it had been more than ten years since she'd been allowed within thirty yards of the store, but she was pretty sure that it still opened early and closed late.

Connor took a left on Long Pond Road, pissing her brothers off if the sound of their horns blaring was any indication. They weren't happy that Connor was going with her. They were also pissed that their pathetic little attempt to get rid of him had failed.

They'd yanked out the battery from Connor's truck along with the spark plugs, a few hoses and let the air out of his tires, probably thinking that would stop Connor from coming with them. Just in case that didn't work, they did the same to her Jeep and explained with smug smiles that they only had room for one more passenger. It was an amateur move.

She knew that Connor really didn't want to spend the day with her brothers and she really couldn't blame him. Even though she wanted him there, wanted to spend a whole day away from work with him, she'd understood and was willing to go without him. Just as she opened her mouth to let him off the hook, he flipped off her brothers and set to work. It wasn't exactly surprising to discover that Connor kept spare parts in his garage. She did the same thing. They'd screwed each other over enough in the past that they were pretty much prepared for anything and everything.

"Do you want to go to Henderson's or do you want to hit McDonalds when we get to the highway?" Connor asked, gently caressing the back of her hand with his thumb as he took a right at the lights.

"McDonald's is a half hour away," she pointed out, starting to feel giddy at the prospect of going to Henderson's for the first time in years. It used to be her favorite store as a child and she'd missed going there every Sunday for a stack of pancakes, bacon and hot cocoa.

As much as she would have loved to blame Connor for getting banned from her favorite store, she couldn't. Getting banned from Henderson's had been one hundred percent her fault. Then again, the ban probably would have been shorter if Alex, her boyfriend at the time, hadn't decided to get in her face and call her a fucking bitch for getting him tossed out as well. That's not what pushed Henderson into banning her for life though. It was Connor grabbing Alex by the throat and shoving him into the shelves of penny candy that got them the lifetime ban, which had been lifted for a probationary period a week ago.

In fact, every ban and restriction in town had been lifted. People were still placing bets on them, but at least they could now go to whatever restaurant or store they wanted to without worrying about restrictions. They hadn't had much time to enjoy the bans being lifted, but they had managed to grab dinner at O'Malley's last Tuesday, a place neither of them had been allowed to set foot in, for over five years. They'd even gone grocery shopping together. Granted, on both occasions the managers had assigned someone to watch their every move and follow them, but still, it was progress.

"You just want to see if Henderson still has those little chocolate balls that you used to love, don't you?" Connor asked, chuckling softly as he pulled into Henderson's cracked parking lot.

"No, I'm just hungry," she only partially lied because she planned on getting three bags of those delicious little chocolate balls and eating every last one of them.

"Uh huh, sure," he said, smiling that sexy smile of his as he handed her two twenties.

Frowning, she asked, "You're not coming in?" and nearly cringed at how needy she sounded. She wanted to share this with him, to enjoy visiting her favorite childhood store with him.

"Sorry, baby," he said, leaning over and kissing her, "but someone has to keep your brothers from going in there and getting you banned again."

She looked past him to see Craig's truck parked next to them and when she saw the anticipatory gleam on her brothers' faces, she realized that Connor had a point. They'd hound her in that store and do their best to talk some sense into her, which of course would annoy her and cause her to do something stupid like get banned again.

"I won't be long," she promised with a pleased smile as she climbed out of the truck and made a beeline for the old familiar white door that used to welcome her as a child. Bryce almost managed to cut her off, but Connor was there a split second before her brother could reach for her.

Knowing that she probably only had a few minutes before her brothers managed to plow past Connor and start the next round of lectures, she quickly made her way through the old country store. She ignored both the curious and frightened looks of patrons and employees and focused on filling her hand basket with chocolate balls, a bag of freshly made donuts that were still warm, ordering two hot cocoas, grabbing some penny candy, a few small white boxes of fruit filled pastries, a couple of waters and a bag of homemade mini peanut butter cups, Connor's favorite, and quickly paid.

"You better watch your back, *bitch*," Johnny said, stressing bitch when she opened the door and stepped outside.

As soon as her brothers spotted her, they backed away from Connor who'd done an amazingly wonderful job of keeping her brothers off her back. Then again, judging by the murderous glares that her brothers were sending Connor, they'd probably forgotten all about her and gotten carried away with another one of their threat sessions that were more annoying than anything.

"Are those donuts for us?" Brian asked, shifting anxiously as his greedy eyes locked on the bag in her hands.

"Nope," she said, smiling when her brothers turned murderous glares on her. "I'd hurry up if I were you. They only have two bags left," she lied, knowing that it was the only way to get rid of them.

Her brothers stood there a moment longer, obviously struggling with the need to keep a close eye on the two of them as the scent of warm donuts surrounded them. In the end, the donuts won and the shoving match began. They didn't stick around to see who won.

"Are you okay?" she asked as she handed Connor a warm donut a few minutes later, noting that he looked sad, again. That expression was becoming more common these days and it was breaking her heart.

"Yeah, I'm fine," he said, forcing a smile as he accepted the donut.

"We don't have to go if you don't want to," she said, hoping that she'd kept the disappointment out of her tone as she said it. She wanted to go. She loved her family, missed them, but she loved Connor more and didn't want to see him sad.

Connor shook his head. "No, it's fine, Rory."

"Are you sure?" she asked, worrying her bottom lip.

"Yes."

She almost asked if this was about Andrew, but decided that she didn't want to spend their first real day off together fighting. With the way that Andrew was acting she knew that it was only a matter of time before they came to blows over what to do. Until then, she just wanted to enjoy her time with Connor.

———

He really was a scrawny bastard, he decided as he climbed out of his truck and for the second time in his life, found himself surrounded by dozens of Bradfords. They were everywhere. Most of them were eating, but a lot of them were setting up the neighboring sites that they'd reserved for the reunion with grills, dozens of them, coolers, tables, a volleyball net, more food and......

Was that a butcher setting up near the grills?

Judging by his collection of knives, his apron and the fact that the short pudgy man was definitely not a Bradford, he would have to say yes. It was definitely going to be a long and interesting day, he thought as he walked around the truck to help Rory out. He had the door opened and was reaching for her when he suddenly found himself picked up and moved aside like he weighed nothing instead of two-hundred and twenty pounds. It was a bit unnerving, but not as unnerving as the wall of muscle that suddenly came between him and Rory.

He heard an excited squeal the same time that he saw Rory's arms wrap around the bastard's neck. The man pulled her out, returned her hug as he turned around and placed her on her feet next to Connor.

"Hey, Jason, how's it going?" he asked, pleased when Rory released her hold on her cousin and wrapped her arm around his.

Jason grinned, looking a hell of a lot happier than he had the last time he'd seen him a few weeks ago. The man had missed his wife and it had taken its toll on him. By the time his week of working for them was over, Jason had been exhausted and his appetite had been pretty much nonexistent, making everyone worried. It turned out that the lovesick bastard missed his wife and couldn't sleep without her. He was glad to see Jason back to being Jason. Sure the man embarrassed the living hell out of him and would annoy the shit out of anyone just for the hell out of it, but he genuinely liked the asshole.

"It's good to see you, Connor," Jason said, reaching out and shaking his hand. "Didn't think we'd be seeing you here today. Thought my cousins would make sure that you…..that you…..," Jason broke off, frowning as he scented the air. "Is that cinnamon, sugar and fruit filling that I'm smelling?" he asked, turning his back on them and focusing his attention on searching through Connor's truck.

Connor was already stepping back and taking Rory with him when several large men around them suddenly stopped, sniffed the air and growled out, "Cinnamon donuts."

"Let's go see if my dad is here yet," Rory said, sounding upbeat and happy while he resigned himself to the day of hell and his truck being ransacked by Bradfords.

"Are you hiding from me or my sons?" the man that he wanted to deck asked as he stepped up beside him.

"Both," Connor admitted, taking a sip of his lukewarm beer as he looked across the large lake at absolutely nothing.

"Afraid my sons are going to hurt you?" Mr. James asked, sounding curious.

"No," he said, his grip tightening around his bottle as he forced himself to stand there and not take a swing at the bastard that had it coming.

For the past five hours he'd been forced to put up with this bastard ignoring Rory, talking down to her and acting indifferently towards her. Several times he had to stop himself from doing something that he'd regret, not that he'd live long if he punched her father with dozens of Bradfords and James around. He honestly didn't care if they beat the shit out of him. Knowing that it would upset Rory was the only thing that had stopped him. Rory deserved so much better than this asshole. She deserved a father that loved her and appreciated her and knew that she was-

"Did you know that Rory is my favorite?" Mr. James said, catching him off-guard.

Connor took a sip of his beer, not sure if calling his future father-in-law a lying sack of shit was the way to go on this one. It was painfully obvious, at least to him, that the man hadn't wanted a daughter. He'd never treated her like she was anything special. All he did was push her away. It was clear that the man didn't have a clue about how to deal with a daughter, but he should have tried. Connor had no clue what to do with a little girl, but if he and Rory were blessed with one, he would damn well do what he had to for her even if that meant dressing up like princesses and playing with Barbies.

"Parents aren't supposed to have favorites, but the moment that I held Rory in my arms she became my world," Mr. James said, sounding pleased and that was pretty much what made Connor snap.

"Bullshit," Connor ground out, moving to take a sip of his piss warm beer when it was suddenly snatched from his hand and just as quickly was replaced with a fresh cold beer.

Frowning, and a little surprised that Mr. James hadn't swung at him, he looked over at the man just as Mr. James tossed his old beer in one of the trash cans that someone placed near the water's edge, not that it was really needed since everyone was still back at the main campsite, eating. He hadn't seen anyone in over an hour and he'd been hoping to keep it that way for the rest of the night.

"I know it's hard to believe," Mr. James said, staring out at the water, "but I love that little girl more than anything and I'm damn proud of her."

"You sure have a funny way of showing it," Connor bit out, taking a sip of his beer and joining Mr. James in staring out at the lake.

Mr. James chuckled. "You were a hell of a lot nicer the last time we had this talk," he said, taking a sip of his beer and still not looking at Connor.

"This talk?" Connor asked, wondering if Mr. James was drunk. He looked over his shoulder to see if he could find one of the man's sons to help him walk it off, but everyone was still off enjoying the party.

"The talk we had when you showed up on my front doorstep on Rory's eighteenth birthday and asked permission to marry my daughter," Mr. James said, reminding him of another humiliating experience that he'd really rather forget.

"Are you going to tell me to fuck off again?" Connor asked, taking a sip of his beer as he did his damndest to ignore the memories of that conversation and how close he'd come to pissing himself.

"That's not exactly what I said," Mr. James said, sounding amused.

"Are you going to go for your gun again?" Connor demanded, still pissed that he'd refused to hear him out and when Connor begged, yes, begged, for his permission to marry Rory if he could make up for all the bullshit he'd put her through. Instead, Mr. James had gone for his gun and fired.

"You weren't ready to get married, Connor," Mr. James said quietly. "And Rory deserved better than that."

"I would have taken care of her."

"I know you would have, Connor," Mr. James said, surprising him. "You would have worked your ass off and taken damn good care of her as best as an eighteen year old boy could, but it wouldn't have been enough and it wouldn't have been fair to either one of you."

When Connor didn't say anything, Mr. James continued. "You would have both struggled. Rory probably would have dropped out of college, because she's so damn stubborn and wouldn't have felt right about you working your ass off to support her. You wouldn't be where you are today if you'd had a family to hold you back. I know the type of man that you are, Connor. You never would have taken a chance at starting a business that could go belly up if you had a family to support. You both had a lot of growing up to do."

Connor chuckled without humor, because that's probably what would have happened, but it still hurt thinking about what could have been. "You're right. We probably would have started a family too soon and would have struggled to get by."

"You were too young and headstrong to see that," Mr. James said, nodding in agreement.

He turned a glare on the older man. "You could have just said that instead of going for the gun!"

"My way was easier," Mr. James said, his lips twitching with amusement.

"For who?" Connor asked, glaring at the man.

"For me," Mr. James said, chuckling as he took another sip of his beer.

"And that's really all that mattered?" Connor demanded, seeing so much of Rory's Bradford cousins in the man at the moment that it actually frightened him a little bit.

Mr. James chuckled. "It's the family way," he said with a wink.

Connor took a sip of his beer as he returned his attention to the lake. For a few minutes neither one of them spoke and he should have been fine with that, but he had to ask, "Do you have a problem with me marrying your daughter now?"

"Absolutely none," Mr. James said, sounding like he meant it.

"Then why have you been glaring at me and pretty much ignoring Rory since you found out?" he demanded, wondering if he'd ever understand this man.

"I can't let Rory know that I'm actually pleased," Mr. James scoffed.

"Why not?" Connor asked, thinking that Rory would probably be happy to hear that her father was happy about something in her life.

Mr. James sighed heavily. "And here I thought you knew my daughter."

"I know her better than anyone," Connor argued, finishing off his beer and chucked it into the barrel.

"Then you know that she's stubborn as hell and will become suspicious if she knows that I actually liked you," Mr. James explained, once again shocking him into silence.

The man actually liked him? That was surprising since he'd done nothing but glare at him since they first met. Of course, he couldn't forget those times that their little misunderstandings went to court the man had volunteered to beat some sense into him, at no charge of course.

"I learned very early on that my daughter doesn't like doing things the easy way. She likes to argue, put her foot down and do the opposite of what's expected of her. Anytime I've tried to support her, she's either shut down or gives up. It's only when I'm a cold bastard that she ends up following her heart. It's what makes Rory, Rory and I wouldn't change her for anything in the world. I'm banking on you marrying her and making her happy."

"I will," Connor promised, hating to admit that the man did have a point. That's what he loved about Rory, but that's also what made him want to bend her over his knees and spank her beautiful ass most days. She was the most stubborn woman that he'd ever met.

"I know you will, because if you don't, I'm going to give in and let my boys do what they've been dying to do for the last twenty-five years and kick your ass."

THIRTY-FIVE

"**I** don't think this is such a good idea," Haley, Jason's wife and the cutest little thing that she'd ever seen, said once again, as she pushed her glasses back up her nose and shot another nervous glance around the dark makeshift parking lot.

"Relax," Rory said as she continued to search through huge toolbox in the back of Connor's truck. "Aunt Megan just had the seventh set of desserts put out. We've got a good twenty minutes before they're done eating."

"Actually, we should have thirty," Zoe said, Trevor's wife and one of the most entertaining women that she'd ever met, said as she risked a glance from their crouched position in the back of Connor's truck.

"You didn't put out any of your baked goods, did you?" Rory asked, trying to mask the fear in her voice as she shot Zoe a look only to find the other woman rolling her eyes.

"I'm not allowed to bake while I'm pregnant," she muttered, lovingly rubbing her very large stomach as she gave up crouching and carefully dropped to a sitting position with Haley's help.

"Trevor's afraid of the babies getting food poisoning," Haley explained, shooting Zoe an apologetic smile and a shrug when the woman gasped in outrage.

"My baking isn't that bad!" Zoe argued.

"Sweetie," Rory said, pausing in her search to reach over and give Zoe's hand a quick squeeze, "there isn't a Bradford alive that will willingly touch your baked goods."

"I overheard Jason and Trevor telling everyone that you baked my cupcakes so that they wouldn't have to share," Haley added softly as she took Zoe's other hand into hers. "Not one single Bradford went near them. In fact, they actually demanded that everything the guys claimed that you baked be taken away and given its own section."

"Oh," Zoe mumbled, her shoulders sagging in defeat. "That would explain why Bradfords kept blocking me from going near the table overflowing with cupcakes, cookies and brownies and telling me that they weren't good for the babies. I thought they were just afraid of the babies getting fat."

"Nope, Bradfords don't get fat," Rory said with a shrug as she once again turned her attention back to the task at hand.

"Lucky bastards," Zoe muttered and she couldn't help but agree.

Bradfords could eat whatever they wanted, whenever they wanted and never had to worry about getting fat. The same could be said for any of the James boys that had Bradford blood. Rory didn't mention to Zoe that she'd also been blessed with that little problem, minus the insane appetite, because it would upset the very hormonal woman who was constantly struggling with her weight. The only time Zoe didn't worry about gaining weight was when she was pregnant, which was understandable since she was pregnant with Bradford twins and it was actually a chore to eat enough to keep her unborn babies satisfied.

"He's gotta have one in here," Rory mumbled to herself as she carefully sorted through Connor's impressive assortment of tools. She'd already picked out a few tools and gadgets that she was going to steal later, but none of them would do for what she needed right now.

"Maybe you should wait until next week," Haley said, sounding nervous, which was a tad insulting. "Your doctor's appointment is on Tuesday. Maybe you should leave it to him to cut your cast off."

"I know how to handle a saw, Haley," Rory said, sighing in exasperation.

"On wood!" Haley snapped. "It's different than cutting something off your arm!"

"It will be fine," Rory said dismissively as she continued her search.

"Um, I kind of have to agree with Haley on this one," Zoe said, shifting uncomfortably and making her wonder how exactly they were going to get the eight month pregnant woman off the back of the truck. Getting her up here had been a miracle. She really couldn't see getting her off working out as well. Nope, not well at all.

"It's not a big deal," Rory said, hoping they'd just drop it.

"If it's not a big deal, then why are we sneaking around?" Haley asked.

"We're not sneaking around," Rory said, carefully moving the large circular saw to the side in hopes that she'd be able to find something smaller and more manageable.

"Then what would you call sending us text messages, asking us to sneak off with you when it's dark out and the men are distracted with food to meet you at Connor's truck and to keep our mouths shut?" Zoe asked dryly, making her lips twitch.

"Female bonding?" Rory suggested, grinning when Zoe and Haley glared at her.

"Over power tools?" Haley asked, laughing.

"Exactly."

"I'd rather bond over cupcakes," Zoe mumbled, rubbing her stomach and Rory could sympathize. She couldn't imagine what it must be like to carry Bradford twins. Trevor let it slip that it cost twice Jason's monthly food budget to feed Zoe. That was frightening, because during that week that Jason had stayed with them, he must have gone through-

"Ah ha! I found it!" she said, cutting off her own thoughts as she pulled out a rather beautiful handheld skill saw with what looked like a fresh blade out of the toolbox. It would be perfect just as long as she got the angle just right and the saw didn't shake too much.

"I-I really don't think this is such a good idea," Haley mumbled nervously as Zoe nodded in agreement.

She opened her mouth to point out once again that she knew what she was doing when two large arms suddenly wrapped around her from behind and yanked her clean from the truck, making her drop the saw and all three of them scream a bit hysterically. Before she could put up much of a fight, she found herself pulled tightly against a body that under normal circumstances she would have loved to touch, but the jackass had scared the living hell out of her and for that he had to pay.

Unfortunately for her, he had her in a pretty good hold, but she wasn't worried because she knew that her cousins had her back. They would kick his ass and make him pay for scaring them. She didn't even bother to bite back the smug smile that played with her lips at the thought of the three of them kicking Connor's ass and bringing him to heel. He more than deserved it and it would serve him right to get his ass kicked by three women.

Any minute now her cousins would come to her defense, she told herself as she waited for the ass whooping to begin. When a minute passed and she still didn't see any movement in the back of Connor's truck, she started to wonder what was holding up her rescue.

"A little help here would be nice!" she snapped, ignoring Connor's rich chuckle as it teased her senses.

"Um," she heard Zoe clear her throat as she tried to make the woman out, but it was too dark now to make out much of anything but a few shadows, "about that. I can't really move. In fact, I think I'm stuck here so you might be on your own for a few minutes."

She'd prefer Zoe's help since the woman knew how to kick some ass, but that was okay. She still had Haley and even though Haley wouldn't have been her first choice in a fight, she always had her friends' backs so Rory knew that she was all-

"If someone could help me find my glasses, I would be more than happy to kick some ass for you, but I seem to have dropped them when Connor scared the hell out of me and I can't see a thing without them," Haley explained and Rory knew that this battle was over and that Connor won.

She really hated it when she lost to him.

Connor chuckled as he pressed a kiss against her nape and let her go, making sure that she didn't stumble. "If I help you find your glasses would you promise not to kick my ass?" Connor asked, sounding deeply amused and making her smile, damn it.

Haley let out a long-suffering sigh before she grudgingly said, "Fine. I won't kick your ass."

"I really appreciate that," Connor said, laughing as he climbed onto the back of the truck from the sound of it.

"As you should," Haley said with a sniff.

Feeling like an idiot just standing there, she quickly climbed back into the truck, thankful for the dim moonlight that stopped her from stepping on someone, and carefully joined the search. Zoe did her best to stay out of everyone's way, only making a sound when she thought someone might step on her. Five minutes later, Haley had her glasses back and decided to commit the ultimate betrayal.

She ratted on Rory's ass.

"She was going to cut her cast off with a saw!" Haley said, smartly moving behind Connor, who she really couldn't see that well, but was guessing wasn't happy with the news.

"Was she now?" Connor asked, sounding thoughtful seconds before a small flashlight was turned on. When the beam of light landed on the toolbox that she may have broken into, she may have made a move to make a run for it. Before she could manage to turn around, Connor had her good hand in his, effectively holding her prisoner.

Haley on the other hand did manage to make a run for it.

Traitor.

"Um, if someone could help me up and off the truck, I'd really like to make my escape now," Zoe said softly.

Not that she could blame her friends for ditching her ass. She really couldn't. She just wished that she could join them and get away from Connor before he flipped out on her for doing something that he probably thought was stupid.

"I'll help you down in a minute, Zoe," Connor said, before his attention shifted right back to her. "Don't move," he warned as he released her.

For a moment, she considered her chances of making a clean get-away and although they were pretty good, she couldn't just leave Zoe here. So with a sigh, she nodded, wondering, hell hoping, that Connor would at least wait until he'd helped Zoe off the truck and she had a chance to waddle away before he laid into her.

"Could you hold this light and keep it pointed on the toolbox?" Connor asked Zoe.

A bit curious, she watched as Connor reorganized his tools while searching through them. When he managed to pull out a smaller skill saw with an even sharper looking blade, she had to smile. He'd bitched a few times over the last couple of weeks about allowing some quack that specialized in runny noses going near her arm with a saw. He was so damn overprotective of her and she loved that about him.

"Do you trust me?" Connor asked, closing the lid on the toolbox as he double-checked the saw's battery and blade. If it had been anyone else, even her brothers who she loved and knew would never hurt her on purpose, she would have said no. But, this was Connor. The man that she loved and the man that she was just starting to realize would never do anything to hurt her. So to answer his question, she placed her arm on top of the toolbox.

Connor leaned in and kissed her. "That's my girl."

"Just be quick. I want to go swimming," Rory said, hoping to do a little more than that actually.

All summer they'd been restricted in their activities because of her arm and tonight she wanted to go skinny-dipping with Connor. She hadn't come to the reunion with that in mind, but when she'd been out walking a little while ago, trying to get over the way her father had been treating her, she'd stumbled upon a secluded little area not too far away with the perfect spot for a small fire and plenty of privacy. It would definitely be the perfect spot for what she had in mind with Connor.

"I don't think that I can watch this," Zoe mumbled, her voice shaking, but thankfully her hold on the flashlight didn't waver.

"Are you ready?" Connor asked, giving her one last chance to back out.

"No!" was Zoe's answer, but she trusted her guy so with one nod, Connor turned on the saw and touched the blade to her cast.

She watched him work and was impressed by his focus and handling of the saw. He kept his cut straight and even, his hands steady. In a matter of seconds he was done, the saw was off and she was pretty sure that Zoe was mumbling something and hyperventilating a tad bit, but she was too excited to finally have this damn cast off to really care.

"How does it feel?" he asked, once the cast was ripped off her arm.

"It feels good," she said, sighing with relief to finally be able to move her hand and arm without that damn cast getting in the way.

"Um, actually it kind of hurts," Zoe said, drawing their attention just as she leaned in to kiss Connor.

"What hurts?" Connor asked, looking like he wasn't about to give up that kiss when Zoe's next words stopped them both dead in their tracks.

"The contractions. My water breaking didn't feel great either, but the contraction definitely hurt," Zoe said as Rory moved past Connor and took the flashlight from Zoe, careful not to flash the light in her friend's eyes and when she saw Zoe practicing her breathing exercises, she knew that their night just got interesting, mostly because they were a good hour away from the hospital.

"Your water broke?" Connor asked, fidgeting and for the first time in his life, not looking all that confident. Not that she could blame him since all she wanted to do at the moment was start screaming for help and give into panic.

"If your water broke then why didn't you say anything?" Connor demanded, truly looking at a loss at what to do next. Give the man a saw and he was cool, give the man a woman in labor and he shattered.

"Because I didn't want you cutting off her arm, you jackass!" Zoe cried out, her words ending in a scream as she grabbed onto Connor's arm and squeezed. Rory could tell by the strain on his face that it hurt, but he took it.

"Sorry," he mumbled.

"You should be!" Zoe snapped. "You scared the hell out of me and now I'm about to give birth to two Bradfords out in the middle of nowhere with no drugs! Do you have any idea how big a Bradford's head is? Huh? Do you?" Zoe demanded, between panting. Rory would have offered Zoe her hand to squeeze, but her broken arm had just healed and she really wasn't eager to another cast.

"I'm going to call for an ambulance," Connor said, pulling his phone out of his pocket just as company arrived.

"What the hell is going on?" Trevor demanded, climbing on the truck. He went to put his arms around Zoe, but stumbled back as the small woman suddenly turned the most vicious glare that she'd ever seen on the man.

"You!" Zoe said accusingly as her eyes narrowed to slits on her husband.

For a moment Trevor simply sat there, looking at his wife until finally he sighed and gestured to Connor. "Do you have any rope?"

"Rope?" Connor repeated as Rory asked, "What the hell do you need rope for? She's in labor!"

"It's to stop her from trying to rip my balls off," Trevor said with a fond smile for his wife, who looked like she wanted to do just that.

Definitely the most interesting family reunion, she thought an hour later when the ambulance finally showed up just as the twins arrived and she decided against telling Connor that she was "late."

THIRTY-SIX

September

"What time is it?" Rory asked around a yawn as she rolled over onto her side so that she could face him as she struggled to keep her eyes open.

"A little after two," he said softly, resisting the urge to go to her, because he knew that if he did that he would want more, need more from her and he couldn't do that to her, not now.

"You're just getting home?" she asked, but made no move to get up or open her eyes this time. For the first time in months, he was thankful for the exhausting hours they put in every day. It was probably the only thing stopping Rory from asking a million questions that he didn't want to answer.

"Go back to sleep, baby. We have to get up in a couple of hours," he said, smiling for the first time in hours when Rory let out a whiny little growl and flopped back over onto her stomach.

He walked in her bathroom, carefully closing the door behind him, wincing as pain shot through his battered hand. For the last couple of hours he'd been able to ignore the pain, but now that he wasn't busting his ass and taking all his frustration and anger out on two by fours and sheetrock, he was starting to feel all the damage he'd done to his hands. He held up his hands and cursed.

Shit!

His hands were torn up, bloodied, blistered and he could hardly move them without agonizing pain shooting from the fingertips and through his arms. Over the past month he'd fucked up his hands with his late night adventures, but never like this. He'd be lucky if he could move his hands today, but with his luck, his hands would probably get infected and he'd be seriously screwed.

He walked over to the bathroom sink and carefully opened the medicine cabinet. When he didn't spot what he needed, he closed the door and looked beneath her sink, cursing as crippling pain shot through his hands, but at least he'd found what he needed. He grabbed the bottle of peroxide and stood up only to have the bottle ripped from his hand.

"What the hell did you do to your hands?" Rory demanded, sounding very much awake now and looking extremely pissed.

"Nothing. They're fine," he said, trying to close his hands and when that didn't work, he tried putting them behind his back and out of her sight. Rory was too damn stubborn to let it go and leave him alone.

She grabbed onto his left arm and yanked it forward. Before he could pull it back, she was holding his bloodied hand and glaring up at him. "Yeah, they're real fine, Connor," she said with a sigh as she released his hand and stepped past him.

"What are you doing?" he asked, kind of hoping that she'd just go back to sleep and forget all about this so that he wouldn't be forced to lie to her.

"Helping you get your hands cleaned before they get infected," Rory explained as she turned on the shower.

"I don't need help, Rory. Go on back to bed and get some sleep," Connor said, trying not to think about how exhausted he suddenly felt.

For the past couple of weeks he'd been running on barely two hours of sleep a night and putting in about twenty hours a day and it was catching up to him. As much as his body was begging for him to stop, he couldn't. He just couldn't. If he didn't stay busy, stay focused on something other than his life he was going to lose it.

"Is this about Andrew quitting?" Rory asked and although he'd been waiting for her to get around to bringing it up since Andrew had decided to quit and cut him out of his life, he wasn't ready to talk about it. He didn't want to talk about it, didn't want to think about it and he sure as hell didn't like waiting around for the phone call letting him know that his best friend died all alone, because the stubborn asshole was too damn proud to let Connor be there for him.

"Leave it alone, Rory. It's over," he said, shoving aside the agony that once again threatened to destroy him.

"I know that you're upset that your friend quit," Rory said, sounding sympathetic as she checked the temperature of the water, "but it's probably for the best. He wasn't showing for work. When he did show up he was late and he always left early. I know you don't want to talk about it, but I think he had a problem."

"Like you said, he quit so let it go," he said, yanking his shirt off and tossing it aside, ignoring the fresh wave of pain that shot through his hands as he forced his hands to remove his pants and boots.

"I can't," Rory said, moving to step in front of him, but he was in no mood to deal with her or anything else right now. He just wanted to take a shower, pass out for a few hours and get his ass back to work where he could work himself into exhaustion and forget about how fucking bad it hurt losing his best friend.

"You can't or you won't?" Connor demanded as he stepped into the shower.

"Both," she snapped, yanking the curtain closed.

He stepped beneath the hot water, allowing it to seep into his pores and work its way down to his hands, stinging his sensitive skin as it washed away the blood. It wasn't enough to make him completely forget, but it was enough to keep him from losing it, something he'd been fighting since Andrew told him over beers and a Yankees game that he had a rare form of Leukemia and that he wasn't going to fight it.

Andrew had type AB negative blood, a very rare blood type. The chances of finding a matching donor were very slim and Andrew didn't hold out much hope of finding a match, but the main reason why Andrew was refusing to look? Because he would rather see the bone marrow go to a child or someone with a family, someone that would be missed. Andrew wasn't married, broke up with his girlfriend last year and his parents died years ago, leaving him all alone so in his book, his death wouldn't be a loss. The asshole was trying to be noble to the end and Connor fucking hated him for it.

"We've put this off for long enough," Rory announced as she stepped into the shower behind him.

"Go away, Rory," he said, feeling his hold on the situation slipping and he didn't want her around when it did.

"Not until we talk," she stubbornly said.

"There's nothing to talk about," he said tightly, forcing his eyes shut while his hands clenched by his sides as he tried to stay calm. He needed her to leave so that he could focus on pretending that everything was okay just for a little while longer.

"Oh, really? How about the fact that I've barely seen you over the past month? You don't smile. You barely say more than a few words to me when you do see me. All you want to do is work. You look like you're going to kill someone anytime someone mentions Andrew. You haven't touched me in a month and-"

"You want me to fuck you?" he demanded harshly as he turned around and faced her, feeling his control snap and even knowing that he was probably going to do something to lose the love of his life, he couldn't make himself rein it back in. He didn't want to hold it back any longer, couldn't. He wanted to put his fist through the wall, scream at the world, and have someone to take his anger out on and right now that person was Rory.

"Is that the problem, Rory?" he asked, stepping into her. "You're pissed, because I haven't fucked you?"

"No, it's not that!" Rory snapped as she tried to stand her ground against him, but he was done playing games.

"Then what's the problem, Rory? Huh?" he asked, stepping into her until she had no choice but to back off and once she did, he didn't stop until he had her back against the shower wall.

"My problem is that you're being an asshole and I want to know why!" she snapped, trying to shove him back, but he refused to move. He moved into her, resting his arms against the wall near her head as he caged her in with the rest of his body.

"It doesn't matter," he said, leaning in to kiss Rory when she turned her head away.

"Yes, it does," she said in that mutinous tone that used to drive him crazy, but now it just simply pissed him off.

"No, it doesn't," he snapped as he leaned in and pressed a kiss to her neck in the spot that he knew drove her crazy. If he wasn't going to be able to work himself into exhaustion then he'd fuck Rory until he couldn't remember his own name, never mind the pain that was driving him out of his fucking mind, he decided as he continued to kiss her neck.

"Talk or stop touching me," Rory demanded, but he ignored her and kept kissing his way down to her beautiful breasts.

Escape, that's all he wanted to do and Rory's body would allow him to do just that. He just needed to escape, he told himself as he moved to kiss his way down to that dark rosy nipple that he loved.

"Goddamnit, Connor! Stop touching me and tell me what the hell is going on with you!" she yelled as she placed her hands on his shoulders and shoved him back, robbing him of the escape that he needed.

"It's none of your fucking business!" he yelled back, knowing that he'd hit a dangerous point and forced himself to step away from her before he did something really stupid.

"Bullshit!" Rory screamed, getting right in his face and cutting him off when he tried to step out of the shower and leave so that he could calm down, but she wouldn't let him.

"Get the fuck out of my way, Rory," he said, tightly through a clenched jaw. When she didn't move, he yelled, "Now!"

No!" she yelled right back. "You're not leaving this shower until you tell me what's going on!"

"Fuck that," he snapped, picking her up and moving her to the side so that he could leave. He needed space, needed to calm the fuck down, but of course the damn woman wouldn't let him have that.

"I told you that you weren't leaving until you told me what's going on," she said, getting out of the shower and moving to block his path, but he simply ignored her as he grabbed a towel and headed for the door.

He didn't make it far. In fact, he'd barely made it five feet into her bedroom when Rory took him by surprise and tackled him, taking him off guard and down to the ground. She hadn't tackled him since she'd started to grow breasts and because of that unfortunate incident in the apple orchard when she'd tried to teach him a lesson, but instead ended up giving him a glance at her developing breasts that had him grinning like a fool for days.

He wasn't grinning now. No, now he was pissed. Barely aware of what he was doing, he rolled them over and pinned Rory to the floor, ignoring her dog's demands to be let in the room and the pain shooting through his hands as he held her arms down.

"You really want to know what's going on, huh?" he asked roughly, settling himself between her legs and grinding his hardening cock against her damp slit. "Huh?"

"Yeah, I'd love to know why you're being a prick," she said, not sounding scared, but pissed, Rory level pissed, as she tried to get her arms free, but he wasn't ready to let her go yet. Not yet.

"Because my best friend is dying," he announced, watching as the anger quickly disappeared from Rory's beautiful face and was replaced by sympathy.

"Oh my God......," she mumbled.

"Mmmhmmm," he said, continuing to grind against her. "Leukemia, but you want to know the real kick in the ass? He has a chance, a fucking chance to live and he's ignoring it. Do you know why?" he asked, barely aware that his voice shook or that his body was trembling as he spoke.

"No," Rory said, her voice hollow, as she lay there, no longer fighting him.

"Because the asshole has a rare blood type and he's afraid that if he takes the bone marrow that he'll be taking away the chance for a kid or someone with a family's chance to live. He doesn't care that I need him and that I'm going to miss him," he said, grinding against her, harder. "He doesn't fucking care!"

He kept grinding against her, not feeling anything as he looked down at her, watching as the tears rolled down her beautiful face. "He doesn't care that I'm going to miss him. He doesn't care that he's making me watch him die and won't let me fucking help him! Now that he quit, he doesn't have health insurance and can't get the medicine that he needs. He won't even let me be there for him. The stubborn asshole doesn't want anyone to see that, but I need it. I need to be there for him and let him know how much I love him and he won't give me that!"

"Shhh, it's okay," Rory said, putting her arms around him and pulling him down, but he wouldn't allow it. He didn't remember letting her arms go or moving to get away from her and didn't care. Suddenly he couldn't stand the thought of her trying to comfort him. It made it feel too real, like his best friend really was dying and there was nothing that he could do. He couldn't deal with it, just wanted to pretend for a little while longer. He-

"Shhh, baby, it's okay," Rory said as she gently pushed him back down until he was sitting on the floor with his back against the bed. Before he could move, she was climbing on his lap and straddling him. He went to push her off, desperate to avoid her touch, but when he moved to push her away he found himself grabbing her and pulling close, suddenly desperate for the comfort that she was offering him, needing it more than his next breath.

"Everything is going to be okay, Connor," Rory said soothingly as she wrapped her arms around his head and held him against her chest. "Shhh, it's okay."

He tried to tell her that it wasn't, but he couldn't. The only thing that came out was an agonized sob, then another and another until all he could do was hold onto her as he lost control and finally gave into the pain.

———

"What do you mean, you and Connor aren't coming in today?" Craig demanded, sounding stressed and for good reason. They had less than two months to finish the hotel and they were barely keeping their heads above water. They should be at work, but Connor needed some rest and she needed to do something.

She leaned over and kissed Connor's cheek as he slept, his stubble tickling her lips and making her smile sadly as she looked down at him. He'd been shouldering this secret for far too long. She hated seeing him in this much pain and she refused to let it continue. With that in mind, she said, "Our cousins aren't coming in today either. I need their help with something."

―――

"This has to end," Andrew said, his legs giving out beneath him, dropping his ass to the ground before he could make a half-assed attempt to hold himself up against the wall. He was tired, too damn tired and couldn't wait for it to end.

He was ready. He'd said his good byes and accepted his fate. He just wished fate would stop fucking with him and get it over with, because he wasn't sure that he could-

"Rory?" he asked, sure that he was seeing things as he watched the stunning woman climb through his window. When two very large men followed her inside, he prayed that they were here to finish him off. The woman hated him, always had and he really couldn't blame her, because he had been an asshole.

He'd love to say that he'd had an excuse for treating her the way that he had, but unfortunately he'd been a dumb kid, a jealous dumb kid who'd crushed on her and hated the fact that Connor loved her. Connor was his best friend, more like a brother and because of him, he'd never tried anything with Rory, but once upon a time he'd dreamed of making her his own. He'd hated that she was off limits, but as the years passed he'd realized that he'd simply been harboring a childhood crush on her and been a complete asshole to her for no good reason.

"Oh good, you're ready to go," she said, smiling when she spotted him.

Frowning, he looked down at his bare chest and boxers and had to wonder what she was talking about. He moved to open his mouth but no words came out as he watched more men crawl through the window, a lot more. A few he recognized, but most of them he'd never seen before. He knew by their builds, their dark hair, and bad boy looks that they were all related and they were all looking at him.

"W-what's going on?" he asked, hating how weak he sounded.

Rory gestured a few of the men forward. "Nothing much. We've just come to get you and end the bullshit."

"Oh shit," he mumbled when they came for him.

THIRTY-SEVEN

October

"**G**et the hell away from me with that, you psychotic harpy!" Andrew shouted, making Connor smile as he headed downstairs, more than ready for this morning's battle.

It had been almost a month since Rory and her cousins kidnapped Andrew. Well, "talked him into leaving his house and coming to live with her," as Rory had explained it to the nice police officer that showed up when Andrew managed to get his hands on a cell phone and called for help. The two of them fought day and night and they seemed to hate each other more than ever, but Rory didn't let that stop her from making sure that Andrew was cared for. She took care of him in the morning, came by several times during the day to check up on him and even had that little snot rag of an assistant of hers help out, and she took care of him at night.

Andrew, who'd been ready to give up, hated every last second of it. He bitched and whined and tried to make several escape attempts, but unfortunately for him, the Bradfords decided to take a special interest in him. They now had three Bradfords a week, two to work on Strawberry Manor and one to hang out at Rory's during the day and keep an eye on Andrew. He'd only managed to sneak past a Bradford one time, but he didn't get very far, not with Bunny on the job. One vicious growl and Andrew was making his way back to the bedroom that Rory had set up for him on the first floor.

Thanks to Rory taking over, Andrew had gained back some weight, had health insurance and all his medication. He also made it to all of his medical appointments and Rory somehow managed to browbeat the man into putting his name on the wait list for a transplant. He had a very rare form of leukemia and was somewhat lucky that a bone marrow donation should heal him. The only problem was that he had a very rare blood type, but that wasn't stopping Connor from praying for a miracle.

"Take your medication!" Rory snapped.

"Go to hell!" Andrew shot back.

"Take it!"

"Make me!" Andrew snapped, making Connor cringe on his behalf as he stepped over Bunny and headed for Andrew's room.

When he stepped inside Andrew's room and discovered that Rory had his best friend in a headlock and was trying to shove a pill in his mouth, he wasn't all that surprised. Andrew had set down a challenge after all.

"Would you two cut the shit? We have to get going or you're going to be late for your appointment," Connor said, ignoring the little power struggle going on behind him and grabbed some clothes for Andrew.

"Actually," Rory said, pausing just as Andrew muttered and made a few gagging noises, "if you have room for one more, I need a ride to the medical center, too."

Frowning, he tossed the clothes he'd grabbed for Andrew, who was chugging down a bottle of water as he glared at Rory. "Are you okay?"

"Yeah," she said, waving it off like it was no big deal, "I just have a checkup."

"Then why do you have to come with us?" Andrew asked, watching Rory suspiciously, probably because Rory had a tendency of taking over Andrew's appointments and interrogating his doctors and making Andrew feel like a five year old.

Rory rolled her eyes as she snatched the tee shirt out of Andrew's hands and returned it to the drawer only to pick out a different shirt and toss it to him. He tried to bite back a smile as Andrew shot him an, "I told you so look." The man bitched day and night about Rory babying him and even though Connor told Andrew that he was imagining things, he wasn't. Connor wasn't about to interfere, for several reasons. One, he knew that Andrew secretly liked the attention. It had been a long time since anyone had taken care of him. Secondly, it entertained the hell out of him and her cousins. It lightened the mood and helped relieve some of the stress of trying to get the manor done and kept their minds off of what would happen if the doctors couldn't find a match.

"Because I lent my Jeep to Max so that he could check up on some orders in town for us and help with the manor. Now stop your bitching, eat your breakfast and get your ass dressed or you'll make us late," she said as she walked out of the room, only pausing long enough to give him a kiss and then she was off, probably to double-check Andrew's afternoon pills.

"I hate her," Andrew said evenly as he picked up the toast that Rory slathered with butter, peanut butter and jelly, part of her effort to put some weight back on him.

Connor chuckled. "No, you don't."

Andrew released a long-suffering sigh as he took a big bite, knowing the little general would just shove it down his throat if he didn't eat it. "You're right. I don't. But if she tries to check up on me in the bathroom one more time, I'm going to throttle the little pain in the ass!"

"I'll let her know," Connor said, chuckling as he headed out the door to give his friend some privacy.

"You be sure to do that," Andrew mumbled and Connor didn't need to look back to know that his friend was smiling. Rory was a hell of a woman and he'd been damn lucky to snatch her up before some other asshole realized how great she was.

Damn lucky.

———

"What the hell is taking them so long?" Andrew asked as he fidgeted in the waiting room chair.

"No idea," Connor said, looking at his watch again. It was a doctor's office so they usually ran behind, but never like this. They were running an hour and a half behind schedule and if Rory wasn't already in an exam room and Andrew needed this appointment, he would have told his friend to reschedule. He had a lot of shit to do today.

"Connor, can you go see how long Rory is going to be?" Andrew asked, sounding tired, which was a side effect of the medication and something the doctors should have considered before making him wait this long.

"Yeah, no problem," he said, trying to figure out how to convince his friend to wait a little while longer.

He walked through the door that led to the examination rooms, not bothering to ask where Rory was since he'd overheard the nurse tell her which room to go into. Plus, they'd just tell him to wait in the waiting room since they weren't related and he wasn't her husband. Next month could not come fast enough as far as he was concerned.

"Rory?" he asked as he knocked on room ten's door.

"Connor?" Rory asked, sounding happy, which of course pleased him.

"Can I come in?" he asked, already opening the door and walking in just as Rory pulled on her shoe.

"Yes," she said, smiling and looking happy, which was a bit unexpected, but he wasn't going to complain since he liked seeing her happy.

"Andrew's appointment is running behind. I just wanted to see how much longer you were going to be," he said, leaning in and kissing her.

"Just a few more minutes. Can you sit with me?" she asked, taking him off guard.

"Is everything okay?" he asked, not that he had a problem with sitting with her, but it was just an unusual request coming from Rory.

"Yeah, it's just boring in here by myself. Do you mind?" she asked, giving him a sweet smile that he was helpless against.

"Sure," he said, returning her smile as he moved to stand next to her as she sat on the exam table.

They didn't have to wait long before a doctor came in the room, looking surprised to see Connor. But when Rory quickly explained that he was her fiancé, the doctor nodded and sat down.

"Your test results all look great, Rory. I ran a pregnancy test," the woman announced, making his heart skip a beat.

Oh shit............

"The test came back negative. You've been under a lot of stress and have been working too hard. I think once you're able to slow down and take a break then your cycle will go back to normal," the doctor announced with a polite smile.

"Thank you, Dr. Hahn," Rory said, quietly.

Connor chuckled as he leaned down and kissed the top of Rory's head. "I guess we got lucky, huh? Maybe you should see if you can get a prescription so that we don't have to worry about this for a while."

"I can write you a prescription for birth control if that's what you want," Dr. Hahn said, smiling. "But, I'd like to talk to you about your other request first."

Connor was just about to ask what the other request was when a nurse popped her head in the door. "We found a match for your friend," she said, worrying her bottom lip as relief surged through him until she added, "We also need you to help pick him up. He may have passed out when we told him the news."

"Aw, shit," he said, giving Rory a quick kiss on the cheek before he followed the nurse out the door, thanking his lucky stars that he'd managed to avoid becoming a daddy and been given a chance to keep his friend for a little while longer.

Definitely a great day.

———

"Do you think that you could swing by and visit Andrew in a couple of hours?" Connor asked, sounding excited when all she wanted to do was curl up in a ball and mourn the child that wasn't meant to be.

It had been foolish to let herself get her hopes up. She should have gone to the doctor sooner or at the very least, bought a home pregnancy test, but she'd been so damn positive that she'd been pregnant. She'd never been late a day in her life before. It had only been natural to assume that she was pregnant. She'd been stupid, so damn stupid and now her heart ached and all she wanted to do was cry, but she couldn't.

Connor was happy and she didn't want to wreck that for him. He didn't want a child yet and as much as that hurt, it would have hurt a heck of a lot more having a child with a man that didn't want it.

"Rory?" Connor asked as he pulled into Strawberry Manor's parking lot.

"Yes?" she asked, feeling like she was in a daze.

"Can you check up on him for me later?" he asked, reminding her that at least she had something else to focus on for a while.

"I'll try to, but I might not be able to," she said, avoiding his eyes as she lied to him.

"Why not?"

"I have to go away for a few days."

"What the hell are you talking about? Now? You need to go away now when Andrew is getting his transplant?" Connor asked, sounding confused and a little disappointed.

"I'm sorry, but I got a call from Trevor while you went to check up on Andrew. I guess with the all the excitement I forgot to tell you, but Zoe's not feeling well and Trevor is running himself ragged between work and taking care of both sets of twins. Everyone else is trying to help, but they really need someone to stay with them. I'll only be gone for a few days," she said, forcing a reassuring smile.

"Okay," he said, sighing and not sounding particularly happy, but at least he let it go. "Drive safe, baby, and give me a call when you get there to let me know that you're okay."

"I will," she said with another forced smile as she gave him a quick kiss on the lips, glad that this at least bought her a few days to get over her heartache.

———

New Haven Hospital
The next day......

"We're not supposed to release you unless you have someone to take care of you," the nurse explained even as she helped Rory out of the wheelchair and into the waiting taxi.

"My brothers are going to take care of me," Rory said as another wave of dizziness shot through her head and threatened to make her lose the green Jello lunch that they'd forced down her throat.

"Are you sure?" the nurse asked, looking uncertain.

"Yes," Rory assured her, thankful when the nurse took her at her word and closed the door behind her.

"Where to, Miss?" the driver asked.

"The Holiday Inn on Tremont Street," she said, closing her eyes and letting her head drop back against the faded cloth seat as she did her best to ignore the throbbing that was starting to make itself known in her hip.

Thirty minutes later she was letting herself in her hotel room and praying for death with each step. She thought a soak in a hot bath would help, but by the time she made it to the bed, it was obvious that she wouldn't be making it that far, at least not today.

THIRTY-EIGHT

"**Y**ou're fired. Get the fuck off my site," Connor told the bastard that he'd caught sitting on his ass and text messaging his girl-friend while the rest of the men were busting their assess.

"What? You can't fire me!" Dave, the man that he'd foolishly hired as a supervisor and had given way too many chances said, getting in Connor's face.

"I just did," Connor said, stepping around the asshole as he ges-tured to a few of his men to remove the prick.

"What the hell am I supposed to tell my wife?" the man demanded as Connor walked away.

"That texting your girlfriend got your ass fired!" Connor yelled over his shoulder, not bothering to waste another second on the asshole.

He pulled his phone out his pocket and after one look, shoved it back in his back pocket and kicked a bucket full of sand out of his way, not giving a damn where it went. Three days, three fucking days without a word from Rory. He'd never gone this long without talking to her or seeing her and he didn't like it, not one fucking bit.

This wasn't like Rory. He wasn't the type of asshole that expected her to check in. He wasn't. He wasn't overbearing and would never try to keep tabs on her, but he was really starting to worry. Three days without a word. The night that Andrew received his transplant, he'd called her to tell her that everything was going good so far and that he loved her, but she hadn't answered. The next day he'd sent her an email update of the project and still nothing.

Something was seriously wrong. He didn't know if he'd pissed her off or if she just needed space, which he could deal with. What he couldn't deal with was not knowing where she was or if she was okay. Rory wasn't the type to leave a project of this size for three days without checking in. She wouldn't do that, not unless she didn't have a choice.

He'd called Trevor and left a message this morning, but he hadn't heard back from him yet and-

"I just got your message. What's going on?" Trevor asked, pulling on a Yankees baseball cap as he climbed out of his truck and headed towards Connor.

"What the hell are you doing here?" Connor asked, frowning as he noted that the parking lot was suddenly overrun with trucks sporting Yankees stickers and Bradfords, a lot of Bradfords.

"Is that really any way to talk to your favorite in-laws?" Jason asked with a *tsk* as he threw a tool belt over his shoulder as he joined them.

"We're here to get this project finished," Trevor said absently as he tossed a hard hat to one of his younger cousins.

"Why aren't you home with Zoe and the babies?" he demanded as he headed for the office, because he knew without a doubt that something was seriously fucking wrong. Rory would never volunteer to play babysitter so that someone else could finish building her dream.

"Mom's staying with Zoe and the babies and so are Haley and the kids," Jason said, following after him. "What the hell is going on, Connor?"

"Why did you call me looking for Rory? Where the hell is she?" Trevor demanded.

"I don't know," he said, opening the trailer door, "but I'm about to find out."

"You'd better," Jason bit out.

"Where's Rory?" he demanded as he stepped inside the trailer, not giving a damn that Jacob was on the phone.

When the man held up a finger, indicating that he needed a minute, Connor walked over, snatched the phone out of his hand and hung up.

"Hey! That was an important call!" Jacob snapped, moving to grab the phone back.

Connor tossed the phone to Jason and leaned over the desk. "Where. Is. Rory?" he asked, biting out each word as he forced himself not to reach across the desk and grab the bastard by his neck and shake him until he told him what he wanted to know, needed to hear, that Rory was pissed off at him and giving him the cold shoulder. He'd rather her be pissed at him than hurt.

Jacob frowned in confusion as he shot a look at Trevor. "I thought she was staying with you."

"No, I haven't seen her since the babies were born," Trevor said, starting to look worried and for damn good reason.

"Then I don't know where she is," Jacob said, rubbing his hands down his face as Jason pulled out his phone.

"Craig, any idea where Rory is?" Jason asked, pacing the office while Trevor and Jacob waited for an answer, but he was done waiting. Something was going on and he was damn well going to find out what that was. When he found Rory he was going to spank her ass until his hand fell off.

"Pull up her bank records," he snapped, pointing at the computer.

Jacob's eyebrows arched in surprise a few seconds before he started shaking his head. "I can't do that."

"Oh, I think you can," Trevor said, crossing his massive arms over his chest as he joined Connor in front of the desk.

"No, I mean, I really can't do that. I don't have her passwords for her personal accounts," Jacob rushed to explain.

"Then who does?" Connor asked, praying that someone had that information, because they were starting to run out of options here.

"Maybe one of her brothers," Jacob suggested, sounding hopeful as he stood up and made his way around the desk.

"Where are you going?" Jason asked as he placed his phone in his pocket.

"To see if she left any clues on her desk," Jacob explained, heading for Rory's office door, but Connor already knew that it was pointless.

"I've been working in there for the past three days and I haven't seen anything," he said, fighting back the urge to slam his fist into something.

Where the hell was she?

Wherever she was, he wasn't going to find her by standing around here, he realized as he headed for the door.

"Where are you going?" Jason called after him as he stormed out of the trailer.

"To find Rory so that I can kill her."

———

"Oh my God, yes! Oh, right there.....yes, oh.......that feels sooooooooo good," Rory moaned as she settled back in the deep tub that she really needed to have her brothers steal for her. It really would make things a lot simpler for her if she didn't have to sneak in Connor's house for these late night soaks.

Granted, this one was more of a mid-day soak, but that didn't change the fact that this tub really belonged in her house. Maybe she could get Connor to install it as a wedding gift, she thought with a pleased little smile as she looked down at the engagement ring that she loved.

She loved this ring, because she knew how hard Connor had worked to buy it for her. He'd offered to replace it for her and had even gone as far as to drag her into several jewelry stores, but she absolutely refused to wear anything else. This was her ring and she loved it and she loved the man that had given it to her.

Since he'd proposed, well, told her that they were getting married only a few short months ago, she'd been stressing out about the future. What if they got married only to discover that they really hated each other? What if he lost interest in her? What if he broke her heart? Not being able to walk for a few days had helped her sort through everything.

It also hadn't hurt that for the first time in years she'd been able to relax. She hadn't been forced to get up before the crack of dawn, put in a twelve-hour shift, work herself into exhaustion to meet a deadline, take care of someone, or run errands. For the first time in years she'd actually had time to relax. She should have left the hotel as soon as the pain started to become manageable, but she hadn't been able to force herself to face the real world.

She'd slept in late every morning, went to bed at a decent hour every night and set a world record for taking naps. She'd lounged in the bathtub, watched television while she'd pigged out on ice cream and junk food and when she wasn't relaxing, she was thinking about Connor. She'd missed him and by this morning she couldn't take it anymore. She decided to end her vacation and come home to him. She loved him and she couldn't wait to tell him. She was also going to marry him, she thought, smiling as she closed her eyes and just enjoyed the hot water. She couldn't wait to see Connor's face when she told him that she loved him.

———

"Time to wake up, baby," that deep sexy voice that sent shivers down her spine said, pulling her away from one of the best dreams that she'd ever had and into one of the strangest moments of her life.

How exactly had she ended up in her bed? The last thing that she remembered was closing her eyes and enjoying a nice long soak in the tub that she decided was hers. It was possible that she'd climbed out of the tub and made it back to her room, but she doubted that's what happened since she was still naked and she wasn't the type to willingly give the neighbors a show. That and the fact that her arms and legs were tied to the bed, putting her in a spread eagle position told her that she probably hadn't got here on her own.

"What's going on?" she asked, thankful that there was at least a sheet covering her naked body. She wasn't normally shy around Connor, but something about this position made her feel a little too vulnerable and she wasn't exactly sure that she liked it.

"How was your nap?" Connor asked, sounding bored and drawing her attention to her left where she found him, half-naked and lounging in a chair, watching her.

"Good," she said absently, wondering if this really was a dream.

"That's good, Rory," Connor said, his eyes never leaving her face and she decided that maybe this wasn't a dream since he looked kind of pissed and she wasn't able to will the ropes away with a thought.

"Why am I tied to the bed?" she asked, giving her restraints a slight pull, hoping the knots were loose. After a moment, she came to the conclusion that Connor was definitely pissed and that he knew how to tie an excellent knot.

"No reason," he said with a one-shoulder shrug, still watching her expectantly.

"I see," she murmured as she looked around her room, but she couldn't find anything out of place or something to clue her in on what was going on.

She did a quick sweep of the bed and was about to move on when something caught her eye and made her stomach drop. Her ring was gone. Oh God, she'd lost her ring! She looked around the bed anxiously, but it was useless. She couldn't see anything, couldn't move and she was terrified that the ring had fallen off in the tub.

"What are you looking for, Rory?" Connor asked in that bored tone that she really didn't appreciate at the moment.

"My ring! I lost my ring, Connor!" she snapped, yanking on her restraints as she tried to sit up, but she couldn't move. "Let me go so that I can find it!"

"No."

"You don't understand, Connor. I think I lost my ring in the tub," she said, letting out a frustrated growl as she struggled to break free.

"You didn't lose the ring in the tub, Rory, so relax," he said, leaning back in the chair, appearing even more relaxed.

"Then where is it?" she demanded.

"It's right here," he said, gesturing lazily to the desk behind him.

"Why's it over there? And why am I tied up?"

"Because I took it back," he explained, getting to his feet.

"Why?" she asked absently as she tried to pull her hand through the rope, but it was useless.

"Because I've decided not to marry you."

THIRTY-NINE

"What?" Rory asked, her voice barely louder than a whisper as all the color in her face slowly faded away.

A few days ago that hurt expression would have done him in. He would have apologized, said anything and everything to make her happy, but not now, not after everything that she'd put him through. For the last three days he'd worried about her, missed her and all this time she'd been less than five minutes away from their houses, shacked up in a hotel with another fucking guy.

When he needed her the most, she hadn't been there for him. He could have used her support while he'd sat in that hospital waiting room, doing his best not to lose it as he'd waited for the doctors to tell him that the Andrew hadn't rejected the bone marrow, that his best friend was going to make it, but she hadn't been there for him and now he knew why.

"You heard me," he murmured as he walked over to the bed and ran his fingers over her leg until his fingers touched the little toes that he loved to kiss. Slowly, he pulled the sheet away, revealing her body inch by inch until the sheet was pooled on the floor by his feet.

"What's going on, Connor?" Rory demanded, not bitching that she was naked and for some reason that made him wonder who the other guy was.

The thought of another man seeing her body, touching her and making her tremble turned his stomach. He had to force himself to focus on something else or he wouldn't be able to see this thing to the end and he would damn well be the one to end this. After twenty years of playing this game with her, he was finally going bring the game to end. Then he was going to walk away from her. After today she was just going to be his neighbor and the woman that he was going to run out of business. She was going to mean absolutely nothing to him.

"The transplant worked," he said, reaching out to toy with one of her toes before he could stop himself.

"I know that. I called the hospital. He's doing well, but he's driving the nursing staff nuts with his bitching," she said, shifting her foot to the side and away from his hand. "Now tell me why you're acting so damn bitchy and give me back my ring."

He ignored her, because there was no way in hell that he was putting that ring back on her finger when she didn't love him. He'd worked his ass off for that ring. He'd been so damned proud and excited when he'd bought it and hadn't been able to wait to give it to her, to the woman that he loved, but that wasn't her. She'd cheated on him and he couldn't fucking believe it.

If anyone would have told him that Rory James would cheat on him, he would have called them a fucking liar and broken their jaw for trying to start shit. Now he just wanted to kill the bastard who'd touched her before he made love to her one last time to show her exactly what she'd lost, because he couldn't say goodbye to her without having her one last time.

"Where have you been for the last three days?" he asked, tilting his head to the side as he watched her, waiting for her to lie, needing for her to lie so that he could hate her enough to push her away.

For a moment, Rory watched him, glared and then muttered a few words that he couldn't quite catch as she squeezed her eyes shut and said, "You know, don't you?"

"Yes," he said, deciding that if she was done playing games then so was he. "What I don't know is why you lied."

"I didn't want you to get upset," she said, shocking him into stunned silence.

"Upset? I'm going to fucking kill him!" he shouted, wondering if he'd ever really known Rory. Up until today he would have sworn that he knew her better than he knew himself. He never thought she would do this to him.

She opened her eyes to frown up at him. "Kill who?"

"Oh, don't play this fucking game with me now, Rory," he said, somehow stopping himself from demanding the name of the bastard. He would find out, but later. Right now he needed to let Rory know that he was done with her. It was over and he was the one that ended it.

"Are you serious?" she asked, laughing without humor. "You tied me up, you jackass!"

"And you fucking cheated on me!" he shouted, regretting the loss of control as soon as the words left his mouth. He was a fucking idiot.

"You think I cheated on you?" she asked, sounding hurt, which he had to admit was a nice touch.

"Yes!" he snapped, hating her even more for trying to bullshit her way out of now that she'd been caught.

"Oh my God, you're an idiot," she mumbled, shaking her head in disgust. "I didn't cheat on you, you jerk!"

"Bullshit!"

"It's the truth!"

"If you didn't cheat on me then why were you shacked up in a hotel room for the last three days?" he shouted, moving closer to the bed until he found himself climbing on it and over her so that he could glare down at her, needing to look into her eyes as she lied to him.

He had to admit that she looked really pissed off as she glared right back up at him. "Because I was recovering from donating bone marrow!"

His automatic response was to open his mouth and call her a liar, but her words stopped him. "*What?*"

"I was recovering from donating my bone marrow, you asshole! If you don't believe me, then you can call my doctor or look at the bruise on my ass!" she snapped, sounding really pissed.

"Then who was the guy that was spotted going into your hotel room?" he demanded.

"Bryce! Someone from the hospital called him to check on me and he put two and two together and hunted me down. He helped me out the first day and checked up on me, making sure that I had food and that I was okay," she snapped and he knew, just knew that if she was loose that she would be going for his balls, but he really couldn't care less.

He was too damn happy to care about his balls.

"You didn't cheat on me?" he asked, knowing that there were a few other things that she'd said that were important, but he couldn't force himself to care.

"No!"

"Oh thank fucking God," he said, sighing with relief as he leaned down to kiss her only to get her cheek instead of those lips that he'd missed.

"Get off me, Connor," she said evenly.

Oh he knew that he'd fucked up, but he was just as stubborn as she was and he wasn't about to back down, not when there was a good possibility that he might lose her. Nope, the best defense here was definitely to go on the offense.

"I forgive you, Rory," he said, making damn sure to sound putout as he leaned back down to get that kiss that she owed him.

This time she was too stunned to move so he got his kiss. Granted, he would have preferred her lips a little softer and perhaps a little more responsive, but he'd take what he could get right now.

Wow, had he fucked up big time......

Not that he was going to admit it, because he wasn't. Her father had been right. If he admitted that he'd fucked up then Rory would just focus on that and the fact that she had every right to be pissed at him and dump his ass for being a fucking moron. Since that wouldn't work for him, he decided that fucking with her head until she apologized to him was definitely the way to go.

"Forgive me?" she repeated in a tone that really didn't bode well for his plan so he kissed her again.

"Yes, I forgive you, Rory," he said against her lips, but the stubborn woman refused to respond.

"For having a needle shoved into my hip to save your friend?" she asked, obviously clarifying what she needed his forgiveness for.

"Yes," he said, deciding that perhaps she needed to be distracted so he kissed his way down to her throat.

She choked out a laugh as he kissed her neck. "You can't be serious!"

Oh, but he was. Damn serious. He raised his head to glare down at the woman who really did deserve a spanking. "You lied to me. No one knew where you were. Do you have any idea how scared I was that something happened to you?"

He expected her to shout at him, but instead her features softened as she looked up at him. "I'm sorry that I lied to you, Connor."

"Why did you do it, Rory?" he asked, his tone softening as he finally allowed himself to think about what she'd done for him.

She'd saved his best friend's life. She'd also done it all alone. From what the doctors had said, the procedure could be difficult and very painful. Unfortunately for people like Andrew, not a lot of people volunteered to donate because of that. He couldn't stand the thought of her being in pain. He hated that he hadn't been there for her.

"I didn't want you to hate me if it didn't work, Connor," she admitted quietly.

Connor sighed as he moved off her and laid down on the bed next to her. He placed his hand on her bare stomach as he said, "That is the dumbest fucking thing that you have ever said."

Her eyes narrowed to slits as she gave her restraints another tug. "As soon as I get out of this your nipples are mine!"

"Not really giving me a reason to let you go, now are you?" he mused as absently ran his hand over her stomach.

"I hate you," she muttered, but he knew that she was lying. She wouldn't have gone through such great lengths to protect him if she hated him. She loved him and he wasn't letting her go until she admitted it.

"No, you don't," he said with a shrug.

"Yeah, I really do. So, since you've decided to call off the engagement then we're over so let me go, Connor," she bit out, once again looking pissed, which wasn't really working for him.

"I have absolutely no idea what you're talking about," he said as his focus shifted to her very naked body. Now that his anger was gone, he took it all in and what he saw had his dick hardening to steel, his breaths coming faster and his body breaking out in a sweat.

Before Rory, sex had just been a way to get off and get his mind off things for a while. Since they'd started having sex his interest in all things sexual had grown. They'd experimented, a lot, but he'd never tied her up, never did anything like this and right now he couldn't help but imagine what it would be like to take Rory this way. Not that she'd ever go for it. Rory liked to be an active participant and would hate giving up any type of control.

"You took my ring back! You tied me up and acted all pissy!" she snapped, clearly hell bent on rehashing something that really should be done and over with by now. He'd forgiven her, hadn't he?

"The ring's yours and we're getting married in less than a month so stop trying to get out if it," he said as he skimmed his fingertips over her stomach and between her breasts, mesmerized by the movement and the way goose bumps suddenly covered her skin.

"Okay, good. That's settled then," she said, her breaths coming faster. "Then you can just go ahead and let me go and we'll um, we'll forget this whole thing."

"Then you apologize?" he asked as he ran his fingertips between her large breasts, watching as her nipples hardened.

"Yes!" she damn near shouted.

"I see," he murmured, sitting up so that he could lean over her and press a kiss against her stomach.

"W-what are you doing?" she asked, her body trembling as he continued to press kisses down her stomach until he came to her navel.

"Touching you," he said before he pressed a kiss against her navel, flicking his tongue out and teasing the spot that usually earned a cute little giggle from Rory, but this time she let out a low needy moan that had him cursing and flicking that spot with his tongue again before he forced himself to move on.

"Do you want me to stop?" he asked, preparing himself to do just that even as he ran the tip of his tongue from her navel to one of her large nipples and traced it with his tongue before he pulled the rosy tip between his lips and sucked it.

"I-I-I-oh, God!" she screamed, her back bowing as he used his teeth on her nipple, scraping it lightly before he licked it better.

"Want me to stop, baby?" he asked, licking a line to her other breast and giving the other nipple the same attention.

Her breaths sped up and he couldn't believe how badly he wanted her to say no, but she wouldn't. Rory James loved being in control and she would never-

"I don't know!"

What the hell was she doing? She wasn't into this kind of thing. She liked regular, normal sex with Connor. Sure, they'd spiced it up and she'd done things with him that she'd only dreamed of, but she could honestly say that she'd never dreamed of being tied down to a bed while Connor took his time licking and kissing her body.

She should be telling him to stop and demanding that he untie her, but God help her, she didn't want him to stop. She wanted him to do a hundred naughty things to her body while she was like this and then she wanted him to do it all over again.

"Tell me to stop and I will, Rory," Connor said, his voice husky as he flicked her nipple with his tongue while he moved a hand between her legs.

Now, she should tell him to stop now! She opened her mouth to do just that when an embarrassingly loud moan escaped her. Why did every touch and kiss feel so much more powerful like this? She hated men taking control in bed and she should hate this, but she realized that she didn't. She wanted to experience this with Connor. For once, she wanted to let go and allow someone else to call the shots while she got to lie back and enjoy herself.

Closing her eyes, she took a slow steady breath, trying to steady her nerves as her cheeks burned with embarrassment and said, "Don't stop."

He stopped.

"You want this?" he asked in a sexy whisper that made her shiver.

"Yes," she said, hating the way her voice shook.

"Open your eyes and tell me that, Rory," he said, cupping her breast.

"I think you can hear me just fine," she said, not sure that she could look him in the eye and admit that she wanted this. She wanted this, more and more with each passing second, but she was actually scared. She wasn't used to feeling like this and she wasn't sure if she liked it.

"Do you trust me, Rory?" he asked, stroking her breast.

"You know that I do," she said quietly, keeping her eyes shut as she moved to turn her head away, but he wasn't having that.

He released her breast to gently cup her face, caressing her cheek with his thumb as he said, "Then look at me, Rory and let me know that this is really what you want."

She turned her head and somehow found the strength to open her eyes. "I've never done this before," she admitted.

"Neither have I," he said with a slow sexy grin that was sweeter than his usual bad boy smile.

"But you want to?"

He leaned down and brushed his lips against hers. "Yes."

His admission turned her on more than she ever thought was possible. "Then yes, I want this."

"I want you, Rory," he said against her lips. "Forever."

"I want you too, Connor," she said on a soft moan as she felt one thick, long finger slide inside her.

"You've got me," he said, giving her one last kiss before he moved his mouth down her neck, kissing and teasing her as his finger began to slowly thrust inside her. She tried to push down, but she couldn't move. It both frustrated and excited her. She was completely at his mercy and she loved it. It made her feel wanted, desired and that was absolutely perfect for her.

When he licked his way down her stomach, she relaxed and allowed herself to enjoy what he was doing. A scream escaped her lips seconds later as his tongue joined his finger. She dropped her head back, closed her eyes and simply lay there, enjoying his touch. She didn't have to worry about pleasing him or worry that she was doing something wrong. She simply let go.

"I love you, Rory," he murmured minutes or hours later, she wasn't sure and didn't care as she struggled to catch her breath. The man took his time, enjoying her body as he touched and explored her at his leisure.

"I love you too, Connor," she said as he carefully settled himself between her legs.

"You damn well better," he said hoarsely, entering her in one slow thrust as he leaned down to kiss her.

"And why is that?" she asked, licking her lips as he filled her.

"Because I'm never letting you go," he swore against her lips.

"Good, because I would hate to have to go for my pliers if you did."

FORTY

November

"I can't believe we did it," he said, pulling into a spot on the freshly paved parking lot of the newly refinished Strawberry Manor.

"And one week ahead of schedule, too," Rory said, beaming with excitement as she looked at the beautiful new hotel. He had to admit that it was beautiful, but that wasn't what he'd meant.

He chuckled as he threw the truck in park. "I meant, I can't believe that we're married."

"Well, I really wasn't left with much of a choice," Rory reminded him, smiling that pleased little smile that she'd been wearing since the nervous Justice of the Peace had announced them husband and wife about an hour ago.

After the initial shock, the Justice of the Peace decided that they needed a little fatherly advice and explained that he believed that they were making a mistake and that perhaps they needed to take some time and come back on December 2nd. At first, Connor had been pissed that he was interfering, but by the time the JP mentioned December 2nd for the third time, it became clear that the man had placed a bet that they would get married on December 2nd. Once the J.P. resigned himself to losing two hundred dollars, he'd married them, scowling at them the entire time until the deed was done and he could storm off.

"You didn't have a choice, huh?" he mused, reaching for his wife as she unclipped her seatbelt and moved to straddle his lap.

"No, not at all," she readily agreed with an impish smile that had him wishing that they could skip the final inspection and start their wedding night early.

"And how's that?" he asked, wrapping his arms around her.

"I had to do it for our deal of course," she said solemnly, looking so damn serious that he couldn't help but laugh.

"For our deal, huh?" he asked with a chuckle, leaning in and stealing a kiss.

"Mmmhmm," she murmured, returning the kiss.

Before he could deepen the kiss, Rory opened his door. She pulled away and climbed out of the truck, laughing and jumping back when he reached for her.

"We need to clear the site so that we can start that insanely expensive honeymoon that you promised me," she said, heading for the manor.

"That wasn't part of our deal," he pointed out as he climbed out of the truck.

"It is now," she said, sounding happy.

"Do I get a veto?" he asked, following after her.

"Sorry. You're a married man now, Connor. Your job is to fulfill each and every one of my needs," she explained, throwing him a wink over her shoulder.

"And you need an insanely expensive honeymoon?" he asked, chuckling as he veered off to the right towards her trailer.

"I really do," she said, sounding happy, really happy and for a moment he was content with just watching her as she made her way inside the manor.

How had he gotten so lucky? he couldn't help but wonder as he turned around, hoping to get this done quickly so that he could move onto the insanely expensive honeymoon that his beautiful wife was demanding when he realized that he had one last problem that he had to handle before it bit him in the ass.

"I heard you tell Andrew that this was all a game," Jacob, the surly assistant from hell, said numbly as he looked at Connor with what could only be described as disgust. "I kept my mouth shut, because I thought Rory could handle herself, but apparently I was wrong."

"It's not what you think, Jacob," Connor said, taking a step towards the man only to have him take two steps back.

"Then you didn't just marry Rory so that you could take over her company?" Jacob demanded.

Connor opened his mouth to tell him that he had it all wrong, that it wasn't like that anymore when he realized that this simple misunderstanding had just blown up into a huge fuck up in under sixty seconds.

"Married?" Johnny repeated, sharing a confused look with his brothers as they quickened their pace as they headed towards him, looking pissed. As he watched the five large men make their way towards him, he realized that there was no way that he could explain any of this without landing in a body cast. They wouldn't believe him, not that he really cared, but he did care if his wife believed him. As he watched them approach and listened as Jacob ratted his ass out, he realized something very important. He was out of options. So he did the only thing that he could think of.

He made a run for it.

"Get back here!" Johnny yelled as Connor shoved past several men and ran inside the manor and into the beautiful lobby.

"Where's Rory?" he asked Andrew when he spotted his friend sitting on the couch, going over paperwork and looking better than he had in months.

"In the ballroom. Why?" Andrew asked, but Connor didn't have time to answer him, not with five seriously pissed off James brothers after him.

"You have some explaining to do!" Reese, one of the Bradford twins and a fucking cop, shouted, drawing his attention.

Scratch that, he had five James brothers, a little prick bastard and two seriously pissed off looking Bradfords after him and he probably only had seconds to convince Rory that he loved her and wasn't after her company before they beat the shit out of him. Not wanting to waste another minute, he made a run for the ballroom, shoving men aside as he ran down the long hallway. The entire way he heard the sounds from the very large men chasing after him, and he'd be lying if he said that he wasn't a little wary of the ass whooping that he was about to receive, but he was more concerned about losing Rory.

He was just about to run through the open doorway of the ball-room when Rory stepped out, looking down at the clipboard in her hands and unaware of all the men barreling down on her. She'd barely looked up when he grabbed her arm and gave it a pull towards the elevators. He didn't have a plan, but he hoped like hell that this would at least buy him a few minutes.

"What the hell are you doing?" Rory demanded as he yanked her into the elevator, pushing her behind him as he slammed his finger against the "Close Door" button just as her brothers and cousins abruptly turned and headed for them.

"Come on, come on, come on!" he muttered, panicking as the door started to close, but not fast enough.

Her brothers were getting closer and closer until all they had to do was put their arms out to stop the doors from closing, taking away his only chance to make this right. Just when he resigned himself to a trip to the hospital and losing Rory, something unexpected happened. The two Bradford twins reached out and grabbed Craig and Johnny just as they reached out to stop the elevator doors and yanked them back, allowing the doors to close.

"What the hell is going on?" Rory demanded.

"First things first," he mumbled as he reached out and pulled the emergency elevator button. The elevator shook hard once as it came to a complete stop. When the alarm began to blare, he flicked it off, took a deep breath and turned around to face the woman that he loved.

"I love you," he said, needing her to know that. "I've always loved you and no matter what happens, I will always love you."

"You son of a bitch!" Bryce shouted, reminding Connor that it probably wouldn't take the brothers long to crack those doors open and kill him.

"I love you too, Connor, but what the hell is going on?" Rory asked, shooting a nervous look past him at the closed doors.

"I need to tell you something," he said, cringing when the banging behind him started.

"Yeah, looks that way," Rory mused, shifting her gaze right back on him.

"Did I mention that I love you?" he asked, shooting her a nervous smile as he tried to figure out how exactly to explain the whole fucked up deal he'd come up without Rory going for his balls.

"Start talking, Connor," Rory said, arching an expectant brow as she folded her arms over her chest.

Since time was a serious factor, he decided to get right to the point. "I fucked up."

"And....."

"There was more to the deal than I let on," he said in a rush. "I didn't think it was worth mentioning, because once I realized that I was still in love with you, I didn't want it any longer."

"What didn't you want any longer?" she asked with a putout sigh, the same one she always used when he was telling her how he'd screwed her over. He felt himself relax, somewhat.

"The plan," he said, searching desperately for the right way to explain his original plan to her without making her hate him.

"And why did Darrin and Reese attack my brothers?" she asked.

"Because of me," Mr. James suddenly announced from behind him, making him curse when he realized that at some point during their conversation the doors had been opened.

At least the doors worked quietly and efficiently, he thought as several pairs of hands grabbed him and yanked him out of the elevator. As Craig pulled back his fist and let it fly, Connor hoped that they didn't break his jaw so that he could beg Rory for a second chance. That's if she came to visit him in intensive care.

———

"Mother fucker!" Connor gasped as Craig punched him in the stomach, causing his legs to give out, but before he dropped to the ground, Bryce and Sean were there, picking him right back up for more.

"Stop!" she cried, moving to help him, but her father stopped her by moving in front of her.

R.L. MATHEWSON

He kept his eyes locked on her as he told the twins, "She doesn't get past me until we're done and you make damn sure that no one interrupts us."

"Sure thing, Uncle David," Darrin said as he stepped in front of the elevator with Reese by his side, standing guard and blocking her view of Connor getting his ass kicked by her brothers.

"Shit!" she heard Connor groan a few seconds later.

"Dad, please tell them to stop!" she begged, panicking as she placed her hands on her face, struggling to keep it together.

"I'm sorry, Rory, but he has this one coming."

"They're going to kill him," she said, trying to stay calm.

"Probably," her father agreed with a shrug.

"Dad, please-"

"Why didn't you call me when you were hurt? For that matter, why don't you call me when you need help? And why did you just get married without me there to give you away?"

"What?" she asked, taken off-guard. "Why would I call you?" she blurted out before she could stop herself.

"Because I am your goddamn father!" he shouted, losing his temper for the first time in her life. While her father could get pissed, really pissed, he never lost control, never shouted and never at her.

"When you're hurt or need someone, I should be the first person that you call! Do you have any idea how fucking scared I was when I found out that you'd been rushed to the hospital? I had to hear it from the fucking mailman that my daughter was seriously injured, because no one called me!"

"Dad, I-"

"Do you have any idea how it feels to have to sit outside your child's house, scared to death that she's in pain or worse that she might not make it through the night? Do you?" he snapped, looking angrier than she'd ever seen him before.

"But, you taught us to be self-reliant. I didn't think that-"

"That's bullshit that your brothers shoved down your throat! You are my daughter and there will never be a time when I don't worry about you or want to take care of you. You were stubborn and didn't want to let your brothers think that you were weak so you tried to act tough. You were my little girl, my little princess and you used run into my arms crying my name every day when I got home from work until you turned five and your brothers decided to treat you like a little brother. From that moment on, you thought that you had to be as pigheaded as they were and you stopped being my baby girl," he said, his voice softening, his expression turning sad.

"You are my baby girl, Rory. I love you more than you will ever know, but you are so damn stubborn," he said with a sigh. "You need to know that you can always call me," he said, stepping aside only to pause and glare at her. "And the next time that you're hurt, sick or you need help, you better call me, because if I have to hear it through the mailman again, you and I are going to have words, young lady," he said, shooting her a wink to soften his words, making her relax as he stepped back.

"I will, Dad," she said, feeling close to crying. Her daddy loved her and she'd probably be rubbing it in her brothers' faces if she wasn't very much afraid at the moment that they were killing her husband.

"Step aside, boys," her father said, as he took her hand in his and led her off the elevator. The scene that met them had her heart skipping a beat and her stomach dropping.

Johnny and Brian held back a struggling and still weak, Andrew while Craig and Sean held Connor up as Bryce pulled back his fist and let it fly, connecting with Connor's face and splitting his lip.

"Stop!" she screamed, releasing her father's hand. She tried to help him, but Reese grabbed her and pulled her back. She went to elbow him, but the large bastard was fast, too fast and he had her arms behind her back and restrained before she could take her next breath with a simple hold, but a damn effective one.

"Okay, let's clear this up, shall we?" her father said, gesturing for Jacob, who looked like he wanted to take a swing at Connor, to come forward. He didn't look like he was going to listen, but one hard look from her father had him swallowing and stepping forward.

"Okay, tell her what you told my boys," her father said, gesturing for him to get on with it. She was just thankful that Bryce had stopped punching Connor to listen.

"Connor's plan was to use you to get your brothers. He was using the relationship to look good in your brothers' eyes to win them over. When the project was finished, he was going to get them to come work for him and run you out of business," Jacob said, shooting Connor a murderous glare, which explained why he'd been acting like such a jerk for the past couple of months. He'd known about the plan and knowing Jacob, he wasn't happy about it, but he'd obviously trusted her to handle it on her own.

"Don't fucking listen to him, Rory!" Connor yelled, but he was quickly silenced by a punch to the gut from Bryce.

"And how exactly did you find out about that?" Darrin asked.

"Because I overheard Connor explain it to Andrew," Jacob said, gesturing to Andrew, who'd closed his eyes in resignation and cursed.

"When?" Reese demanded.

"In June I think," Jacob said, looking thoughtful, "he was just using her. He wasn't in love with her. As long as he didn't hurt her, I stayed out of it. I didn't know that marrying her was part of the plan. I thought he was just going to screw up and Rory was going to end their deal."

"That's bullshit!" Andrew snapped, but thankfully no one hit him, probably because none of them were mean enough to strike a man recovering from a life threatening illness.

"I heard every word!" Jacob said firmly, crossing his arms over his chest.

"I love her!" Connor shouted.

"Then why are you after her company?" Jacob demanded.

"Okay, let's get this over with, I have somewhere to be in an hour," her father said, gesturing to her brothers to drag a bloody and panting Connor forward.

"I'm a little confused about something," Johnny said. "If he was trying to get on our good side, then why didn't he try sucking up to us?"

"He only kept telling us to fuck off," Sean said, sounding confused.

"He punched me," Bryce bitched.

"That's because I didn't want any of you!" Connor snapped.

"What the hell do you mean that you didn't want us?" Johnny demanded in outrage.

"We're a fucking catch!" Sean snapped.

"You'd be lucky to get guys like us! Lucky!" Bryce said, sounding pissed and insulted.

"I don't want any of you!" Connor snapped.

"*You bastard!*" Johnny gasped as her brothers glared at him.

"Rory?" her father said, drawing her attention, but not enough to look away from Connor, who was looking up at her through one swollen eye.

"Yes?"

"Do you love him?"

"Yes," she said softly with a small nod that had Connor noticeably relaxing.

"And what are you willing to do to prove to my daughter and my boys that you're telling the truth and that you love her?" her father demanded, watching Connor intently as he waited.

For a minute, Connor stood there, not saying anything as dread twisted in her gut. She wanted to tell her father that he didn't have to prove anything, but she needed to know that their deal was truly a thing of the past.

Connor looked up and met her eyes as he said, "Anything. Everything. She can have my house, my business, everything that I have. I don't care about any of it. The only thing that I want is her."

She bit back a smile as she walked over to him, making a show of thinking it over. "What about the bathtub?"

"It's yours."

"Will you stop stealing my hot chocolate?" she asked, reaching up to cup his slightly bruised handsome face.

"No," he said, turning his head so that he could press a kiss against her palm. "But I'll learn to make it the way that you like so that I can make it for you."

"Highland Construction is mine?" she asked, already deciding a month ago to combine their companies into one and run it with him.

"Yes," he said with absolutely no hesitation.

"You'll work for me?"

"Yes."

"Fetch my drinks?"

"No."

"Be at my by beck and call?" she asked, loving the way his poor abused lips kicked up into a grin.

"No."

She sighed heavily as she said, "You really suck at interviews."

"Do I have the job?" he asked, giving her that bad boy smile that she loved.

"I'll have to think about it," she said with a shrug as she turned to walk away.

"Uh, Rory, what do you want us to do with him?" Johnny called after her.

"Give him the official welcome to the family," she said, laughing as she walked away.

"Rory?" Connor called after her, sounding uncertain and for good reason. "Rory!"

She paused long enough to look over her shoulder and wink as she announced smugly, "Checkmate."

EPILOGUE

1 Year Later…..

"Who do you think we should call?" Rory asked as she snuggled closer to him.

"Your dad?" Connor suggested, not sure that calling his father-in-law at two in the morning to come bail them out of jail was the best idea, but that's all he had at the moment.

"No," Rory sighed, laying her arm across his chest as she did her best to get comfortable, but the small bench and cement wall behind them made it impossible.

"Why not?" he asked, pressing a kiss to the top of her still damp head.

"Because I'd have to explain to him why we got arrested," she said with an adorable little pout.

Connor chuckled as he wrapped his arm around her and pulled her closer. "In a couple of hours everyone in town is going to know what happened."

"This town sucks," she muttered, making him laugh.

"You have no one else to blame but yourself," he said, wincing when she poked him in the side, hard.

"You could have just said no," she said, tilting her head back so that she could glare up at him.

"True, but then you would have gone for my nipples," he said, laughing when she poked him again.

- 327 -

"At least it's not the worst thing that we've ever done," she muttered, giving up on trying to get comfortable on the wooden bench and moved to sit on his lap.

"Put some space between you both, now!" the police officer manning the desk barked at them.

Connor placed his hand on the large swell of Rory's belly as he stared the officer down, "If you want to put some space between us then let my wife out of here."

"I can't do that and you know it," the officer said, not looking too happy about having a pregnant woman locked up in a cell. Connor wasn't exactly thrilled about it either. If his hormonal wife hadn't reached over while he'd been driving them home, after they'd made another late night run for burgers and shakes, and started rubbing him through his pants, he would have used better judgment. He sure as hell wouldn't have pulled into their old high school's parking lot to help her take care of another craving.

In his defense, he really hadn't thought that anyone would be able to spot his truck from the road, not with that storm making it difficult to see anything. At least this time they hadn't come banging on the window until after they'd finished and Rory was dressed. He really hated anyone else seeing his gorgeous wife's body, but it did happen on occasion when things got out of hand, kind of like tonight.

"Let's call my brothers," Rory suggested, laying her head on his shoulder.

"Can't. They're refusing to bail us out for five years, because of what happened last month at the Strawberry Festival."

"That wasn't my fault!"

"Shhh, I know, baby," he lied. It was completely her fault, but he wasn't about to point that out to his hormonal wife. He wasn't a fucking idiot after all.

"Andrew?" she suggested, sounding hopeful.

"Nope, he's down in Boston for the weekend, helping with the walk to raise money for leukemia."

"Oh, damn," she said, sagging his arms. "What about Jacob?"

"Not until after six. You know his rules," Connor said, pressing another kiss to the top of her head as he shot another glance at the clock, wishing that it would speed up so that they could call their assistant. If the man wasn't the best at what he did, Connor would have fired the bastard's ass months ago, but he couldn't because they'd be lost without him.

For a few minutes she didn't say anything and he actually thought that she'd fallen asleep, so when she climbed, with difficulty, off his lap and waddled over to the door, he was taken by surprise, but her next words had him groaning.

"I have to use the bathroom," she announced, cradling her stomach as she leaned against the wall.

"You have to wait for a female officer," the officer said, shooting her a sympathetic look, probably thinking that would be enough to make Rory waddle back over and sit down.

It wasn't.

"No, you're going to have to take me," she said, shifting.

"I'm sorry, ma'am, but you'll have to wait for a female officer."

"I am nine months pregnant with a boy whose idea of fun is to play kick ball with my bladder and you really think that I can wait?" she demanded and he knew that if there hadn't been a set of bars separating them that she'd already be kicking the shit out of the officer's shin.

Connor stood up and joined his wife at the bars. "Just let her out. She doesn't need to be in here. Have someone take her home and I'll stay."

"How is that going to work?" Rory demanded, turning a murderous glare on him and he knew that the hormones had taken over once again.

Yup, pregnancy was a fucking blast.

"I need help getting up the stairs and with Andrew in Boston, there won't be anyone to help me!" she snapped and he really wished at that moment that Andrew had stayed home. Eleven months ago Andrew had bought his old house so that Connor didn't have to watch it go to strangers and it had been the best decision that any of them could have made.

Rory and Andrew still liked to give each other shit, but they'd grown very close over the past couple of months. Andrew went out of his way to help Rory whenever he was home. He was also very protective of her. She'd saved his life after all and was always there for him.

"Well, I-"

"All I want to do is to use the bathroom and maybe get a snack and he," she said, gesturing to the stunned officer, "won't let me and now you're willing to stay in jail just to get away from me!" she sobbed just as the first tear entered the picture and he knew, just knew that she was going to go for his balls this time.

For years he'd wished that she'd act more like a girl and cry a few tears and now he was getting that wish and more. She cried at everything and he meant everything. If he got her a cup of cocoa, she cried. If he told her that he loved her, she cried. If Bunny did something cute, she cried. If the mail was five minutes late, she cried. He could not wait for his sane, normal, happy wife to return to him. God, he missed her.

When she buried her face in her hands and sobbed loudly, he threw the bastard keeping him locked up with her a murderous glare. The crying didn't stop, oh no, it got worse and soon the officer was fumbling with his keys and couldn't open the cell fast enough.

"You know what? You can both go home. I'll talk to my sergeant. You don't need to be here and I'm sure that you can clear this whole misunderstanding up with the school board tomorrow," the officer said, opening the door and gesturing for them to leave, looking close to begging them to go.

"Are you sure?" he asked as Rory somehow managed to sob louder. "Yes!"

"Thank you," he said, comforting Rory as he guided her out of the cell, but the poor thing was still pretty upset and wouldn't stop crying. She didn't stop crying while they were being signed out, handed their personal items, walking out of the building and he by the time he helped her in the truck he was started to panic because she couldn't seem to stop crying.

As he walked around the truck to the driver's side, he resigned himself to a night of sitting in the damn nursery that he'd built so that she could gush over every little sock, diaper and teddy bear just to make her happy. He took a deep breath before he opened the door, climbed in, and started the truck. It wasn't until he pulled out the parking lot that he realized that his wife was no longer making rather frightening sobbing noises.

"Do you think we could stop at Roy's Dinner on the way home? I have a craving for their apple pie and hot cocoa," Rory said, sounding chipper and scaring the shit out of him.

"You want to stop and get pie?" he asked cautiously, knowing that the wrong tone could get him killed.

"Mmmhmm," she said, nodding as she reached over and started playing with the radio.

"Okay………..," he said, not really sure how to proceed so he went with a safe question, or at least what he hoped was a safe question. "Do you need to use the bathroom?"

"No," she simply said with a shrug.

"No?"

"No, I'm good," she said, shooting him a sweet smile.

"Then what was all that back at the jail?" he asked, wondering if her hormones were starting to make him go crazy.

"I had a craving for pie," she said with another shrug as she settled back in her seat.

He pulled to a stop at the light and for a moment he could only stare at her in wonder. "You did all that for pie?"

"And cocoa," she clarified with a nod.

He laughed, he couldn't help it.

"What's so funny?" she asked, reaching over to hold his hand.

"You are a dangerous woman, Mrs. O'Neil."

"And don't you forget it, Mr. O'Neil," she said teasingly.

"Or what?" he asked, raising their entwined hands so that he could press a kiss to the back of her hand.

"Or I'll go for my pliers," she promised, making him smile, because he knew damn well that she would. She didn't take any of his shit, drove him out of his mind and he loved every single minute of it.

THE R.L. MATHEWSON CHRONICLES

If you've enjoyed the characters from this book or any of R.L. Mathewson's books and want to see what happens to them after they get their happily every after, then the R.L. Mathewson Chronicles are definitely for you.

Every week a new chronicle is posted to the website, continuing their stories.

Sign up for the newsletter to keep up to date of all the R.L. Mathewson Chronicles.

A look at Truce: The Historic Neighbor from Hell
And where it all began.......

PROLOGUE

Present day Massachusetts

"**Y**ou're not doing it right."

He was going to strangle the son of a bitch with his bare hands, Jason decided as he ignored the bastard hovering over him. The party was in two hours and he wasn't even close to finishing Haley's present. Four months of working on this damn thing first thing in the morning and late at night and it still wasn't done.

Thank God his father had started bugging the shit out of him six months ago to get this done. At first, he'd shrugged it off, deciding that it could wait until the last minute, but then his father, uncles and a few of his cousins started to share their horror stories with him until he'd decided that perhaps it would be better to just get it over with.

Four stitches, one citation for trespassing, two second degree burns, ten migraines, one wrecked pair of jeans, two-thousand miles on his car, more than a dozen sleepless nights later and he was cursing his great-great-great-great-great grandfather to hell and back for starting this bullshit tradition in the first place. Would it really have killed the inconsiderate bastard to go out and buy his wife a necklace for their fifth anniversary instead of making one and dooming all his descendants to this bullshit tradition? He really didn't think so, especially since the man had supposedly been the brother of a very wealthy earl.

"What the hell is that supposed to be?" Trevor asked, taking a big bite out of-

"Those are my brownies, you bastard!" Jason snapped, snatching the half-eaten brownie out of his cousin's hand.

With a roll of his eyes and an annoyed sigh, Trevor reached over and plucked the brownie out of Jason's hand and shoved it in his mouth before Jason could steal his precious brownie back. Mangled necklace momentarily forgotten, he stood up and shoved his cousin out of the way so that he could make sure that the rest of his precious babies were okay. He felt his heart break as he neared the kitchen counter and saw what was left of the platter of brownies that Haley had made him for his mid-morning snack.

"How could you?" Jason asked hollowly, picking up the empty plate and praying that his cousin had missed a delicious morsel or two, but there was nothing left.

The bastard had probably licked the plate clean.

"I was bored," Trevor said with a shrug as he sat down at the kitchen table and leaned over to get a better look at the mangled necklace that Jason was desperately trying to finish in time for the party.

"If you're bored then help me," Jason said, shooting a nervous glace up at the clock and trying not to wince at the amount of time he'd lost bitching over the loss of his precious treats.

"Can't," Trevor said with a shrug.

"Why the hell not?" Jason demanded, sitting down next to Trevor and picking up the small white stone bead that he'd made out of one of the rocks he'd managed to steal from the pool at Haley's old house.

He really wished that they hadn't sold her house to that crabby old bastard. He'd taken great joy out of refusing to give Jason a few rocks from the pool area so that he could make Haley a necklace for their fifth anniversary. Actually, he really wished that he'd brought a steak with him later that night when he'd been forced to jump the fence so that he could grab a couple of rocks. Then again, the steak probably wouldn't have saved him from the psychotic little dog with the pink bow that had taken his job as guard dog a little too seriously.

"Because you have to make the necklace by yourself from start to finish," Trevor pointed out, unnecessarily since all Bradfords knew the rules for this tradition by the time they were ten years old.

"The party is in less than two hours," Jason pointed out, hoping that his cousin ignored tradition and helped him. He didn't want to disappoint his wife and he sure as hell didn't want to break a tradition that the men in his family held sacred.

"Then I suggest that you stop bitching and get threading," Trevor said with a smug smile as he gestured for Jason to get working.

"Your fifth anniversary is coming up soon, asshole, so I wouldn't get so damn cocky if I were you. You're going to need help," Jason said pointedly as he gestured to the thin silver chain.

"In three years," Trevor said in that smug tone that was starting to piss him off.

"You'll need help then," Jason bit out tightly as he arranged the tiny plastic bags in order, or at least, what he hoped was the correct order.

"Unlike you, I didn't wait until the last minute. As soon as I realized that Zoe couldn't live without me, I started to work on her necklace," Trevor explained as he leaned back, making a show of relaxing.

"Didn't you have to beg her to marry you?" Jason pointed out, simply to piss him off.

"I just let everyone think that."

"Uh huh," Jason said, switching the bag holding a small gray stone bead with the bag holding the small dark, almost black, stone bead. He'd made it from the stone he'd picked up from the bar's parking lot where he'd carried Haley that fateful night when she'd released her adorable fists of fury for the first time.

"You're still not done?" his father snorted in disgust as he walked past them on his way to the kitchen counter.

"Almost," he said, hoping that it wasn't a lie.

"Where the hell are my brownies?" his father demanded.

"Jason ate them," Trevor said quickly, making sure to sound properly appalled as the rat bastard did his best to screw him over.

"You selfish bastard!" his father hissed in outrage, making him wish that he didn't have to finish this necklace so that he could kick his cousin's lying ass.

"Haley brought ten platters to the party," Jason pointed out, hoping that his father and cousin would take the bait and get the hell out of here so that he could focus on the task at hand.

"Goddammit!" his father snapped, yanking a chair away from the table and sat down. "There won't be anything left by the time we get there," his father bit out with a pout.

With a muttered curse, Jason rolled his eyes at his father's whining even as he frantically rearranged the order of the small bags. He should have marked these rocks better.

"Party's not for two hours," Jason pointed out, not bothering to look up as he placed the handmade stone beads in what he prayed was the correct order. "If you leave right now Haley will probably let you have an entire platter to yourself to hold you over until the party starts," he murmured absently.

"Can't leave yet," his father grumbled.

"Why the hell not?" Jason demanded, chancing a look up at the clock and wincing when he realized that another ten minutes had gone by.

Shit!

"Tradition," his father and cousin said in unison, making him frown in confusion.

"What the hell are you talking about?" Jason asked, shooting the clock on the microwave one last anxious glance before looking back down at the bags of rock beads.

"As your father, it's my job to tell you the story behind this tradition," his father started to say, only to shoot Trevor a wink, "it will be my job to tell you the tale as well."

"I've already heard this story," Jason said, sighing heavily as he stared down at two gray stone beads that he couldn't for the life of him remember which one was which.

"Well, you're going to hear it again, so stop your bitching!" his father snapped before he grumbled, "I'm starving," and making Jason chuckle.

"Besides," his father continued in a calmer tone, "your Uncle Ethan is telling Haley the story even as we speak."

"Tradition?" he asked with a smile as he looked up to find his father throwing the empty brownie platter a wistful glance, no doubt hoping that another batch of brownies would suddenly appear.

"Haley left a small platter of finger rolls in the fridge in case I got hungry," he said, taking pity on his father.

"Sit your ass back down!" his father snapped at Trevor when the greedy bastard shoved away from the table and took a step in the direction of the refrigerator.

"I'm starving!" Trevor bitched, but he did sit down.

"Too goddamn bad! I need sustenance if I'm going to tell this story," his father said, sounding irritated as he stormed over to the refrigerator, grabbed the platter of sandwich rolls, leftover cherry pie and the gallon of chocolate milk.

"That's the kids' milk," Jason pointed out, returning his attention back to making the necklace.

He heard his father grumble something as he shut the refrigerator door. When Jason looked up a few seconds later, he wasn't surprised to see that his father had returned the milk and grabbed the gallon of ice tea instead. His father might be obsessed with food, but he would never willingly take food away from his grandchildren. No Bradford male would. Their children and wives came first and they made damn sure that they were well provided for.

"Those look good," Trevor said, gesturing to the platter of sandwich rolls. "Can I have one of the-"

"No!" his father bit out, glaring as he shifted the large platter away from Trevor.

"I'm starving!" Trevor whined.

"Then starve!"

"You selfish bastard!"

"Can we get on with it?" Jason asked, off cutting his father, who looked seconds away from taking Trevor to the ground in a chokehold.

"Fine," his father said, throwing Trevor one last glare before he picked up a tuna salad roll and returned his attention to Jason. Clearing his throat, his father shifted in his seat before he started.

"Once upon a time..."

"Are you fucking kidding me?" Jason asked, shaking his head in disgust.

"What?" Jared demanded, taking a bite from his sandwich roll.

"You're really going to start it like that?" Jason demanded, sharing a look of disgust with Trevor, who was inching his hand toward the platter of sandwich rolls.

His father narrowed his eyes on him. "If I want to start this story off with 'Once upon a time,' then that's how I'm going to damn well tell the story!"

Jason rubbed his hands down his face. He really didn't have time for this shit. "Fine, tell your damn story," he said, focusing his attention back on the necklace.

"I will," his father said with a sniff followed by the sound of a hand being slapped.

"Ow!"

"Those are my sandwich rolls!"

"*Dad*," Jason said, not bothering to look up as he prompted his father to get on with it.

"Oh, right," his father said, pointedly clearing his throat. "Once upon a time......."

ONE

1809
London, England
Hyde Park....a little after 4 pm.

There he was, her prince, Elizabeth mused, sighing happily as she watched the man that she was going to marry. She smiled wistfully and moved around to the other side of the tree to get a better look at James, her James, before her governess could find her and drag her away.

Even though his family's London townhouse was close to theirs, she hadn't seen him since they'd arrived a week ago. Their townhouses weren't as close as their country estates were, but James rarely ever visited his family there. The only time she had the chance to see him anymore was when they came to London for the season and even then she hardly ever got the chance to see him as much as she would have liked. He was a very busy man about town after all. Knowing that it would probably be some time before she saw him again, she had to take another look at James and make it last.

Could any man be more perfect? No, she didn't think so. Only James, only her James was absolutely perfect. She bit her lip and watched as he bowed over her mother's hand. He pressed a gentle kiss to the back of her hand before releasing it. Elizabeth sighed happily when he stood back up, mostly because it granted her a better opportunity to stare at him. He wore a stunning black suit with a crisp white shirt. His brown hair was cut short today, but she could still make out the small curls that she loved.

He was, in a word, marvelous.

At twenty-four years old, he was beyond perfect. He was handsome, educated, wealthy, smart, funny, and lovely. Everyone thought so. Men wanted to be him and women wanted to marry him. That last thought made her face squish up. No, Mama said that he was much too young to marry. She'd said that most men of his station wouldn't marry until they were older and more established, whatever that meant. All she knew was that he was here and he was perfect. With that thought in mind, she released another dreamy sigh.

"Boo!" someone suddenly yelled just as she was shoved forward, making her jump and scream in terror. Heart pounding in her little chest, she turned around to see what kind of monster had descended from the tree to attack her.

"You!" she mouthed the word perfectly, giving the little tyrant in front of her the coldest, haughtiest glare that she could muster. Thankfully, she had two older sisters who'd taught her well.

The boy was momentarily dazed speechless by her reaction before he bent over with uncontrollable laughter. "Oh…..you….should….. see…..your….face!" he said through loud, rather annoying bouts of laughter.

Elizabeth ran her small hands over her pink gown and looked down her nose at him. Well, she tried to at least. It was rather difficult to look down her nose at someone taller than her.

"You, Robert Bradford, are a beastly boy!" she said loudly, perhaps a little too loudly if the laughter erupting around them was any indication.

Robert's face turned an interesting shade of red as Elizabeth narrowed her eyes on her nemesis and studied his face, hoping to find some proof that *this* boy was an imposter. It was simply impossible that such a crude, distasteful little boy could be related to her James. This boy had darker, almost black, hair, green eyes instead of James' brown eyes and wasn't in the least bit good looking. The boy was rather homely looking. Even her mother had said so, so it had to be true.

"And you smell like the backside of a mule!" Robert shot back loud enough for everyone walking past them to hear.

Elizabeth felt her face flush hotly. She looked back in time to catch her sisters trying to hide their smiles from their overbearing mother. Their mother threw them a look of warning before turning her attention back to Elizabeth. The glare that she sent Elizabeth was a clear warning to behave and not to make a scene.

The other children around them stopped playing to watch as they giggled and pointed at Elizabeth and Robert. Lady Bradford looked horrified at her son's behavior or Elizabeth's, she wasn't exactly sure and she didn't care, because at this very moment James was laughing.

At her!

She turned away before he could see the tears streaming down her face.

"Are you crying?" Robert demanded, sounding horrified.

"Leave me alone."

She tried to push past him, but being only seven years old it was rather difficult to push past a towering twelve-year-old boy who'd planted himself firmly in her path.

"I know you fancy my brother. He laughs about it, you know. We all do," Robert said proudly.

She gasped loudly.

He knew?

He laughed?

Oh no, this was bad. This was very bad. Had she been that obvious? Her family had never said anything. They'd smiled at her when they knew they were going to see the Bradfords, but that was only because they liked the Bradfords, wasn't it?

Oh no, everyone knew, she realized with something close to panic. She had to get out of here, fast. She made another attempt to step around Robert only to have him move quickly to block her. "What's the rush? Running off to plan the wedding?" he asked mockingly.

Slowly, Elizabeth turned around to see her parents, sisters, Lord and Lady Bradford, and James walking towards them. She wanted to cry all over again when she saw that her sister Heather was hanging on James' arm. She was eighteen and this was her first season. She was plain, boring and annoying, but at least she got to touch him. Elizabeth felt her little heart break.

"You know that you're the ugliest sister, don't you? And you're fat, too!" Robert added. He looked around, beaming at the chuckles the other boys were sending his way and clearly enjoying himself at her expense.

Elizabeth had baby fat, but she would grow out of it. Her governess and father had promised her that is was just a phase. She caught one of the boys making rude gestures with his hands, indicating a fat stomach before he pointed at her for his friends.

"Stop it!" she cried.

That only made them laugh louder and Robert grin hugely. She looked back, hoping Mary would come to her aide. Her sister was no longer smiling. She cared about Elizabeth, she truly did. Unfortunately, Mary was still a good ten yards away. Elizabeth could tell that her sister was upset, but she knew that Mary couldn't rush over and help her. Married woman or not, their mother would be devastated if any of them did anything improper that would bring the family embarrassment, especially since it was Heather's first season.

They didn't seem to be coming to her aide quickly at all. In fact, they appeared as though they were taking a relaxing stroll through the park. They actually stopped to talk to Lady Newman. Lady Newman! She was the biggest gossip of the *ton*! Her annoying daughter Penelope was with her. She was just as mean as her mother. She was also glaring down her too thin nose at Elizabeth.

"Come on, Beth, what's the matter? Don't you want to go over there give your betrothed a big fat kiss?"

"Enough, Robert," James said, chuckling.

Elizabeth couldn't look back. No, she wouldn't do it. He was laughing at her, again. Her sweet, understanding James, who'd kissed her scraped elbow when she was five, was laughing at her.

That was it. She didn't care if all the children of the *ton* laughed at her and made fun of her. She didn't care if she was the fattest, ugliest girl in the world. She would not be forced to stand here and listen as James laughed at her.

This was all Robert's fault.

At that moment, she decided to do something that her parents had specifically forbid her ever to do. In fact, after it was done she knew that her father would spank her soundly, but it would be worth it. Somehow she forced herself to stop crying and smiled sweetly up at Robert as she prepared herself for a month without pudding and a sore bottom.

———

His smile faltered as he looked down at her. Her pudgy little cheeks were pushed up by a smile that was rather unsettling. She looked.... dangerous. He licked his lips nervously, wondering what was she up to.

"Robert, I don't understand why you're being so silly right now. You know how dangerous that can be," she said, a little too loudly for his liking. All the children watching them stepped closer, eager to see how this was going to end. Some of the adults also seemed quite amused with the afternoon's entertainment, but not him. He suddenly felt the overpowering need to get away from the little brat.

Robert tried to take a step back and get away from her, but Elizabeth took a step closer, refusing to grant his escape. She suddenly looked oddly dangerous in that light pink dress. Looking thoughtful, she tapped a finger to her chin. "If I recall correctly you've been told to be careful when you laugh, get too excited, nervous..." she started to explain.

Robert knew where she was going with this. The little witch was about to break the promise that her parents had made to his. "Shut up!" he screamed as desperation and fear coiled in the pit of his stomach.

She continued as if she hadn't heard him. "When you're anxious or upset, because...." this is where she leaned in conspiratorially, but she didn't whisper.

Oh no, she didn't whisper it at all, she yelled, "You will wet your pants, again! You know we still can't get the smell out of the parlor rug, but then again, it was only last week that you wet your pants when my puppy jumped on you! In fact, I don't know what was worse, your crying or the smell!"

Loud hoots of laughter seemed to fill the park as he stood there, momentarily frozen in shock as the realization that his deepest, darkest secret was out hit him.

"Robert Lemonade!" she said in a singsong voice, further taunting him and making him hate her more than even he thought possible.

The boys were all pointing and laughing at him. Robert felt his lower lip tremble. These boys attended school with him. This wasn't happening, couldn't be happening. This was bad, very bad and even as he hoped beyond hope that this was a dream, he knew that it wasn't. He also knew that his life was going to become intolerable now. Suddenly every boy around them pointed towards his pants and laughed louder. Many of them stumbled and fell to the ground, unable to curb their amusement.

Robert hadn't been aware of the hot liquid running down his legs until that moment. He looked down, praying that it was just his imagination, but it wasn't. His brown trousers were soaked thoroughly around his crotch.

"Robert Lemonade!" the children chorused. "Robert Lemonade!"

He turned to glare at Elizabeth, who wore a pleased little smile on her face. This was her fault! He shoved her soundly. She stumbled back, but didn't fall. Her eyebrows came together and she stepped up to him, looking determined. Robert was prepared to shove her again or pull her hair when he saw her small fist sail through the air towards him.

He stumbled backwards, tripped over a root and landed on his backside. New laughter erupted around them. Not only was he crying and had wet his pants, but now a seven-year-old chubby girl had knocked him down in front of everyone!

"Better make sure to bring your nanny with you next semester, Robert Lemonade!" a boy yelled.

"Yeah, don't want any unseemly yellow stains on the mattress!"

"I'd hate to be his roommate. Can you imagine smelling vinegar all year?" the boys yelled, taunted and teased.

Robert dragged himself to his feet and glared at Elizabeth Stanton. One day….one day he would get her back for this. He would have his revenge.

In front of everyone she turned her back on him just in time for her father to discreetly grab her and haul her off.

Robert stood there, his hands curled up into fists, ignoring his family's concerns, the laughter and jeers and focused on the receding image of Elizabeth as she left the park. One day soon…..

ABOUT THE AUTHOR

Writer, Facebook stalker, mother of two and hot cocoa addict, R.L. Mathewson lives life to its fullest.

When she's not chauffeuring her children to and from school or their various activities, she runs a Lego Club for a bunch of chocolate addicted children, blasts Sirius XM's The Highway, writes, edits, cooks, cleans and oh yeah, she even watches movies on Netflix.

It's safe to say that she does it all…………..

Intrigued?

Of course you are…..

If you would like to know more about this author, her latest books or information on the latest methods to stalk people on Facebook, visit her site

www.Rlmathewson.com

Or you can email her directly at, Rlmathewson25@gmail.com

Thank you for purchasing this book.
Sign up for my newsletter and receive the latest news about
the Neighbor from Hell Series as well as my other series at:
www.Rlmathewson.com

Made in the USA
Lexington, KY
10 August 2015